The
SHATTERED
SUN

ALSO BY RACHEL DUNNE

THE BOUND GODS NOVELS

In the Shadow of the Gods
The Bones of the Earth

THE
SHATTERED
SUN

A BOUND GODS NOVEL

RACHEL DUNNE

HARPER Voyager
An Imprint of HarperCollins *Publishers*

Harper Voyager and design are trademarks of HarperCollins Publishers LLC.

FIRST EDITION

Designed by Paula Russell Szafranski

Library of Congress Cataloging-in-Publication Data has been applied for.

ISBN 978-0-06-242819-6

18 19 20 21 22   LSC   10 9 8 7 6 5 4 3 2 1

For Grandma Diane—

I'm sorry I made so many characters.

Prologue

Memories surfaced like waves as he slept, cresting and curling and retreating. It was a strange thing, to have memories that were not your own.

Etarro sat in one of his hiding spots—or, more accurately, one of his sister's hiding spots that he'd discovered and claimed, since she used it so little. Still, Avorra knew right where to find him, and she peered under the stone overhang to meet his eyes.

"What happened?" she asked. She knew he hid only if something had happened that made him want to be away from all people. Usually he could stand the company of others, but not always. She knew when he wanted to be alone, and mostly she didn't let it happen, because she also knew he didn't really want to be alone.

"I went outside," Etarro said, not meeting her eyes, shrugging one shoulder as though it were nothing.

Avorra saw through it, of course. "You went to watch the sunrise," she said flatly. It was never overt, but there was always disapproval in her voice when the topic came up. "Who caught you this time?"

Embarrassment made his cheeks burn, and they burned brighter with the anger that he had to feel embarrassed about something he shouldn't be embarrassed about. "Valrik," he muttered, and hunched his shoulders against his sister's laugh.

"Uniro himself caught you at it? I'm sure he had plenty of words for you . . ."

"He did," Etarro said shortly.

"Ah, Brother . . ." Surprisingly, Avorra began to wedge herself into the cubby beside him, squeezing and wriggling until they both somehow managed to fit into the hiding place. She clasped his hand, and their shoulders pressed together, and she leaned her head against his. "You've got a choice to make. You can learn to love the moon as much as you love the sun—they'll accept that. They'll love that. Or—" She squeezed her fingers around his, and he felt her cheek pull up in a smile. "Or you'll have to learn to be sneakier."

The dream receded as Fratarro woke, leaving him holding one hand to his head in long silence. He was used to sleeping—he had spent long centuries doing little else—but he was not used to dreaming. Dreaming was for mortals. A god did not need to dream.

But his mortal body, the one he had taken—*borrowed*, he had tried to tell himself for a while, but the lie rang hollow—from a boy named Etarro, was still full of dreams, full of the shining memories of a young life.

"I'm sorry," he whispered, even knowing it meant nothing.

Fratarro stood, because there had to be more that he could do with this second chance than sleeping and wallowing. There had to be a reason he had been freed, a reason he had stolen this body and stolen the boy Etarro's chance at making any more memories.

The hallways were short, and barely higher than his head. It had taken so much work to make them even that high, but he knew his sister would not be reduced to crawling. Fratarro had poured buckets of sweat, and he'd bitten his lip so hard it covered his chin in blood—something that had startled him badly afterward—but he'd managed to make this shelter for them, a place far beneath the earth. Far from prying eyes, and far from the place where their old bodies still lay imprisoned.

They were both careful to never point out how much their new home looked like a prison.

Walking tired him; he was more tired now than in all the centuries he had been forced into sleeping. Just the act of leaving his old body to take a new one, of rising to freedom, might have been enough to exhaust him for days, but they had immediately ousted the sun, and all of their own power had not been enough to accomplish that. They'd had to steal the power needed for it, and sapped all their own strength in the process. He'd not yet recovered.

He found Sororra pacing, and it was still unsettling to attach her name to the girl's body she had stolen—the twin of the one he wore. The girl's name had been Avorra, and Fratarro had so many memories of her that were not his own. He was still, too, getting used to the strange double vision that overlaid his sister's true form atop the mortal body: a shining pillar of light, compacted and compressed and forced into a too-small vessel. The world itself would be too small to contain Sororra.

The room had little space for pacing, forcing her to make short circles and tight turns, for a great white mound lay against the wall. It lifted its head when Fratarro entered, reptilian features shifting in a way that most would not recognize as a smile. Straz, first of the *mravigi*, who had so loyally guarded the Twins for centuries—and how could he not have, when Fratarro was his creator, Sororra his defender? Straz was too old and dignified for something like joy, but he glowed with pride each time he saw the Twins.

Fratarro gave him a tired smile in return, and then called softly, "Sister."

She hadn't noticed him, and her shoulders went stiff as her head swung around to face him. "How are you feeling?" A smile that was mostly a mask plastered itself on her face. She didn't mean for him to, but Fratarro saw the way her eyes flickered down to his hand—his left hand, that hung open-fingered at his side. It wasn't for more than a second, was hardly even noticeable, but these mortal bodies were so unsubtle.

He curled his fingers into a fist, but only the right hand managed it. The left hand stayed still, unmoving, unresponsive. Sororra saw that, too, and Fratarro saw disappointment wash over her face.

Fratarro gave her a weak smile, so brittle it felt like it would shatter. "Any other ideas?" he asked. Nothing they had tried so far had given him the use of his left hand—the hand which, on his real body, his old body, had been destroyed by an enterprising group of traitors. He'd used his stolen power to seal off the damage and keep the destroyed hand from eternally leeching his power away, but ever since he had risen from imprisonment to take this new form, the left hand had been useless and unusable.

Fratarro's power had always been to shape—to make something where there had been nothing, to pull beauty from ugliness, to change and twist and unfurl. His power had been to create with his hands—and now. Now it was *hand*. It should not have been so, it felt disproportionate, but its absence had locked away half his power. His shaping was weak and ineffective, and left him sweaty and weeping and cursing.

And because they were tied together, two halves of a whole, Fratarro's weakness made Sororra weak, too. He knew weakness was one thing she could not abide.

She walked the short distance to stand before him and took his left hand, the useless one, using her own fingers to curl his into a fist. She held his hand there, between their stolen host bodies, and said soothingly, "I promised you I would make this right. Do you still have faith in me?"

Before their Parents had cast them out, they had shaped the world to their will, and their will had always been one. They had lasted centuries, trapped far beneath the earth with nothing but each other. Together, they had removed the sun. There was nothing they could not accomplish, so long as they had each other. Fratarro had always believed it to be so.

"I do," he said, because it was what she needed to hear. She needed his trust, and his belief that she could fix everything. They relied on each other as much as anything. It was how their Parents had shaped them. He would always ask for her protection, because she needed to protect him; she would always press him to creation, to creativity, because she knew shaping ran through his blood. They were two halves of a whole, and they would bend the world for the other—*had* bent the world.

"Soon," Sororra murmured, fury and longing mixing in her voice, "you will make something beautiful from this miserable world. I vow it."

Fratarro reached up with his good hand to cover hers, squeezing lightly. "I know," he said, hoping it was true.

Etarro stood watching the sunrise from a secret door his sister had shown him, one she swore was never used, was entirely unknown. So far no one had caught him at it, and he took a different path to the door every time so that no one would be able to find a pattern in his wanderings. They thought him a strange boy—let them wonder where he went, so long as they never found him.

Avorra would always find him.

She stood by his side, watching the sun climb above the treetops far below their feet. It made her uncomfortable, that was clear enough, but she didn't chide him or leave him. Only after the sun was more than halfway past the horizon did she ask him, "Why?"

Because his heart was full of a simple joy, and because the sun still shone in his eyes, Etarro answered her truthfully. "Because one day we won't see it anymore. And I think it will be one day soon. And I want to remember." He swallowed the sudden prickle of tears, and for the first time didn't swallow the words he'd always been too scared to speak: "I want to remember the reason we'll have to die when that day comes."

Avorra didn't answer him—not with words, at least. After a long, silent moment, she reached out and twined her fingers through his, and they watched together until the sun's belly cleared the horizon.

Part One

When the Long Night comes, there will be peace. All will thrive without the disapproving eye of the sun.

—The Fall and the Rise

CHAPTER ONE

The grass was just the right height that it tickled against Anddyr's elbows as he walked along through the unending darkness, and it made him want to scream. There was no time for screaming, though. He had to keep walking, they had to get as far away as they could. That was what the others kept telling him, at least.

"I shouldn't be here," he said. He never meant to speak aloud, didn't know he did it half the time, but they all told him he had a bad habit of mumbling. It came out of him like a gut-punched whine, sounds he couldn't help making. "I should have stayed." The unrelenting darkness made it easier to sink into the miserable puddle he kept shoring up with guilt and grief. The darkness made it easier to pretend he was alone, abandoned as he rightly deserved to be. "I made the wrong choice."

And then the grass tickled his elbow just right, and a shrieking laugh burst out of him.

Rora turned and thumped him on the shoulder, none too gently. She had impeccable aim, considering the darkness, but Anddyr supposed she was used to working in the dark. He'd seen the Canals. He'd heard enough of her brother Aro's stories. Or it was possible she'd been aiming for his face, and the darkness truly did throw off her aim.

She was just a dim, silent outline in the darkness, lit around the edges by faint starlight and nothing more. Still, Anddyr couldn't look away from her. Even in the unending night, he saw her clear as daylight. If he focused on her, he could ignore the tickling grass, ignore the Long Night itself. Looking at her, he could sink quickly back into his misery.

I made the wrong choice.

The thought played through Anddyr's head like a tide: rising to a scream, crashing and shattering, and then leaving nothing save a deceptively calm surface, until it rose screaming once more. It drowned out everything else, no room for anything but the thought and the emptiness it left in its wake.

He stared at the back of Rora's head, watched her march stubbornly on ahead of him, and his hands groped uselessly at his sides. It had seemed such a simple choice at the time. He'd seen Rora's face in his mind, clear as he could now, and *not* choosing her had seemed such an intolerable thing. It was Rora. He could face any wrath, for her. He could face the end of the world.

He'd seen the Twins rise in their new bodies, gods freed from their centuries-long imprisonment. And because of Anddyr, the Twins hadn't taken Rora and her brother as hosts— instead they'd done the very thing Anddyr had been meant to prevent, and stolen the bodies of a different set of twins. Etarro and Avorra had been groomed from birth for that very purpose, to become hosts to their godly counterparts, and at least one of them had gone to it willingly enough. But Anddyr had seen Etarro's face, his gaze stretching across the distance, and the boy had been almost unrecognizable. Lost inside himself, or cast out . . . gone . . .

Etarro had been the closest thing Anddyr had to a friend inside Mount Raturo. A sweet boy, painfully intelligent, and more insightful than he had any right to be. He'd given Anddyr a stuffed horse named Sooty. Etarro had freed him from the drug-locked prison that Joros had made for him, given Anddyr the chance to fight for his own wretched life. Etarro had given him everything.

And now he was gone, because, to Anddyr, Etarro hadn't seemed an important enough choice. That alone felt like ten belly punches, to his mind-stomach *and* his real stomach.

Maybe it would have been bearable, if not for Rora being so—

"Shut your fecking hole," she growled at him, like a wolf in the night scenting its prey. He didn't know he'd been mumbling again.

Maybe it wouldn't feel so much like the wrong choice if she didn't hate him so much.

A pained groan boiled out from behind Anddyr, which brought Rora to a sudden stop—Anddyr learned that when he ran directly into her. She was so much shorter than he that he almost went tumbling over her completely, but her helpful shove kept him on his feet. In the darkness of the night without end, Anddyr could see so little . . . but he could see the stars in her eyes. He wasn't sure which burned more furiously. There was anger and sadness there, and a small lost part of him ached for her, wanted to reach out and comfort her—and yet. *I made the wrong choice.* It was no less true. She still made him hurt, but there was a new layer to the pain. She, so heartless and cold and distant, was still here with him, throwing her anger like a fist, while a boy's sad soft smile was gone from the world. And that was Anddyr's doing, his choice. Perhaps her wrath was his punishment, for choosing so poorly. If that was the case, then maybe she was exactly what he deserved.

The groan again, and the sadness in Rora's eyes briefly flickered stronger. But it vanished when she turned away, her footsteps whispering through the tall grass. It was left to Anddyr to deal with. It wasn't fair, but nothing was.

Anddyr turned away from the dark outline of her, turned instead to the very similar, groaning outline huddling behind him. If Rora was his punishment for choosing her, then this was a different kind of punishment . . . but a punishment all the same.

Looking at Aro, her brother, was like staring into a mirror that looked a decade into the past. Once, Anddyr had been just as Aro was now: shaking, twitching, wide-eyed in terror and need. Truth be told, it hadn't been so long ago that Anddyr was *just* like him, a slavering mess, but it was worst early on. The mind-twisting drug got easier to bear over the years.

Anddyr walked to the younger man's side, put an arm around his hunched shoulders. Aro was taller than Rora, but otherwise the two of them had been made on the same loom, their eyes full of the same stars. "You're all right," Anddyr lied. "Remember what I said before?" Aro just mumbled, shuddered inside the ring of Anddyr's arm. Anddyr jostled him a little to get his attention. "Come now. Remember it? You said you would remember."

Voice shaking as badly as his limbs, Aro said slowly, "It will pass. And I'll be better."

"That's right," Anddyr said in his best encouraging voice. Those were the same lies he told himself, and they'd always made him feel better. They weren't entirely lies either—occasionally, mixed in with feeling like he was about to die or feeling so awful that he wanted to die, Anddyr felt like his old self, before Raturo, before Joros, before the foul black paste that had twisted his mind. It would be the same for Aro. He'd only gotten one dose of skura, but that was enough of the drug to do its nasty work. Anddyr would make sure that no more of it twisted Aro's mind further, but Rora's brother had already become an abacus, the measure of his days balanced in madness and sanity until the days reached their end. Anddyr was still trying to decide how to tell Aro that he'd now have a much shorter life than he might have expected, but that conversation might remind Aro that it was Anddyr who had done this to him.

Anddyr tugged gently with the arm around Aro's shoulders and the younger man obligingly walked forward. Aro was still a muttering, twitching mess, and he was only getting worse, his bad spells coming more and more frequently. Anddyr knew from personal experience that he would get much worse before he could get better—after forcefully weaning himself off the skura, Anddyr felt as though he were finally on the upswing of his own downward spiral, but that had been a process of nearly a month, during which he'd very nearly killed himself or the others multiple times entirely by mistake. The loss of control was the true issue of the detoxification process; a mage without his carefully instilled control was a danger to anyone unlucky enough to be nearby. Aro hadn't reached truly dangerous levels yet . . . but it was only a matter of time.

Anddyr looked up at the star-dotted sky, always dark now, save when the moon deigned to make an appearance. Those were happy hours, the closest thing they had to a sun anymore. But the moon was smaller, darker, each time it visited. Anddyr worried that the moon was vanishing like the sun had, just at a much slower rate. None of their group could remember how full the moon had been before the start of the Long Night, or how full it should be. All they could do was hope that once it disappeared, it would grow slowly back as it always had.

"Stop."

Her voice brought him up short, and his arm around Aro's shoulders was as good a restraint as a guide. Rora had stopped and, squinting, Anddyr could see why: their leader had stopped. It was a statement that applied to the moment—where he seemed to have simply chosen to sit down among the waving stalks—as well as to his general state of mind since the rise of the Twins. Joros had stopped. Stopped thinking, stopped leading, stopped speaking. He had become a walking, breathing corpse.

Joros spent much of his time trudging along either far ahead of or far behind the rest of them, so quiet Anddyr wouldn't have known he was there if not for the sound of his footsteps. He stopped and started on his own whims, leaving the rest to follow his example or leave him behind.

Somewhere inside his working-or-not mind, Joros had decided that it was time to stop, and there was no arguing with that either. He was sitting amid the waving grass, staring just as vacantly as ever, and Anddyr knew from the three previous attempts that there would be no moving him. Rora could only shout so much at a slab of stone.

"We're done for now," Rora said. She said it as though it had been her choice, rather than an inarguable fact beyond her control. This was the fourth time they'd stopped since leaving the seething hill behind—the fourth time she'd had a halt imposed on her. She grew unhappier each time.

Anddyr could understand it. She'd had a bad time of things at the hill. She'd been offered up as sacrifice to the gods whose very existence made most of the world want to kill her, she'd watched her brother poisoned, she'd perhaps felt the brush of the newly freed goddess Sororra against the edge of her existence, and her brother had betrayed her in some way Anddyr couldn't understand but that seemed to have cut to her core. Things hadn't been going particularly well for her, and so, in the logical part of his brain that bubbled up every so often, Anddyr could see why she was so angry and so sad . . . and he didn't think Cappo Joros was helping with her mood at all.

Anddyr knew she blamed the cappo for her brother's condition at least as much as she blamed Anddyr himself, but the issue with Joros was that he refused to be antagonized, refused to let her make him a target of her rage. He seemed to have locked himself inside his own mind, and Anddyr knew how dangerous that could be.

Anddyr carefully patted down a section of the tickling grasses, and lay down in such a way that they wouldn't be able to get to his elbows. He had to admit he was grateful for the rest—Rora set a grueling, unforgiving pace. They all wanted to be away from the hills and the Twins as quickly as possible, and Rora seemed determined to make it happen at superhuman speeds. Anddyr, though, was only a regular human, and a poor excuse for one at that. He was tired.

As Anddyr drifted off to sleep, wrapped around the miserable knot of his guilt, the only sound was Aro's low muttering.

Anddyr couldn't make out the words, didn't really want to—he didn't want to know what horrors his actions had put into the younger man's waking nightmare. He didn't want to listen, but as sleep finally claimed him, he could make out two words, repeated endlessly, not quite Aro's voice but a constant stream of the words, *Find me. Find me. Find me . . .*

It's a tower. Anddyr knows that, somehow. A spire that hangs in the air, built from clouds, floating like a puff of down on the wind, but its wall feels solid against his back. It might even be real.

At the tower's center there's a boy staring into a mirror, but no—he's facing a girl whose face matches his. The boy's is softer, but the girl's has smile lines. A lot of grimacing can carve those same lines into a face, though. Anddyr knows their faces, can name them even, factual as reciting to a professor: Etarro and Avorra. He knows he should feel something, looking at them, but he doesn't. He's shaped out of cloud and air, too, just like the skytower.

The twins are talking, and as Anddyr watches, the boy lifts his left arm. At the end of it, his hand flops like a useless piece of meat. "You said it would work," the boy says, accusation and hurt in his voice, both barely held in check. "You said it would be like it was before."

"It did work, Brother! Just look." She spreads both her working hands, though they only encompass the inside of the floating tower. "Look at all we've done. And this is only the beginning . . ."

The boy drops his arm, shoulders hunching. At his side, one hand curls into a fist, though the other doesn't so much as twitch. "I see it. I see how you have everything you've ever wanted."

"Everything we've always wanted."

"I never wanted this!" The outburst shakes the stone at Anddyr's

back, makes the skytower tremble and waver. "I only wanted to shape, and now even that has been taken from me—"

"They'll pay," the girl interrupts, fierce as a mother cat. "All of them, I swear it. Our Parents will pay for all they've done, and their people will, too. They're all guilty, all of them, and soon they'll learn. Soon they'll know."

Softly, quiet as clouds, the boy whispers, "I only want to shape." He wraps his working hand around the useless one, looks away from his sister, and his eyes find Anddyr. He sees the surprise grow in those eyes, sees the outrage forming on the girl's face, her mouth shaping a curse—he sees all these as facts, as a historian at the center of a war, careless of the surrounding danger. He observes this, and he observes when the clouds swallow the girl, dragging her down through the floor of the skytower, soundless. He observes the confusion in the boy's eyes, and the war raging within him.

The boy stands in front of Anddyr sudden as blinking, and his eyes are different. Younger. More human. "Find me," he breathes, and he raises his left hand, the one that didn't work, and in it now is clutched a stuffed horse. That had been Anddyr's stuffed horse, which he'd loved beyond all reason. Her name is Sooty. "Find me." The boy's hand is wrapped around her, bone and muscle working beneath flesh. He holds her toward Anddyr, the toy closing the space between them, and Anddyr reaches, too. "Find me . . ." His hand touches the boy's, and the shock that springs between them makes the skytower crumble, clouds swirling away to wisps, and he plummets through the open air, down and down and down . . .

Anddyr woke flailing and choking, clawing his way up through the ground that had swallowed him. A hand grabbed his shoulder and yanked, and Anddyr sucked in air as he stared up at stars, grateful just to be alive, grateful he wasn't trapped beneath the earth like the Twins had been.

"Fecking idiot," Rora muttered at him, and Anddyr was, for the first time, grateful for the darkness of the Long Night—it hid his burning cheeks as he realized he hadn't been swallowed by the earth, only sleeping on his stomach with his face pressed to the ground.

The dream almost slipped away from him in a sleepy haze of shame, but with another gasp of air, Anddyr grabbed on to the edges of the retreating dream, and pulled it back.

"Etarro," he blurted.

Rora glared at him, along with two other half-asleep sets of eyes. "Shut up about him," she said. Anddyr didn't realize he'd been talking about the boy, apparently often enough that it had started to prick at Rora.

"No, he's . . . he's not gone. He's still there, still fighting."

"Sounds like you shouldn't've stopped taking your *medicine*," she said, and since she knew very well now how the mage-enslaving drug skura worked, that cut especially deep. The guilt and self-hatred threatened to overwhelm Anddyr once more, but he clung to the dream. It had been *more* than a dream, he could feel that in his bones.

Anddyr crawled clumsily toward Cappo Joros, and went rifling through the pockets of his robe. Any other time, he never would have done such a thing, not even when gripped by the deepest madness, but he was desperate to prove himself right—no, not even that, he was desperate to prove that Etarro still lived, that he could be saved . . .

Luckily Joros was half asleep and slow to react. By the time he growled and began to turn away, Anddyr had already found what he was looking for, pulled the smooth stone out of the cappo's pocket—

It was like a punch to both his mind and his body. He could tell, in a very disconnected way, that he went tumbling over backward to land on his back with all the air exploding out of his chest, but that was the smaller of the two concerns. Dark flames blossomed before his eyes and tore through his mind, a wildfire made of starlight, and it scorched everything it touched. There was nothing it *didn't* touch. Anddyr's world narrowed to the pain of its burning, and he could see nothing but the flickering flames, hear nothing but their roar in his ears, and there was a *tug* like a child at a sleeve, an inexorable pull south—

His fingers released the seekstone, or one of the others knocked it from his hand—Anddyr didn't know or care which, he only knew that he could breathe again, and see, and think. Still, he lay there for a while longer, reeling. The world seemed to spin around him, or perhaps he spun around it, and his stomach churned.

"What in all the hells was that?" Aro's voice, high and nervous. He reached for the seekstone and Anddyr lurched upright, knocking the younger man's hand away. Aro looked back at him with the saddest eyes.

Anddyr ran his shaking hands through his hair, trying to pull back any composure he might have left. Even if he'd ruined the man's life, Aro was still his pupil. Even if Aro's sanity now faded like a tide, he could still learn. "What do seekstones do?" Anddyr asked in his best, calmest teacher's voice.

"They let you see out of someone else's eyes." Aro's tone suggested that he expected it to be a trick question, that he was bracing for the blow of a wrong answer.

"And what else?"

"Give you a . . . a directional pull on where the other person is, so you can—"

"Enough with the witch-talk," Rora growled. "What'd it fecking *do*?"

It was incredibly hard, but Anddyr ignored her and spoke only to Aro. "Exactly. And this seekstone"—he pointed to the one sitting so innocently at his side—"is attuned to Etarro." He waited for that to sink in, but three blank expressions told him it wasn't going to. Gently, he prompted, "Etarro, who is . . . ?"

"Dead," Joros said flatly. It was the first word he'd said in hours, if not days.

Anddyr winced, but ignored that, too. He fixed his gaze on Aro, willing him to think through the answer. Aro looked between the others, curled his shoulders up to his ears, and made a timid guess: "Dead?"

"*Not* dead." Anddyr sighed. "He's host to Fratarro, his mind and body usurped by a god. When I touched the seekstone, I touched Fratarro's mind, saw through the eyes of a god. That's . . . not something any person is made to withstand. It *burned* me . . ."

Joros snorted, and with a corner of his robe wrapped around his hand, he reached out to grab the seekstone and drop it back into his pocket. "You think because you saw through Fratarro's eyes when you touched *Etarro's* seekstone, that means Etarro is still alive? Sounds rather like the opposite, to me."

Anddyr opened his mouth to argue, and stopped. The only argument he had was the dream, which had felt more real than a dream, but was even now starting to fade, the urgency and surety drifting away like wisps of cloud. The cappo was right—the seekstone didn't prove anything aside from Etarro's body still being to the south. A few seconds of touching Fratarro's mind had nearly burned away Anddyr's own mind—how could he expect that Etarro would be able to withstand constantly sharing his body and mind with a god?

With all of them awake now, there was no reason not to keep moving on—as far as the others were concerned, the sooner they could be away from the Plains, the better. But Anddyr hung back, staring south, staring back the way they'd come. He could still feel that pull, that insistent tug, and no matter how often he told himself it had just been a dream and nothing more, he couldn't forget Etarro whispering, *Find me*, as he'd clutched the stuffed horse that had belonged to both of them. He couldn't help wondering what he'd find if he were to go back to the hill where the Twins had risen to steal the bodies of the children that had been provided for them. Would he find only a boy with an ancient god's eyes, or—worse—would he be able to see the trapped boy's eyes behind the god's?

CHAPTER TWO

There was a tension to the darkness. A feeling like a held breath, like a narrowed eye. A waiting, watching and impatient and still as a startled hare. A silence, but one that begged for an end.

Scal was not good at filling a silence. He never had been. Words came slow to his lips, slow as falling snow, and they were so easy to swallow. He was a man made of silences, made of all the words that he had never said. And so the quiet dark wrapped around him, familiar and foreign both. An old cloak, a favorite, that no longer fit as it had. A tune, so close to one he knew, but with notes that jarred like nails. He was a man used to silences, but this one fit poorly.

Silence, too, walked at his side. Vatri, wrapped tight in her yellow robe, was as quiet as when she searched for meaning in a fire. Eyes fixed, unblinking, waiting to hear the Parents speak. But she could not read the darkness like a fire. The Parents would not speak their voices into the Long Night. Still, though, her silence held. Her eyes held, looking anywhere but at Scal. He did not know how to ask her to speak, how to ask her to fill their silence.

Between them the makeshift torch. Not a torch at all, but a sword that burned with soundless fire when Scal's hand touched it. It gave them a pool of light in the darkness, making the dark grass sea dance with shadows. The tall grass that brushed against the burning sword came away unburned. Untouched, by the quiet fire. The sword filled the space between Scal and Vatri, filled it with enough light that it could hide the shadows between them. That it could hide how deep that chasm ran, and how wide.

Scal thought, again, of reaching across that space. He had thought it often in their walking. Of reaching out to touch her arm, her shoulder, her face seamed by old scars and new worries.

But the sword was in his hand, and there was the light. The sword *changed* when he held it—grew flames from the touch of one hand, and ice from the other. Powers she had given him, though she said she simply worked the will of the Parents. He was the man she had made him. The sword burned, when he touched it. He did not know if she would burn, too.

His hand stayed on the sword. Tight, and unfeeling.

She had not reached across the space either.

The edge of the light from his sword touched against something taller than the grass. Sudden, a thing that did not belong. Scal shifted his grip, angled the sword, ready to strike. Vatri faltered, stumbled, and unthinking Scal reached with his other hand to pull her behind him. The tall thing did not move. Scal stepped forward, feet sure upon the ground, and still the other did not move.

"Tree," Vatri breathed behind him. Her fingers touched his arm, a calming gesture. "It's a tree." A breathy laugh escaped her, as surprising a sound as any. Her fingers were warm through the thin fabric of his shirt.

"It is a tree," he agreed. Said the words, useless as they were, so the silence would not swallow them back down.

Vatri laughed again, still softly, as though scared the world would shatter like the silence if she were too loud. "Like children spooking at shadows . . ." She shook her head, shook the laughter away. "We're close to Fiatera, then. Once the moon comes up, we might be able to see Mount Raturo, see how much we'll have to adjust our path. Here . . ." Her fingers pulled at his arm, pulled him forward closer to the tree. It was a small one, but the light from his sword showed taller trees behind it, and many of them, stretching away into the darkness. The edge of the Forest Voro, that stretched along the southern border of Fiatera.

Vatri's fingers slipped from his arm. She looked at Scal, and he could not tell if the space between them was smaller or larger. She said, "We should stay outside the trees until moonrise. It will be harder to tell where we're going otherwise. We . . ." She blinked. Looked away, and he could not tell whether she was looking to something else or looking away from him. "It's been too long since we had a proper rest."

"Yes," Scal said. Voice like a croak. Hoping she would keep talking. He did not know how to keep a silence at bay. Of all the things that made him, he was a fighter, but silence was not a thing that he could fight.

She was facing away, and he could not see whether her eyes were on the distance or on him. "I'll . . . gather some wood." The sentence started a question, ended harder. A statement. A sureness. "A fire will be fine. There's no one else around to see it."

Scal kept his lips closed. Kept his silence. He did not want to argue, not now that they were speaking. Did not want to tell her that if they had come this far, there was no reason others could not have come as far in as much time. Did not want to say that there could be black-robed priests moving through the Long Night behind them, hidden in the darkness, hidden in the pool of black that stretched beyond the sword's glow. Did not want to scare away her certainty or her words. Instead, he said, "I will help."

Under the sparse cover of the young trees, they stayed close together. It was not wise to part, in the darkness lit only by stars. There was no knowing what danger lay beyond, and so they stayed close, the space between them like a chain, a bar. Never farther apart, never closer together. A turning wheel.

His one arm that was not holding the sword could still carry more than Vatri's two, and so she piled sticks into his arm. Deadfall, where her roving hands found it, but there was not much. She jumped into the air, fingers wrapping around a half-dead branch, and for a moment she hung there. Arms stretched and feet swaying, and there was a small and child-like joy on her face. He stood far from her, distant, separate. Her joy was not a thing he could share. The branch snapped, and her feet thumped to the ground. She put the branch in his arm, and though she had to step closer to do it, the space between them felt no smaller. The silence had burst free, and it filled the circling, turning space.

"You are so calm," he said. The words came before he could think of not saying them.

Vatri paused, bent in two as she poked through a pile of brush. Her still hands resumed, plucking at branches, and her voice was light: "Why shouldn't I be?"

"This is not right." Scal waved with the sword, the flaming

sword that should not have been, at the unending dark around them. Her back was to him, but he thought, still, that she would see. "The world has gone wrong."

"It has." Vatri straightened. Put her small branches into the pile in Scal's arm. Her eyes slid away from his.

Scal could not think of the right words to ask the question that shivered through him. He might have let the silence take hold again. Let it fill the space between them until they were nothing but two strangers. Divided by the sole piece of light in the dark world. But the thought of it made him ache. "You are so calm," he said again. The closest he could come to asking, *How?*

She walked past him, back to where the trees shrank to tall grass. He followed. There was nothing else for him to do.

He dropped his armful of sticks and branches, and it made a mighty crashing, cracking sound that set birds screeching somewhere not so far off. He remembered a night—a short night, but just as dark—when Vatri's shouting had woken birds, and Scal had laughed until his belly hurt. It had been a life ago. He had been a different man then, and there was no laughter in him now.

How many rebirths since then? One, surely. Waking in Aardanel, beneath the glow of the everflame, where the shadows of all the other lives had seemed small. But Aardanel had burned, and he had gone south again. Was that a new life? The wandering, the waiting. He had stepped unburned from the great bonfire Vatri had built—that, surely, was an ending and a beginning. But he felt no different from the man who had woken before the everflame. No different, truly, from the boy who had seen the everflame for the first time. Felt its slow warmth reaching to the tips of his fingers. Flames as warm as the voice of the red-robed priest. He had not come so far from that boy. Lost, alone for all that another body stood nearby, cold for all that fire licked near his skin. Seven lives, or one?

"Scal," Vatri said. "The fire."

He knelt, set aside the sword so that its fire-glow died. Only the stars to guide him, and the pads of his fingers. He arranged the twigs and the sticks and the branches, and a few careful strikes of his flint set a spark alive among the twigs. He fed it, let it grow strong enough to chase back the darkness. He looked across the tops of the flickering flames, to where they shone in Vatri's wide eyes.

There was the look in her face. The searching look, the listening look. Waiting for the flames to speak, or her gods. She had never told him how it worked, but he knew better than to interrupt her. And so he sat in silence, watching the flames, too, and ignoring the twisting in his stomach that was half hunger and half fear. Clinging to the pop of wood, the hiss of fire.

"I'm calm," she said, hardly louder than the fire's sound, but still it might have startled him if he had not been listening for her voice, "because this isn't the end. Not yet."

Scal thought of all the black-robed preachers, the sea of them gathered around the hill where the Twins would rise. Shifting and writhing like a swarm of flies on a corpse, their number beyond counting. "You think we can fight them."

He could not tell if her eyes were on him, of if they were only on the flames. "I think we don't have a choice." She almost smiled. "And that makes things simple, doesn't it?"

Scal looked to the sword that lay at his side, that would line with fire or with ice if he touched it. He did not let his fingers near it. "I am only one man."

"You're not alone. We're together in this, Scal."

"We are only two."

The fire-sounds filled the night again. It was not a large fire, nothing like the one that Vatri had built for him to walk into, nothing like the flames that had licked at the belly of the sky. But it was a fire, in a world where the sun had died. Anyone walking through the Long Night would see the flames. Perhaps no one would see, no one would come. Perhaps it would draw fellow travelers, grateful for the light and the warmth, grateful to stack their numbers against the night. Perhaps it would draw in the black-robed preachers, the endless sea of them, with their anger and their triumph and their hatred of the light. He knew he should turn from the fire, let his eyes soak in the darkness so that he could see any moving shadows. See any threats before it was too late. But he could not look away from the flames. Could not look away from the woman beyond them.

"You don't see it, do you?" Vatri's voice was still soft, and the screen of flame between them made her moving lips seem to dance.

He had tried so often, when they had traveled together, to see the things she saw within the flames. It had never worked. He was not touched by the gods. He was not chosen. He did not know, sometimes, if he believed there was anything to be seen within the fire. "No," he said. "I do not."

"Look," she whispered. *"Look."*

For her, he tried. Staring into the fire as it blackened the wood he had fed to it. Bark curling away, the strong wood beneath cracking and fracturing, spreading open a dozen mouths of fire. A line of smoke twisting into the air, lit by the flames below. Almost like a dancer. He had seen a woman dance at a festival once, beauty and grace, and it had hurt that nameless place in his chest to watch her. The flames reached, always reaching, always hungry. They would eat the world, given half a chance.

"I see nothing."

The flames twitched toward him with Vatri's sigh. She rose, not as graceful as that long-ago dancer, but nearly. When she sat beside him, it stirred that same nameless place. Without the fire between them, with her arm almost touching his, he did not know how small the space was between them. Smaller, surely. Her head only reached his shoulder, but her eyes were wide and clear when she looked up to him, and the flames did not reflect in them at all.

"Are you cold?" she asked.

"I am not." The blood ran warm in his veins, his own flesh a shelter against the cold of the North. "Never."

"Am I cold?" She held her hand toward him, her fingers near his knee, but he hardly saw it for her eyes. Wide and bright as the slow-waning moon, clear and lovely. The dancing light and the shadows it cast played across her face, and they melted away the damage a different fire had done. Smoothed away the old scars and the warped ridges of flesh, made her soft. She was so close. Nothing between them, nothing at all. "Scal?"

He reached for her hand, held her fingers gentle in his. They were warm as summer, and the skin of her palm was smooth, untouched by that old fire. "No," he said. She was warm. She was life.

"Do you see?" Her voice rose with excitement, fingers tightening in his. Her other hand rose to clutch his. There was a touch of fire in her eyes, the flames creeping in from the edges.

He saw her. Fire or no, he saw her. But with the flames in her eyes, he did not think she saw him. "No," he said. Regret, for the things he could not see, and the ones he could.

She sighed again, heavier this time, and dropped their clasped hands to his knee. Did not let go, but her fingers were looser. Her eyes slid away, looked to the fire, flame-bright, before she looked down at their joined hands. She ran her thumb across his knuckles, and he could not see her eyes. "It's warm, Scal. It shouldn't be, but it is. The sun's fire warms us all, and with the sun gone, it should be worse than winter. But it's not! It's no colder than before they took away the sun." Thumb over his knuckles, smooth skin trailing back and forth over the roughness of his hands. "Do you understand what that means?"

Scal did not want to think. There was so much, too much, and he did not know how to handle any of it. Better, surely, not to think. To be led again, to follow. To not have to think, or to hurt. "No," he said, staring at her thumb drawing shallow circles.

"It's still there. The sun. It's not gone, not at all, and that means they've done something else to it. It means they're not nearly as powerful as they want us to think. It means we can *fight* them."

Too much. Always, too much.

In another life, or perhaps it was still the same one, he had asked Vatri to shape him. To make him whole, to make him a better man. A good man. He had asked, and she had done what she could. He had asked, though. "Yes," he said, squeezing her fingers, looking up to meet her soft smile and her flame-touched eyes. It was easier. "We can fight them."

CHAPTER THREE

The Plains stretched on like an ocean—Keiro could say that, for he'd seen the wide ocean that swallowed the western half of the world. He'd watched the tides hide and reveal beaches of sand and stone, seen the earth crumble away in sheer cliffs that the ocean crashed against, and he'd seen how the water went on endlessly, stretching far and away to nothing more than a shimmer.

He'd seen the ocean swallow people, too: swimmers who thought they were stronger than the tides, boats tipped by a sudden storm, whole villages washed away by angry waves. In one of his darker times, after Algi's feet had taken her away from him, Keiro had stood shoulder-deep in the cold water, his toes clinging to the stony floor, waves lapping beneath his chin, and he'd wondered what it would be like to walk deeper. A wave had slapped into his face, filling his throat with water, and he'd flailed back to shore sputtering with fear and regret. The ocean was a fickle thing, and Keiro had not been unhappy to put it at his back.

He'd found himself thinking of the Plains as an ocean more often of late. In the glow of the stars, the way the grasses moved in the wind looked very much like the ocean at night.

He wondered, if he walked deep enough into the grass sea, if it would swallow him, too, and take his body far away.

"Brother Keiro," a voice called softly, timidly. Keiro didn't need to turn to see who it was; the cringing tone was enough to mark Laseneo. The man had installed himself as Keiro's attendant, without giving Keiro much choice in the matter. He'd tried more than once to dismiss Laseneo, both gently and firmly, but the man had looked so wretched each time that Keiro had given up on it. Trying to dismiss Laseneo made him feel more guilty than the fact of having an attendant. "They're ready for you . . ."

Keiro let himself stare over the dark grass for a moment more, pretending it was all there was to the world. But it wasn't. There was so much of the world—he should know, he'd walked much of it—and much more that needed doing in it. The Long Night had come, and in it, there was little enough time for sleep.

Keiro stood, and a shadow stood with him. His constant companion was like a piece of the sky fallen to earth: glowing with pinpricks of starlight and as dark as the space between each star. Though most of the world would call him a *mravigi*, here in the Plains his kind had been named Starborn. Cazi's reptilian face peered up at Keiro, attentive and keen as ever, red eyes steady. Not so very long ago, he had perched on Keiro's shoulder, rather like a big gray bird; now he was the size of a dog, and a big dog at that, his shoulder reaching halfway up Keiro's thigh. Cazi rarely left Keiro's side, and with his scales gone to black, there was more than one reason Keiro thought of the *mravigi* as his shadow.

Laseneo stood on the edge of the hill, wavering between

trying to disappear in the grass and trying to do what he considered his duty. The man had the nervous habit of rubbing the back of his neck with both hands, as though he thought wringing his own neck might be the kindest thing he could do. He had the tendency to rock as well, swaying back and forth, always looking truly caught between staying and fleeing. He was almost worse than the mages, some days. If Keiro had felt he needed an attendant, Laseneo would have been near to his last choice, but one of the things Keiro had come to accept was that one wasn't usually given a choice in life.

As Keiro walked down the hill, Cazi kept pace, a proper shadow, while Laseneo tried to walk as close to Keiro's heels as he could without actually stepping on them. Keiro was too tired even to sigh at the man. In the dozen days—or, Twins' bones, nights? spans? how was he supposed to track the passing of time?—since the sun had been torn from the sky, Keiro had gotten so little sleep. He was kept busy, his long hours filled with questions and commands and reassurances . . . but he was given plenty of time to rest, to sleep. They wanted to make sure his head stayed clear, his mind focused. It was simply that Keiro, alone among the uncountable bodies that filled the hills, could not seem to sleep in the unending dark.

You should be sleeping the sleep of a triumphant hero.

It was the whispering certainty, the voice that tickled so unobtrusively through his thoughts that he hadn't even noticed it at first. Even now, knowing the whispers were Sororra's careful manipulation, knowing to listen for them, it was so hard to tell. The suggestions always seemed so reasonable, the conclusions so natural, the assurances so comforting. Why would he ever have cause to doubt the thoughts in his own head?

There are more important things to worry about. There was so much that needed to be done, so much Keiro alone needed to do, that it was a small wonder he was having trouble sleeping. Responsibility was an ill-fitting, uncomfortable coat.

The sound of the assembled Fallen was like a moan, loud and ceaseless and wordless: too many voices talking, too many bodies shuffling. He heard them well before the smaller hills parted to reveal the largest hill, the mound that, until so very recently, had housed a pair of gods. The Fallen were gathered around the base of this hill, a shifting, swelling, writhing mass of them, more like an angry ocean tide than the Plains. Keiro paused for a moment, Laseneo stepping on his heels and quickly jumping back. He was far enough away that they wouldn't have seen him yet, for he was nothing more than a dark-robed spot of black against the greater blackness. The longer he watched them, the less they looked like an ocean tide. No, they looked more like maggots, wriggling atop a corpse—

"Brother Keiro?" Laseneo prompted timidly, the wince in his words.

Keiro sighed, and started forward once more.

The Fallen parted for him, bodies pressing back to make a space wide enough for Keiro and Cazi to pass side by side, closing again on Laseneo's heels. Laseneo stopped at the edge of the crowd, the base of the hill, but Keiro continued on with Cazi. The silence came gradually, but it was fully quiet before he even reached the top of the hill, no sound but the wind stirring the grass, the scrape of dirt beneath Keiro's feet.

There was no good place to stand where they could all see him, for the center of the hill was a crater, its smooth edges beginning to crumble. Keiro stood as close to the hill's crest as he dared, and he turned in a slow circle, taking in all their silent expectations, their held breaths, their tempered excitement. For all that had been done since the Long Night had fallen, so little had been shared with the common preachers. They didn't know what they were meant to do now, or why the Twins hadn't issued commands, or why the Twins hadn't been *seen* since the sun had disappeared. They didn't know why so many of their brothers and sisters lay buried in the vast, shallow pit they'd spent long hours digging to the south. They didn't know why they'd been spared the Twins' judgment, or when the next wave of their appraisal would come.

This would be the first time, in the long days or nights or spans since the rise of the Twins, that the mass of the Fallen would be addressed. And of course, that task fell to Keiro.

He opened his mouth to speak and then paused—he'd almost forgotten. He wasn't a loud man, and even a loud man's loudest shout wouldn't have reached the far edges of the living sea in any useful way. He noticed, finally—how were they always so unnoticeable?—the dark shape huddled some lengths away. With an uncomfortable lump in his throat, Keiro went to the folded-small form, touched its shoulder. He recognized the man who lifted his face from the curl of his arms—some distinctive Highlands features in the mouth and the hair, but an otherwise nondescript Fiateran face. Still, the blue robe marked him for what he was: a mage. This one was named Terstet; Keiro had made a point of learning as many of the mages' names as he could.

"It's time?" Terstet asked, his voice shaking as badly as his hands when he unwound his limbs.

"It's time," Keiro agreed. Thanks to the flippant explanation offered by one of the Fallen, he knew now that the mages were unable to resist any direct commands, and he'd vowed to never issue one—*foolish as that was*. So he waited while Terstet flexed his hands, rubbed his arms, blinked owlishly. Keiro didn't doubt someone else had given the mage his commands, and he didn't mind waiting for Terstet's damaged mind to find its way through the mire.

The mage finally worked his fingers in the dancing way that wove a spell, and though Keiro didn't sense any difference, Terstet nodded to him. Keiro turned back to face the crowd, still waiting so attentively.

"Brothers and sisters," Keiro began, and he *heard* how his voice echoed throughout the gathering—not a mighty boom that reached to the far edges, but some trick that spread his voice evenly to any who might hear. "You all know that our time is upon us. The Twins have been freed, and they have risen to walk among us once more. They have pulled Metherra's sun from the sky, and they have brought the Long Night to the world. All that they vowed, through their long imprisonment, they have done. But they are not alone, for they have all of us."

The cheer that arose startled him, and it spread like wildfire, until all of the giant ring around the hill was cheering, screaming, hands raised in triumph, and the sound of it all nearly overwhelmed Keiro. He took a stumbling step back, and his hand caught against something warm and solid—Cazi. The *mravigi* steadied him, Keiro taking strength from his presence, and then Cazi flowed forward from his side. Cazi was young still, and not near to his full size, but the screech when he opened his mouth seemed to shake the ground. It silenced the

Fallen more effectively than anything Keiro could have done. In the echoing quiet, the only thing he could hear was Terstet, softly sobbing somewhere behind him.

Keiro took a deep, bracing breath. "Your faith and your eagerness are . . . inspiring. The Twins are honored beyond words to have all of you to serve them. But you must understand: we do *serve* them, and servitude is not always an easy thing." Keiro managed not to look at Terstet, to instead face a different section of the Fallen. "The Twins have set us a task—an important undertaking, but not an easy one. It will take all of our faith, and all of our strength."

Keiro made his voice louder, harsher—not to be heard better, but so that they would hear the words and *listen* to them. "Hear me, for I am the voice of the Twins. You will leave this place, all of you. Return to Fiatera. You must—" They began to shout then, to complain. Keiro raised his voice further, and with the aid of Terstet's magic, he shouted over their cries. "You must prepare the world for them. They will march on Fiatera soon enough, and claim the land for their own, but there is much that must be done for them first.

"Go. Return to Fiatera, and spread the word of the Twins. In every city, town, village—any collection of hovels large enough to merit a priest, anywhere that has a merra or parro promising the Parents' salvation—there should be, too, a preacher, welcoming new followers with open arms into the Long Night. Our brethren should have a chance to prove themselves true before the Twins' judgment falls.

"For too long, we have had only Raturo to shelter us, only Raturo to call our home. No longer. We must make havens all across the land, strongholds where the Twins' power is unquestionable and unassailable. We must show that it is not only the Twins who are strong, but that we have grown strong alongside them.

"Go, my brothers and sisters. Return to Fiatera. Only we can serve the Twins' will in this. Hear me, for I am the voice of the Twins. *Go.*" Keiro sagged, his hand finding Cazi's warm, firm shoulder once more. With his other hand he made a motion, hoping Terstet would see it, too tired to speak anymore.

But of course, that was not the end of it.

The Fallen swarmed the hill, those who could not find the inspiration in his words, or those who had not understood that this was not a choice. They scrambled up the sides of the hill, an unstoppable rising tide, and Keiro resigned himself to long hours of repeating the same command, again and again and again . . .

He was saved from that, at least.

Valrik, the ostensible leader of the Fallen, stepped in front of Keiro. He was the first, but others followed, a ring of preachers appearing around the crown of the hill, and they all had two red stars sewn above their hearts. No matter how often Valrik insisted there was no hierarchy among the Fallen, there was no one who questioned that these Eye-marked preachers were leaders. They no longer called themselves the Ventallo, the leading faction of the Fallen, but everyone else did.

The Ventallo alone wouldn't have stopped the mob, for there were only a dozen of them, but they were not alone. Filling the gaps between the preachers were black-armored mercenaries, and their swords were drawn. They were called blades for the darkness, and they were meant to be the Fallen's own army. Keiro had only seen them serve as bodyguards to the Ventallo.

He had grown so uncharitable of late.

The naked steel stopped the mad press of bodies, replaced anger with the first inklings of fear. The blades stood completely still, their swords held ready but not attacking. It was a very simple and very effective warning. An equal warning was the mages, still unseen, that had made the sudden appearance of the Ventallo and the blades possible.

"Brothers and sisters!" Valrik's voice boomed over the Fallen. It was amplified by Terstet as Keiro's voice had been, but Valrik still shouted. He seemed not to mind hurting all the listening ears, and given how quickly the last traces of anger melted away through the crowd, Keiro wasn't about to argue the man's methods. "You know as well as I that Brother Keiro speaks for the Twins. His words are their words—so why do you think to argue with him? He has spoken the will of our gods, and it is not for us to judge the will of the Twins. We—faithful servants that we are—must listen, and obey. Even when we cannot understand their commands, still we must listen. Even if we dislike what we have been ordered to do, we must obey. That is the nature of the Fallen."

Valrik had a way of putting an edge on both sides of his words—exhorting his people to listen to Keiro while speaking to the doubt in their hearts about the wisdom of the Twins' orders. In so short a time knowing the man, Keiro had learned already that he needed to be careful in trading words with Valrik.

"Rest," Valrik went on, his voice less a thunderclap and

more the distant rumble of a storm. "You are not expected to leave *now*. There is much preparation to be done still, and you will have the time for it. Go, and sleep, and listen to your hearts. The Twins have always guided us true, and we must have faith that they will continue to do so."

The Fallen listened to him better than they had to Keiro, better than they ever *would* listen to Keiro. There was no help for that. Still, questions rumbled up through the ranks, shouted forward from mouth to mouth until the words found their way to the top of the hill: "Where have the Twins gone?" "When will they go to Fiatera?" "Why did they strike down so many of us?" "Why haven't they shown themselves?" "We can be useful here!" "Where are the Twins?" "Where are the Twins?" "Where are the Twins?"

They were used to getting answers from Valrik, their leader, and Keiro was sure he would give them *something*. He didn't need Keiro hovering at his elbow, ready to catch his words if they faltered or slipped into knowledge they shouldn't give. Valrik knew better than that.

So Keiro left. There was nothing more for him to do there, nothing for which he was needed among the anger and the hurt and the endless questions. No way through the pressing mob, but there were other paths through the Plains. Keiro walked to the edge of the great crater into the hill, and his feet found the familiar ladder that hung over the edge, and he descended into darkness. He didn't even have Cazi's faint glow for light. *Mravigi* claws were not meant for ladders, and so the Starborn would be taking his own path into the hill, ways that were hidden to all humans, even Keiro.

He was glad for the darkness, when his feet reached the

bottom of the great cavern that sat far below the hill's crest. In the dark, he couldn't see the bodies that slumped against one wall. Still, the image was burned into him, floating in the empty space behind his missing eye: the old bodies of his gods, their *corpses*, empty and broken. Thinking of them made his gorge rise, and seeing the bodies was so much worse. He hurried across the cavern, and was not sad to drop to his hands and knees to crawl away through one of the countless tunnels that branched from the cavern.

By the time a faint glow caught up to him—Cazi, who could move faster than Keiro and knew more shortcuts—Keiro's faint nausea had passed, and he'd managed to push the image of the Twins' bodies from his mind. He didn't bother greeting the Starborn; one didn't greet one's shadow each time it made an appearance, after all.

After a few quiet, crawling spans, Cazi said softly, "*You did well.*" His voice was slightly shrill, an off-key version of the beautiful music all *mravigi* spoke. He was growing still, barely an adolescent by their measuring, and Keiro remembered well how his own voice had cracked and warbled at that age. "*You spoke strongly.*"

"Thank you," Keiro murmured, grateful for the thought if not the lie itself.

Keiro paused at a branching of the tunnel. The left would take him back up, to a cluster of bushes near the edge of the hills, where the grass turned from chest-high to taller than a man. That way lay the plainswalkers, who had given him home and protection and purpose. He longed to turn left, even though returning to the plainswalkers would only show him how many faces were absent, how many had been buried in their own peaceful graves after the Twins' rise. The plainswalkers had kept their distance from the Fallen ever since. Keiro truly didn't know if he would be welcome among the plainswalkers ever again because of his part in the horror of the Twins' resurrection. Still. He wanted so badly to know, one way or the other—to see them, even if all he saw was fury on their faces.

Cazi nudged his foot. Keiro swallowed his wanting, and took the right branch.

Their path tilted ever downward, each branch leading deeper into the earth. Keiro's fingers felt heavy and clumsy, the cold ground seeping into him. For a long while, the only sounds were the pad of Keiro's hands and knees against the tunnel, the *snick-snick* of Cazi's sharp claws, the scrape of his tail dragging behind him.

A sound like a rockslide made Keiro flinch, but he did not pause. It was a wonder, how quickly a man could grow accustomed to the impossible. The shouted cursing was faint at first, gradually louder as Keiro continued on. The words set a pressure between Keiro's eyes—not quite pain, but something very close to it. The rumble sounded again.

"—not working, *helesani chornya pero* made me useless. *Prene te elora, vsint*—"

Keiro did pause this time. Very softly, he said to Cazi, "You should wait here." When he started forward once more, there was no *snick-snick*ing behind him.

Finally the tunnel flattened, and opened into a wide space lit by pale blue light. Keiro kept his eyes fixed to the ground between his numb fingers.

"—even make a simple *chentaya*." The words slipped fluidly between ones Keiro understood, and those that made the pressure behind his skull pulse, that made his teeth ache. *"Mserin tevarro, tor* swear by all the *sverein stahn*—" Keiro pressed his face against his arm, clenching his eyes and his teeth as the pressure built, built almost beyond bearing. The words took on a new cadence, a chant, each word like a dagger between his eyes, and it was sure to rip his skull open if it went on too much longer. *"—elune ment, treteine bero vosha lon, helesani pero—"*

"Brother."

The single sharp word cut through the invective. Silence crashed as sudden as a wave, the horrible pressure fizzling away so quickly Keiro almost sobbed with relief. A different sort of pressure filled the room, but the weight of fury against his skin was much more bearable than when the fury had pulsed within him.

"Control yourself, Brother," the second voice said. Though she spoke quietly, there was nothing soft in her voice—all sharp edges and clipped words, as though each sound was a heartbeat away from a scream. Keiro knew the flavor of her anger: a slow-building rage that lurked always beneath the surface, but rarely broke free. It wasn't her anger that palpably shivered the air.

Keiro dared to look up.

Two adolescents stood at the center of an empty, circular chamber. They faced each other, identical glares plastered onto their young faces—their *identical* young faces, for there could never be any question that they were cut from the same cloth. The girl's dark hair was longer, her face slightly more angular, and the boy was a good handspan shorter—but for those minor differences, they could have been the same person.

Their eyes were the same, too—ancient eyes, that had seen

the birth of the world and seen their own deaths. Incongruous eyes, in such young faces.

As the children continued to stare each other down, the pressure of the anger built. A sheen of frost spiderwebbed out from the boy's feet. One of his hands was balled into a fist, pounding rhythmically against his thigh, though the hand closest to Keiro hung motionless. The girl stood completely still, not blinking, not even when the frost stretched beneath her feet, spread across the whole floor, rimed the smooth walls of the chamber. The pale blue light, emanating from a single lantern hung above their heads, began to flicker crazily.

Keiro tried to make himself smaller, sitting back on his knees, wrapping his arms around himself, tucking his head. He still shivered violently.

It was not an easy thing, to sit before two bickering gods.

Finally, *finally*, the girl's voice broke the silence: "Enough." Softly spoken, but it held the weight of command. The girl had been named Avorra, but Avorra was gone—replaced, instead, by the goddess Sororra. When she'd wandered the earth long ago, wearing her own body, any who had dared to disobey her had not lived long. The very ground had trembled at her will. "That is enough."

The flickering light stilled as Keiro lifted his head. The frost receded slowly from the walls. The boy's clenched fist loosened, and his eyes dropped to the floor. He didn't utter an apology, but the slumped lines of his shoulders spoke it as well as words.

Sororra stepped forward, the last of the frost crackling gently beneath her feet, and set her hands on her brother's shoulders. "We will fix this," she said, and the command had drained from her voice, leaving in its wake a fierceness that burned as bright as the sun had. Her hands slid down his arms to grasp his hands, and his fingers curled around hers—except for the fingers of his left hand, which lay still within her grip. "I promise you, Brother."

"I know." His voice was barely a whisper as he pulled his hands gently free. He turned his back to her, shoulders hunched, his good hand tugging at the bad one as though trying to work feeling back into numb fingers. Keiro couldn't see his face, but he could see Sororra's, written with a fierce pride and a love that would see the world burn.

She had always protected her brother. Championed him, fought for him, killed for him. All the old stories, the ancient tales that glowed in Keiro's heart, were full of inconsistencies and the chaos of the time before the Parents had imposed order upon their world . . . but there was a constant, no matter the tale, no matter who told it: in all their interminably long lives, Sororra would do anything for Fratarro.

There was another constant, too, one that burned less bright, that often flowed by unnoticed: Fratarro never truly understood what his sister was capable of.

Fratarro, who wore the body of a boy that had been named Etarro, asked, "Did it go well?"

It took Keiro a long moment to realize this question was directed to him; he hadn't thought either of the gods had noticed him at all. Before he could answer, though, Sororra said, "It did." Of course she would know.

Keiro bowed his head. "I sent them away, as you asked." All the old stories told how much Fratarro had asked from his followers, but he had always *asked*. He'd never needed to command, not with Sororra at his shoulder, her eyes carrying all the command his words didn't. "Valrik and the others will see to it that they leave. Two more da . . . moon-passes, and they should all be gone."

"Good," Sororra said, her voice lowering, almost a purr. "You've done well."

"Thank you, Keiro," Fratarro said softly.

Sororra went on, "I know I can trust you to see to things here, and to attend to my brother, while I'm away."

"Away?" Keiro asked, before he thought to strip doubt from the question. If Sororra heard any, she didn't show it.

"There's much to be done, as you said. My brother needs more time to return to himself, but this time is vital—I need to know the tilt of the world; all that has changed, and all that needs to change. It is something I can do, while my brother regains his strength."

Fratarro still had his back to the room, shoulders tight as he ignored that he was being talked about as though he wasn't there, but Keiro could see how his thumb pressed into the palm of his motionless hand, pressed hard enough that red, mortal blood began to well around his thumbnail. *They can't see, no one can see.*

Keiro looked away, so that he could pretend he hadn't seen, pretend he didn't know. "I have always lived to serve the will of the Twins."

CHAPTER FOUR

One of the guiding tenets of Joros's life was that the application of enough willpower, enough intelligence, enough *pressure*, would lead to his success. It was a simple arithmetic, and a lesson he'd been able to grasp very early in his life. Though the values of each variable shifted constantly, he need only do *more* than they required to guarantee the result. With enough hard work, Joros would never fail.

The sun's vanishing had turned that philosophy to ash.

Trudging through the Plains and the sudden edge of the Forest Voro, away from the blasted hills where everything had ended, Joros had realized that sometimes there simply wasn't enough effort available to win out. He had given everything he had and everything he was, had tried harder than a drowning man fighting for air—and all for the same result. Eternal darkness. No matter how much he tried, one man couldn't hope to beat two ancient gods newly freed from their long prison. Joros had tried to keep them from being freed, to stop them before they were a true threat, but he'd lost. He'd played a good game, and now it was over. Everything was done. All of his trying had, in the end, amounted to nothing.

Joros wanted to feel his usual fury, because the fury at least was something he understood, knew how to process. But he just felt . . . sad. A genuine sadness, the sort of thing he hadn't felt when he'd left his home and family, or when he'd realized his two decades of service to the Fallen had been an utter waste, or when he'd killed Dirrakara, whom he might even have loved if that was a thing he'd ever learned how to do. This was a child's sadness, brought on by a world-twisting realization that booted one unceremoniously toward adulthood. The last time Joros had felt the like was when his oldest brother, bastard that he was, had told Joros he'd been a mistake, and that everything would be better if Joros had never been born. Joros had been nine then, and the words had held enough of the flavor of truth to send him running into the surrounding fields, wiping tears from his cheeks. After the first dozen minutes of running, he'd decided he didn't actually want to run away, but by then nothing looked familiar, and the wheat reached higher than he could jump. He hadn't stumbled home until an hour after the sun had gone down, and no one was relieved to see him or startled he'd been gone.

Now he felt nine again, full of the same world-crushing pain of a child realizing that the world didn't give a shit what he wanted. All his years spent plotting, charting the course of his life and the world he would shape around himself, planning a solution for every possible contingency . . . all of his careful planning had failed. Everything had ended when the Twins rose, and since then he hadn't been able to plan any further ahead than where he'd put his foot down next. If there was anything that *could* be done to stop the Twins now, he didn't know how to go hunting for it, and the solution certainly hadn't drifted magically into his mind.

There was a metallic sound to his left, and Joros froze. Some instinctive part of his brain put a name to the sound—*the jangle of armor*—and lurched to life—fractionally. It was enough to send his hand to grip his short sword's hilt, but not enough to draw it. His eyes flickered, searching, between tree trunks— and then he saw them.

Walking shadows, moving toward them through the moon- lit trees. Two, five, more—all wearing black robes. Preachers of the Long Night, and Joros could only imagine how bold they'd be, surrounded by their ultimate success.

At his side, Rora had drawn her daggers, hopefully as many as she could hold at once. The air around Joros crackled as one of the mages—probably Anddyr, since Aro had been clawing at his own arms until recently—raised an invisible, protective shield around their small group. That would keep them safe for a while, but if it came to a fight—if the preachers struck first and fast and hard—the four of them wouldn't be enough. No matter how hard they fought, how hard they tried, they would die. That was the way of the world.

"Hail, Brothers," one of the preachers called across the distance, and surprise sealed Joros's lips for a moment. Joros remembered in a rush—without being stupid enough to gape down at himself—that he was still wearing one of his old black robes, that Anddyr was as well, that perhaps Rora and Aro's clothes were dark enough to pass for black . . .

Joros's mind lurched into sudden, frantic activity.

"Hail, Brothers," Joros repeated, keeping the surprise from his voice. His hand didn't leave his sword, though—they might see through the lie at any moment. Joros didn't want them com- ing any closer for a lot of reasons, but short of outright fleeing, there weren't many options for keeping them away.

"Have you come from the south?" the same preacher called. There were at least eight of them—no, nine—fanned out among the trees, and that was a number that looked rather intimidating compared to four. "Did you see it happen? Did you see them rise?" There was that fervor in his voice, the all-encompassing kind of faith that was equal parts annoying and terrifying.

"We did," Joros said shortly. He'd never learned how to talk to those sorts with anything but condescension, and that seemed like a poor route to take, what with being so outnumbered. Two mages evened out the numbers a bit, but at the same time, it really didn't. Anddyr was dependable, to an extent, even when he was trapped in his madness. The right spells could make him worth three fighters. Aro, though, was generally a useless lump. So long as he was in one of his sane moods, he could cast spells effectively enough, if erratically—but when the madness was on him, he couldn't be counted on for anything, and was more often a danger than he ever was a help.

With the Twins freed, with Joros's last plans an utter failure, perhaps he could finally get rid of the useless twin.

That was a thought for later. There was more immediate business at hand. The preachers were drawing closer, close enough that, soon, they'd bump into air that was unexpectedly solid.

Joros made a subtle motion with his hand, one he hoped Anddyr would see in the darkness. The mage must have, for the crackling air faded until all the hairs on Joros's arms lay flat once more. The preachers drew closer, sensing nothing at all amiss.

"It's true, then?" the talkative one went on. "I mean, of course it is, just look around!" He laughed, the others joining in, like a pack of hyenas cackling as they circled their prey . . . There was nothing particularly threatening about them besides their greater numbers, but Joros knew how quickly camaraderie could switch to enmity. "We got the summons, but we couldn't make it back in time . . . we were in Montevelle, important business with the Duke, but you don't need to know that. Tell us everything!"

They were close enough now that, even in the darkness, he could see the expectant looks on their faces, their excitement and their zealous faith.

Joros stood there, staring back at them, his tongue frozen to the roof of his mouth. The part of his brain that had been running on adrenaline ran out. He couldn't think of the lie that would make the preachers leave, couldn't think what attack would be best, couldn't *think*.

He stared, and the silence stretched. The eagerness faded slowly from the preachers' eyes, replaced by confusion.

"No time," a voice croaked from behind Joros's shoulder. "We're on important business, too. We need to get to Mercetta as fast as we can."

Aro. Foolish, thoughtless Aro, speaking when he shouldn't have, daring to say anything when Joros himself couldn't think of the right words . . . but at least they *were* words, any words. It was an imperfect plan, a flimsy lie, but at least it was *something*. Sluggishly, Joros's mind started turning once more, rust flaking away from the gears that had always been plotting.

"Yes," Joros said, straightening his back, tipping up his chin—little affectations that could add a sense of superiority better than any tone of voice. "They'll be able to tell you more in the hills, but we have no time to waste. And you'd best hurry—important things are afoot." That was too grandiose, he realized too late, but they didn't seem to notice—the talkative one widened his eyes, the eagerness creeping back in.

"The hills . . . ?" he asked carefully.

Joros waved his hand back in the direction they'd come. "Almost directly south. Through the Plains. I don't doubt you'll encounter others who have more time to spend giving simple directions." Not even a year ago, Joros had been a member of the Ventallo, one of the elite rulers of the Fallen, and that position had brought with it an extreme level of haughtiness—and that was something that couldn't be shaken easily. Joros could throw on that haughtiness like a cloak, and he saw how it cowed the preachers.

The talker actually *bowed* to him. "As you say. Forgive us, we'll be on our way. Strength in the night, Brothers, and may the Twins guide your steps."

And they left, easy as that. Joros stared after them, not sure what he should feel first or strongest. Satisfaction, of course, that a few sentences had been enough to chase them away. Relief that his planning mind hadn't been shattered and broken beyond repair. Resentment that he'd given up the cow-eyed scraping his position in the Fallen had brought him for the band of fools he was now saddled with. Curiosity that Aro, perhaps, wasn't quite as stupid as Joros had always thought.

Joros turned away once the darkness had swallowed the preachers, and he began walking north once more. There was nothing else to do—but the gears were slowly waking in Joros's mind. Turning, still sluggish, still gummed up by failure and the fog of sadness—but beginning to turn nonetheless.

Later, as Joros's thoughts spun faster and faster, even walking became a distraction. He stumbled over his own feet more than once, ran into the others' backs or had them run into his. His numbed mind had shrugged off its shroud, and as though attempting to correct for its previous paralysis all at once, his thoughts were racing, crashing and colliding, spinning too quickly—spinning out of control. It was almost worse than the numbness—at least then, he hadn't been able to feel the crushing weight of his failure.

Joros called a halt, hoping that stilling his body might still his thoughts. They made a rough camp, with the scarce remains of the supplies they'd brought south: a battered pot, two ratty travelsacks filled with a grain that made a tasteless porridge, a flint and steel that had survived the rest of Joros's fire kit, and their own cloaks. No bedrolls, no tents, no shelter from the wind that rattled the tree branches around them. Winter was fading, but it still held ground in the forest beyond the Plains. It felt colder without the sun's light . . . but not as cold as it should have, not a winter to beat all winters as he would have expected. Joros still didn't quite know what to make of that.

He insisted on a fire, now that they had trees for both kindling and shelter, and Rora was too tired to argue with him. That was disappointing. He stared at them each in turn, Rora poking at the fire, Anddyr stirring the porridge as it bubbled thickly over the flames, Aro muttering to himself as he stared up at the stars. Joros hoped one of them would be foolish enough to open their mouth, to give him an excuse to talk, to argue, to stop *thinking*.

But no. They were caught up in their own thoughts. And Joros's continued to race, uncontrolled, unabated.

Joros stood abruptly, startling all of them. "I'm going hunting," he said, not that he owed them any explanation. The mages stared like they couldn't comprehend the words, but Rora raised an eyebrow at him—a disbelieving eyebrow, as if she thought it was a joke not even funny enough to laugh at. Joros could remember a time when that might have thrown him into a rage, but he felt only the sadness and the reeling of his thoughts. "Give me your knife," he said to her, utterly inflectionless, holding out his hand. That made her other eyebrow go up, but after a moment she fished out one of her daggers from its hiding place, flipped it up to catch it by the tip, and laid the hilt into his palm. Ignoring the blatant braggadocio, Joros closed his fingers around the dagger and turned for the trees.

The sun's disappearance had thrown the animal kingdom into as much of an uproar as Joros imagined any city across Fiatera was in. Normally diurnal animals were now forced to venture out in the night, animals that didn't know how to survive when they couldn't see their predators. That generally made it an easy task for Rora to bring down a bird or a squirrel to supplement the bland porridge, but she'd had less luck since leaving the Plains, with trees and branches now getting between her and her prey. Joros was sick of being constantly hungry, his stomach lined only with porridge.

Joros tucked the dagger into his belt near his shortsword—not a hunting tool, and he wouldn't risk its edge—and skimmed his fingers over the rough ground, searching for stones among the deadfall and gritty patches of snow. He found a few that fit comfortably into his hand and tucked all but one into his cloak's biggest pocket—far away from the damned seekstone that was now linked to a god—and put his back to a tree, waiting. He would have preferred to sit, but the ground was too cold and damp to be comfortable, and he didn't want to get his cloak soaked *now* when he'd need to sleep in it later.

Then it was just waiting for a bird or a rabbit or a fecking deer and hoping that he could stun it long enough to cut its throat. And waiting on animals was nothing like the sort of distraction he'd been hoping for.

The problem was—and he'd begun to realize this slowly—that he *believed* now. It was hard to deny the existence of a god after he'd watched two of them burst through a hill and steal the nearest bodies for their own, carving a swath of death to power their rise. Only a fool would try to deny the evidence of his own eyes. That made the Twins real—and if the Twins were real, that made the Parents real, too, and if the Parents were real, then why in the name of every bleeding hell hadn't they done anything to stop their wayward children from returning to power? Joros had done everything he could to keep the Twins bound—and the Parents, who should have been doing far *more* than a mere human, had instead done nothing. They had let him fail, and left him with nothing.

Things had been easier when he hadn't believed—when he'd been a simple preacher, seeing an opportunity for power among a band of lunatics who actually believed the stories they told about gods bound beneath the earth; or when he'd started to actually wield that power, building a network of preachers that spanned the kingdom, shadowseekers all acting on his command, for his benefit. He knew the moment when it had all begun to fall apart: when Dirrakara—sly, conniving, *insidious* Dirrakara—had given him a pet, a mage to do his bidding, and told him so guilelessly that she was sure he would find a use for the mage. *Like calls to like*, Anddyr had told him. A thought had burrowed into Joros's brain that perhaps he could find the gods he feigned belief in by using the mage and that disturbing relic of the Fallen—an enormous fleshy, burned leg that cast doubts on his own doubts but was easy enough to avoid thinking of, the wondering kept as securely locked away as the leg. *Like calls to like*, and the mage had done it, somehow, found *something* and there was no denying it. It was hard to maintain disbelief in the face of five flickering points laid out like a constellation across a map of Fiatera, five *likes* the mage had found with the leg, *flung to the far horizons*—

There was a rustling in the brush, and Joros's hand flung out instinctively, the stone in his palm going crashing through the sparse foliage. Surprisingly, there was a shrill scream, and instinct carried him again: he jumped forward, using the tree's trunk for leverage, and pulled out the dagger with one hand as the other pushed aside the branches and deadfall where the scream came from. He found a rabbit half on its side, back or leg broken, and he slashed with the knife just as he'd planned, a quick cut across the throat. He grabbed the rabbit by the ears, and it felt *good*. He'd heard others talk about how it could make a person feel powerful, taking a life, and he hadn't understood that. When he'd killed Dirrakara, he'd only felt frustrated that it had come to that point—that was how he chose to remember it, at least, just the frustration and none of the other uncomfortable, complicated things. He knew, at least, that killing her hadn't made him feel powerful.

Looking at the rabbit he'd killed, Joros felt a touch of that—"powerful" wasn't the right word, though. "Satisfied" was closer, or "gratified." He'd set out to do a thing and done it. "Useful" felt like the right word.

Joros tucked the rabbit into his belt and started collecting wood, clearing a space among the sparse, dirty snow to start a fire. He still had his flint and steel, and it took him longer to get a spark than he would ever admit, but he built up a nice fire and split his time between feeding it more sticks and skinning the rabbit. That was something he'd never done before, but if it was something *Rora* could do, there was no reason he couldn't. Though a good amount of meat came away with the hide, he was left with plenty of rabbit to put on the sharp end of a stick. The smell of it roasting made his stomach roar, but he'd be damned if he'd eat half-raw meat and wind up shitting out his innards; he'd have a proper meal. He sat watching the rabbit brown and char, listening to his thoughts spin.

There was a thing Dirrakara had taught him, or tried to at least. "You get so *angry*," she'd chided, not understanding, never understanding how impossibly frustrating it was to be constantly surrounded by so much madness. She'd told him it was all right to feel anger—"Or any emotion," she'd said lightly, but with unmistakable reproach—so long as he didn't let it consume him. "Feel it," she'd said, "feel it entirely . . . and then move past it. I know you believe your anger sharpens you, but there's a point where it makes you . . . unproductive."

To the cooking rabbit, since Dirrakara wasn't there, Joros said aloud, "Made me pretty damned productive when I killed you, didn't it?" There wasn't any emotion behind the words, though, no anger or sadness, just a statement flat as a path that had been walked a thousand times. She'd been wrong about so much. His anger sharpened him to a fine point, deadly and unstoppable. It was the little-boy emotions, the sadness and the fear, that made him unproductive. Dirrakara had been wrong about so much . . . but not all of it.

Joros prayed, for the first time since he'd been a boy, since he'd realized that no one cared about him in this world or all the worlds beyond it. He prayed to the Parents, whose existence he could no longer deny, and his prayers were full of all the sadness and the fear. He felt them, felt them entirely, let them consume him . . . and let them fade away with the words of his prayers. They left behind a great emptiness, and in the wake of those foolish, childish emotions rose the familiar anger. Was it still prayer, if he screamed at the Parents? His anger shouted at the stars above, at the missing sun, at the Parents sitting secure in the godworld beyond the sky, and any lingering sadness morphed into hatred, fear into frustration. They had let this happen to the world, let this happen to him.

He had failed in all else—so be it. But he had wallowed long enough, been directionless long enough. There was one clear path left to him, one thing that he could yet do. He could still destroy the Twins, show the Parents that he didn't need them, that he was *better* than them. He could still be useful.

When the shouting fury subsided, Joros pulled his rabbit from the flames. It was overcooked, blackened along one side, but it tasted delicious nonetheless. Meat that he had caught and killed with his own hands.

Joros ate all of the rabbit, even the parts that were more char than meat, and he sucked the bones clean. When he was done, when his belly was full and his head was clear and his core was filled with the familiar clear-burning anger that had always driven him forward, he rose and stomped out his half-dead fire, kicking the scraggly patches of snow over the embers to be sure. He began walking, his feet generally following the direction he'd originally come, but in the darkness one tree looked very much like any other. He might not be heading back to the others at all.

Would it be the worst thing, if he turned his feet north right now?

He saw the fire through the trees—likely Rora and Aro and Anddyr, though he supposed it could be a group of preachers, or a group of commonfolk hiding in the woods from the end of the world. There was enough doubt that he could justify it, even, if he were to turn away from the flames. What kind of fool would approach strange fires during the Long Night? Better, surely, to leave, to strike out on his own. He didn't need anyone but himself.

Joros stood for a long time, staring at the fire, and then he began walking again.

He heard their voices before he reached the fire: Aro and Anddyr, their madnesses synchronized as they muttered at each other. He made enough noise as he approached so that Rora wouldn't be startled and put a dagger in him, but she was standing and ready to do just that when he stepped into the circle of light. She deflated with a strange mix of disappointment and relief and put her daggers away. Then she sat once more, studiously ignoring the two mages arguing. "You were gone awhile," she said.

"You should rest up," he told her as he shook out his cloak, wrapping it snugly around himself. "We'll need to start moving faster from now on." He didn't *need* anyone else, and that was true enough—he'd take on all the world with his hands if need be, cut the throat of anyone who got in his way—but things would be easier, far easier, with drudges.

It was simple arithmetic, an equation done in reverse: he *needed* to succeed, and so it was simply a matter of finding the values: How much effort, how much skill, how much blood? If he had failed before, it was only that he had not given enough. If he had failed, he simply needed to try harder.

"After all," he said, staring at the fire's flickering, and he felt a small smile twist his lips, "we have some gods to kill."

CHAPTER FIVE

Even with the moon not yet risen, Scal could make out Mount Raturo. It was a darker shape against the dark sky. A space with no stars, an emptiness. Like the sky had torn open to show the nothingness the winking stars hid.

The night was silent around them. All the creatures of the forest lost and confused without the protection, the consistency, of the sun. No other humans nearby, or at least none that he could hear. It was quiet because Vatri did not speak. Quiet because Scal had never learned the trick of breaking a silence.

They were too close to Raturo, far too close, and Scal could not help staring at it as they walked. His neck began to ache, from turning so often to where the mountain lurked at his left shoulder. Even when the trees blocked it from his sight, he still thought he could feel it. His eyes would not leave it alone.

There had been a time, not so very long ago though it felt like another life, when he had almost walked willingly into the mountain. He had been a different man then, trying to find his place, trying to find the shape of his life. It had been before he had found Vatri again. A group of the black-robed preachers had found him, had been kind to him. Had offered him a place among them. Had offered him purpose. He had ached with need, but he had turned from them, turned from the mountain, turned to Vatri. *She* had shaped him. It had been a better choice.

And yet.

The mountain called to him like a toothache. Unavoidable, nagging, sharp. *Dangerous*. He did not know why.

In time, Raturo dropped behind his shoulder. This made it harder for him to look, easier to ignore, and he was grateful for it. He had known a man with a bad tooth, who had hardly been able to eat without pain. A fellow caravan guard, whose jaw had slowly swollen around the tooth. When the swelling had spread to his neck, there had been nothing they could do but listen to his wheezing breath grow louder, more strained. When the wheezing had stopped, his hands clawing at his swollen neck as his eyes went huge, killing him had been a kindness. The ache in his tooth had ended, though. It always did, one way or another.

Scal followed in Vatri's wake, and ignored the way his head wanted to twist over his shoulder. Ignored the pulse of the mountain.

He heard the sound before Vatri did. It was not a surprise—she was always in her head, lost in her thinking and planning. At least she did not startle when he wrapped his fingers around her arm, pulling her to a stop. She heard it, too, when her eyes focused on him.

Talking. Voices low, but they carried through the silence of the dark forest.

Scal watched Vatri, watched all the thoughts flicker behind her eyes as she stared into the night. Waited. She would ask, and he would do whatever she asked. It was all he could do.

Finally she looked to him, jerked her head in the direction of the sound, the direction they had been going. She was smart, to speak without words. He did the same. Reaching out both his hands, pressing them firmly on her shoulders, holding his palms toward her as he stepped back. She frowned, but she nodded. She did not follow when he began picking his careful, quiet way through the trees.

His eyes had adapted to the darkness, in the long dark walking hours. Even with the tree cover, even when the moon hid beneath the edge of the world, Scal's eyes could still pick out shapes well enough. He had torn strips from his tunic, looped them around his belt to hang the sword at his side. It swung to his right; his left hand was slower, but he would rather pull ice than fire. He did not draw it now, as he walked forward. He would not until he needed to.

The two voices, talking together, grew louder. Dull light guided his feet, calling him closer to the edge of a small clearing. He hung back among the trees, but he could see well enough: a small house, a smaller shed where a handful of pigs milled. Farther in, two men, one younger and one older, moving in an awkward crouching walk along lines of thick logs. Picking mushrooms, he finally saw. Farmers. But they both wore black robes. Had tied their hair back with black cloth. Farmers, but preachers of the Long Night, too.

He watched them for a time, listening. They talked of the mushrooms, of the pigs, of the darkness. Things that did not matter. They talked of the Fallen, of all the preachers who would surely be returning in triumph soon. Scal heard movement inside the house, another person. A family, alone and peaceful and happy.

He stayed longer than he needed to. Longer than he should have. He would have stayed still longer, silent and watching, but he heard the steps behind him. Careful steps, but loud to his own ears. He did not turn to see; there was no point. He did not look as Vatri came to stand at his side.

She watched, and the edge of the moon crept above the trees, shining its light into the little clearing.

Vatri touched his arm, and Scal turned to face her. Her face was tight as a mask, the eyes carved grim, pitiless, unyielding. He had seen carvings of Metherra, where the face looked much the same. Vatri's hand fell, and landed on the hilt of the sword that hung at Scal's hip. She did not say it. She did not need to. Scal had known, from the moment he had seen the black of their robes.

Scal had never tried to count how many he had killed. From the start, it had been too many, more than he could remember. Five lives he had lived, all washed in a sea of blood, an ocean, a world of it. So many lives taken that one more, three more, could not possibly matter. Could not make any difference.

He left her side. Walked quiet around the shadowed edge of the clearing, closer to the men. The elder told a joke, the younger laughed, the sound shivering through the trees. Under the cover of that noise, Scal drew his sword. Drew it with the left hand, the hand of ice, and crystals danced along the blade. They did not see him when he stepped from the trees. Did not hear his feet, silent on the ground.

He took the elder first. It was a kindness, for no man should have to see his child dead. The blade went smoothly through the man's neck, and the spiny ice shards did not catch when Scal pulled the blade free. The younger man did not react in the time it took Scal to take three steps toward him. He fell as silently as his father. The woman screamed when he entered the house, but it did not matter. There was no one for her to warn.

After, when it was done, the moonlight whispered across the floor to the woman's body, and it shone off the killing wound in her neck. Shone, for her neck was pale and shimmering, frosted with ice halfway up her cheeks and beyond the neck of her shift. There was no blood. Frozen, likely, within her veins.

The sword, too, was clean. Perhaps it was meant to be a kindness, less blood added to the sea of it that could drown him so easily. A kindness, from the gods who would use him as their tool . . . but it did not feel like a kindness.

Outside the pigs were shuffling nervously. He let them be; his stomach rumbled with hunger, but he had no taste for flesh. He did not even think of the mushrooms.

Vatri met him near the edge of the clearing, her yellow robe bright in the moonlight. "I'm sorry," she said, reaching out to touch his wrist. Not the one that had held the blade. The words felt true, though. "Will you gather wood?"

There was nothing else for him to do. Vatri went into the house, likely to search for anything valuable, anything useful. Scal did not know if she meant to make a camp or a pyre, and so he piled sticks between the house and the mushroom logs, in the empty space where—if he kept his eyes straight, did not let them see anything to the edges—death had not touched.

Vatri piled her own findings nearby: a bedroll and a sturdy travelsack, three blankets that were thin but better than nothing, pots and spices and a tiny jar of salt, wooden bowls and utensils, needle and thread, candles and oil, the lantern, a tinderbox, two small knives and a hatchet, a whetstone, a long length of oiled canvas, scraps of leather, dried meat, hardbread. The belongings of people used to travel. It would be foolish not to take it all.

She began arranging the sticks for a fire. No pyre, then. Scal took the tinderbox from the pile she had made, but she stopped him with a word: "Wait." Building the sticks higher, a pile big enough it would drown a spark, not enough small pieces to catch. "The sword," she said at last, and Scal drew it. The flames licking along the blade turned her face once more to a mask. Vatri motioned to the pile of sticks before her, and the mask murmured, "Now make a fire."

Scal frowned. He had walked through the long grassy Plains with the fire-sword live in his hands, and the flames had brushed against the grasses, but they had never caught fire. He had touched his free hand to the flames, and felt nothing save heat. The fire seemed harmless.

Vatri sighed. Dug through the pile of her new belongings. Pulled free one of the small knives, no longer than her hand, and she threw it to Scal. It was a foolish thing, but he managed to catch the knife, even with his slower left hand. And dropped it in surprise, when ice shards swept along the little blade. Unease churned in his stomach. Scal crouched down, set the sword aside so the flames died along its edge, and instead he lifted the knife with his right hand. Stared, as the same flames flickered.

He had thought—*hoped*—that it was the sword. Taken from one of the Fallen's mercenaries, it was surely some of their strange magic that turned the sword to fire and ice.

But no. It was him, his own hands.

In this same forest, Vatri had drawn on Scal's body with ash, symbols that hurt his eyes if he looked at them too long. She had drawn two symbols on his palms that were like a mirror to each other, and she had sent him into the bonfire. He had almost convinced himself it was a dream. No memory of the flames, no memory until he had woken in a pile of ash with not a mark of it on his naked flesh. He remembered his palms had hurt, but the ache had faded.

"This," Vatri said softly, "is the will of the Parents. *You* are their will. Metherra and Patharro have put their faith in you to help in this fight against the darkness."

She had told him, in the great grass sea, though he had not listened. A weapon for the Parents, to match the mercenaries of the Fallen. She had said he was made to serve the Parents, shaped by the hands of life into a tool for them to use. It had not been the explanation he wanted. He had not wanted to hear, and so he had not truly listened.

"The power they've given is yours to bear, yours to use *as you will*. You need to learn now how to use it. There is so much we must do."

Scal laid down the knife, raised the sword instead. A sword had always felt better in his hand. Even when he hated the things a sword could do, the hilt fit perfectly in his hand, an extension of himself. The flames that danced along the blade whispered, and Scal thought of Vatri. Of how she had gotten her scars. The fire had spoken to her, and she had leaned in to hear better, leaned too close. Scal let the fire whisper. It could say nothing that would draw him in.

So. She wished him to make a fire with the sword, with the power of the Parents. Scal reached, and touched the tip of the sword to the piled sticks. The flames touched and skimmed harmlessly against the wood.

Fire. It was what his name meant, one of the Northern runes, the oldest words in the world. It was what he had named himself in his second life, the life after the killing snows, the life of warmth and smiles and nothing but brightness. It had been the only word in his head, at the start of that life. But flames had burned Aardanel, burned away his home and his life and his hope. Burned them all over again in his third life, burned away what little peace he had found in the frozen North. *Fire.* The tool of the Parents. Metherra's sun, brought to earth. Warmth and death and life and destruction.

Perhaps he had only ever had one life, built of blood and built of fire. In all his days, those had been the only constants.

Fire, Scal thought, and the sword's light flared, and the sticks caught with a roar.

When the flames settled, and Scal looked across the crackling fire, Vatri was smiling, pleased. It hardly looked a real smile. Her face a mask still, mouth carved in the proper shape.

Scal set aside the sword, and held his hands in his lap. Staring at the lines that marked his palms, the scars, the calluses. Trying, somehow, to see the sigils she had drawn there. To see the mark of the Parents on his skin.

"I don't want you to hate me," Vatri said, her voice soft from the other side of the fire. "I understand you, Scal. You wish the world had made you differently. You wish you could have a simple life—if not free of blood and pain and death, then at least with less of it. You wish you could be happy. I understand you." Scal looked up from his hands. She was watching him through the flames, and her face was less a mask. More open, behind the old scars carved into her face. Honest, and sad, and hopeful. "I want you to understand me, too. My whole life, I have served the Parents. They're what I live for. They chose me, and I *must* be worthy of them. But it's not easy. They ask so much . . ." She looked away, and a gust of smoke hid her face from him completely. "You wanted guidance. A hand to point you, a voice to direct you. You asked me . . . but I've only ever served the Parents. If you follow me, it's them you're following. Any orders from me are orders from them. The gods ask much of us, but they never ask more than what we can bear. Anything I ask of you, anything you do for them through me . . . it may hurt, but it won't break you." The heavy smoke cleared, and Vatri had turned back to him, her face set once more. "The world sits at a delicate balance, now more than ever. The return of the Twins will change things even more than it already has. We have to maintain balance, Scal. We have to do whatever we can to make sure the scales don't tip too far in *either* direction. And that means the coming days, weeks, months, will not be easy for us. But they will not be impossible."

Scal stared into the fire. Tried to pull the important pieces from her speech, tried to decide if she wanted him to say something, if there was anything he could say. She had said so much, enough to drown his own thoughts. He could think of nothing to say before she spoke once more.

"The fire is always full now . . . full of Metherra's voice, full of Patharro's will. I know you can't read the flames like I can, but they're full of hope. We *can* fight the Twins, and fight the Fallen. We can restore the sun, return the world to its proper balance. I see all this."

Scal stared into the fire between them. She was right—he

had never seen the future in the red-gold flares. He only ever saw the dancing, indistinct shapes as the wood snapped and the flames wove about each other.

"I see Raturo," she said, and he thought of the mountain, felt it over his shoulder, and stopped himself from twisting to look at it. He stared at the fire instead, and perhaps the flames did dance in the shape of a crooked thumb. Perhaps he saw. Perhaps he only wanted to. "I see its peak crumbling, falling— the mountain destroyed. It's the symbol of their power, the Fallen and the Twins both, and we will *crush* it. I see them flee- ing, scattering like dust, and the fall of Raturo crashes like a wave upon them."

A twig snapped, sending embers dancing high. If he could see the shape of the mountain within the flames, perhaps, too, he could see the preachers spreading out from the mountain. But Scal had seen the Fallen assembled in all their numbers. If he saw them in the flames, reaching out from their mountain home, he did not think they were fleeing. He had seen the Fallen, seen how they carved their path upon the earth like a mighty river, how they swallowed the ground like a sea. If Vatri saw the tide of the Fallen receding from Mount Raturo, it was only so they could crash against a different shore.

But Scal had never seen the future in the flames. It was a thing that was beyond him, and so he said nothing.

She spoke little after that, and after a time she rose and said there was much still that they needed to do. Before he stood, Scal looked to the sword that lay stretched along the grass next to him. He had thought, *Fire*, and the wood had caught. The power of the Parents, answering his will.

He waited until Vatri's back was to him, before he held a

thought in his mind and reached to hold the sword in his right hand, the hand of fire. When he raised it, the blade remained cold steel, showing only the light of the stars, of a piece of the moon. He returned it to the makeshift sheath at his belt so that Vatri would not see. So that she would not ask why he had looked into the dancing flames and held the thought: *Darkness.*

CHAPTER SIX

They avoided roads when they could, not that it made all that much difference. Rora'd seen few enough people out, even when she'd circled close to the road. Most folks seemed to've locked themselves up inside their houses, and she couldn't say she blamed 'em for that. Every time they passed by a house, its windows glowing like stars in the darkness, it put an ache into her. She'd only lived in a real house twice in her life, both times when she'd barely been old enough to remember things, but maybe that was why *home* called to her so strong. Both those times, she'd felt more safe and happy than she'd ever felt since.

And it was a small, stupid hope, but Rora thought maybe she was heading toward home now.

She recognized the land they were walking through, all the fields that were shit for hiding in and the big stretches of nothing but grass with maybe a bush to break up the boring. Even in the dark she recognized the area, because the last time she'd been through it, she'd been holding her head proud as she led her new charges, all the knives and fists that answered to *her* now. She'd spent so much time scouting, because she'd wanted them to see she'd do her fair share, see that she cared about doing a good job of it all.

Funny—in that really-not-funny way that was right on the edge of tears—how quick things could change. She felt more like a beaten dog now, creeping back with head and tail low, hoping for scraps of food, attention, love, anything. Hoping her stupid little hopes.

Hoping that her family—the family she'd chose, not the family her blood had chose for her—would take her back. Hoping they'd somehow be able to make everything right.

"This feels bad," Aro muttered. He had his back against a low stone wall that some farmer had put up around his field. Seemed a pretty bad fence—it hadn't stopped Rora stepping over it and helping herself to the farmer's tasteless corn. That was the good thing about being back in Fiatera proper— there was a lot more food, and it was a lot easier to steal. "It's all wrong . . ."

Nothing had been right for a while, but Rora kept that thought to herself, hard as it was to do. She'd spent her whole life listening to her brother, answering his questions even when they were stupid, taking care of him. Even if he was broken, even if he'd broken the trust they had, even if he some- times wasn't much like the brother she remembered at all . . . he still *was*. Taking care of him was a hard habit to break.

But Rora'd made a promise to herself not to let him off easy like she had her whole life. He'd taken away her teeth, taken away all her power when he asked her not to kill Joros and Anddyr for what they'd done to him. He'd asked her to go against everything that made up who she was, and forgiving him for that felt like a long, faraway thing. And all the killing- hot anger she still had inside her had to point somewhere, so Rora felt like she spent most of her days wrestling it away from

Joros or Anddyr to point at Aro instead. He'd asked her not to kill the others, and she wouldn't because he was her brother and he'd asked—but that meant she got to be mad at him for a good long while.

And she'd seen the look in his eyes when he was mostly sane, when he realized how mad she was at him. Aro'd always had more pride than he deserved. He hadn't said he was sorry, and she knew he wouldn't. He'd just let her be mad until she forgave him, the same way she always had. Rora ground her teeth. Old habits broke hard, but they *could* break.

"It's bad," he whispered, "it's bad, it's bad . . ." He trailed off into mumbles, probably the same words over and over just too quiet and tangled up to hear.

Even if Aro was lost in the mess of his mind, he wasn't wrong. This place felt *bad*. There were no people around at all, just dark houses you could barely see and an empty road stretching off to nowhere. Even farther south, farther away from real civilization, there'd been *some* people; here, closer to the capital, they should've run into people or seen 'em locked up in their houses like sensible folk.

But there wasn't any kind of life around, and the closer they got to the old crumble-down estate where they'd left Whitedog Pack, the more worried Rora got.

Anddyr tugged at one of the cornstalks, his eyes going bigger as it swayed toward him. The witch'd been clear-thinking for a while, which probably meant he was due for a crazy spell anytime now. It was always great, when him and Aro got crazy at the same time. "We're close," Anddyr whispered. "I don't . . . I don't know what's waiting . . ."

Joros snorted. "Then we'd best not waste any more time in

finding out." He stood up from the rock he'd been sitting on and gave Rora a half glare, probably waiting to see if she'd argue with him.

She almost wanted to—because even as bad as she wanted to get to her pack, she was more'n a little scared what she'd find. Waiting wouldn't make the finding out any better, though, so she didn't argue. "Get up," she said to Anddyr, and he lurched to his feet like a baby horse who hadn't quite learned how to stand yet. She went over and nudged her brother—she couldn't order him around, especially not when he was in one of his bad patches. She had once, back in that heavy forest that'd swallowed them for a few days: she'd got so frustrated with the way he couldn't take more'n five steps without falling down and crying about giants or birds—he was blubbering so much she never could hear it clear—that she'd shouted at him, "Gods damn it, Aro, stop crying and just *walk*." And his face'd gone totally slack, his tears drying up as his eyes changed into a stranger's eyes. There hadn't been anything left of her brother in them, not for the handful of heartbeats it'd taken him to stand up and take a few shaky steps. She'd stood there frozen, horrified, but the strangeness had faded from his eyes once he got walking. Still, those few seconds he hadn't been Aro, those few seconds he hadn't been *anybody* . . . that'd stuck with her.

So she shook Aro's shoulder, grabbed his arm to help him to his feet. He was still her brother. He followed behind her—he was usually pretty good about that—and she led the way through the fields, picking their roundabout way toward the old estate. Mumbling was the only sound, Aro and Anddyr and occasionally Joros—she didn't hear what he said or who he said it to, and that put a twitch under her eye. The witches kept up their mumbling over the next few hours, even when Rora made everyone stop and hunker down behind some wild shrubs, staring across the empty road.

The estate sat as dark as all the houses they'd passed by lately, dark and dead. The gate hung half off its hinges, just like it'd been the day Joros'd shown 'em the place and said it belonged to Whitedog Pack now. If the pack'd made any changes since, it didn't show. If there was anyone alive inside the walls, it didn't show.

"Wrong," Aro whispered, "wrong, wrong, wrong . . ."

Rora hushed him gently even though he was right. She could taste her heartbeat, sour with nerves and fear.

"They can't be dead," Joros said, soft and shocked, but sounding like he was right on the edge of tipping into a good shout.

"We have to go in," she said. "See . . ." She didn't know how to finish that, didn't know if it'd be worse to see them all dead or to see that they'd left, that she'd never know where they went, that she'd never get their forgiveness or have a family or have a home . . . "We have to go see."

She stood up, and led the way across the road.

As they passed through the gate, moonlight flickered dull off the spots that weren't covered in rust. The moon wasn't more'n halfway up the sky, so it threw long shadows across half the courtyard, the old walls stretching across the ground. Rora searched all the windows of the dark house, looking for any movement, any light, anything . . .

Anddyr screamed.

It made Rora near jump out of her skin, whirling around to face the witch, and he was scrabbling at his chest . . . scrabbling at something *in* his chest. A plain hilt, the rest of the dagger buried in his flesh. His fingers were already starting to turn black where he pawed at the hilt, darkness taking all the color out of the blood. Rora spun back around in just enough time to duck under the arm that would've slammed into her throat, but she didn't avoid the jab to her kidney that sent her down to her knees. Fingers grabbed enough of her hair to hold on to— she had the crazy, stupid thought that she should've taken the time to cut it back to short enough it couldn't be grabbed—and yanked her head back. She wasn't even surprised when she felt the dagger against her throat.

Anddyr was still screaming, but it was more muffled; Rora could move her eyes enough to see he was facedown on the ground with a whole pile of people on top of him, grabbing at his arms. They were smart enough to know he couldn't cast any spells without his hands.

She couldn't find Aro with her eyes, couldn't turn her head enough to see him, and she couldn't hear his voice at all. What in all the hells was he waiting for? Anddyr'd trained him enough he could save them, stop this, at the very least put a shield up around her and the others.

She felt the crackle in the air, and if Anddyr was too tied up to do anything, it meant her brother'd finally shaken the cotton out of his head enough to do something useful. The world got sharp and heavy and full of iron, something big building, something horrible, but at least it had to be better'n dying at the hands of whoever'd killed her pack or driven them out. She couldn't avenge them if she was dead, so whatever awful thing Aro was building, she knew it'd keep them alive, him and her at the very least, and—

Two people stepped out the front door of the old house, and the sour fear in Rora's mouth turned to full panic.

"Aro!" she screamed, ignoring the pain as the dagger scraped against her throat. Bloody gods, would he be able to hear her over Anddyr's screaming? "Aro, *don't do anything.*"

Somehow, she heard the little whimper. She'd know her brother's voice from anything, and all the sharpness fell out of the air, sudden as letting out a held breath. Rora sagged a little, even though it tugged at her hair, even though it pressed the dagger harder against her throat.

Of the two people that'd walked out of the house, the slower one stopped, looking around the half-dark courtyard. The other one kept going, heading straight for Rora, hands curled into fists. "Listen," Rora said quickly, the knife scraping on her throat, "it's not how it—"

It was a good punch, Rora'd give her that. Tore out some of her hair as the person holding on to her kept holding on. There was the taste of blood, the burn of split skin across her cheek, but she'd been half expecting the punch. She'd earned it, kind of. Maybe she'd even earned the second punch, the one that slammed right into the same spot on her cheek, and this time the hand let go of her hair. She fell hard against the ground.

Rora's head was spinning, but she could've got up. She had daggers all over the place, and she could've pulled out any of them, used her knives and her own fists to fight back. That wouldn't've done her any good, though, and maybe it'd even make things worse. So she just lay there, letting her head spin, blinking away the red fog. She got a good look at Tare, the older woman's face written clear with pure murder, and then she got a much *closer* look at Tare as she landed on top of Rora. Fingers wrapped around Rora's throat, digging in where the dagger had nicked her, and Tare's other hand went back to slamming into Rora's face.

Far away, Rora could hear shouting, but it was just like Aro and Anddyr's mumbling, soft and unclear. All she could really hear was Tare, snarling in time with her punches: "I knew. I couldn't. Trust. You. Traitor. I'll. Kill you."

The punches stopped, and Rora blinked back blood, saw others had finally managed to grab Tare's punching arm and were yanking it back. That only slowed her down for a second, though—she unwrapped her fingers from around Rora's neck and curled them into a fist instead, worked on pulping the other side of Rora's face. She'd been the one to train Rora to use her off hand just as good as the other one, so the punches didn't feel too much different. The others eventually got control of that arm, too, hauling Tare up, but she got in a few good kicks to Rora's middle before they lifted her up completely.

And then it was just Rora staring up at the stars, wheezing and gurgling and trying to figure out if she really was still alive. Even lying still hurt, and she knew how priests always said all your hurts went away when you died, so that meant Tare hadn't killed her. Yet.

After a while, before the buzzing cleared out of her ears, it felt like something was crawling along her skin. No, more like there were a hundred hands, all pressing down on her, like they wanted to push her through the spaces between the cobblestones, but they were light as butterflies. She didn't even know what it was until her ears opened up and she heard someone screaming her name, over and over and over. She'd know her brother's voice from anything.

"I'm okay," she tried to say, but she could hear how her own voice was just bubbles of blood. But he had to know she was fine, or he'd do the bad thing, she could feel it in the air again. "Aro, I'm okay." How could they not feel it? If she could, Rora would've curled into a ball and cried—but if she could move that much, then she would've raced across the courtyard, tackled Aro to make him stop, stop, *stop* . . .

The screaming rose up louder, and the stones shook under Rora, and then Tare's weight hit her chest again, hands pounding her face, Tare holding nothing back—

The air *snapped*. The pressure against Rora's skin burst like a hundred fires, and Tare's weight that'd landed on top of her was suddenly gone. The screaming died for three heartbeats, long enough for Rora to painfully twist her head to the side. Tare was sprawled next to her, mouth gaping open, eyes staring. Rora couldn't tell if she was moving, couldn't see clear enough if there was any life left in her eyes, oh gods, Aro, Aro, *what'd you do?*

Bodies blocked her sight of Tare, others crowding around, shouting. "Is she alive?" they kept asking, but no one ever answered the question, just kept asking it, and over their gabble she could hear her brother's high wordless wail. She knew the meaning behind it anyway, he'd said the words so many times he didn't need to anymore, *I'm sorry. I had to. I'm sorry.*

Rora squeezed her eyes shut, closing out the hovering bodies, closing out the winking stars. She shouldn't've come here, she'd just been selfish, selfish and stupid to think she could ever have a home here, to think she could ever belong with her pack again. She only ever made their lives worse. She only ever got them killed.

The shouting changed—but it was still shouting, so she almost didn't hear the difference. When she peeled open her eyes, sticky with tears and blood, all the hovering bodies were standing now, starting to move. Through a split between the press of bodies, she saw a body hanging from two shoulders. Tare, her head lolling, but her eyes blinked dizzily, and her feet stumbled against the cobbles as they pulled her along. Not dead.

Not dead.

A gurgling sound of relief was the best Rora could manage, but even that took a lot out of her.

Sharra Dogshead, leader of Whitedog Pack, she had a trick of making her voice heard no matter what. Even though her people were still shouting, even though Aro's wailing still carried over everything, even though Rora was right on the edge of leaving consciousness behind, still Sharra's voice cut through: "It seems we have a lot to talk about, doesn't it?"

Rora closed her eyes, and fell away.

CHAPTER SEVEN

Joros had no fond memories of the cellar; one of his sisters had locked him inside it once, and her laughter on the other side of the door had been louder than his pounding fists or his screams. When he'd grown older, he'd spent a night alone in the cellar, just to prove to himself he could. The cellar didn't *scare* him anymore, but that didn't mean he liked it.

Still, he couldn't deny that it was probably the most secure place in the estate, large enough to hold Sharra and her second, Tare, and the dozen fists and knives they brought for protection—large enough to hold all of them, but not large enough to make Joros, dropped against the far wall with his hands tied, feel small and powerless. He wasn't quite charitable enough to think that was intentional, but even a blind pig would find a mushroom now and again.

Anddyr and Aro had both been pushed into one of the nearby corners, their fingers elaborately tied—*that*, at least, Joros was impressed with. For people who still called them "witches," the pack at least knew how to efficiently disable a mage. Rora was sprawled near them, unmoving, the only sign of continuing life the loud wheeze of her breath through a nose that was likely broken. At least they'd laid her on her side so he didn't have to worry about her choking on her own blood.

They'd tried talking to Aro—after they'd made sure his fingers were securely tied, because they weren't about to take their chances with even a suspected witch. Sharra Dogshead in particular had tried coaxing and cajoling the boy, grabbing his arms and shaking him and demanding to know what had happened even as tears stood in her eyes. Aro had just blinked at her owlishly and stayed silent. The traces of skura still running through his veins compelled it—earlier, Joros had gripped the boy's shoulder and murmured, "Don't talk about what happened. If they ask, tell them it's too painful." Aro wouldn't tell them anything.

Which meant, when the pack finally accepted that Joros was the only one in any condition to tell the tale, there would be no one they trusted to refute his carefully woven mixture of truths and lies.

"Tell me," Sharra Dogshead said, eyes and voice both level as she settled before Joros. "Tell me everything."

What a stupid thing to ask for. "I'll tell you everything you want to know, so long as you keep your rabid dog chained up." He jerked his chin in Tare's direction, and the woman bared her teeth in response. "This is the second time she's tried to kill my hireling."

Tare snarled, "She was ours before she was ever yours."

"And with a welcome like this, I can't imagine why she ever left."

The Dogshead lifted her hand before Tare could make any response, and the way Tare fell into sullen silence spoke to Sharra's leadership. Joros had noted it on their last meeting, but Sharra had that precarious balance of respect and fear from her people. He knew there were plenty of leaders who would covet such a reaction, but Joros had never seen the point in wasting time earning the respect of underlings. Fear was so much easier.

"Tare acted foolishly," the Dogshead said, holding Joros's eyes. "But can you blame her? We trusted Rora—trusted *you*—with our people, and it seems like Tare was right when she said we shouldn't trust her. I think we're owed a little payback. An explanation, at the least." And she stared at him, waiting for the answer to a question she hadn't actually asked, and Joros could play that game. He stared back, innocent as a kitten, until the Dogshead flexed her jaw and asked, "What happened to the knives and fists who went with you?"

Joros sighed. "You think so *small*. The Twins have risen and the world's gone dark, and you're worried about a dozen lives?"

"Fifteen," Sharra said levelly.

"Fifteen, then."

Sharra's lips thinned, and Tare looked a handful of words away from casting aside all her fear and respect and leaping over to strangle Joros. The others looked equally unhappy, but no one moved or spoke, all waiting on word from their leader. Sharra finally said stiffly, "Tell me how it is that all my people died while all yours survived."

"That can't be something you want to hear. Rora is one of your own . . ."

Tare gave a low growl as she drew her dagger. "That's all I need," she said as she started toward the slumped form in the corner. Aro squawked and tried to weave his hands into a spell, but his fingers couldn't move in their restraints. Anddyr simply moaned, his shoulders twitching, too far gone in his madness to be any use. Rora stayed silent as death.

The fists took halfhearted steps forward, ready to stop

Tare no matter how badly they didn't want to. Joros suspected they'd only put up a token resistance. Even the Dogshead seemed willing to allow the inevitable to happen.

That was good. That was where he needed them. Now he had to redirect them.

"Rora may be the *reason* your people were killed," Joros said loudly and calmly, "but she is not to *blame* for their deaths. That blame lies with the Twins. And if you kill her, I won't tell you how to save the rest of your pack."

Sharra's eyes sharpened on Joros, and even Tare turned. The silence lasted for a few heartbeats. "Speak," Sharra said tightly.

"I'd like to see that dagger disappear, first," he said to Tare. She would have refused on principle, he knew, but after a moment the Dogshead nodded in concession, and Tare scowled as she returned the dagger to its hidden home. Joros could *hear* her teeth grinding.

"I sent Rora and Anddyr into the mountain, as we'd discussed, along with all the knives. But Aro . . . well. He wanted to help, and he followed them." It almost sounded genuine to his own ears. "I've managed to piece together what happened. Aro was captured by the Fallen, and it was they who discovered him as a mage. Anddyr is the result of what they do to mages . . . and Aro couldn't escape them on his own."

"He really is a witch, then?" It was Tare who asked it; the words seemed to lose themselves somewhere in Sharra's obvious anguish.

"It's rare, I'm told, but not unheard of for mage-powers to manifest so late in life. When Rora learned of his capture, she risked everything to save him—the mission, your people, her own life." He paused, deliberate, the moment before an uncomfortable truth. "I'm given to understand such behavior is not unusual for her."

"No," Tare said, her voice hard, her hand going back to her dagger, "it's not."

The first time he'd met any of the pack Joros had seen their resentment toward Rora for abandoning them in favor of her brother—the way they saw it, pack was more important than blood. That resentment was so easy to use.

A small bubble of emotion gurgled in his stomach, easily ignored. He needed the pack on his side; that Rora had to suffer for it was an inconsequential by-product.

"Many of the knives perished in the escape, and many of the fists in fighting off the pursuit," he went on. "Of those who remained, I offered them the chance to return here . . . but they had seen what we were up against. With our initial failure, our chances were even slimmer. They knew that they could help stop evil from spreading across the world, from reaching their home." Let the pack see their lost family as heroes, as martyrs. Their deaths would serve him better as a rallying cry than as a meaningless footnote to his failure. "Together, we found the Fallen, and together we faced the rising Twins themselves."

The pack's anger turned to a simmer, edged out by curiosity, the fists and knives and even Sharra leaning closer. Only Tare wasn't looking at him, her glare staying on Rora.

Joros let real bitterness into his voice when he said, "We failed. We were so close—but." He paused, mentally shifting the lies and the remaining truths into better alignment; let them think he struggled to relay what had happened. "My last hope of stopping the Twins demanded great sacrifice. Aro and

Rora . . . well, like calls to like. There is power in twins. Their sacrifice could have saved the world.

"Aro understood what we asked of him, and he was willing to lay down his life. But Rora lost sight of all reason—even as we watched the Fallen kill scores of their own to give the Twins power, even as we watched the world begin to darken." It was such a careful balance he had to strike. Rora was the last of his group who could discredit his story, and so he needed the pack to hate her enough to ignore anything she said—but not enough to put a dagger in her heart. Joros needed them on his side, even if that meant losing the only competent member of his little band. The pack as a whole was more valuable than one disgraced knife. "She fought—convinced that her brother needed to be saved. Anddyr, the poor fool . . . love can make even the strongest men into fools, and Anddyr could never be called strong. He turned alongside Rora. Your fists and knives were loyal to the end, but by the time it was over, the Twins had already risen. We had already lost everything."

They stayed buoyed on the echo of his words, but the Dogshead sank faster than he would have expected. "Why would Rora come back here?" she asked. Her words popped the bubble of simmering rage and retribution that his tale had built. "If what you say is true . . . she must know coming back here would be as good as slicing her own throat, and you didn't bring her in chains. Why would she come back?"

The Dogshead had always been clever, Joros would give her that; but even—or especially—with the cleverest of people, simple explanations tended to work best. "She wasn't in her right mind at the time—far from it. I don't know if she remembers what she did, but her only concern was getting her brother to safety." Joros spread his hands in a gesture of supplication, and braced himself; this particular truth scraped like thorns on its way out, far more painful than any lie. "I need help. There's only so much I can do alone. I was able to convince Rora that we would find safety here, and she was willing to believe it.

"Do not mistake me—though we failed to keep the Twins from rising, hope is not lost. Now is the time to *strike*. The Twins are weak—weakened by their years of captivity, weakened by their mortal flesh, weakened by pulling down the sun. Right now, they'll be little better than mortals, no more dangerous than any man. With your help, we can hunt them down, and even a small group like this could—" Joros faltered, stumbled to silence. The Dogshead was staring at him aghast, as though he'd just offered to kill her family.

Joros realized belatedly that, in her mind, that was precisely what he'd done.

"No." That one word was enough to still any fervor that had been rising in the pack. "I won't lose any more of my people to one of your schemes."

"It's not a *scheme*," Joros said, "it's the last chance to save the world! The Twins will recover, and then they'll come storming up through Fiatera. If you think they'll spare anyone from their wrath—"

"We've got a chance at surviving," Sharra said. "Better odds than we've had before, sometimes. These"—she raised both hands to gesture at her pack—"are very close to the last of my fighters, the last of my protection. They're very close to the last of my *family*. I'd rather give them a short life of freedom and happiness than a shorter life of fear and death."

"Why not let their deaths mean something?"

"Because the lives of my people are not coins to spend." It was the first time he'd heard Sharra sound truly angry. "You gave us this place, gave us a chance at life, and we'll always be in your debt for that, I won't deny it. But you're asking too much. You've already taken more than you've given us, and I can't let you take any more." Though he glared, she met his gaze steadily, undaunted. He could see why her people so feared and respected her. "But you did bring back a traitor for justice, and you brought Aro back to us. We're thankful for that. So you can stay here as long as you like—we don't have anything fancy, but we live well enough. We'll deal with Rora, and we can deal with your witch, too, if you'd like—"

"No," Joros said quickly, his stomach twisting in sudden concern. "Just because you won't help me doesn't mean I'm giving up. *Some* of us still care about saving the world . . . and for that I need Rora and Anddyr, and Aro, too. They're still mine. You won't harm them, or have them."

The silence was rife with tension, the knives and fists shifting uncomfortably from foot to foot, stretching muscles sore with standing. The Dogshead stayed quiet for a long while—to make it starkly obvious, Joros imagined, just how outnumbered he was. "Is that so?" she finally asked. Not angry this time; just not used to being challenged.

"It is." Joros smiled tightly. "Let's say I'm calling in my debts. Asylum—shelter, a home—for myself and Aro, for as long as we may need, and Rora and Anddyr are kept alive. I don't care if they're kept comfortable; I just need them alive."

Sharra lifted an eyebrow, searching his face. She didn't seem unhappy with whatever she thought she saw. "That seems—"

"And you and your people help me in any ways that they can, provided they don't risk their lives."

Her jaw tightened. "Let's get this right. You come here and won't let me kill a traitor, tell me how you would've killed my boy and promise to take him from me again, and demand home and help. What am I getting out of this, exactly?"

"Your short, pathetic life, and the short, pathetic lives of your people. Help me, and I won't burn every last brick that builds this place." It had been a recurring dream throughout his early years inside Mount Raturo. If no other good could come of this place, he would do that, at least.

Sharra laughed. "So why shouldn't I just kill you now, too? Kill you, kill Rora, kill your—"

A wailed *"No!"* was accompanied by a *thump* as Aro lurched forward from his place against the wall. He fell on his side and flailed, ungainly, fighting desperately to get his tied hands free and looking as though he might tear his arms from their sockets in the process. Joros saw Sharra's face crumple as she watched, and she moved quickly to the boy's side, cradling his head and making comforting sounds until his flailing stilled. "You can't," Aro sobbed. "You can't kill them. Please."

"Shh," Sharra murmured, stroking Aro's hair. "Shh. I won't."

Sharra Dogshead might have the respect and the fear of her people, but she was a fool to let them see her as human, too. More a fool to so blatantly show Joros her true weakness.

Softly, almost tenderly, Joros said, "This is what the Fallen do to mages. They *break* them. It's taken me so long to help Anddyr find the pieces of himself . . . but your Aro's a clever boy. He didn't get so lost, or so broken, and he's learned quickly. I've been able to help him grow better, bit by bit. There's still a long way to go, but . . ." And he waited.

The Dogshead turned her eyes up to Joros, and they were full of suspicion drowned in the desperate need to hope. "You're saying you can cure him."

"Yes," Joros lied, smoothly and earnestly. "Not quickly, not easily—but yes."

Sharra took a few deep, slow breaths. If she'd looked to her second, she might have seen the distrust writ clearly across Tare's face—but the Dogshead had returned her eyes to Aro's face, resting tear-streaked against her leg.

"We can make this cellar secure," Sharra said to Joros. "Rora and your witch can stay here. They won't be comfortable . . . but they won't be dead. You can stay in the house, and you'll help Aro to get better." She gave him a hard look. "I won't stop you if you want to go off and save the world, but I won't make any of my people help you. You can ask, but it's their choice."

She'd make him go through the pack like a beggar, pleading for help? So be it; he'd seen the fervor in the eyes of her fists and knives when he'd told them of the Twins' rise. He didn't doubt many of them had been devout followers of the Parents—the poor always seemed to cling to the hope of true belief. They would help him. He could manage the charade of curing Aro well enough; being separated from Anddyr was an inconvenience, but a minor one; and while Rora had proved useful to him, he'd rather have her jailed but alive than dead. It was simple arithmetic: the benefits outweighed the costs. "Agreed," he said, and lifted his bound wrists. "Now untie me. You've wasted enough of what little time we have left."

CHAPTER EIGHT

S cal had never taken joy in hunting. It was only a necessary thing, to keep himself alive, to keep alive those he
protected. Like fighting, hunting was killing, and he had never
truly had the spirit for it.

He enjoyed it even less when it was men he was hunting.

Vatri had told him what needed to be done, and as always,
as ever, he would see to it. So he hid among the dense trees
of the Forest Voro, listening to the soft sound of approaching
voices, and his hand waited ready near the hilt of his sword.
He had not drawn it yet. The fire would give him away, and
he could not think *Darkness* at the flames, for Vatri would be
watching.

The trees hid much, with only the faint moonlight between the shadows, dancing and twining upon the ground. In
the depths of the forest, little enough snow had reached the
ground, and spring was beginning to breathe through the
trees. The first shaking gasps of warmth. There was only deadfall, and patchy brambles, and they were the same shade as the
shadows.

Little to see, but he could hear their voices, hear their feet
crunching upon the deadfall. Their sounds made them clear as

sight, and in the darkness, Scal moved toward them on silent feet. He did not like to hunt, but there was an endless difference between liking a thing and being able to do it well.

There were four of them. One in chain armor that rattled with each step. One that kept a constant stream of muttering. The other two speaking softly to each other, too quiet to make out more than the worried tone. A fighter, and a witch, and two preachers. He knew how to deal with a fighter, for it was a language Scal spoke well. He knew how to deal with a witch, for he had known a mad witch and he knew the ways their minds and bodies worked. The preachers would likely be useless, and so he was not concerned.

Scal moved silent through the trees. Closer, until he could make out their conversation—a long journey, forced upon them, spread across the country—until he could make out the witch's mumbling clear as speech. He let them pass, the fighter and then the preachers and then the witch, and then Scal stepped from the trees. Stepped to the witch's shoulder, and he pulled his sword free. Fire along the edge, brighter than starlight, sudden as held breath. Scal let the draw carry forward, a low swing biting sideways, and it cleanly sheared the witch's arm at the elbow and sank into his side. The fire sealed the arm—no blood.

He still did not know if that made it kinder. Certainly not to the witch, who let out a low wailing screech. It felt dishonest. To kill a man, there should be blood. Scal ripped the sword free and brought it back around higher. To take a life, he should be reminded of all he was stealing. Bathe in all the lost possibilities, walk away drenched in stolen moments. But the sword, fire-dancing, sealed, too, the wound it carved into the witch's neck. He did not bleed, but he died all the same. Scal stepped from him spotless, untouched. Clean and clarified and shining.

Scal bore his scars like a written history. The tale of all his bloody lives, told across the fragile canvas of his skin. Beneath the scars were all the marks unseen, the bone-deep stains left by all the blood he had shed.

He stepped from the dead witch, and his skin was clean, and Scal did not think that he knew himself any longer.

The chain-mailed fighter had turned at the witch's scream. Drew his sword as the witch's cry gurgled to fiery silence. Stepped, now, as Scal stepped, and their swords met, and they shed fire and sparks where they clashed.

Scal and the fighter danced in the shadows and the flickering light. Dimly there were whispers in Scal's mind, faint voices, the men who had shaped his past lives. One saying that violence was weakness. The other saying that a man fought with what he was given. But as Scal's sword swung, one voice rose from the dusty whispers: *We only do what we must,* Vatri had said. *All that we do, we do in the name of the Parents.*

Scal kicked out his leg. His foot bounced against the fighter's knee, and Scal felt the bone crack, and the fighter began to fall with a curse, with a wild swing of his blade. Like the witch, he did not bleed. Like the witch, he still died.

There was a line of fire along Scal's forearm. In his sword's light, he could see the blood welling from the thin slice there, where the fighter's last swing had scored. Blood that was black in the moonlight, shimmering, and it spilled down his arm and over his fingers where they held the hilt of the sword. Scal drew in a breath that seared his lungs, that tasted of winter and faraway ice. He did not know himself half as well as when blood stained his hands, spattered his face.

The two preachers had tried to flee. Tripping over each other, wailing, stumbling against trees. They would have been smarter to separate, but fear made fools of all men. There was no joy in hunting, but it was a thing Scal could do well. There was little enough difference between a man and a deer, when fear chased, when blood boiled, when the trees rose shadowed and strangling.

Scal caught them, and he sent one to join the others in death. But the second preacher he held, arm tight around the man's neck, denying him air. The preacher clawed at Scal's arm, and his legs kicked where they hung off the ground. *I have so many questions,* Vatri had said, with the fires in her eyes, and so Scal held the preacher tight against his chest. Waiting for his breath-starved body to still, waiting for the fight to flow from his limbs. Scal thought that he could almost see the man's blood flowing beneath his skin. That he could feel his heartbeat, like a caged thing through his ribs, pounding against the calm thud of Scal's own heart. His left hand curled around the back of the preacher's head. He had touched Vatri, touched things that were not weapons, and they had not burst with flames or with ice. He had not willed them to.

His fingers buried in the man's hair, arm tight around his neck, Scal wondered what would happen if he willed the ice to flow from his fingers. No blood. No questions. If the end was the same, it could hardly matter what means.

I have so many questions. Vatri would ask them at the point of Scal's blade. And when it was done, whether she got her answers or not, it would end the same.

Branches rustled, brambles snapping beneath soft feet. Scal did not turn. Only held tighter to the preacher as his limbs went slack, breath washing over Scal's arm, fingers slipping from the furrows they had carved in flesh. More scars, that would make him whole, make him himself.

"That was neatly done," Vatri said at his shoulder. Scal opened his arm. Let the preacher fall boneless to the ground. He did not open his mouth, because he did not know what would come out of it.

He leaned down and tied the unconscious preacher's wrists together behind his back, tied his ankles together for good measure. He propped the man up against the trunk of a tree, and then Scal stepped away, back, letting the shadows swallow him. He might have gone farther, if he could.

Vatri crouched before the preacher, and she reached out to roughly pat his cheek. Bleary, slow-blinking, the preacher woke. He made a strangled noise when his eyes fixed on her scarred face. A monster escaped from the realm of nightmares.

"Where were you going?" Vatri asked.

The preacher said nothing, pressing his lips together tight. Anger and pride and faith flickering in his gaze.

"Where are the Twins?"

Silence.

Vatri was undeterred. "What have your leaders told you to do?"

"What have you done to the mages?"

"Where are the Twins?"

The preacher twisted his shoulders, rested more comfortably back against the trunk of the tree. There was almost a smile on his lips. A tilt to his head that seemed to say, *You can waste as much of your breath as you would like.*

"What will be the Fallen's next move?"

"Where are the Twins?"

"Scal."

He came forward, obedient as a dog. Stepped to Vatri's side and he drew the sword once more, right hand around the worn grip so that the flames danced bright along its edge, and the preacher's eyes flickered with fear. Scal stretched the blade out until its tip almost rested against the preacher's throat. Scal did not will it to burn, but the preacher's neck and cheek reddened with the heat.

Scal's hand had never shaken, holding a blade. It did not now either, but he almost wished it would. That, somehow, someone might see a piece of the quaking within him. That someone might see his jaw, held as tight as the preacher's.

"I give you one last chance," Vatri said, voice steady and even. Pleasant. "Where are the Twins?"

The preacher swallowed hard, throat bobbing closer to the sword. There was sweat on his brow, on his upper lip, and the fear was growing more wild in his eyes. He stared at the tip of the blade, and his eyes flicked to Vatri, to Scal, to the blade, and rested finally on Vatri. There was no less fear in his eyes when he said, "I won't tell you anything."

Vatri sighed as though the words truly made her sad, but Scal could see the fire of his sword matched in her gaze. "Then you're choosing your own fate. Scal."

There was a cry trapped behind Scal's teeth. A screech like the witch had made, dying, or like the wails of the fleeing preachers. A cry that would carry endless, and shake the roots of the trees, and make the stars tremble in the sky, and shatter the world in half. Shatter Scal in half.

He kept his teeth pressed tight together, and he drove the sword forward. There was fire, and there was no blood, and the scream clung to the roof of his mouth. Fighting, fighting to break free.

"May the Parents watch over your soul," Vatri intoned. It sounded almost like she meant the words. She rose from the dead man's side, said, "There will be others," and then she made her way through the trees. Shadows fluttering like moths' wings across her scarred flesh, the darkness pulling her deeper into the forest.

Scal, obedient, loyal, followed.

CHAPTER NINE

Keiro sat cross-legged far beneath the earth, his back straight, hands loose upon his knees, chin tilted upward. Every inch of his bearing spoke to calm confidence. Every inch was a lie, but it was a good lie—a necessary lie.

For around him, the earth trembled.

Keiro forced his breath to come steady, even though his heart thundered and every instinct screamed that he should flee. He sat still, and he breathed, and he waited.

Across from where he sat, a god-storm raged.

Fratarro was in the middle of what Keiro would have called a tantrum, if Fratarro had truly been the child whose skin he wore. But Fratarro was no child, and even a god's petulant anger was a frightening thing to behold. His pose mimicked Keiro's, legs folded and back straight, and though Fratarro's hands rested on his knees, the right one shook like a leaf in a tempest, while the left lay utterly, disturbingly still.

Showers of dirt pattered onto Keiro's shoulders, onto the ground. Somewhere not so far away, the earth groaned with the stress of staying put as Fratarro worked, however unintentionally, to shake it to pieces.

Left unchecked, it would not be very long until he succeeded.

Keiro strove to keep his voice steady, to keep the words from breaking into a scream, as he recited, "Gentle Fratarro, warm and kind." A child's rhyme, words he'd heard recited countless times through the halls of Mount Raturo . . . but there could be power in even the simplest words. "Though deep beneath the earth confined, good children know they'll always find his loving heart and caring mind." As Keiro repeated the rhyme, the words coming stronger to his lips, Fratarro's shaking hand began slowly to still. The fury faded from his eyes by slow measures, until he squeezed them shut; and they were summer-breeze calm when he opened them once more.

Keiro said the rhyme again and again until the dirt stopped raining on his shoulders, until the floor stopped trembling beneath him, until Fratarro sighed and said softly, "Thank you."

"Of course, my lord."

Fratarro made an unhappy noise at the back of his throat, and faint tremors started once more beneath Keiro. "I have told you—"

"Brother," Keiro amended quickly, and the tremors stilled. It felt wrong to address his god so casually, but self-preservation was stronger than propriety, and he would do nearly anything to keep Fratarro's frustration in check. If he wasn't so exhausted, he might have remembered better how carefully he needed to step. "You're doing better, Brother."

"I'm not," Fratarro said, and he sounded so much like a sulky teen that Keiro almost smiled. That was a dangerous line to walk—no matter that Fratarro *looked* like an adolescent, he was centuries old, older than all the stars in the sky. To forget that, for even a moment, was dangerous.

"Control will come," Keiro said, hoping, *praying*, that the words were true. They all needed them to be true. "Power must come first, and you're certainly showing that. The rest will follow. You were . . . bereft for so long. No one expected you to rise to your full power immediately."

A wan smile twisted Fratarro's lips. "You tell sweet lies, Keiro Godson." Keiro opened his mouth to babble an argument or defense, but Fratarro lifted a hand to halt his words and wave them away. "You've done enough today. Go. I know there is more to be done above. You're more useful above."

It wasn't meant to be a cut against him, Keiro knew that, but there was still a dull ache beneath his breastbone at the words. He rose slowly to his feet, leaving Fratarro sitting alone at the center of the chamber. Walking between pools of flickering blue light, Keiro paused to lift something that had fallen to the floor during the tremors, incongruous by its very presence in the nearly empty chamber. It was lumpy and ratty and faintly musty. Turning it in his hands, Keiro recognized the shape of a horse, an old and poorly stuffed toy.

"Leave it," Fratarro said, and Keiro fought back the urge to shout, for Fratarro stood suddenly at his elbow. The unnatural silence of a child, combined with the powers of a god. "I don't know why I keep it . . ." But he held out the fingers of his good hand, and Keiro handed him the stuffed horse. He watched Fratarro run his thumb down the yarn-mane, staring into the horse's button eyes. Fratarro's own eyes were . . . different. Keiro could not quite say how, and he left before they could change again. As he crawled into the tunnel from the chamber, his last glimpse was of Fratarro reaching up to place the horse on a shelf sunk into the wall, dark with shadows.

Keiro had grown very skilled, of late, at not questioning

the things he saw. His mind was a study in emptiness as he crawled through the bowels of the earth. He did not—very carefully, did not—think of the second part of the child's rhyme: *Patient Sororra, trapped in sleep, her anger brightly burning deep. If you've crossed her, run and weep, for she has promises to keep.* The tunnels were long, and he was alone with his mind as carefully empty as the tunnels themselves. Best to be safe—there was no telling when Sororra might be listening.

Above, on solid ground beneath the dark, open sky where clean air blew across his face, there was almost, *almost*, peace. There was a single moment of it, at least, where Keiro knelt with his eyes closed and his face upturned, and felt relief like a tide through his veins. It felt so like the first time he had visited these hills, when he had seen the Starborn sing to the full moon and felt a moment of heartbreaking peace. Yaket, Elder of the plainswalkers who had lived in the grass sea since the Plains had been only knee-high, had shown him the *mravigi*, and he'd thought he'd understood the message she'd been trying to teach him. He should have listened to her better, then and later. In the piling mountain of Keiro's regrets, it was a firm foundation stone. He might have had more peaceful moments like this if he'd learned her lessons better. He might not have been so terrified of his own thoughts.

He supposed it was fitting, that Yaket found him there. "These are troubled times, Godson," she said as she lowered herself down next to him, startling him from his melancholy.

Keiro swallowed heavily, and could not look at her. "It has . . . been a long while, Elder." She did not often leave her people, the few that were left of her tribe, and Keiro couldn't bear to see them—or, rather, to see all the faces that were missing. He kept telling himself it was better for Yaket and the plainswalkers—the last thing they needed was for the Twins or the Fallen to turn their attention and their ire on the plainswalkers.

"It is better for us, away from the hills. Your people are not so welcoming of strangers . . . especially not of strangers they believe have wronged them."

They are not my people, Keiro wanted to say, but the words stuck to the roof of his mouth and his tongue could not free them. Instead, he said, "You must understand their suspicion. They think that if you and your people did not come to the Fallen with the location of the Twins, that can only mean you intended to keep them hidden away forever. There is no room in their minds for any other option."

Yaket did not answer right away. "That was what you thought, too, at first."

"It was," Keiro agreed softly. He could not say any more, keeping his mind carefully blank of any thoughts. It was dangerous, certainly, to say anything else, and dangerous enough even to think beyond the constant pressure in his chest, the endless exhaustion, the fear, the fear, the fear . . .

"I think you know, now, why I made the choices I made," Yaket said, not hearing the warning in his silence. "You know why my people have stayed here for so long, and kept our silence for so long. We, who lived so close to them, knew the stakes better than your people ever could."

"Yaket—"

"We are not without hope, Keiro. We never were, and we never shall be." Her words came in a rush, fierce passion lighting through her voice. "My people are old enough to remember the lessons of the past. We can find a way to fix all of this, to restore—"

"Yaket!" Keiro nearly shouted it as he surged to his feet, hands clapped over his ears like a child, desperate not to hear, desperate not to let Sororra hear. Yaket stared up at him, her wrinkles smoothed by wide-mouthed surprise. Keiro put his back to her and wrapped his arms around himself, trying desperately to slow his heartbeat, to calm his thoughts—these would be like an open door to a thief, for a goddess ever listening for opposition. "You cannot ever speak these things, Yaket. Do you hear me?" His hands still shook, but his breaths came more even. He was so, so tired. "These are troubled times," he said heavily. Her own words, echoed back to her. "We must all be faithful, loyal followers of the Twins in their path to victory. They have risen, and they will rise further." He stopped the words before they could leave his mouth, but he could not stop them drifting through his thoughts: *And there is nothing we can do to stop them.*

He heard Yaket start to rise, knew the compassion he would see on her face if he turned, knew she would touch her crabbed hand to his shoulder and he would break. There was so much danger here. He fled before it could consume him.

He wanted to pray, but there was no safety in prayer anymore. Sororra would hear, and that was what he did *not* want. He kept his teeth clenched, and did not let himself hope that she hadn't been listening, that she hadn't heard the whispering of blasphemy—

No. Dangerous to even think the word.

I am loyal, he thought. *I am a good and faithful servant of the Twins.* But he didn't know if the words were his own, or Sororra's.

They would need to be his own, if he was to survive this. He could give the Twins no reason to doubt him.

He thought of Yaket, likely staring after him, her heart heavy with grief—for herself, certainly, but he did not doubt that most of it would be for *him*. The thought made his own heart heavy, but he pushed away the pain. She had to understand. Everything had changed now. Everything was different.

He very carefully did not think, *Everything is wrong*.

If she had heard, if she had been listening through Keiro when Yaket was talking, it might already be too late. A seed of doubt would be all it took, a single ripple enough to turn into a capsizing wave. She might even now be returning from wherever she whiled away the long hours waiting for her brother to regain his power, her course set on Keiro, set to destroy anything that might get in her way—

"Brother Keiro!"

Ripped from his apocalyptic thoughts, Keiro stumbled over his own feet and nearly fell. Laseneo was huffing toward him, eyes huge in his moon-pale face, and one of his hands was already inching toward the back of his neck as he ran.

Keiro stared at him in stark disbelief. As Laseneo stopped, panting, before him, Keiro said, "You're supposed to be gone." Blunter words than he might have chosen another time, but his nerves and his mind and his soul were frayed. Laseneo should have left hours ago with the rest of the Fallen. Keiro couldn't allow disobedience, couldn't be seen as weak—not by the Fallen, and certainly not by—

Laseneo curled into himself, taken aback. "Brother Keiro, I serve you . . ."

Keiro cut him off with a sharp motion. He had to find a way

to salvage this ruin of a night, so that Sororra need never know any of it. "*All* of the Fallen save those specifically named were to leave. Were you named, Laseneo?"

"N-no, but . . ." Laseneo began rubbing his own neck again, his fingers leaving red marks like claws. "That's w-why I came to find you . . ."

Keiro's pulse grew loud in his ears. "Show me," he said, before Laseneo could say any more. Something had gone wrong, but there had to be a way for Keiro to fix it, and to do so without Sororra ever hearing. He was her voice and her hands, her will among the Fallen. He *couldn't* fail her.

Laseneo scampered across the hills, eager as a puppy, and Keiro followed with a lump in his throat that might choke him, and his thoughts carefully blank. Raised voices soon led him as much as Laseneo, and they came across a large crowd of people clustered in the valley between two hills—a larger crowd of people than there should have been.

Earlier, when Keiro had crawled beneath the ground to make his way to Fratarro, the Fallen had been leaving, finally, the great mass of them packing up and beginning the long trek back to Fiatera. From what Keiro had seen, it had all been going smoothly—there was anger, grumbling, but they all seemed to accept that they had no choice. Valrik had been supervising it all, along with his chosen leaders, the ones who didn't call themselves Ventallo but were. Most of them would be staying, along with a complement of the black-armored mercenaries and a small cadre of mages. Only two score total, staying behind to guard the hills, to serve the Twins until they regained their full strength.

At a quick look, Keiro would guess there were close to two hundred people gathered now between the hills.

No. The despairing thought lurched through his mind before Keiro could stop it. And on its heels came a much harder thought, unforgiving, merciless: *You should have known.* Sororra had said she would be watching . . . and Keiro was her eyes and her ears. Of course she would know of his failure.

If you've crossed her, run and weep . . .

Keiro had been so focused on Fratarro's capricious moods that he had forgotten that the world was swaying and lurching beneath his steps. In this new and singular world the Twins would see made, there was no room for failure, no allowance for missteps. Sororra would—

He had to fix this. If he didn't, he was as good as dead.

He hurried forward, past Laseneo and into the throng. They parted for him, some with guilty looks, but many with open hostility. Keiro had not been well liked among the Fallen from the beginning, for all that he had found the Twins. He had been branded an apostate before that, banished, and he had done nothing since to be worthy of their good graces. Ordering the Fallen to leave their gods behind had only cemented their hatred. They wouldn't listen to him willingly, not these who had already chosen to disregard his orders. They wouldn't care that their disobedience would be deemed Keiro's fault.

The shouting voices died as Keiro passed by, pulling a shroud of silence behind him. As he had expected, Valrik stood at the center of the crowd, waiting with his hands on his hips, his empty eye sockets pointed directly at Keiro. "Brother Keiro," he said in his rumbling voice.

"What is this?" Keiro tried to make his voice authoritative, but it came out reedy and weak.

"Some of our loyal brothers and sisters have elected to stay," Valrik said, and there were murmurs of agreement throughout the crowd.

Keiro shook his head, and felt fear-sweat eke down from his hairline. "My instructions were clear. *Your* instructions were clear. The Twins need time to rest and recover, and they cannot do so with so many people ar—"

"There aren't that many of us," Valrik interrupted, spreading his hands in an empty gesture of conciliation. "Surely the Twins will be heartened by the faith of these remaining few."

Keiro thought of Fratarro, cloistering himself far beneath the surface—just a different kind of prison from the one that had held him for centuries. He didn't want to show himself in his weakened, broken state, not with so many of his followers around; Keiro had seen the longing in his eyes when he had asked how long until the Fallen left. How long until he could climb free of his prison and walk beneath the sky once more. *It should have been now.* "I promise you," Keiro said, "they will not be." He turned his back to Valrik, facing the unhappy masses. "Leave, as you were commanded. A truly *loyal* follower would do as his gods have ordered."

"How do we know they did?" The heated shout came from somewhere in the crowd, Keiro couldn't pinpoint where. "We've only your word for that!"

"Now, now," Valrik rumbled, stepping to Keiro's side and reaching out to place a heavy hand on his shoulder. Keiro resisted the impulse to shrug Valrik's hand off. How things had changed: not even months ago, Keiro would have thought it an honor to stand in the presence of the leader of the Fallen, the earthly embodiment of the Twins' will. He knew better now, in so many ways. "Sororra and Fratarro have named Brother Keiro their voice; we must trust that he is serving them truly." The words did nothing to soothe the grumbling, but then they had not been meant to. He spoke to Keiro next, though his voice was loud enough to carry. "Still, Brother, I hardly think a few dozen more of us will do any harm. No doubt we'll raise the Twins' spirits—a perfect reflection of Sororra's own stubbornness, eh?" He shook Keiro's shoulder in what was likely meant to be a brotherly way, but that was too much. Keiro twisted out of his grip, knocked away his extended arm, and the grumbling died into shocked silence. Who would *dare* assault Valrik Uniro?

Keiro would. *He had faced the Twins, and he had nothing else to fear.* "There is stubbornness," he snarled, "and there is stupidity. You are fools, all of you, if you think the Twins will be *pleased* with disobedience—and you, Valrik, are more the fool for encouraging it. If you are wise, you will leave. The others can't have gotten far, and a group your size will move faster. You can likely catch them up before the moon rises. Listen, and *go*." His voice broke on the last word, his throat thickening unexpectedly. He knew already that it was hopeless.

He could not face them any longer—not without screaming or sobbing. So Keiro turned, and pushed through the crowd until he broke free of them. As he walked through the hills, the murmur of their voices followed him, and a smattering of laughter, of jeers.

If you've crossed her, run and weep . . .

Laseneo found him, jabbering and plucking at his sleeve, his voice like knives through Keiro's skull. Keiro spun on him, and his hand stung—and he did not realize until two breathless moments had passed that it was because he had struck Laseneo. The smaller man stood there, staring and quivering, tears already welling in his eyes, and guilt and fury surged within Keiro, so strongly that he could not tell them apart, could not tell which was stronger, could not tell which was real. He fled, hillsides looming in the darkness, his feet clumsy on the uneven ground until he stuttered to a halt only long enough to yank the ill-fitting boots from his feet. They had belonged to a dead man. He left them behind as he continued racing through the hills, bare feet firm and confident against the ground, his toes pressing into the cool dirt. He ran and ran until his breath was like rocks in his throat, and the ground reached up to grab him. It was not quite falling, but it was not so very far off.

Sitting beneath the slow-spinning stars, Keiro wrapped his arms tight around his churning stomach. He wanted to stand and keep walking, to choose a direction and let the stars guide his feet, but that was hopeless. There was nowhere else in the world left for him, nowhere he belonged, nowhere he would be safe. When Sororra returned, she would mete out the punishment for his failures, and there was nothing he could do to stop it.

Was there?

Sororra had no mercy for those who opposed her. She was strong, and she respected that same strength in others. She would not stand for disobedience, and Keiro was her hands and her eyes and her voice. He would not stand for it either.

Keiro's racing pulse slowed by steady beats. The lump eased from his throat. As he stood, his hands were steady.

Keiro made his way toward the largest hill under which

the Twins had been buried for centuries. He walked at a slow and measured pace, and his thoughts were empty of everything but his singular purpose.

The mages weren't allowed to congregate, weren't allowed to even be near each other, and so the ones who had been chosen to stay behind had each carved out their own space. Keiro hunted down all of them, ten in total, said to each of them, "Come with me," and they did because of the drug that ran through their veins. He hated using that against them—it made his stomach churn, to see their faces go slack with mindless obedience—but there was no choice left to him. His life hung in the balance, and Keiro had never wanted to be a martyr.

Perhaps the mages would thank him, when it was all done. The thought was cold comfort, and little enough even of that.

He gave them more tremulous orders as they went, telling them what to do and making sure they knew the signals he would give them. They retained commands so well, even in the throes of their madness. Keiro simply had to hope they wouldn't falter.

With the ten mages stumbling along behind him, Keiro climbed to the top of the tall hill on the side opposite from where the remaining Fallen had gathered, walked around the crater gouged into its center until he could look out over them all. The few who had been asked to stay, and all the ones who had chosen to.

Keiro made a motion to Terstet—he would always know the mages' names, always—and saw the man's hands weaving a spell in response. It was the same spell he had used the last time Keiro had addressed the Fallen, the spell that made his voice loud enough to reach thousands of ears. For the two hundred left, Keiro's voice would be like thunder over the hills when he called, "Valrik. Ventallo. Blades for the darkness. To me."

They came slowly, all two score of them—but they did come. Keiro made a mask of his face as they approached. Perhaps they would thank him for this, later—when they began to see how precariously their own lives perched along a dagger's edge.

Keiro had to make them see.

Keeping his expression masked, Keiro said, "You were asked to stay." His voice still boomed loud, and he saw some of the two score gathered before him wince, but he did not signal to Terstet to break the spell. He wanted to be sure they heard him, even if it meant shattering their eardrums. "*Only* you. You were chosen for your loyalty, and your faith, and your usefulness. You were deemed worthy of trust."

"The Twins handpicked us, did they?" It was one of the youngest among the Ventallo, his voice dripping with scorn.

"No," Keiro said flatly. His voice had all the authority he had wished for it earlier, drawn up from the dark and desperate place within him. "The Twins wouldn't waste their time on you. They chose *me*, and I chose you."

There was silence, long enough for a dozen heartbeats. Silence, as they waited to see who among their number would be the first to refute him. He gave them those moments, to see if there were any who were exceptionally brave or exceptionally foolish. If any of them were, they hid it well. Fools did not survive long among the Fallen, and the brave did not survive long at all.

Into their waiting silence, Keiro's voice boomed once more: "You all were there beneath the hill, when I showed you the faces of our gods. You heard when Sororra pardoned Valrik for the sin of declaring himself a leader among men." Keiro turned his eye to Valrik, whose jaw was clenched, tendons and muscles dancing stark around his eyes. "Do you remember what she said to you?"

"She said the Fallen would need guidance," Valrik rumbled, and it sounded as though each syllable pained him. "She said I would continue to lead the Fallen."

"She said more than that, Valrik."

Keiro imagined that if Valrik still had his eyes, he'd be giving a truly formidable glare. Even if he could, Keiro still would have levelly stared him down. "She said," Valrik ground out, "that I would lead, with you advising me."

"You will heed the voice and the hands and the eye of Keiro Godson." The words flowed through Keiro, empty and easy. "Does that sound familiar?"

"Yes." Reluctance clipped the word short.

Keiro skimmed his eye across the others, the Ventallo who had cowered before their gods and babbled praises. He knew them, knew their names and their histories—but he couldn't let those matter. They would understand, soon. "You should all remember Sororra's words . . . but it seems you are in need of a reminder. *You will be our voice,* she said to me, *and our eye, and our hands. Your word is as our word, and silence shall fall at your speaking. Your actions are as our actions, and none shall doubt you.* All of you were there when she said this. Do you remember now?" They didn't answer, but they didn't need to. Their hatred was a sharp stench in the night air, their silence answer enough.

Keiro stepped past them and faced the gathered hundreds,

the willful Fallen who had thought their faith was more important than their obedience. They should have known better, should have learned the lessons buried so shallowly in all the old stories passed through the Fallen. Sororra had no tolerance for betrayal, no mercy for traitors. *My actions are their actions. My hands are not my own.*

They all watched, as silent as the Ventallo, for they'd heard Keiro's words just as clearly. From so far away, Keiro couldn't make out individual faces, couldn't see whether they gaped with fear or with fury, couldn't tell if they were on the edge of fighting or fleeing. It didn't matter, either way. "You have an excuse, all of you. You did not hear the Twins speak, did not hear them name me their voice. You can be excused your doubts— after all, it's a poor servant who never questions the reasons for doing his master's bidding. The Twins are kind, and merciful, and they will understand why you doubted that my words were truly theirs." They must have been at least a little frightened, for Keiro could almost taste the relief that now washed through them. He quashed it. "They will not understand your disobedience, though—that's one thing they cannot abide."

Without turning away from the gathered Fallen, he called to one of the mages, Enil, to create a shield, watched the lines of its power crackle along the crown of the hill, surrounding Keiro and the Ventallo and the mages and the black-armored mercenaries. A line, drawn definitionally between those who obeyed and those who did not. He called on the other eight mages, called them each by name. With his voice still loud as thunder, and flat as a dead man's gaze, Keiro commanded the mages, "Kill them all."

If you've crossed her, run and weep . . .

They all doubted him, Keiro thought, all of them—doubted him even until the fires began to blossom among the gathered Fallen.

The Ventallo shouted, though their cries were not louder than the ones from below that rose shrieking into the night sky. With face fixed in a mask of impassivity, Keiro watched the fires spread—eight fires, tendrils reaching and joining and growing. A hand grabbed at Keiro's shoulder, and without thinking, Keiro grabbed the offending wrist, twisted and yanked so that a wet *pop* registered briefly below all the screaming. No one else touched him. Some of the Ventallo battered themselves against the shield, straining to be free, but not so many of them. Fools did not survive long among the Fallen. The brave did not survive long at all.

Somewhere in the conflagration would be nervous Laseneo, who had wanted only to serve. But Keiro had not asked him to stay, and Keiro could show no mercy, and no remorse.

Sororra would not tolerate disobedience, and she would not tolerate those who allowed it. If the disobedient Fallen were here when she returned, she would kill them anyway. Was it so terrible, then, to take their lives sooner? Take them, to spare his own? The end result was no different, save that Keiro might survive it this way. He couldn't—shouldn't—wouldn't be held accountable for their foolishness. They had chosen their fates.

A few of the Fallen broke free of the spreading inferno, stumbling shrieking into the surrounding hills. The mages— ever obedient—sent tongues of flame skittering after these runaways without even being told. *Kill them all*, Keiro had said. He could as well have shouted, *Save me. Help me. Please.*

He watched, his face an impassive mask, as a hundred and

a half of his sworn brothers and sisters burned. It would surely draw Sororra's eye, and the righteous fire of vengeance would drive all other thoughts from her mind.

It had to.

Once all the screaming had stopped, and the fires had turned the bodies to ash upon the scorched dirt, Keiro made a motion with his hand. His hand didn't shake at all, the mask spreading like a creeping vine to hold him steady. The fires, never anything natural to begin with, died quickly as snuffed candles. The shield fell away, though none of the Ventallo made any move to pass beyond where its line had been drawn. Hot air rushed forward and hit Keiro like a slap, but his toes curled into the soft earth, and he didn't stumble or sway. He made himself draw a dozen deep breaths, the heat and the burned-meat smell tearing at his throat, until he could speak without choking. Speak without letting the mask shatter.

"I am their voice, and their eyes, and their hands," he said, and his voice still shook the air atop the hill. He had not asked Terstet to dismiss that spell. He needed to be sure they heard him. "My word is their word, and my actions are their actions."

Finally he turned to face the Ventallo, looked at them without looking *at* them. He didn't want to see their fear or their hatred or their horror. He didn't want to see what he had done, reflected back to him in the emptiness of their eyes.

I'm so sorry, he whispered into the blank mouth of the mask.

"Heed me," he said, "for I am the voice of the night."

CHAPTER TEN

Anddyr pressed his ear to the chest below him, listening to the fluttering uncertainty of a heart trying so desperately to fight. It was almost a physical ache for Anddyr, to watch Rora struggling to stay alive and not be able to do a damned thing to help.

They'd bound his hands exceptionally well: wrists flat together, fingers tucked around each other with strips of fabric wound between each digit. His hands were of little more use than a club at the end of his arms, and it kept him from shaping his fingers into the sigils necessary to cast any spells. He couldn't heal Rora, couldn't help her at all. He didn't think she was close to death—though without his magic, he couldn't be *sure*—and he'd guided Aro through as much healing as he could . . . but healing was complicated, and Aro had had so little time to learn even the basics. He could have done more harm than help, his magic stumbling through Rora's battered body, and they wouldn't even know it until blood started bubbling from her lips, or her eyes were bulging from the swelling of her brain, or . . .

The cellar door opened, and as the darkness rushed in from outside, Anddyr thought it actually felt *darker*—as though the little lantern they'd left him was able to fight back a cellar's worth of gloom, but quailed in the face of the unending night. It was easier to fight the smaller problems; the bigger ones had a tendency to suffocate.

Anddyr, holding tight to the pieces of his fraying sanity with two clubbed fists, was struck by how very much he felt like that lantern. Strong and bright if given the chance, but shuddering like a breath and flickering into obscurity when faced with anything too *big*.

Anddyr realized he was still half lying on the ground, his ear pressed over Rora's heartbeat. He quickly pushed himself up, clumsy with his bound hands, but he'd had what felt like a handful—*Hilarious*—of days to get used to how useless he was. He made it to sitting before the first person descended fully into the cellar, boots clomping down the ancient ladder. The ladder would crumble away to nothing someday, leaving Anddyr trapped down in the cellar with his useless hands and the life he couldn't save.

The first face was unfamiliar, but it was a woman whose every inch screamed *fist*, and she was followed down by another before Anddyr finally saw one he recognized: Aro, of course. He was a loyal brother, and he visited every day.

"Hullo," Anddyr said. He raised both fists in the best he could do to approximate a weak little wave. None of the three responded to him, but they rarely ever did.

Aro gave him a guilty look, though his gaze quickly slid away as he knelt at his sister's side. He felt her forehead and her throat, careful around the lumps and lacerations Tare had left, careful around the manacle at her wrist. "She's still stable," Anddyr told him. No response, of course, but he'd begun to suspect that didn't really mean anything. "She's been awake off and on . . . mostly off, but some is better than none. Her breathing still concerns me, and her heart hasn't leveled out yet . . . I think there's something we may have missed." That last bit he said very carefully. There was no *we*, but Anddyr had to be cautious about placing any blame. A man with no means of fighting back, trapped in a small dark place with two shovel-faced fists glaring harder with each word he said . . . it wouldn't be a surprise or a mystery to anyone if Anddyr ended up laid out along the floor just like Rora.

The fists moved around the cellar, the man collecting the pail of refuse Anddyr had pushed as far into a corner as he possibly could, while the woman leaned her back against a wall, arms crossed and glare ever present. As the man carried the pail up the ladder at arm's length, Anddyr turned his shoulders slightly, putting the woman more to his back, ducking his ears into his shoulders. "You need to check her heart," he said as softly as he could. It was a command, plain and true, and he saw it touch the twisting skura-sickness within Aro, saw it shiver down his spine before Aro went stiff all over. Anddyr ignored the twisting in his own gut; that was a different flavor of disgust, and he knew how to live with self-loathing. "Like we did before, remember?" Aro's fingers faltered, fluttering, hovering over Rora's neck. Her breath wheezed in through her mouth, hitched, stalled, and then rushed out painfully. Aro's breathing was, in that moment, much the same. Finally he lowered his hand, fingers splayed, thumb and forefinger bracketing his sister's neck. "Good," Anddyr breathed. "Blood is easiest, remember. Follow the blood, find where it stalls or pools or poisons."

He could taste the magic in the air, and stared, breathless, at

Aro's eyes flickering behind their lids, darting as he searched, not knowing enough to know what to look for. Sure enough, his eyes opened and met Anddyr's briefly, darting away with a quick shake of his head. If he'd had use of his hands, Anddyr might have torn at his hair.

The woman-fist grabbed his shoulder roughly, pulled him back from Aro and Rora. "Enough whispering," she said, and this time her glare turned to Aro. "Tare said to do your plan and then go back up top. Plenty to get done without wasting more time on them."

A muscle jumped out in Aro's jaw, and his fingers curled reflexively where they still lay below Rora's throat, but he didn't argue that he was wasting his time. Anddyr could understand some of that—the pack all viewed Anddyr as a waste of breath, it really wouldn't be all too surprising if they'd brought Aro around to their way of thinking—but if they'd done the same to Aro's thoughts about *Rora*? They'd had their fight, to be sure . . . but they were twins, bound tighter than blood, bound tighter than anyone beyond them could understand. Aro would never think of her as a waste of his time.

Surely.

"Up," the fist said, hauling Anddyr to his feet. A shove sent him sprawling against the back wall of the cellar, his nose bouncing off his bundled hands as he landed and making bright stars dance before his eyes.

"Wait," Anddyr said muzzily, stretching his hands up like he could stop them somehow, and trying to fix his eyes on Aro. "What plan?"

Silence was his only answer for long enough that he began to wonder if, somehow, his head-bounce had damaged his hearing as well as his nose, but no, when he managed to focus on their faces he saw that none of their lips were moving either. Both fists, the woman and the man with an empty bucket at his feet, both simply glaring with their mouths set. Aro stared down at his sister, and Anddyr had seen the look in his eyes before, that lost glimmer; the twins had their own silent way of communicating, and this was the way Aro asked Rora for help, asked her to tell him what to do, asked her to choose so that he wouldn't have to. Only this time Rora couldn't see it, couldn't help him. And maybe, with the way things had been, she wouldn't help him even if she could see.

"What plan?" Anddyr asked again, whispered it like a prayer.

Aro's jaw worked, the muscles in his throat jumping and twitching over and over. They stood out starkly in Anddyr's blurred vision, as though the scope of his world had narrowed to the war being fought along the length of Aro's neck. "To give you more . . . freedom," he finally said, the words fighting free, "while still keeping you contained. Harmless." A sickly smile shivered across his face. Anddyr wondered who it was meant to be directed at, him or Rora or Aro himself. "You should make yourself comfortable, Anddyr."

It was like the slam of a prison door, walls dropping down all around Anddyr with a horrible finality, and it threw the world into sharp relief. He'd wondered how long it would be, how much longer they'd let him stew in his filth and hatred and fear before they sealed him up. Bound hands could only provide so much security—bonds could be slipped, chains could be loosed, and after all, the Twins had been bound and then broke free . . .

"Wait," Anddyr said, trying to keep the desperation from his voice. "Please . . . let me heal her first. She needs help."

He could see the uncertainty waver across Aro's face, watch his eyes dart to the two fists and settle on the damaged sprawl of his sister. That was when his shoulders squared. "He's going to heal Rora before I seal him up," he declared, voice stronger than Anddyr had expected.

The woman-fist jerked forward. "Tare said—"

"*I* say he's healing Rora," Aro interrupted, and then he took a step toward the woman.

There was nothing inherently threatening about the motion, but the woman still took two quick steps back, fingers of one hand curled into a warding sign. Anddyr could only see half of the bleak smile that twisted Aro's face, and it had vanished by the time he turned back around. He crouched down in front of Anddyr, and though he had his back to the fists as the woman scurried quickly up the ladder, Aro said in a low voice, "You'd better be quick about it."

Aro put a shield up around Rora and Anddyr, a heavy barrier to contain them both. It took the younger man a few tries to correctly weaken the barrier so that he could stick his hands through the barrier—a few false starts while Anddyr watched sad-eyed as his knuckles thumped against solid air without passing through. His face twisted with frustration, sweat glossing his forehead, but he got it right, finally, and quickly undid the binds around Anddyr's wrists and palms and fingers.

It was like the first breath after drowning, flexing fingers that had gone stiff and bluish.

Anddyr wasted no time—the fist would be back soon,

with others who could override what little authority Aro had scraped together for himself. Though his fingers were less than nimble, they were good enough to weave sigils in the air, good enough to press against the soft flesh at Rora's elbow and temple, and send his magic skittering down into her.

Follow the blood, he'd told Aro, and he did just that, skimming through from toes to skull, steadying the flutter of her heart, sealing a slow-leaking tear here and there, and finding, finally, that nagging problem, the source of her painfully slow recovery: a swelling in her brain, a bruise on the soft tissue, and Anddyr could pretend the bruise was in the shape of knuckles so that he could sharpen his anger against that certainty. It was easy enough to heal, a steady flow of magic and gentle coaxing. Perfectly easy, if one knew what to look for.

With his hands curved into healing shapes, Anddyr couldn't make fists, but *oh*, he wanted to . . . He wanted to punch and bite and tear, to scream, *This is easy. You should know this. You must know this.*

His anger was meant for the woman who'd beaten her, made her brain swell, left a tapestry of bruises over her body . . . but it was a broad anger, and there was enough of it that a little could be spared for Aro.

It was a broad anger, and unreasoning. When he saw Rora, slowly dying and so easily saved, he thought of Etarro. The boy was dead now, probably, or perhaps worse than that, and it was because of Anddyr. *I chose her,* the voice of his anger screamed, and it turned howling to Aro, *I chose you. And look at what you have made of my choice. Look at what you have done.*

Anddyr opened his eyes a few breaths before Rora opened

hers, and he held her brother's gaze above her. "You have so much to learn," Anddyr said softly, came close to spitting it, and then Rora's eyes opened.

Aro's eyes widened and then narrowed, and he barely spared a glance for his sister as she shrugged herself awake, began to tug against the chains around her wrists. "Back against the wall," Aro said, deepening his voice, as though that were all it took to make someone listen. Anddyr did listen—the fists would make him otherwise, and he knew how fists hurt—but he obeyed slowly, his fingers trailing reluctantly over the manacle on Rora's wrist before he shuffled away to the far end of the room. Aro's barrier slid across the floor around him, leaving Rora behind, containing only Anddyr.

He huddled against the wall, wrapping his anger tightly around himself, glaring out at Aro as the boy began to weave his hands through the air. There was already sweat streaming down Aro's face, and as he wove his new spell while still holding the barrier around Anddyr, his face turned bright red, a slight bulge around his eyes, a wheeze around the muttered words.

The spell settled, and the barrier fell away from Anddyr along with the rush of Aro's breath. What was left behind was a different kind of barrier.

Intrigued in spite of himself, Anddyr pushed himself to standing against the wall, stalked toward the new barrier. It was visible in the same way air grew visible on a hot day, a shimmering distortion, and it was perfectly solid when he pressed his hand against it—just like any barrier Anddyr had ever made. But it *felt* different. He slapped it lightly with his palm, and beyond the distortion, he saw a faint twist to Aro's face—almost like a wince. Almost like he'd felt the blow.

Through the shimmering wall that sealed Anddyr off at one end of the cellar, he stared at Aro, his captor, and the boy's sister slowly waking at his feet. Aro still had so, so much to learn.

At the Academy, where Anddyr had learned to control the fire in his blood and bend it to his own use, the masters there had a special way, sometimes, of teaching their most recalcitrant young mages. "Loosen the leash," he'd once overheard the masters muttering to each other. "Let them run. They'll learn their own limits quick enough. Or they'll run too far, and snap their necks when they reach the end of the rope."

Anddyr was a good teacher. He'd done all he could to teach Aro well in what little time they'd been given. It shouldn't reflect on the teacher if the student was unwilling or unable to learn the lessons he was given; it shouldn't reflect on the teacher if the student ran too far too fast and snapped his own neck.

Circles and circles, the masters at the Academy had taught. Malefaction and justice. Always and eternal and balanced. A meed to fit the deed.

He stayed silent as he watched Aro through the shimmer between them, his sister at his feet with her chains rattling as she pressed a hand flat to the side of her face, to the myriad bruises there slowly fading.

Let the boy learn.

The skytower hangs empty, or nearly so. Anddyr stands upon its floating clouds, solid beneath his feet but soft like swampland. Anddyr does not fill the space of it, though. The loneliness does. Oppressive as a summer's heat, and it presses Anddyr's back against the insubstantial wall, flattening him, making him small.

Almost as small as the boy curled against the wall across from him.

The boy lifts his tear-streaked face from his knees, and the shape of it wavers between Etarro, Rora, Fratarro, Aro, Avorra. It never stills, never settles. Etarro whispers, "Please," and Fratarro, "Find me." Rora, "Leave me," and Avorra, "Cold," and Aro, "Don't," and their whispers surround Anddyr in a choking cloud as he is pressed back and back through the wall of the skytower. He passes through layers of cloud and air spun glimmering, until the tower releases him and he stands on air alone, and then Anddyr is falling. He can only shout, "I'm sorry. I'm sorry," and hope that they hear him.

Anddyr lands, and he is scattered, and he is broken.

CHAPTER ELEVEN

In his dream, Keiro stood at the center of the fire.

Bodies crashed and raced around him, in terror and pain and fury, and their screams wheeled like the stars. They shouted at him, begged him to make it stop, crumpled writhing at his feet. He saw their flesh cook, their blood boil. In the red ruins of their faces, their eyes stared wide, accusing, hateful and hurtful. They could not flee the flames, and so they watched him as the fire devoured them. Watched him with bubbling skin and lipless mouths frozen in ringing screams.

Keiro stepped toward the closest one. His hands passed through the flames, the heat of them flickering against his skin, but he did not burn. He found a face. Resting one hand against the top of the hairless head, he slid his other hand down to the neck, to cup the jaw where the scream vibrated against him. It was all bare, sticky flesh beneath his palms. Still the flames danced around this body, devouring, eating away—and still the body stood before him, screaming, staring. The fire burned, but it would not kill them.

Only he could do that.

Keiro's hands moved, his arms flexed. It was an unfamiliar motion but it came to him easily. The *snap* echoed loud through the night, louder than the flames, louder than the screams. His hands fell, and the body fell to the ground, silent and closed-eyed and completely consumed by flames.

All the bodies surged forward, their hands reaching, pressing, leaving behind pieces of black flesh so their bones scraped against him. Screams tore through their throats, a thousand voices begging for relief, begging for release.

Keiro reached for the next one.

He jerked awake, a scream halfway out of his mouth, and tried to thrash weakly free of the reaching hands. There was one wrapped tight around his arm, another pressing hard against his chest, more and more and *more* crowded at his back, the heat of their burning flesh suffocating—

A soft, soothing rumble vibrated through Keiro's body. He lay still, panting with his eyes wide open in the dark, telling himself that it was Cazi like a pillow beneath his shoulders, Cazi whose chin rested against Keiro's chest as one clawed foot held his arm firmly but gently, that it was the *mravigi*'s warmth rather than the heat of a fire. When Cazi's eyes opened, their dull red glow was not the comfort Keiro would have wished: in the darkness, the light made Keiro's flesh look mottled black and red, the skin sloughing away . . .

The rumble again, a wordless reprimand and consolation both. Keiro forced his breath out through his teeth, his hands clutched into motionless fists at his sides. "I had to," he croaked aloud. Surely a sound would shatter the dream, send it skittering away to the dark corners of the room, to the dark corners of his mind. But his voice didn't sound like his own voice. Keiro turned onto his side, knees drawn up to his chest and arms wrapped around them, his face pressed into Cazi's flank. If he pressed his eyelids tightly enough together, his vision turned white, both eyes seeing the same.

"You're allowed to feel pain," a soft voice said. It was not Keiro's voice, *truly* not his voice, nor was it Cazi, and Keiro's shoulders went stiff with alarm—not because it was a stranger, but because he knew that voice. "I made an old friend of pain. It's easier, to think that a friend would hurt you. That way, at least, you can justify that it's done out of love. It gives a reason to the mindless screaming inside you."

Keiro sat up slowly, swiping at his cheeks with the back of his hand. Behind him, Cazi shifted, wrapping himself into a smooth ring around Keiro: head on one knee, tail tucked over the other. Keiro could just barely pick out the lines of the slight form crouched in the cave's entrance. "Good evening, Brother," Keiro said, and there was only a faint waver in his voice.

"There are some people," Fratarro said, "who attract pain. It's always been so, since the start of time. People who pain follows like a second shadow. You seem to be one of those people, Keiro." His eyes shone, but in the darkness Keiro could not tell whether it was with fury or with tears. "You would do well to make a friend of pain, too. I do not think it will be leaving you anytime soon, and a friend is easier to bear than an unwelcome guest."

"I . . ." Keiro fought to find anything intelligent to say to that, anything that was not simply a bitter laugh that sent his innards spilling out through his mouth. "I will keep that in mind. Thank you."

A sigh. "I wish you wouldn't patronize me." It wasn't said with any malice—a simple statement—but Keiro still rushed to deny it and to beg forgiveness at the same time. A sharp motion stilled his words, Fratarro's hand chopping through the air. "'Patronize' was the wrong word. I wish you wouldn't just *placate* me. There's no joy in a one-sided conversation. And I have no one else to talk to."

Keiro closed his eye, focused on the steady, sturdying warmth of Cazi at his back. "I was alone for seven years," he said. "Completely alone for most of that. I know it's nothing compared to your centuries, but . . . I do understand what it's like. How the silence invades and twines so deeply around your soul that to speak feels like to kill. That the sight of another face, any face, would be at once the world's greatest blessing and a punishment to set your very being ablaze."

He thought of all the people his own lonely life had touched—sharing the road as a wandering preacher, the Fallen who had cast him out, the plainswalkers who had taken him in, mages and broken mages, the *mravigi*—so many lives he had touched, and he did not know if any of them had been made better by him. He knew some, like the plainswalkers and the disobedient Fallen, were far worse for having met him. He thought of the burning bodies, remembered his dream-self so carefully snapping their necks, and shuddered. Perhaps that was why his throat twisted and his voice grew rough with touches of anger and venom, and why he said something he should not have said: "At least you were never truly alone. You always had Sororra."

He tried to bite back the words, but it was too late. They'd slipped past all his careful defenses and filled the darkness with heavy acrimony. Knowing the fraught relationship between the Twins, Keiro expected the silence to come alive and grow teeth, to rear back snakelike and swallow him down in smooth, smothering gulps. Keiro gripped the fabric of his robe so tightly that he almost thought his knuckles glowed in the darkness.

But the silence between them slept. "Yes," Fratarro finally said softly. "There is that."

Keiro's held breath left him in a soft *whuff* at the unexpected surprise of not being obliterated. At still being *able* to breathe. He held his own silence for a while, wrapped around the shock of such an obvious misstep not having cost him his life. Another low rumble from Cazi shook down to Keiro's bones, but the *mravigi* did not take his glowing eyes off of Fratarro.

"My sister will be coming back soon," Fratarro said. His voice held none of the simmering frustration Keiro had become accustomed to—that had, in fact, been absent from everything Fratarro had said so far—and more of the spiraling despair than Fratarro usually let show. That realization chilled Keiro more than his own brush with mortality, but he couldn't have said why. "She'll be proud of you, I think. She always did have her favorites." Fratarro lifted his eyes, and the red glow softened his face, smoothed out all the lines a god's eternal worries had put into it. He looked almost like the boy whose body he had stolen. "I worry she won't be as pleased with me."

Keiro saw the dagger between his feet again, the sharp edge that would slice him to pieces at the first misstep. It felt like there were more daggers now, more edges to dance along, more ways to slip. "Sororra loves you." It felt like the only safe thing to say. "She'll always love you."

"Do you think so?" The red light shone off tears, gathering, falling. "Truly?"

Keiro's lips parted, but no words came out—all swept away by the tide of a god's tears.

Fratarro, still crouching, moved forward on the balls of his feet and the palm of his good hand, a feral thing, uncertain and alien. As Keiro reached out, his fingers only trembled slightly. Fratarro took his hand, and then the boy fell against his side, head buried in Keiro's shoulder, hands curled against his chest. "I feel so alone," he said, and the words sounded strangely doubled, as though two voices were speaking them. "Trapped."

"You're not alone." Keiro put a tentative hand against the back of Fratarro's head and, when he didn't flinch or snarl, petted his hair as he would a dog's. Keiro had always understood how to soothe a child's capricious moods.

Behind them, Cazi shifted with a sigh, moving to bring Fratarro into the curl of his body, draping his tail over Keiro and Fratarro both. Keiro made wordless, soothing sounds, and he thought of how Sororra had done the same as Fratarro had screamed with the pain of the distant destruction of his hand. This was a much softer pain, but that did not mean it cut any less deep.

With his face pressed against Keiro's shoulder, Fratarro's voice was low and muffled as he said, "He's sorry about Cazi."

"What?" Keiro leaned back, gently gripping Fratarro's shoulders so that he could search his face by Cazi's red-white glow.

Fratarro blinked, a small frown on his face. "I didn't say anything." There was no trace of deceit in his voice, and Fratarro had never been called anything but honest. He scrubbed at his cheeks with his good hand, twisted his shoulders under Keiro's hands to free them, and leaned back on the balls of his feet—a boy distancing himself from hurt, and a god pulling his mask back down.

When he spoke again, his voice was firmer and more certain, even if the words were little different. "I'm sorry about Cazi."

A chill crept down Keiro's back.

"I wish it could have been different," Fratarro went on—thinking, perhaps, that Keiro's silence was anger. "And I wish it could be undone. But it's so much harder to reshape a made thing." He reached out—not with his good hand but the bad one, dangling limp from his wrist. He turned his hand and rubbed his knuckles across Cazi's snout. The Starborn didn't move, didn't blink. "I wish I could give you back your wings, but some things can't be undone. Not even by a god." He pulled his hand back, fingers hanging uselessly. "I hope you don't hate me." It took Keiro long moments—too long—to register that those words were for him.

Still, Keiro did not respond even when he realized he needed to. He had spoken both foolishly and brashly this night, and both had been dangerous steps. He thought, now, before he spoke, turning his words and feelings over in his mind, feeling them crash against the terrified pounding of his heart. A more considered answer did not necessarily make it a better one. Cazi's tail flicked against his leg—a warning? An encouragement? "I don't," he said finally, and the words were at least mostly true.

He had the ancient eyes of a god, but his face, when he raised it beaming to Keiro, was the face of a boy and nothing more. A boy named Etarro, who had been born and raised in the darkness and—the preachers whispered—who had had an unnerving fondness for watching the sun rise.

It didn't last nearly long enough, the boy's happiness twisting away into a god's concern. His hands rested on the ground, the fingers of the good one scraping fretfully at the dirt. Perhaps it was only a trick of the light as Cazi shifted, but the fingers of Fratarro's bad hand almost seemed to twitch. "What will happen," Fratarro asked softly, one hand moving against the dirt from a claw to a fist, "when she comes back?"

"Don't you know?"

The shadows played eerily across Fratarro's face, lit from below by Cazi's scales. "Don't you?"

Keiro wanted to sink into the earth and stone, or to run beneath the stars until his feet bled and hardened. He wanted to *sleep*, to hide himself away from all of it if only for a short time . . . but there was fire in his dreams, and fire was such a dangerous thing.

"She always said she wasn't any good at shaping." Fratarro dug his fingers into the ground, twisting and scraping. "She never understood she was just good at a different *kind* of shaping. Not all shaping is done with hands and matter." When he pulled his fingers from the earth, there was dirt caked beneath his nails, streaking his skin, and Keiro remembered his dream—how the flesh of the burning dead had clung to his own skin after he had snapped their necks, and how easy it had been. "She never understood herself, and so she never understood her strength. I don't know if she ever truly will." With his dirty fingers, Fratarro reached out to cup Keiro's jaw, fingers boy-small but god-strong. If his other hand worked, Keiro wondered, would Fratarro rest it on the top of his head, waiting for that so-easy twist? "You're strong, too, Keiro. You have to be."

A laugh shook its way out of Keiro's throat, past the press

of Fratarro's palm. If he screamed, Keiro wondered, would that feel any different? "I am whatever my gods need me to be."

Fratarro dropped his hand and his gaze. "She'll be proud of you," he said, echoing his own earlier words and the fatalistic tone. His face hardened to flint, any trace of boyishness sloughing away. "Well. I should be as prepared for her as you are. You're awake now." He shifted away and settled, crossing his legs, his back straight, palms upward on his knees. There was no trace of movement in the left one.

Keiro pushed himself away from Cazi, folded himself into a mirror of the boy. His mouth was death-dry, and fire danced behind his missing eye. Still, he made himself say the words, a rumbling intonation plucked from that deep well inside him that had been shaped by careful, cautious, calculating hands: "Power first, for without power there is nothing. Control, mastery, and finesse can come later. First you must regain your power."

Fratarro's face creased with effort and concentration, and the world around them trembled. As showers of dirt pattered on his shoulders, as the heavy air thrummed against his ears, Keiro sat motionless, waiting. And he did not stare at Fratarro's left hand—he didn't need to look at it to know it wouldn't twitch, wouldn't move, wouldn't ever be what it had been, or what it needed to be. There were some things written so indelibly across the stretch of time that not even a god could change them. Some things could not ever be undone.

"She'll be proud of you, too," he said anyway. He did not know if Fratarro heard him, and did not know if the words were his own or if they belonged to the voice that sometimes used his mouth. He didn't know if there was a difference, anymore.

CHAPTER TWELVE

The house was so much smaller than Joros remembered it.

He'd been young when he'd left his home and family, but a man by any count—old enough to work, old enough to marry, old enough to kill. He'd left and seen enough of the world to begin to understand the shape of power and influence, to understand how a man could move through the world and twist it to fit his designs.

Perhaps that was what made the house seem so small. When he'd lived in it, he'd been little more than a seed, watered by anger and resentment but with no room to sprout. The house had been confinement in more ways than one.

Joros walked the halls of the place he'd lived decades ago, and his feet still remembered the careful steps to avoid the creaking floorboards. Though all the belongings and personal touches were gone, dusty furniture remained. Beds crowded together where he and his brothers had slept piled like puppies to make space for all his father's wares. The desk in the study where his father had conducted his tedious business of ledgers and letters, and his mother had screeched at him for tracking in dirt, *you useless foolish boy.* The countless rooms full of now-empty shelves that had always been piled high with whatever next thing his father had been *so sure* would remake the family's fortune. The space in the dusty attic where a small body could wriggle through and sit sealed away from the rest of the house, and watch the stars through a peeling section of the roof. He half expected to see memories of the people, too, but those ghosts lay silent.

He'd checked the sad little mausoleum that housed ashes from seven generations of his good, Parents-fearing ancestors, all the way back to the forebear who'd made his fortune brokering sales for fishermen who'd never realized they were being robbed blind. The man had made more than enough to pay for an extravagant house, and an ash-casket too heavy to lift so he could be housed in eternal glory. But he'd left little else for his descendants. The casket stood dull and rust-spotted at the center of the mausoleum that was crumbling around it, as untended as the house. Still, Joros found new names faithfully carved into the wall among the list of interred: his father and mother both, all three sisters, and two brothers. There was no one to bet against save himself, but Joros would have wagered all the coin in his purse that the family's lingering debts had forced the other two brothers to flee or to prison.

He didn't wonder where they'd gone. He didn't care. If any of the pack had asked, he would have told them so, in no uncertain terms.

He'd claimed a room for himself—kicked out the fists who'd been living in it while he'd been trudging across half the world to try to save their skins. This was still his house, *his*. He hadn't wanted the room he'd shared with his brothers, nor his parents' comparatively large room, nor even his father's office. Just a simple room, fairly small, so unimportant he couldn't even remember what furniture had filled it so long ago—a room that held no shadows or ghosts. It served its purpose well enough, with a rickety bed taken from a knife who Sharra had ordered to give it up, a wooden chair that smelled faintly of rot, a desk that was too small—a desk whose worn surface felt familiar beneath his restless palms. He'd found the desk squirreled away in one of the other rooms, and a foolish whim had made him drag that one old shadow into his new haven.

Sitting at the desk, he could reach his hand beneath it and his questing fingers eventually found the rough-carved letters chicken-scratched into the underside. A boy had lain on his back under the desk, a dagger held clumsily in both hands, squinting up through the falling wood splinters as he carefully carved the letters of his name. That had been a boy who'd thought all the world was his for the taking, that he could hold power like a dagger and carve his mark on the world.

He tugged open one of the desk's drawers and stared down at the stone it held. He'd thought, almost daily, about picking it up, even just pressing a fingertip against its smooth surface. Thought of letting the old magic flow through him, to see out of another's eyes, to let it give him direction. But this seekstone, linked to Etarro, would make him see, now, through the eyes of the god who had stolen the boy's body, and Joros was not at all sure a mortal could survive seeing through a god's eyes.

But perhaps he could. Perhaps it would be no different from looking through any seekstone, and he could learn the Twins' whereabouts and the shape of their plans. Perhaps it was worth the risk.

The stupid, foolhardy, power-hungry boy he'd once been would have done it.

Joros pushed the drawer shut. It had been decades since he'd been that boy, and he'd learned since that power wasn't something that could be wrested and held like a dagger. Power was more like water in a desert, and if the years had taught Joros anything, it was how to make a waterskin, and that a smart man wouldn't brave the desert without as much water as he could carry.

Joros prowled through the shadow-touched hallways of his youth, feeling like the walls got a little tighter each time he passed between them, and he was grateful to find Sharra Dogshead watching her fists drill out in the courtyard. Despite the oppressive night, the air outside, at least, didn't smell of rotting memories.

Someone had brought out a chair for the Dogshead to sit on; with whatever damage had been done to her leg aeons past, she started wobbling if she stood for too long, and it didn't do for a leader to remind her people of that any more often than necessary. Better to seem lax or lazy than weak.

Joros skirted around the fighting fists and went to stand at Sharra's side, his hands clasped behind his back, not at all minding the height difference. He stood in silence, waiting, and as he'd known she would, the Dogshead spoke first. "My people tell me you've been making the rounds."

Joros shrugged. "You said you wouldn't commit them. It might surprise you how many of them are willing to commit themselves for hope and justice."

"Justice?" She raised a hand, palm flat, and tipped it sideways as though dropping something useless. "They already fought a losing war for me. They should be a lot less eager for another one, but they're young." She turned an eye up to him, needing to twist her neck awkwardly for even that. Gods, being tall was a blessing. "*Too* young."

"Some would say that giving your life in service of the gods is the surest path to eternal exaltation." A good vocabulary was almost as great a blessing as his height around these people; he never tired of the flicker of consternation when he used a word that was beyond them.

"Would you?"

"I would *say* it is."

The Dogshead snorted, and looked back at her fists.

A dark shape detached itself from a wall and stalked over: Tare, Sharra's second. He was genuinely surprised he'd gotten in more than a handful of words to the Dogshead before her rabid dog had shown up. Tare took up her post at Sharra's other shoulder, but Joros didn't spare her a glance as he asked, "Isn't there a cellar you should be haunting?"

He felt her anger burst toward him like the first breath of winter, and he allowed one corner of his mouth—the one she couldn't see—to turn upward. Ever since Rora's health had improved, Tare had made a habit of playing escort to the fists who tended to the captives, bringing food and cleaning filth. When he'd asked, the fists had told him with broad smiles that Tare spent her time threatening to cut more pieces off Rora. The fists seemed to think it a good show of strength on Tare's part.

"Don't you have a world to save?" Tare returned, mockery heavy in her voice.

Joros shifted his jaw until it popped. He had indeed been making the rounds, telling anyone who would listen how their dear departed pack mates had martyred themselves so valiantly, and how the Twins could still be defeated. Their eyes always shone with fervor after he was done talking—but Tare had been making her rounds, too. Preaching caution and safety and security, whispering aggrieved reminders of all the members of the pack who had died under Joros's supervision. Oh, she was always careful not to imply that it had been *his* fault—she was happy enough to rest that blame on Rora's shoulders, as he'd intended—but the fact still stood that members of the pack had been given into Joros's keeping, and he had not been able to keep them safe and alive.

He'd hoped, by now, that he could muster up at least *some* support—a handful of the thickheaded fists, or a few of the quick knives, kindled by faith and fear and the promise of glory. He wouldn't need more than a few to start; once he had enough to strike out into the world, more would come, falling into line like herded sheep. Once it had begun, it wouldn't stop.

It was simply the beginning of it that was proving to be difficult.

Joros shook himself, aimed a flat and meaningless smile in Tare's direction. "Patience is a virtue of the Parents, isn't it?"

Tare snorted. "Who's failure belong to?"

"The weak."

Someone streaked across the torchlit courtyard and threw themselves at the torch, dousing the light and plunging them all into darkness. The fists immediately ceased their sparring, and Tare's response died in a puff of air, so that it was completely silent when the light-killer hissed, "Danger on the road."

It sent them all into a quiet, organized commotion. The Dogshead stood up so suddenly that her chair toppled backward, and with her unsteady leg she almost toppled with it. Joros, close as he was, was likely the only one who saw Tare steady her leader. The fists broke apart in all directions, moving soundlessly to apparently preordained locations. Dimly, Joros made out bodies climbing up the crumbling walls. When he looked back, Tare had vanished, and the Dogshead was limping toward the house.

Joros stood alone in the courtyard, impressed at the efficiency of it all and looking forward to the day when he could turn that efficiency to his own use.

There was a small gardener's shed set against the wall behind the house. The shed had been decrepit when Joros was a child, and he was amazed it still stood now. He was more amazed it held his weight as he climbed up the makeshift ladder someone had leaned against its side. There were a few others perched atop the shed, their heads poking over the edge of the wall, and two children at the edge of the roof, ready to jump down and relay messages as needed. Joros joined the adults at the wall, stepping carefully across the roof until he could rest hands and chin against crumbling stone.

Starlight showed him a familiar face, a young knife named Harin who seemed to hate silences and would fill them with her chatter. She'd proved to be an excellent source of information, the cost of which was occasional inane prattling until he could redirect the flow of her word-stream. Harin was perfectly silent now, though, simply pointing over the wall to the west.

Over the fields, a little blue orb bobbed and its light showed a group of five walking beneath it. Though it was hard to tell with the night and the shadows and the orb's hue, Joros would wager his soul—what little of it there was left— that those five were wearing black robes.

With the distance, he couldn't be certain—but with his

knowledge of wasted decades, Joros was *sure* that one of them would have robes that were actually blue, a muttering and dangerous mage; and at least one of them would be wearing black-dyed leather armor beneath the robes, for Valrik didn't trust his people's safety to the mages alone.

They were some distance away, and not skewing toward the estate—assuming they maintained their pace and direction, they'd pass right by the walled house without ever seeing it. No trouble, no danger, no damage done.

Joros had the strange impulse to stand up to his full height, to bash his sword against the stone wall and scream until his throat tore, to draw the danger in and bring it crashing down and show Sharra that it could be fought and destroyed.

He quelled the urge, but it was a near thing.

"Do you think we could take them?" he asked Harin, soft as possible.

Harin gave a little snort. "Not a chance. They have a witch."

"We have a witch, too."

The woman turned to looked at Joros with something like shock, or perhaps wonder. When she turned her gaze back over the fields, Joros could see the calculations behind her eyes. He could see opportunity opening its arms to him.

"If you had to fight them," he asked, because for all her talking she was shrewd enough, "how would you do it?"

And she told him, and the others watching from the wall listened with held breaths and shining eyes. The group of Fallen had moved out of sight by the time she finished outlining her plan—all entirely hypothetical, of course—but everyone on the roof wore feral grins. Harin, with her quick words and loose tongue, would likely talk to the rest of the pack within hours. If the Fallen showed themselves within sight of the estate again, he doubted the pack would simply watch from the walls.

If Sharra wouldn't give him the help he needed, Joros would have to make his own help.

Joros returned to the room he'd claimed, sat at the too-small desk and stared at the dangerous stone it held. *Not yet,* he thought, closing the drawer. He knew Harin's plan would spread through the estate faster than a plague, and by the time it reached the Dogshead, her people would be straining against the protective chains she'd wrapped around them. They wouldn't let themselves be stopped or swayed from the plan—*their* plan, thought up by one of their own, and carefully and completely free from outside influence. *Not yet,* he thought, staring out the foggy window at the star-dotted night, and his lips curled in a smirk that might almost have been a smile, *but soon.*

CHAPTER THIRTEEN

The town was small, quiet within the unending night, but Scal could see faint light outlining doors and windows. Fires, candles, lanterns—light, to fight back the darkness. It was the first town they had seen since leaving the Forest Voro, and it made Vatri look pleased. Not so pleased as when they found wandering preachers. Not so pleased as when she prayed over their bodies. But pleased, still, and her steps were brisk as she led Scal into the town.

He had known Vatri long enough now to know that it was not in her to be shy. She spent too much of her life being stared at to flinch before the threat of attention, and she had the surety that Metherra's hand rested firmly on her shoulder, guidance and protection both. Both things made her bold. Too bold, sometimes, for Scal's comfort.

Her voice rang loud through the small, quiet town. "Divine Mother, Almighty Father, shapers of the earth and keepers of the flame, we ask you hear our hearts." The start of an old prayer, and simple. He could hear the sound, like twoscore breaths being drawn and held. A wavering sort of hope. "Gentle Metherra, we offer you our fears and beg you soothe them." Shutters creaked. Doors cracked. Eyes, peering carefully out, to prove what ears alone could not believe. "Stalwart Patharro, we give our hearts unto your keeping, and beg you keep the darkness at bay." Vatri spread her arms wide, scarred face glowing in the dull light as doors opened wider. As faces poked from houses, as feet crossed thresholds to step careful upon the ground. "Holy Parents, we give you all that we are, and ask only for your shelter, now and for always." The crowd formed tentatively. Held-breath hope and careful feet ready to turn. "We are the tenders of the flame, and we keep it burning in your honor." Vatri made a motion to Scal. Obedient, loyal, his fingers wrapped around the hilt and pulled his sword free. Twoscore breaths released sudden in surprise, in an explosive moment of renewed faith. Fire reflected in the eyes that stared at the sword he held over his head. "Mother preserve us," Vatri finished, triumph ringing in her words, "and Father shield our souls."

There were cheers and prayers and sobs. Hands grabbing at Vatri, grabbing at Scal, and he stood unmoving in the surge of them. Stood before the fire in their eyes, the hope spilling from their mouths. He was not like Vatri. He did not like crowds, did not know, often, how to deal with people. He knew, less, how to deal with people who looked upon him, flaming sword in hand, as though he were a god come once more to earth. But Vatri held on to his raised arm, held it so he would not lower it and so all the townsfolk would stare at the sword, and she told them, "See, loyal followers, the tool of the Parents. See their answer to the darkness. See Nightbreaker!" They cheered, and Scal stared above their heads. He could pretend he was not at their center, if he did not see their eyes and the fires shining within them. Thought only of Vatri's hand on his arm, like a tether. Wondered when she had decided the name of his sword.

The town's joy continued, but they were wise folk. Practical. They, too, had seen all the wandering preachers, seen the new purpose in their wandering steps. Preachers were drawn to the hint of a flame, and the town glowed from all the open doors. Scal and Vatri were half pushed toward a long, low building, the town flowing behind them.

The building was part meeting hall, part chapel. Its windows were all covered, to hide the light from the everflame hanging in an iron basket at the center of the room. Vatri sat herself below it, and Scal at her side. He could not keep his eyes from the everflame. He had been a boy once, and he had lived with a priest, and he had helped to tend the everflame. It felt, often, like the only time in all his lives that he had been happy. Scal wrapped his fingers around the flamedisk that hung from his neck. The snowbear claw strung next to it dug into the meat of his palm, tip sharp enough to draw blood.

Vatri wove for them the story of the Twins' rise, talking over their cries of distress. She told them all of it. And when she told them of Scal, cutting down preachers and their mercenaries with his mighty sword, they stared at him once more like he was more than a man. He felt their eyes on him. He stared at the everflame, held his two pendants as they sank their shapes into his skin.

"You can't give up hope," Vatri told them. "All is not lost, for we have a gift given by the Parents themselves . . ."

Scal stood. Sudden enough it startled the townsfolk, startled even Vatri. The seated crowd parted for him, fear and awe mixed on their faces that he could not entirely avoid seeing. He was careful not to step on any of them, and so he had to look. But none of them, not even Vatri, called to him as he walked out into the night.

The town was quiet, and dark. Only the faint outlines of doors and windows, and if he stood the right way, they all fell from his sight. When Scal drew a slow breath, it coated his tongue with the taste of spring. Mud, and heat, and rain. No faint winter left.

Scal released his pendants. Let his hand fall to his side, where it brushed against the sword. Nightbreaker. Just a sword, a normal sword, stolen from a mercenary of the Twins. There was no power in it. Nothing special, nothing deserving of a name. He could drop the sword here, now. It was only a sword.

No, the power was in him. In his hands, and in his will. He was the ice, and he was the flames. He could leave the sword behind, and it would not matter. There were always other swords. It would not change anything.

This is the will of the Parents, Vatri had said.

Scal had stared at the everflame, and he had heard nothing but Vatri's voice, seen nothing but fire-shining eyes. Had stared at the everflame and thought of the red-robed priest who had tended the everflame of his childhood, a man who laughed often but smiled rarely, sadness hanging from his shoulder like a shadow. And Scal could not remember his voice.

You asked me to shape you, Vatri had said.

The sword was nothing. Scal was the true weapon—Vatri had made it so. He stood staring up at the dark sky, the thousand stars. He remembered the boy he had been: the boy who had lived in the cold, who had been raised by a priest who was so close to a father. Almost. The boy who had wanted nothing more than to tend the everflame, and to one day go on a grand adventure with his friend. Scal did not know if any piece of that boy still clung to him. Could that boy have survived all the other, bloody lives that had followed his peaceful one?

The creak of a door. Soft steps. A murmur, from a nervous-swallowing throat.

Scal had known he would be followed. From the moment he stood at the middle of their chapel and stepped through and around them, he had known he would not be left alone. Vatri would not be the one to follow him; she had larger concerns— *Where are the Twins?* He did not know if she would send some-one after him, or only not stop it from happening. It was the same thing, in the end. Soft breathing, behind his back, and a waiting silence.

And, finally, a small voice. "Are you gonna bring the sun back?"

He had not expected it to be a child. Had not planned to speak with whoever had chosen to follow him, but this voice made him turn. The child was nothing like the boy he had been—she was a girl, and small for her age, and her hair was so dark that her face seemed framed by the night sky. And yet. The fearless set of her shoulders. The words flat, like a chal-lenge. Eyes that wanted to hope but did not know what hope looked like. She looked nothing like the boy he had been, but there was more to any person than looks.

Scal looked down at the girl, and he looked away, to where his hand still brushed the hilt of his sword. Nightbreaker. There was a time, not so long ago, when he had made a word-less vow to himself alone that he would not ever carry a sword again. He had broken that vow, and not even thought of the breaking. Even when it danced with flames, even when it was sheathed in ice, the sword fit in his palm like it was a piece of him. Like his arm was not complete without it.

It was just a sword. He could leave it, and it would not matter. He could find another, always. *Nightbreaker.* Vatri had not named the sword. Her fingers had tightened around his arm, eyes fire-bright. *Nightbreaker.* She had shaped him, and a thing was not truly shaped until it had been given a name.

The girl stared up at him, cautious and curious and fearless. Asked again, "Are you gonna bring the sun back?"

Scal raised his palms. Clean, with no shadow of all the blood that had stained them. Scarred, but there was no trace on them of the ash-marks Vatri had pressed into his flesh, no sign of the gods' touch. Only his own skin. Only himself.

Vatri had said, *The gods ask so much of us . . .*

Scal closed his fingers over his palms. Felt the bite of his nails, deeper where the snowbear claw had pierced his palm. He dropped his hands and felt the left one rest against the hilt of his sword. He looked up to meet the girl's fearless eyes, and he said, "I am going to try."

She nodded once. Satisfied. And when she turned from him to walk back into the meeting hall, he followed after her, a single step behind.

Scal spent the night in prayer. He knelt beneath the everflame with his hands pressed to his forehead, and his prayers were made more of thoughts than of words. He did not know what to ask the Parents, or how to ask it. But an old red-robed priest had taught him prayer, and if Scal could not remember the priest's voice, at least the words of countless prayers had sunk into him. Carved into his mind by long nights and crackling flames. Flowing beneath his skin.

Vatri snored softly at his side, and the only other sound was the crackle of the everflame above his head.

He had sat in the same place as she had told the town that the Long Night would end. That Scal would fight the Fallen and their risen gods, and restore balance to the world. That this was indeed a long night, but the sun rose at the end of each night. The night would need to grow darker first, but it would end, as all things do. The townsfolk had cheered her every word. Cheered her declaration of war, and looked at Scal like a hero stepped from legend.

He had sat quiet.

She stared at him for a time, after she woke. Her eyes still soft with sleep, and the everflame smoothing the deep-lined scars across her face. She only said, though, "We should find more towns like this. Hearing from me, seeing *you*, raised their spirits. We give them hope against the Long Night." Scal nodded, said nothing.

The town leader walked with them to the line drawn by the last row of houses, thanked them for coming, wished them all the luck of the Parents. There was a knowing smile that would not stay off his face. They learned why, no more than a handful of minutes from the town.

Footsteps, and close enough that Scal drew his sword, fire dancing out. It shone on six faces, familiar enough in his sword's flickering fire. Townsfolk, from the town they had just left. Younger, mostly, those who had reached adulthood but were barely past its edge, their eyes eager for adventure. The weapons they held were mostly tools and makeshift things, eager for blood.

The oldest of their number took another step forward. A woman of middling years, who carried an unstrung bow taller than she was. "We'd like to come with you," she said. Said it to Scal, her face open and earnest, but her gaze slid to Vatri. "If you'll have us."

And Vatri's answering grin was the only answer they needed.

CHAPTER FOURTEEN

Rora sat in the same place she always sat, back slouched against the wall so it didn't press the bruise on her shoulder, with her arms and her chains wrapped around herself, and looking anywhere but at the shining not-wall down at the other end of the cellar. Even a glance would send the witch into fits, and she'd got so damned tired of his fits.

Most of the time that she wasn't sleeping—and she spent more time sleeping than any person should, but even moving around made her head spin and her mouth yawn—she tried hard as she could to listen through the cellar door. The world was out beyond it, and she could always hear footsteps and voices, but never the words, not until they were standing right outside the door. Still, trying to hear was better'n anything else she had to do.

It got so bad, sometimes, that she'd start counting how many times the witch'd try to talk to her before he either went to sleep or drove himself into a fit. Highest she'd gotten so far was three sets of five times, and he'd capped that one off by pounding his whole body against the not-wall and screaming at her to *Look at me, please, God, please just look at me.* That'd been damn near the most exciting day she'd had since waking up.

"It's quiet," the witch said, and she could *hear* his wide-eyed look. He was right, though—she couldn't hear any steps across their ceiling, couldn't hear any muffled voices. It was like the whole world'd gone dead above them, and that was a thought that was as frightening as all the hells. If everyone else was dead, that meant no one to bring her just enough food to keep her from starving, no one to have awful little conversations with between slop-bucket cleanings, no one to someday, maybe, unlock her chains from the wall and let her go walking out the cellar door, too . . . Rora didn't spend much time thinking about her own death, but she could say for sure that wasting away under the ground with only a damned witch for company wasn't how she wanted to go.

Rora counted her breaths. Five, and then five times five, both hands ticking off the fives until she ran out of numbers and it twisted her head to think how to count more. And still it was death-quiet.

"Rora," Anddyr whispered, his voice cracking around her name, and she almost looked at him—she might've, even, if the loudest hell hadn't come crashing down right at that moment.

It sounded like an army was running over their heads, feet pounding on the ground, and dirt rained down around Rora. There was shouting, loud enough she probably could've heard the words if there'd been any, but it was just the kinds of sounds you made to make yourself feel braver and your enemies feel scareder. There were metal sounds, too, like weapons hitting; and solid thumps like bodies hitting the ground hard. Rora wrapped her arms tighter around herself. Usually she hated the chains, but now with the way they wrapped tight around her, too, they made her feel small, and small felt like the safest thing to be now.

The witch was crying, his blubbering a lot softer'n whatever was happening above—but when the above-sounds stopped almost as sudden as they'd started, the witch's crying felt like having knives jabbed into her ears.

Rora counted her breaths again. If she listened real hard, she thought maybe she could hear soft voices beyond the door. It was hard to tell around Anddyr's crying, and around the way she could hear her own blood racing like a wildfire. Five and five and five and five . . .

She knew the next sound well as she knew anything. The slow scraping sound of a body being dragged.

Being dragged *closer*.

Since she'd been a kid, since she'd first pushed a knife through a man's heart, Rora'd usually been the kind of person to run toward danger, as long as it wasn't a stupid fight that'd get her killed for no reason. Most times when she faced a fight, it was—sometimes straight-cut, sometimes roundabout, but almost always true—to keep her and Aro safe. She could go charging at danger if she knew it meant keeping her brother safe.

But with a body being dragged over her head, and closer to the cellar door, Rora sure as shit didn't want to run toward it, but she wasn't about to run from it either, even if she could. All she felt was froze up, like the ground'd swallowed her halfway, or like she couldn't get enough air even to think. All she could do was stare up at the slow-dragging line the body was making over her head.

The door swung open, thumping against the ground and showing Rora a little piece of the night sky above. Then the opening was full of bodies spilling down the ladder, boneless and tumbling and covered in blood—

But the bodies landed on their feet, and their grins shone through blood-covered faces, and under all the blood she could recognize some of those faces. It was the pack, and once she could hear anything besides her blood in her ears, she realized their low voices were tight with held-back cheers, like they were just a few seconds away from breaking into some kind of celebration.

Two carried a body between them, trussed up good and tight, and a big hunk of the robe it wore dragged along the ground. It looked like a black robe at first, but as they hauled the body past Rora, down to the far end of the cellar where Anddyr'd made a never-dying little light to keep them from going madder, Rora could see the robe was the same dark blue as the one Anddyr had been wearing when she'd first met him.

Whitedog Pack had trapped itself another witch.

And like two witches in one room wasn't too many already, Aro was the next one to come down the ladder.

His face was glowing, same way it did when someone told him he'd done right, like he was just a dog who needed a pat on the head to keep happy. There wasn't any blood on him, but he was grinning just as wide as the fists and knives who had red spattered everywhere. His face fell a little, when his eyes flicked over to Rora, but they flicked quickly away and he pushed the smile back on his face. No one else probably knew him well enough to see it wasn't the same smile it'd just been. He hurried after the witch carriers, to help, sure, but probably also just to put Rora behind him, where he wouldn't have to see her. That was fine by Rora. She kept telling herself that as she stared at his back.

There were enough people in the cellar now to almost fill all the free space there was, and still more heads crowded at the door opening, peering down like owls. The crowd left a half circle of space around Rora, and a bigger one near the not-wall, where Aro and the two witch carriers stood. Rora couldn't see much through the forest of legs between her spot and the not-wall, but she heard Aro's muttering and Anddyr's surprised gasp and the cheering that finally broke out of the pack. Some of 'em even started chanting her brother's name, but mostly it was just celebrating the good work they'd all done. Through the legs, she could see her brother grinning again as hands slapped his back, and behind him, behind the not-wall, she saw a flash of Anddyr kneeling down next to the blue-covered body that was now on his side of the not-wall.

"Wouldn't get too used to this much company," said a voice to Rora's side, and she didn't like how much it made her jump, how unsettling it was that someone'd managed to sneak up on her so good. She could blame it on the crowd and the noise they were making, or maybe her distraction with her brother, or—when she turned to face the voice—it could just boil down to Tare being good enough at sneaking that it didn't matter how good you were at not getting sneaked on.

Tare was leaning against the wall next to Rora, not more'n a few handspans away, arms crossed, one shoulder pressed to the mucky stone, one ankle hooked behind the other. Anyone who didn't know her that well would probably think she was relaxed, that the smile on her face was just any regular smile.

But Rora saw tension in every line of her, saw the way her pointed canines showed more than any other teeth—it was a smile that was more snarl, same as it was every time she looked at Rora. She wasn't looking at Rora, was staring off over the heads of the pack, but Rora could feel her attention like an arrow pressed to her forehead.

Tare went on, "The novelty of a new prisoner'll wear off quick enough, and then you'll be stuck down here all on your own again."

Rora tried to hide her hard swallow, to hide how much fear those words sent skittering down her back. "Seems like I'll be less alone by one more person, even after you all leave." She tried to make it sound light, like she didn't care either way, but her voice came out raspy and croaky, same it did every time she tried to talk now. Some of it was from when Tare'd nearly killed her, but some of it was just from Rora only talking when Tare came to mock her.

"I'm sure witches make great company," Tare said, snorting.

Rora looked away, back through the forest of legs, catching a glimpse of a face that was a less beat-up version of her own. "Doesn't seem like you've had a problem keeping company with one."

"Some betrayals are easier'n others to forgive."

"What's honor to a thief, hey?"

Like Tare'd said, the pack was starting to lose interest. The cellar stank—Rora knew that better'n anyone—and there was nothing to look at besides a few pathetic prisoners, nothing to do besides mock those prisoners, and two of 'em were stuck behind a not-wall while the other one was already being mocked. Wasn't much there to hold the pack's attention, and so they were starting to drift up the ladder, back into the dark air. Aro was with them, and he glanced at Rora again as he passed by, looked away just as quick as he had before. The smile stayed on his face this time, and he was up the ladder and gone before Rora could tell how forced the smile was.

The ones who were left, who were drifting slower back up to the real world, Rora could hear them talking over how great the night'd gone. How they were so happy the black-robes'd been dumb enough to fall for their plan, how easy it'd been to lure 'em in, how they'd died simple as anyone—"Seems like following the Twins don't do much good, yeah?"—how Aro'd disabled the witch like it wasn't even hard, and how Tare'd tried to get answers out of one of the black-robes before putting a dagger through his eye and into his brain.

"Sounds like a good plan you've all got," Rora said, looking at the not-wall, where, now that the cellar had cleared out some, she could get a better look at the two witches. Anddyr'd untied the new one and was probing over his body, likely checking for damage.

"It works well enough."

"Did Joros give it to you himself," Rora asked, "or is he still wanting you to think it was your own idea?"

She was looking away from Tare, and so she didn't see the older woman's reaction—but she could imagine Tare going even more tense, like a bowstring ready to snap. "It was Harin came up with the idea."

"Harin?" The name sounded familiar, which was a rare enough thing with how little of the pack was left from Rora's days in it. "She the one with the big teeth who was always underfoot?"

"No, that was Kera," Tare said distractedly. When Rora sneaked a look up at her, Tare was staring off at nothing, her upper lip pulled down between her teeth. "Harin's good. Harin's solid."

"Might want to see who she's been hanging around, then. Joros's got a twisty way with words, Tare. He's good at giving you ideas without you knowing it."

Tare's eyes snapped down to Rora, and the snarl went back on her mouth. "I don't need advice from you. I don't have any reason to trust a traitor." She pushed away from the wall, went to join the last few people hanging back before leaving the cellar. Halfway up the ladder, Tare paused, looked back at her. "You shouldn't've come back," she said. "You should've just kept on running."

It wasn't the first time Tare'd said that to her, but it didn't hurt any less, the more often she said it. Put a dull ache in Rora's chest. She slumped back against the wall, closed her eyes to the woman and the witches and the world. "I've done enough running," she said. Let the smart people decide what it meant if she didn't run or fight, if she just stayed put while the world rushed on around her. Wasn't anything different she could do anyway. "But you should find out what Joros wants witches for." She didn't open her eyes, but the cellar door slamming shut was answer enough.

And then it wasn't too long after that when the new witch woke up and started screaming, and Rora pressed her head against her knees. Way she looked at it, at least things couldn't get too much worse than they were now.

CHAPTER FIFTEEN

Keiro felt like he had only just closed his eyes when a trembling hand on his shoulder shook him awake, and he looked up into Terstet's twitching face. Keiro might have scolded the mage, but Terstet had a panicked look about him that instantly woke Keiro. "There's . . ." Terstet said, but his words trailed off almost before they'd begun, and he shook his head furiously—whether in denial, or in an attempt to shake his thoughts free, Keiro couldn't tell. Finally Terstet managed to choke out, "Need to see," before he fled from Keiro's chamber.

Cazi, curled at Keiro's side, rose to stretch, his forked tail flicking across the ground. Half turned, he met Keiro's questioning look with one red eye and rolled it toward the ceiling. *"Need to see,"* he repeated, and Keiro followed him through the tunnels and out into the night.

There was the moon, low on the horizon, and little more than a slice of it—not enough, certainly, to make the night as bright as it was. No, the light came from what seemed a great comet, streaking slowly through the sky, flickering with reds and whites. As Keiro stood staring, he saw what all the others had already seen: the comet was growing steadily larger.

One of the Ventallo whispered, "Is this the Parents' vengeance?" He did not speak loudly, but in the hushed silence, the others scattered across the hill heard him. None seemed surprised by the question—no sudden realizations dawned, only a calcifying of fear.

"If it were the Parents," Valrik said, "they would not give us the time to flee their wrath." He might have meant the words to be comforting, a reassurance, but they didn't have that effect.

They were all looking up, even those without eyes, staring at the comet, so distracted by the uncertainty of their fates that they did not see what Keiro saw: the *mravigi*, emerging slowly from their hidden tunnels and burrows, scales gleaming star-bright as their snouts turned up to face the comet, their eyes the same red as the comet's heart. And none of them saw the different-shaped form that crawled alone from a different hole, moving slow and low across the ground, as though called by Keiro's gaze. The dark shape crouched at Keiro's feet, fingers of one hand splayed against the ground for balance, the other hand draped motionlessly over a knee. Barely visible in the crook of that arm was the lumpy shape of a stuffed horse. He turned his face to the sky, eyes wide, and Keiro thought he had never looked so much like a child. "She'll be here soon," Fratarro said softly, voice reedy and wavering. All the others shuddered visibly at his words, but they did not turn their eyes from the sky. They had not seen their god since his rising, but even his presence now could not pull their attention from the comet-that-was-not streaking ever closer.

Keiro alone did not stare at the sky. He looked from face to face, from the eyeless preachers staring raptly, to all the scaled Starborn who had begun a low humming that was not quite yet a song, to the boy-god crouching below him whose face shifted between fearful and glacial.

What will happen, Fratarro had asked him, *when she comes back?*

Don't you know?

Don't you?

Neither of them had had an answer. Keiro's hand shook ever so slightly as he reached out to rest his fingers on Fratarro's shoulder. Fratarro didn't move or react—only stared up into the sky, waiting beside the rest of them for the return of his sister. The comet grew closer, moved faster, and Keiro turned his eyes upward to watch in silence. There was nothing else he could do. Had there ever been?

Seconds or hours, they all stood watching, the faithful chosen of the Fallen, and their protectors, and their mages. And finally, with the comet hanging like a sun above them, the red fire faded and great white wings snapped out, slowing. Straz, first of the *mravigi*, landed gently upon the ground in the hastily cleared space. Fratarro, mere feet away, did not move from his kneel. Keiro, hand still gripping the boy-god's shoulder, stood firm as well. All others shuffled back, faded away, became insignificant or made themselves so.

And from Straz's back, Sororra leaped down, her young face alight with elation and a sharp-toothed grin. "Brother!" she crowed, and danced over to haul Fratarro to his feet, to wrap him in a hug. He hesitated a moment, and then the stuffed horse fell from his arms as he wrapped them around her in turn, and he leaned his face heavily against her shoulder.

She'll always love you.

Do you think so? Truly?

Keiro, standing so close, saw the moment when Sororra realized only one of her brother's hands held her back—that the other still rested dead and useless at the end of his arm. Keiro saw the anger and the pain that suffused her face, saw how her grin melted into bare-toothed fury. By the time she pulled away, holding him at arm's length, her smile was back in place. Keiro wondered which was the mask.

"It is good to see you again, Brother," she said, and Fratarro choked some reply that Keiro could not hear.

They stood together, side by side, arms at shoulder and waist, and faced all those who had gathered to greet Sororra's return. She saw Keiro first, and grinned. "I trust you've been keeping everything in order?"

Keiro did not think anything at all. "I have, my lady. Sister."

"I'm glad to hear it, Keiro," she crooned. "And what of my brother—have you been keeping him in order as well?"

"He hardly needed me at all," Keiro said. She would know it for a lie, but the lie wasn't for her benefit—it was for all those spread at Keiro's back, who needed to believe their gods strong, infallible. She would hear the truth in the lie, if she did not know it already.

"Good!" she crowed, her smile not slipping. "And I see only the most faithful remain. The others are off doing our bidding?"

"They will spread across the land, and prepare it for your coming."

"You've done so well, Keiro," she said, and he remembered Fratarro whispering, *She always did have her favorites . . .* To all those gathered behind Keiro, the Ventallo and the blades for the darkness and the mages, she said, "You should get some rest, all of you. There's so much we must do, and little time to waste. Come with us, Keiro. There are things you must hear and do."

Bowing his head, Keiro stepped forward—and faltered when a harried voice called out at his side, "Glorious Twins, if these are matters that involve my people, surely I should join you as well." It was Valrik, who pointedly did not look at Keiro. "You named me the leader of the Fallen, and I cannot lead my people well if I do not know how they can best serve you."

Sororra tilted her head to the side, as though considering, and Keiro's heart raced in sudden panic. Since his arrival, Valrik had been at war with Keiro—Valrik having the trust of the Fallen, Keiro the trust of the Twins. They had been playing a deadly game of balance, one set up by Sororra herself: the Fallen needed only one leader, the Twins needed only one proxy. If the scales tipped—if the Fallen began to follow Keiro, or if the Twins' trust in Valrik grew—the other would become unnecessary.

Though he still dreamed of fire and bubbling flesh, though he often found himself clutching his elbows and pressing tight against the roiling in his gut, though the thought drifted through his mind not infrequently, *How can you live with yourself?*—still, Keiro could not bring himself to want to die. He had walked shoulder-deep into a far-off ocean, and had not been able to walk any deeper. And if he did not wish to die, he had to fight for every moment of life.

"I will be sure to tell you anything you need to know in order to perform your duties," Keiro said to Valrik, and Sororra smiled amicably, and did not invite Valrik to join them. Fratarro, after a moment's hesitation, bent to pluck the stuffed horse from where it had fallen and tucked it into his shirt, where it would be unseen but not forgotten.

Fratarro would have led them beneath the ground, to the

cave he had made into his home, but Sororra laughed. "Brother, we spent centuries belowground. Why would I ever go back there?"

And so Keiro led them away, through the long grass that would warn them of any who dared try to follow them. Keiro thought it might have been the first time Fratarro had truly explored the world since being freed—as far as Keiro knew, he'd spent all his time in the tunnels and caves, working with Keiro or surrounded by his *mravigi,* who adored him. Because of the trepidation he could see on Fratarro's face, Keiro led them to one of his favorite places: where butterflies whose wings glowed blue would rise fluttering into the night when their slumber was disturbed.

He didn't realize until they arrived how tainted the place would feel: the last person he'd brought here was the mage Nerrin, whose life had been taken—*given*—in order to restore some measure of power to the Twins when they were still bound. The butterflies had made Nerrin so happy, and it had lightened Keiro's heart to bring a measure of joy to the poor mage's life. She had laughed the same way Sororra now laughed, spinning in place with arms outstretched as the glowing butterflies spread around her.

There were so many people he had tried to protect, and failed. With the mask that was shaped like his face, Keiro smiled.

They sat among the butterflies, Keiro and his two gods who wore the bodies of children, and young Cazi, who always trailed after Keiro. That, at least, brought a smile to Fratarro's face—Cazi curled in Keiro's lap, but resting his chin upon Fratarro's knee. Sororra spoke at length, not needing anything besides a listening audience. At the end of it she held her brother's hand, the one he could not move, and she told him it didn't matter. She looked to Keiro and asked, "You told them what to do? The Fallen?" Keiro nodded; the instructions she'd given him to pass along had burned through his mouth, clear goals for all the mass of the Fallen even now likely reaching the edges of Fiatera. It would begin, very soon. Sororra squeezed her brother's hand. "You see? All will be well, Brother. *We* will be well."

Fratarro pulled in a deep breath and slowly released it as he lifted his good hand. It shook slightly, and for a long moment nothing happened—and then a butterfly shimmered into being on his palm, its wings white-speckled black, like the *mravigi*, like the night sky. It fluttered uncertainly upward until it found its balance, and then it swirled among the multitude of blue. Fratarro met his sister's grin with a smile of his own. He said, "I'm ready."

Keiro left them with Cazi at his side, feeling like an intruder. Sororra had given him his instructions, and there was nothing left that they needed to share with him. There was much he had to do among the Ventallo: they needed to be ready to leave by the moon's next rising, for there was nothing left to keep them in the Plains. The Twins had shattered the sun, and brought the Long Night, and it was time for them to go forth and do all that they had promised.

Keiro found Terstet and brought the mage with him before he went to speak to all the others—Keiro had learned that reminding them of the power he had brought to bear never hurt. Terstet stood shaking at his shoulder as Keiro assembled all the others, the Ventallo and the blades for the darkness and the mages, and told them to make ready to leave. "It is time for the Twins to return to their homeland," he said, "and we will be their escort. We will lead them back to their home, and to their glory."

Keiro was not surprised when Valrik stepped forward, his face tight with fury. "Did you not think," he asked, the words edging closer to a shout, "that I should be told of this first?"

"No," Keiro said. "I didn't. The Twins bid me prepare the remaining Fallen to leave. It seemed a task I was perfectly capable of handling."

"You impudent whelp." Valrik took a step closer, fists clenched at his sides, and then another step. "If you think—"

"Terstet," Keiro said, steadily and clearly. The mage at his shoulder jerked forward, obedient. Keiro's heart was slamming within his breast, and he left the rest of the threat unspoken, hoping it would be enough.

But Valrik *laughed*. "You think your pet scares me? The mages are *mine*, and they will heed me above all else. Sit," he commanded Terstet, and the mage sat. The certainty in Valrik's voice was so strong that Keiro knew he would fail if he tried to give Terstet an opposing command, and so he stood silent with racing heart. He would not make a fool of himself before all these people. Valrik went on, "The mages are mine. The blades are mine. The Fallen are mine. You have nothing and no one—you are an apostate, cast out, and you will never lead the Fallen. It is time for this charade to end." He took another step.

Ever since finding the Twins bound below the earth, Keiro had been fighting—fighting for them, certainly, but fighting, too, for his own life. They had named him their most loyal follower, they had chosen him, but they had not given him any tools beyond their faith in him, which rang a hollow thing when faced with weapons of steel and magic.

All his life, he had never wanted anything more than to walk and share stories and find simple joys. He had never thought to find his gods, or to become their voice, or to be shaped into their tool. He had not wanted any of this.

As Valrik took another step forward, Keiro took one stumbling back. It was not in his nature to run from things—he would rather walk away bruised and beaten, but with his chin raised. But the racing of his heart made his breaths come short, made his vision swim with rising panic, and he could feel his legs tensing, ready to flee, because the only other option was to stand still and wait for his death to find him.

Another step bumped his hand against Cazi's waiting snout, and the Starborn pressed reassuringly against his palm.

A cry of some sort nearly burst out of Keiro, but it stayed behind his teeth. He had been there when Fratarro and Sororra had taken Cazi's wings, had stolen his ability to fly in nearly the moment of its discovery; Cazi was not large, but perhaps if his wings had not been taken, he might have been able to get them to safety. Instead he was as trapped as Keiro, though surely Valrik and the others would not be so foolish as to kill one of Fratarro's own creations—surely they would not stoop to profane so vilely the race shaped by their god's hands.

"Cazi," Keiro murmured around the heavy scream in his mouth, "I'm sorry."

The *mravigi* pressed his snout firmly against Keiro's hand once more, and then the press of it was gone, Cazi's light-speckled body streaking forward.

There was the half-moon, and the stars in the sky, and the faint glow of Cazi's scales, but all that was not enough to clearly see what happened. Keiro heard a cry, and a gurgle, and Valrik fell to the ground. Keiro's racing heart stuttered as the moonlight outlined Cazi, crouched atop Valrik's unmoving form. Stopped, as Cazi turned to face him—moonlight turned red blood black, but Keiro could see it around Cazi's muzzle, on his deadly-sharp teeth when he opened his mouth to say, *"I am sorry."*

The frantic racing of Keiro's heart resumed, and the scream behind his teeth battered for freedom, and he wanted to run until his legs fell from his body. But his feet stayed still, and in his mind he felt a gentle tug, a careful twist, and a certainty that this was *an opportunity.*

With his heart shattering in his chest, Keiro swallowed his scream, and he stepped forward to Cazi's side, to Valrik's. The leader of the Fallen was dead—that was obvious at a glance. Fratarro had shaped the *mravigi* for beauty, but he had not neglected their safety. Sharp teeth and powerful claws were more than enough to kill the fragile humans that the Parents had shaped. Cazi gazed up at him with glowing eyes. It felt like another failure, another Keiro had vowed and failed to protect—

The mask settled on Keiro's face once more. His heartbeat slowed. He faced the Fallen, who stared in shock, unable yet to process what they had seen. Keiro said, "I have told you that I am the voice of the night, that I speak for the Twins, that my actions are their actions. If you doubt me, then take this for proof: Fratarro shaped the *mravigi*, and they know his heart better than any save Sororra. The *mravigi* have found Valrik wanting. The *Twins* have found Valrik wanting." His hand was steady as he reached down to rest it atop Cazi's head, where the Starborn perched on his kill. "If there are any yet who doubt me, please—now is the time to speak."

His answer was an echoing silence.

"Good. Then we have wasted enough time. When the moon rises next, we will be gone, and any who are not ready will be left behind."

Keiro turned and left them—left Valrik where he lay, left Terstet sitting with a blank stare, left the Ventallo and the mercenaries watching openmouthed—and Cazi followed smoothly after him. They disappeared together below the earth, winding through tunnels until they came to the cavern at the center of the hills—the place where Sororra and Fratarro had been bound for centuries, where their first bodies still sprawled. The air was heavy and musty, for the Fallen had sealed the place away once more, and did not visit it. Their gods had new bodies, and the old ones did not matter.

The two bodies towered over Keiro, slumped shoulder to shoulder, burned and empty husks. The faint stench of ichor still lingered—though Fratarro's limbs had been returned and sewn in place, there was still the black spine that pierced his heart, and that wound still leaked even now. Keiro's mind and heart were too full of other things to know what to make of that.

In that abandoned place, Keiro curled himself around Cazi, the Starborn's tail draped around him in an embrace, and they sat together in silence. Keiro wanted to weep, but he could not.

Before their banishment, Sororra and Fratarro had both been considered great leaders. Fratarro had amassed followers who adored him, who prayed to him and for him out of love, who would have cut their own arms for a smile from him. Sororra . . . those who followed her had done so largely out of self-preservation, out of the assumption that if her anger sparked, the fire of it would at least touch her followers last. Her followers had been no less passionate in their fear than Fratarro's had been in their love.

Keiro had never dreamed of being a leader, had never wanted it—he had always been happy enough in his solitary wandering. But he wondered—if the circumstances were different—which kind of leader he would have become. He worried less that Sororra's careful plucking at his mind had shaped him into someone different, and more that she had merely peeled back the cover of something dark and festering at his core.

The light of someone's approach stretched across the cavern far ahead of them. Keiro waited with the patience of stone to see who it was, to see who would have dared start a fire, to see who would dare seek out the old bodies that did not wish to be found. In some way, he knew who it would be before she emerged into the cavern, the light of her torch nearly blinding Keiro. It burned, in the same way his dreams burned.

Yaket, Elder of the plainswalkers, sat down on the ground near him, and planted the torch so that it was between them but to the side, so that he could see half of her face without being blinded, and so that half of her face was gone to the darkness. "You're leaving," she said.

"Yes."

"I am glad." Yaket's voice was heavy and full of regret, but the half of her face that he could see was determined. "You are not the man I knew. You've changed, and you've changed the lives of my people. I think things will be better, when you're gone."

Keiro gazed at her as Cazi's heartbeat thumped steadily in time with his own. He said nothing. What could one say, in the face of their own failures pointed out so starkly? He hadn't *wanted* to think about how badly he had failed the plainswalkers—how he had promised them safety and then stood aside as so many of them were killed; how he—the thought didn't want to finish, he'd trained himself so well to avoid thinking such dangerous things—how he had played a part in their destruction, bringing forth the change in the world that had needed their deaths—

"You have heard many of my stories," Yaket went on, jolting Keiro from the grim spiral of his thoughts. "Almost all of them, I think. But I know there is one you haven't heard. Will you let me tell it to you? It is short, I promise."

Keiro felt his arms tighten minutely around Cazi's body, and there was a sudden thickness in his throat. He remembered all the nights—when there had been *true* nights—that he and Yaket had sat up late, sharing stories, laughing and questioning and prying brazenly. She had welcomed him into her tribe that was her family, and guided him. She had shown him the Starborn on the night they gathered to sing to the full moon, had given him that moment of untouchable and indescribable beauty. She had stood at his side when he sought to free the bound Twins. She had let him help put to rest all the plainswalkers who had died in the Twins' first judgment.

"Yes," he said again, around the needles in his throat.

She turned to stare at the old bodies of the Twins, their

dark forms lined with firelight. "My people are old," she began, "older than yours, older than most of the peoples who have walked the earth. We have long memories, and truths as old as the sun.

"My ancestors bore witness to it all. They watched Fratarro build his paradise, and they watched the beautiful creatures he had made soar above the trees. They watched that paradise burn when Patharro unleashed his fury—watched all the land south of their home burn for days and nights, and watched the beautiful creatures burn as they flew. They saw two mighty shapes plummet from the sky, and crash to the earth.

"My ancestors were not of Fiatera. They did not know the full history, and did not know of the politics and jealousies among gods. They knew only that there was trouble, and that they could, perhaps, help.

"I promised you a short story. My ancestors found where the Twins had fallen, a deep and mighty crater sunk into the earth, the ground and their bodies still smoldering. They thought the Twins dead, and so they buried them and built a barrow around them, and it was the undertaking of years. In those days, we honored the gods of others even if they were not our own, and so my ancestors stayed nearby, to guard the bodies of the fallen gods. In time, the *mravigi* came, those who had burrowed beneath the earth to escape Patharro's fire, and who had searched endlessly for their creator since. They were welcomed, and lived peaceably beside my ancestors for a century.

"You know the way a story is shaped. You know the Twins were not truly dead. And so it will not surprise you, I think, that some of my ancestors began to hear a calling—a command. They could not help but obey. A group of two dozen went below the earth, and found that the *mravigi* had hollowed out the barrow around the Twins, that they merely slumbered, that Fratarro bled from the wound through his heart, and that Sororra, in dreaming, could still touch the minds of men."

Yaket stood—slowly, as though her knees pained her—and retrieved the torch from the ground. She gazed down at Keiro, the light dancing across her face, and said, "Come. Sometimes words are not enough. It is easier to see, and know."

Cazi uncurled from Keiro's arms and padded to Yaket's side, and Keiro followed after them both. Yaket did not lead them far: a tunnel that led off the main cavern and plunged down deeper before opening onto a round room that seemed to be about a dozen lengths across. The size of it was hard to tell, though, or at least hard for Keiro to determine—for he was distracted by the bones that lined the room.

There were full skeletons posed, and there were individual bones shaped into symbols and shrines, and there were patterned piles. Keiro gaped, unable to think clearly, unable to truly see what he was seeing.

"My ancestors were faithful followers," Yaket went on softly. "They were true believers, for they knew the faces of their gods. We have always had Elders, who passed down the stories and the tales and the old ways. It was an honor to be chosen as Elder, to learn the ancient stories and older truths. It was a sacred duty.

"There are some things you do not notice happening until they have already happened. When I became Elder, once a year, I would bring one of my people here, as all the Elders had before me. One each year, chosen to leave the tribe on the longest night, chosen for a sacred journey. For long centuries, we have kept our faith in the Twins. Every one of my people I brought before the Twins was struck with awe, with wonder, with devotion. Every one went willingly to the knife. It was an honor, to serve the Twins."

The torchlight shone off the tears tracking down Yaket's cheeks, and when she faced him full, the shadows hid her milky blind eye, and showed only the good one, full of ferocity. "It has been a very long time since my mind has been clear. But since you came to the Plains . . . you changed things.

"All my life, I have been the guardian of the Plains and my people and the secrets that lie slumbering beneath the long grasses. But you made me unnecessary. You pulled the attention that had so long been focused on me. And for the first time in all my long life, my mind is clear.

"You are leaving. My people and I will leave as well. We were the guardians of this place and its secrets, but there is nothing left for us to guard. What secrets we have, I would prefer to leave buried here, beside the departed. I am the Elder of the plainswalkers. My people are old. We know the shape of the world. We know the ways of keeping balance." Yaket shifted, passed the torch to her other hand and made the shadows dance. Now it was her clear eye buried in shadow, so that the blind one stared at Keiro in stark accusation. "You knew, once. But you have forgotten. You have been lost. I do not think I will see you again in this life, Keiro Godson. I will take my people far enough away that we can be sure of it."

She turned from him, and Keiro's heart lurched within his chest, a sudden pounding ache to go with her and the plainswalkers who remained, to walk with them wherever their feet would take them and feel the calluses build up on his soles once more, to have the taste of the wind embedded in his nose, to feel the sharp and bracing hunger of the long road. He had been made for walking. "Yaket," he said to her back, but his voice sounded like scraping rocks. She did not hear him, or she did not choose to. Either way, she did not turn.

She walked from the bone room, putting her people, both ancient and recent, behind her. She took the light with her, leaving Keiro surrounded by the darkness and the dead, and finally he wept.

Part Two

They talk of life being some grand tapestry, but hells below, whoever's weaving it has had too much to drink.

—Anon.

CHAPTER SIXTEEN

The harsh whisper came past Joros's door like a flash of lightning, there and gone almost before he could register it: "Preachers on the road."

Joros set aside the old book he'd been reading, and as easily as if it were a part of him, his hand found the scabbard leaning against his chair. The new leather of his shortsword's hilt felt strange against his palm; one of the knives had rewrapped it not so long ago, and Joros was trying to put some wear on it, to make the leather smooth as that of a sword that saw daily use.

"Everyone helps" was the Dogshead's rule, and her rabid dog Tare was more than happy to enforce it. As far as Joros was concerned, the two of them and their rule could go hang; but luckily, the long years of his life hadn't been entirely wasted: among the Fallen, he'd become an expert at seeming to be something he wasn't. That, if nothing else, was a skill Joros had aplenty. He spent much of his abundant spare time just palming the sword's hilt, rubbing sweat and oil into the leather, making a show of swinging it around when the knives held their practices in the courtyard. The appearance was the thing that mattered. Oh, he could use the sword well enough if he needed to, but he shouldn't *need* to. There were others for that.

Tying the scabbard around his belt, he stepped out into the hall.

The lightning-flash messenger was a girl, hovering on that awkward edge between child and adult, all long limbs and gracelessness. She was already dashing away, but Joros followed her low calls down the hall: "Preachers on the road." Loud enough to hear, quiet enough not to carry beyond the corridor. "Preachers on the road." Others joined Joros in the hallway, a motley mix of weapons held ready, every set of feet pointing toward the courtyard.

There were more bodies moving out in the cold night— children dousing torches or scampering toward the cellar, men and women piling more wood within the crumbling walls or moving to their assigned places, one woman holding a burning torch as others shielded its light with their bodies. They knew what they were doing; Joros left them to it and took his place inside the old stables. It was crumbling and rot-smelling, but the building miraculously hadn't yet fallen entirely to pieces. So long as it kept standing, it was a good enough place to lie in wait. A few others were there already, more trickling in to take their places among the rotting hay piles and warped stalls. Joros ignored them, pulling his sword free in a graceful arc that rattled the scabbard so pleasingly. He'd practiced it, out in the dark fields surrounding the estate.

Outside, the cellar door closed loudly, too loudly, and Joros muttered a curse. Peering through a broken place in the stable wall, he watched the torchbearer thrust the flame deep into the pile of wood, and by the faint glow that swelled, he saw the rest running for their own hiding places, leaving the courtyard empty.

And then it was just waiting. Watching the flames eat the piled wood and hoping they grew fast enough, hoping even if the fire couldn't be seen over the broken wall that the fire's light would show the smoke climbing into the night sky . . . hoping the light would bring the shadows.

And they came, of course. Preachers these days couldn't resist the opportunity to douse any bit of light they saw. There were six of them, only six, all in dark robes—though, when all was darkness, one learned to see the difference in small shadings, and one of the robes was a deep blue instead of black. So very predictable—the preachers hardly went anywhere without a mage to wipe their arses.

Joros flexed his fingers around his blade's hilt, and glanced at the others in the stable; there were two hulking, bulky fists. He'd let them go first.

The preachers moved cautiously into the courtyard, heads turning, checking the corners of the old walls, peering at the crumbling buildings as they moved forward with small, careful steps. They weren't stupid. They never were that.

But all the preachers had grown so very damn cocky.

They stood before the fire, the mage beginning to weave some spell for drowning the flames. That was the only signal they needed.

The burly fists went charging first from the stable, the sort of men one would expect to give bloodcurdling battle cries as they charged, but they moved surprisingly quietly. Joros gave them five steps before he followed, he and the others in the stable, the less bulky bruisers and the sneaks. Joros moved at a run, matching his steps to the knife at his side—not a second slower or faster. All the others broke from their hiding spots as well, the courtyard suddenly full of bodies and all of them converging on the gathered preachers. If one of the preachers hadn't made a gurgle as a cudgel hit the side of his head, the rest might not have noticed their impending doom at all.

The pack was hungry for vengeance, or possibly just hungry for blood—either way, it was red slaughter. It always was. There were at least three weapons for every preacher; plenty of stabs and slices and thumps to go around, and that didn't count the leftmost preacher, wide-eyed as he was ringed by daggers and cudgels. They always kept the leftmost preacher. It didn't count the mage either, who was busy battering herself against the sudden barrier that surrounded her. Joros slowed his steps, came to a stop. His blood didn't boil with the need to spill other blood, and no matter how careful one was, there was always danger in combat. He watched, and waited.

It was over in minutes, save for the excessive stabbing and bludgeoning that always went on for a while after. It was all so very efficient. Joros sheathed his sword; he'd been seen, had been a part of it all. The appearance was the thing that mattered.

He stood near the center of the massacre, and he gave a small smile. He'd done this. Not directly, of course, he wasn't an idiot—but the right words said into the right ears, and his will was done. It was a paltry, pathetic comparison, but it was the most power he'd felt since leaving the Fallen.

The Dogshead hobbled out of the house when it was over, as she always did, her eyes taking in everything. The first few times, she'd tried to stop her people from desecrating the recently dead, but she'd given that up; she was smart enough to see it only made them angrier. It was easier to let them take out their rage in a . . . constructive way. Sharra Dogshead, leader of her miserable band of misfits, was no fool.

She was flanked by her constant attendants, who bristled every time Joros called them that: pinch-faced Tare and blank-eyed Aro. Neither of them supported her or even touched her, but both were ready to catch her if she stumbled at all on her gimp leg. They made their rounds, stopping to talk to all those who weren't busy bludgeoning preachers, and finally making their way to the living preacher and the immobilized mage. Joros went to join them, because questioning their new-est prisoners was something he was actually useful for, if the Dogshead was in the mood to prove that Tare didn't have com-plete free rein.

Two of the fists held the preacher's arms, and a third was busy delivering well-placed punches to his abdomen while Sharra watched with crossed arms and an impassive face. Like a well-made machine, the fist stepped aside and Tare took his place. Joros had grown to like her just as much as he hated her—she was a ruthless thing, and driven by anger, which Joros could relate to perfectly well; but she was also too damned canny and didn't know her proper place. Joros would have called her an insolent bitch countless times, but she carried five daggers openly and likely had at least that many hidden away.

Tare grabbed the preacher's chin and forced his head up as he gasped for air. From the fists and knives desecrating corpses, there were still distant wet thumping sounds to un-derscore the coldness in her eyes as she demanded, "Tell me what you're doing here."

To the preacher's credit, he faced his inevitable and likely slow death without flinching. "The Twins' holy work," he wheezed. If he'd still had eyes, they probably would have shone with religious fervor; as it was, his smooth-skinned sockets, and indeed his whole face, glowed with his zealotry.

"Come on, now," Tare clucked, "we're all friends here." She punched him in the armpit, connecting solidly and precisely with the cluster of nerves there. The preacher screamed; zealotry didn't provide any sort of shield from pain. Just another reason to avoid that sort of thing. "Let's have some honesty, friend."

A bit of the fervor went out of the preacher's face, but all the punches still hadn't seemed to teach him that he wasn't immune. "Fuck you," he said.

Tare shook her head like she was truly sad. "I tried to be friendly," she said, and gave his cheek a few sharp pats. "I hope you'll remember that." Her eyes roved around the courtyard, the reflected flames of the high-burning fire turning her gaze demonic. "Pedri," she called, interrupting one of the men who was still busy finding out how many holes he could put into a dead preacher before it didn't look like a person anymore. But Pedri left off the corpse and ambled over, a smile curving his lips that didn't come close to touching his dark eyes. He held a dagger, a wicked curved thing, and both the blade and his hand were well soaked with blood.

There weren't many of them left in Whitedog Pack, but even if there had been a hundred of them, each one would be just as valuable—the soft-footed sneaks, sharp-eared spies, quick-handed assassins. There was a reason they were called *knives*.

Pedri knew just where to stick his dagger, in and out and in again, the places to draw blood and screams without touching on the edges of death. Tare crouched by the preacher's head, stroking his hair back from his face in a twisted loverlike way, her questions flowing even and steady under the man's screams: *Where are the others? Where are the Twins? Were you looking for us? Who commands you? Where are the Twins?* He sobbed out all the answers he had, few and useless as they were, but Tare kept asking and Pedri kept digging.

Joros, still finding no use for his sword, moved through the watching crowd until he stood at Sharra's side, in Tare's empty spot. In the light of the fire, Sharra's face was smooth and her eyes bright—not the face of an old woman at all. The limp was the confusing thing, each of her steps as careful as if she thought it would break her. He forgot, most of the time, that she was no older than he was.

On her other side, Aro stood tall and straight-backed, his eyes fixed on the preacher, his throat working in spasms. He'd vomited all over the courtyard the first time they'd lured a band of preachers to their deaths, the first time Tare had gone searching for answers with the point of a dagger. Granted, it may have been his madness rather than the violence that had made Aro sick.

Sharra had been so careful in ensuring Joros was never alone with Aro. It seemed his confession that he would have killed the boy to save the world hadn't sat right with her. Or perhaps she just feared that if given the chance, Aro would leave again. She was so determined to thwart Joros's planning.

They stood silently watching Pedri and Tare work for a while. "This one doesn't know anything," Joros finally said softly to Sharra, not wanting to interrupt the show for any of the crowd. Sharra gave a noncommittal shrug, and after another moment Joros prompted, "The mage?" Aro twitched at the word, but Sharra nodded and the three of them moved through the pack. Everyone stepped aside for limping Sharra, moving and turning as though they were hinges, fixed in place by their eyes on the preacher and Pedri.

The preachers' mage had curled into a ball on the ground, knees drawn up to her chest, arms wrapped over her head, looking altogether rather pathetic. "I can talk to her," Joros offered, running his fingers over the hilt of his sword.

"No," Sharra said, and made one of the signs her people occasionally used to communicate. The other man was already moving forward when she added, "Aro will speak with her."

Aro knelt down outside the impassable barrier he'd put around her, and with the two of them so close together, it was easy to see that his eyes were hardly less crazed than hers as she peered at him through her arms. Aro reached out, pressing his palm flat against the barrier, fingers splayed. "I know it hurts," he said softly. "But we can help each other. You can—" His words were swallowed by the preacher's screaming and blubbering as Pedri kept up his work, but Aro's lips kept moving, and the mage must have been able to hear him. She sat up slowly, her hands slipping from around her head, and she finally reached out to press her palm against his, the barrier between their skin. As the screaming faded away into ragged sobs, Aro turned his head very slightly, his eyes never leaving the mage's, and said, "She understands. She'll stay."

It had been a stroke of luck for Joros when Harin, all atingle over the pack following the plan even she thought she'd come up with all on her own, had suggested a new aspect to the pack's preacher-hunting plan: if Joros was already rehabilitating one witch, and if they already had a sure way to confine a witch . . . what harm could it be to add another witch? Joros had made his full support for the plan known, and even the Dogs-head hadn't fought hard against it—everyone knew how useful mages were, even damaged ones. That a weapon was nicked wasn't cause to throw it away. Sharra, consumed with keeping her doomed family alive as long as possible without actually doing anything proactive about it, thought some extra witches would be just the thing to help them survive the Long Night.

Let her believe what she needed to. So long as she kept a stockpile of mages, Joros could utilize them whenever the time was right.

Standing at Sharra's side, Joros said, "Your people have got-ten good at this."

"They have." She didn't say it with the pride she should have.

"I can only imagine how—"

"No. I won't tell them to die for you."

Joros ground his teeth. "You put their lives at risk each time you lure in a group of preachers. They're already fighting the Twins—why not let them do *more*?"

"They chose this," Sharra said, making an expansive mo-tion to the courtyard at large. "I told you, if any of my people choose to help you, I won't stop them. But I won't send them to die in another war."

Joros hadn't expected any other answer, but he had to keep trying. He was fairly certain persistence was one of the virtues of the Parents. And badgering, at least, made him feel like he was doing *something*.

He tilted back his head to look up into the sky, the sky that was always night-dark since the sun had vanished months ago. Three months was the general best guess, based on patched-together memories of how full the moon had been after the sun had been stolen away. It was as good a guess as any—and, anyway, time had stopped holding any meaning. Most things had.

Joros knew that somewhere, the risen Twins were consolidating their power, gathering their allies, spreading their sneaking fingers far across the realm—but that seemed to be a slow and tedious process. They'd made no strike, had not even been *seen* by anyone outside their order, and potentially not even by those within—all a far cry from the sweeping justice that had been promised. He'd been sure that the sun's fall would herald the end of the world and, more importantly, the end of his life—but both were still spinning on. No apparent end to the Long Night, but no consequences of it beyond a creeping lethargy and slightly more danger beyond secure walls.

On the one hand, it gave him more time to desperately pull together some kind of defense or offense, and he needed that time based on how poorly it had been going so far. On the other hand, how could he fight something that wasn't making itself known? How could he fight a shadow, or a whisper?

Joros turned his back to Sharra and roved his eyes over the courtyard—the blazing fire, the three bodies and the blood running between the cobbles, the gathered crowd of Sharra's people, her pet Aro and his pathetic new friend, the one living preacher and Pedri working very diligently to make him not, and beyond them all the old house still standing against all odds. He paused by the messy remains of the preachers and did what he could in the way of looting the bodies—Sharra's people, for all that they were scavengers and thieves, were too wrapped up in their anger to ever remember to check pockets first. The preachers each had a seekstone on them, which Joros was careful to hold only with his sleeve wrapped over his fingers before he tucked them into his own pockets. There were a few coins, some worthless trinkets, a piece of paper too blood-soaked to read, and a little jar. The jar was chipped but still sealed and unbroken, and that was worth keeping.

With nothing better to do, Joros returned to the house, to the room he'd claimed and its little desk. He added the new seekstones to the drawer full of them, each a different shade of blue or green or purple. With little enough else to do, he'd had plenty of time to sort and organize them, to figure out who was linked to the stone on the other end. There was the walker, who never stood still, and the sitter, who hadn't seemed to move an inch in all the time Joros had held the stone. There was the flapper, whose hands were always moving when Joros looked through his eyes, and the director, who owned the partners to at least five of the seekstones Joros had. And there was the boy, or the god, whose seekstone Joros had not touched; that one was too dangerous.

Joros closed the drawer of seekstones and stared out the small window. Beyond the warped glass, the moon was rising through the sky, the closest thing to daylight there was any-more. Joros drew his shortsword and laid it across the top of the desk, turning the blade to catch the moonlight. It was sharp and hungry, ready to fight, ready for war . . . he just had no idea which direction to swing it.

With a sigh, Joros went to lie on the bed, leaving the sword bare on the desk. That was the good thing about always-night: there was never a bad time to sleep. And there was little enough else to do.

CHAPTER SEVENTEEN

It was a morbid kind of funny, Anddyr thought, the way all their individual madnesses seemed to synchronize, as though mania followed moontides. No, that wasn't quite right—it was more like yawning, an innocuous little thing caught and passed around. One would start screaming, or singing to a child none of the rest of them could see, or weaving a spell to combat an assailant that didn't exist. And once one of them had begun, it wouldn't be long until another began muttering and scratching at invisible bugs beneath their skin, and then another would start clawing desperately at the stone floor. Once it had begun, it was only a matter of time before they were all trapped together, alone in whatever unique shape their madnesses took that day.

Anddyr sat in the space he'd carved for himself, his own private circle pressed against the cellar wall and the barrier keeping the mages contained—sat there, and tugged with both hands at his hair, just hard enough to keep himself focused. Four of the others were deep inside their madnesses, and Anddyr was using every tool he possessed to keep from joining them. His tools, though, were woefully few and manifestly inadequate.

He pressed his face against the barrier, staring out into

the cellar beyond, trying to distract himself by watching the shapes moving beyond his reach. Usually it was a shape, singular—a very singular shape—but there were *bodies* now, plural, all massed halfway between the barrier and the ladder leading up from the cellar.

There would be the usual planned chaos going on above, and so the pack had sent down their pups, all the children too young or foolish to be useful. If the rest of the pack was killed, well, at least the children would survive longer by whatever number of minutes it took the pack killers to find the cellar door. It was a charmingly optimistic pessimism.

The first few times, the children had been hushed with fear and excitement, practically cowering. They stood as far as they could from the specters lurking at either end of the cellar: the mages taking up breath and space at one end, the shadow of treachery chained at the other. That was how *they* saw Rora, anyway. It felt like a long time since they'd been like that. Now the children were fearless and foolish, returning to whispers only when one of the older pups wisely hushed them. They were never forced into the cellar for long, but even a minute can feel like an age to a child, and these ones particularly were easily bored. They spent their time breaking things, throwing things, playing blind man's wager, and—most frustratingly—pressing against the barrier of solid air and pulling faces at the mages.

That was their newest game, and they seemed tickled by how their silly faces could drive a mage into fits, if the mage was in the wrong state of mind. Anddyr had considered throwing fire at them the next time, to teach them a lesson—they'd be perfectly safe beyond the barrier, and it might put enough fear in them to leave the mages alone. He knew he wouldn't, though.

They were playing a betting game, now, using chips of wood as coins. At least three of them were cheating, and that was only obvious enough for Anddyr to notice it; more likely they were *all* cheating, but some were better at hiding it than others.

And as Anddyr watched them, the children's legs sank down like roots into the cellar floor, and they began to sprout mushrooms from their shoulders and backs.

Anddyr groaned, pulled harder at his hair. It cleared the mushrooms from some of the pups, but not all, not all. "My name is Anddyr," he whispered to himself, "and I am a prisoner, and I am in a cellar." A chant to ground himself, to keep his mind where it was meant to be. That had been Travin's idea—the first mage who had been tossed through the barrier into Anddyr's end of the cellar. Anddyr had been clawing his way steadily toward recovery—or as much recovery as he could ever hope for—and holding on to his sanity with a tight-fingered grip. He'd been able to maintain that grip even in the face of Travin's deterioration, enough so that he could nurse Travin through the painful process of freeing himself from his skura addiction. Now Travin was showing immense improvement: his stretches of sanity were nearly as long as Anddyr's, his hallucinations more mild, his whole demeanor calmer.

But each new mage stretched them thinner, and wore away at their tightly held grip on sanity. Anddyr would try any madcap idea to keep his sanity, and Travin's chant worked well enough. Most times.

"My name is Anddyr," he said again, flinching as one of

the children turned entirely into a mushroom that stared at him with accusing eyes. "I'm a prisoner. I'm . . ."

The cellar door above swung open, and the mushroom-children scattered like spores, flying up the ladder to freedom. Anddyr breathed out a half-sigh, half-sob noise of relief, resting his forehead against the cool of the barrier, closing his aching eyes.

When he opened them, four new bodies had come down the ladder. They'd gotten another mage, another prisoner of the pack, another new tool for whatever precarious plan the cappo had planted in their brains. Anddyr growled. It was always hardest when a new mage joined their group. Within the madness they all shared, routine and regularity were more than simple comforts—they were vital to staying sane, and sanity was very close to life. A new addition threw off every routine, forced the ailing mages to adapt. The coming days would be unpleasant indeed, and Anddyr was not—

He noticed, then, the three people leading the new mage forward. He watched them come closer, and he tried so desperately to hold on to the knowledge that their names were Aro and Skit and Badden, because his eyes were telling him that they were all Etarro, and each iteration of the boy was weeping blood where his eyes had once been.

Anddyr groaned and pawed at his face, trying to shake the double vision loose. "I am in the cellar," he told himself. "I am a prisoner. I am Anddyr, and I am trapped beneath the pressing earth . . ." When he looked up, his vision had mercifully cleared: Skit and Badden stood a handful of paces back, thick arms crossed over ale-barrel chests, glowering at the multitude of smells wreathing their faces. And the new mage stood before the barrier, young, likely not very long out of the Academy, and wasn't that her poor luck to end up twice a prisoner in so short a time. If she ever had grandchildren to tell—she wouldn't, though, none of the Fallen-touched mages ever would—maybe that would be enough time and distance for her to laugh about her misfortune.

And holding the new mage gently by the arm was Etarro, weeping blood.

"I'm sorry," Anddyr moaned, "I'm so sorry." He thumped his head against the wall, hard enough to hurt, hard enough to make white spots dance before his eyes. Etarro was staring at him in that eyeless way, mouth curved into a sad and unforgiving frown. "I was supposed to be stronger. I should have chosen you."

Etarro reached out to press his hand against the barrier, looking away from Anddyr. He stood there, motionless, holding to the mage with one hand and the barrier with the other, and the blood coursed down his face. He swayed where he stood.

"Falcon?" Skit took a step forward, gently touched Etarro's shoulder. "I mean, Aro? You okay?" Birds fluttered about Skit's shoulders, roosted in his hair, plucked at the ties of his shirt like they were worms, and the birds screeched, *No, no, no.*

Etarro straightened with a jerk, fingers curling to claws, then smoothing again. "I'm fine," he said, and his voice was deeper than Anddyr had ever heard it before, gruff with age and exhaustion, and that was Anddyr's fault, he'd done that to the boy. "I'm fine." He took his hand from the barrier to wave Skit away, then pressed his palm flat once more and rested his forehead on the barrier beside it. His eyes closed, but the blood didn't stop. Skit took a few steps back, frown tight across his face, the birds huffing annoyance, as Etarro began muttering spell-words, his fingers against the barrier tracing sigils. His shoulders were hunched, and the hand that held the mage's arm held hard enough it would leave bruises, and Etarro still swayed in an unseen wind though most of his weight was leaned against the barrier.

The air frizzled, like a hundred simultaneous electric shocks, just the wrong side of pain to make Anddyr cry out. And Etarro stumbled forward, two jerking steps before he caught his balance, as the barrier that had been supporting him vanished.

As the barrier that had been containing Anddyr disappeared.

Anddyr stared openmouthed, and Etarro stared back, and the boy's empty bleeding eyes begged, *Help me.*

Redemption flared through Anddyr like wildfire. He'd been consumed by regret since that day in the Plains when he'd sentenced Etarro to oblivion, had been wallowing in self-flagellation, wondering if he'd made the right choice, and tormented by the growing notion that he hadn't. And here, finally, was what he hadn't dared to hope for: a second chance. He could save Etarro this time.

Anddyr lunged forward and threw an arm around Etarro's waist, lifted the boy over one shoulder, and began to run. That was what he intended to do, at least. But Anddyr had been in the cellar for long weeks, years, aeons—he was weak, and newborn-calf clumsy. He stumbled heavily into Etarro, bore them both down to the ground screeching like cats, and Anddyr's forehead bounced against damp stone. He reeled back and up, tasting blood but desperate to keep moving, to not waste the chance he had been given, to not—

When he looked down, Etarro had faded away into smoke, and in his place sprawled Aro.

There was another surge of redemption, and flaring alongside it was raw fury. "I chose you," Anddyr screamed, and his fists fell like a hailstorm, beating and battering, and Aro bucked beneath him but could not escape. "You've wasted the chance you were given." Anddyr chanted low, words of power, words of destruction, and between strikes his fingers traced sigils upon the air. Aro's hands raised, but only to guard his face, not to cast any spell—he didn't have the instinct. "You don't deserve to be here." There were shouts and pounding feet—irrelevant. They could not reach him. "I shouldn't have chosen you." There was a spell he had sworn he would never cast again, one that had destroyed a town and all the lives in it. His fingers wove the structure and scripture of that spell. "You must learn." This *was* a second chance, but Anddyr could not undo the choice he had made. He could only seek retribution for that choice. He could destroy the fruits of his choice, and all that it had touched. "You must learn." The air grew warm, burning hot, and—

"Anddyr! Stop."

He almost toppled backward. Much of it was the ready-to-burst spell leaking away, exploding out and quickly retracting, jolting through his arms and chest and leaving his hair crackling. But it was also that she had spoken to him, directly to him, for the first time in a very long time.

Hang-jawed again, he stared at Rora where she knelt in her corner, stretched to the limit of the chain at her wrist. She stared back, horror in her eyes. But she didn't look away. Anddyr reached a hand out toward her, and that was when Skit tackled him.

Anddyr screamed into the floor of the cellar as both shoulders were wrenched so hard he was sure they would pop from their sockets. He could hear Skit yelling for Aro to get the barrier back up, could hear Badden threatening death to the other mages, could hear the mages all wailing in confusion, could hear Aro coughing blood between the muttered words of a spell. Anddyr lay perfectly still as Skit continued to twist his arms, keeping his fingers from moving though Anddyr wasn't trying to move them. All the fight had gone out of him along with the spell. He'd failed, again.

The barrier rose once more, sealing off the end of the cellar, sealing off the six mages who huddled behind its subjective safety. Skit pushed Anddyr through to join them, and he collapsed into his usual spot, pressing his face to the corner made by the barrier and the wall. He cradled his arms against his stomach, his shoulders aching.

Badden was half dragging Aro to the ladder, muttering, "What in all the fecking hells *happened*?"

And Aro's soft wail of a reply: "I—only for a second, I only lost it for a second . . ."

"You have to learn," Anddyr shouted to his back. And then he added a whispered, "I'm sorry," because when Aro turned to face him one last time, he was Etarro again, and the blood pooled from his eyes. "I couldn't help you . . ."

The cellar door slammed shut with a resounding, final sort of noise. Intermittent sobbing broke out through the mages, particularly the new one, who Anddyr would hazard was having a rather horrible day altogether. Travin had taken it upon himself to dole out soothing words and pats. Anddyr left him to it. Sat there, nursing his varied wounds.

From Rora's corner came a mutter so low Anddyr was likely the only one who heard it: "Fecking witches."

CHAPTER EIGHTEEN

It must have been cold. Scal could see his breath frosting in the air. Thousands of little crystals forming and dancing and disappearing. At his side was Vatri, shivering. Chattering teeth loud in the still air. Gloved hands scraping against rough wool as she chafed her arms.

It must have been cold, but the cold did not touch Scal. He stood among the trees, and his hands were still at his sides. Waiting, patient. If his heart or his soul was uneasy, it did not show in the scar-marked stretch of his face, still as cut stone.

He heard footfalls, on the road that wound between the trees. They were expected. Six travelers, and they would not pass unnoticed through this wood. The forest was Scal's, and he knew every breath that stirred its air, every arm that brushed its hanging branches, every foot that marred the lingering snow. They had been seen, and they had been marked.

Hands hanging still at his sides, Scal stepped from the trees. The moon made silver lines of the scars that scored his bare arms. His sword lived over his shoulder, its hilt reaching for the moon, but he did not draw it. He walked to the center of the road, and he turned to face the travelers. They had stopped, and though most of their faces had no eyes, he knew they saw him still. "You will leave this place," Scal said. He would give them the chance, but only the one. "You are not welcome here." He had argued long for it. They deserved the chance to leave. Everyone deserved one chance.

They never took it.

"Stand aside," said the one man with eyes, pulling his sword free. He walked toward Scal, the sword held across his body, and there was a fight gleaming in his eyes. "We'll not be commanded by anyone but the Twins themselves."

Scal had given them their chance, and so the time for talking was done. There was only one way to end now. All that was left was the blood.

Scal raised his hand to his shoulder and drew his sword. His right hand, and so when the sword came free of its scabbard, it trailed fire along the line of the blade. Bright and burning, and he saw the fear in the other swordsman's eyes. Too late. Scal had given him his chance, and there would not be another.

Feet steady upon the ground. Not fast. He did not need speed. There was fear in the swordsman's eyes but he would not run. There was a way a man held himself, to show he would not run. Steady steps forward. Scal, closing the distance between them, the fire-sword lighting the air, lighting the fear in the swordsman's eyes. Scal swung his sword and their blades met, and again, and again, and a feint put the fire into the soft unarmored place beneath the swordsman's arm. The blade bit deep, but the fire bit deeper. For a moment the man's eyes showed pain. Regret. And then the light left them, and he slid heavily off the blade and to the ground.

It seemed a painless enough thing, as deaths went.

The preachers reacted in different ways. One screamed,

fell to his knees, howling. One turned and ran. One solemnly drew a dagger shorter than Scal's hand. The other two simply stared with the puckered skin over their eyes, shocked or sad or scared. It was hard to tell, without the eyes.

Scal stepped forward again, toward the preachers. From the trees came an arrow, chasing after the running priest. It missed, but the second did not. Scal's sword, trailing flame, took off the dagger-holding arm. Twisted back to take that preacher's head. A step to the right and one of the silent staring preachers fell to the biting flame. The other staring one backed away, hands raised, mouth making useless movements. Scal stalked after him, and put the sword into his heart.

And then there was only the howling man. On his hands and knees, he had crawled to the swordsman's side. Clutched his shoulder, empty sockets weeping. Scal walked to him slowly, steady as a falling storm, and he passed the sword to his left hand. The flames died. Ice in their place, shards of it along the fullers, crystals on the edge of the blade. Darkness fell, in the absence of flame, but the half-moon watched like a disapproving eye.

Scal set the ice-blade against the side of the man's neck, breath-light. His sobs changed, but he did not lift his head where it was bent over the swordsman. It was a small thing, but brave.

They came from the trees. Yellow-wrapped Vatri, straight-backed and head high. A slim woman with a longbow as tall as she was, and a face sharp as an arrowhead. A young man wrapped heavy in armor that shone in the moonlight, his dark hair braided so that its tip brushed against the backs of his knees. Together they came to Scal and the preacher, and as they walked Deslan drew an arrow from the quiver at her back. Set it to the string, but did not draw it. Waited, patient, muscles ready.

Vatri reached out, her flesh rippled and warped, her fingers like claws, and filled her hand with the preacher's hair. Pulled, so the man's head raised and the puckered pits of his eyes met hers. Tears to fury. Scal raised his weapon with the movement, and Deslan's grip shifted on her ready arrow.

Vatri, with her voice like lightning, twisted the preacher's hair and demanded, "Where are they?"

The preacher tilted his chin higher. "They'll come for you," he said, and his voice was steady. There was hard iron in him.

"Where are they?" Vatri asked again. At her side, her other hand curled to a fist. Released. Curled again.

"They will come, and they will bring their judgment." The words seemed to give him strength. To make him more brave. His back straightening, his breath coming faster. "The unworthy shall fall—"

Vatri's hand cut the preacher's words short. A sharp sound, flesh to flesh, and in the moonlight the preacher's cheek shone red. "Where are the Twins?"

There was defiance on the preacher's face, and his hand lifted. Scal pressed the blade harder against his neck. The ice and the steel drew blood, and the preacher flinched, but it didn't stop his finger. Pointing, at the body of the man between himself and Vatri. The swordsman Scal had killed first. "Maybe he would have told you," the preacher said, and he would say no more.

The young man with the long braid spit onto the ground

before the preacher. "Useless," he said, and put his boot into the preacher's gut. The preacher doubled in half, the sudden movement scraping his neck against the sword and its icy spines. Not enough to slice, but enough to draw blood. Edro was thoughtless like that.

Scal put his sword away. Shards of ice chipping away against his scabbard, falling across his back. He left them—the gasping preacher, and Deslan, who drew her arrow to point at his eye, and Edro with his face set in fury, and Vatri glaring hatred. Scal began to collect the bodies. Five of them, the swordsman last. A sturdy rope to tie around their ankles, and the rope over his shoulder. A brace of preachers. They were heavy, hard to drag, but not so hard that he could not manage. Vatri prodded the remaining preacher to his feet, and there was less defiance in his face now. More fear, on top of the bravery. He marched behind Scal, behind the dragging bodies leaving a trail upon the ground. The blind preachers saw more than they should have, but if he saw that he walked upon the blood of his comrades, he did not mind it.

Vatri had chosen the place earlier. The perfect place, she had called it. An old oak, tall and broad and greedy. It had choked away all the other trees, making a wide clearing around itself. Wood sat in a neat pile nearby. The ends of each log fire-charred. Any weapon Scal held sprang with fire or with ice, even a simple woodsman's ax. It had an edge, and could be used easily for killing. That was all that mattered to the magic of the Parents. That was all that mattered when Vatri was watching.

The preacher and the archer and the man and the merra

waited. Silent, sullen. Scal pulled the bodies to the spreading oak, and he piled them around the trunk of the tree, and he piled the cut logs upon the bodies, and kindling atop the logs. And then he took the rope, fraying and bloodstained but sturdy, and he walked toward the preacher.

He saw Scal coming, in the strange way the blind preachers saw things. There was little bravery left on his face. Scal thought he would run. Readied himself to chase the preacher, so Deslan would not put an arrow through his leg.

The preacher swayed, but did not run. When he stood before the man, Scal bowed his head briefly. The most respect he could show. The most he was allowed. With the rope in one hand, he put his other around the preacher's hand. The man's fingers were cold, clammy, shaking. But he let himself be pulled. Forward, forward to the tree and the bodies and the piled wood. He let Scal guide his steps, let Scal lift him atop the pile. His back against the tree, his feet upon one black-clad body. It was the swordsman, Scal realized. The man whom the preacher had cried over. Scal had not intended that. Too late, now. He wound the rope, around the preacher, around the tree. Sturdy and steadfast, unshaking. The preacher's face was pale, but it was as brave as could be.

Winter held hard to the northern part of Fiatera, keeping the air and the ground cold well after the rest of the country would have begun to see warm weather and grass and kind skies. Scal did not know if the weather to the south was as normal, or if it had been changed by the sun's absence. But here, against the Highlands, close to the frozen North, it had stayed cold. There was little risk of a fire spreading.

Vatri stood before the tree, and her scarred face was as unyielding as a mountain. "I ask you once more," she said. "One final time. Where are the Twins?"

The preacher turned his pucker-eyed gaze to Vatri. His voice shook, but the words came hard and ringing. "They will find you. They see into all shadows. Soon enough, they'll come for you."

"I look forward to it," Vatri said. Iron in her voice, in her spine, in her face. Her hand motioned, and Scal drew his sword once more. The right hand, so that flame danced along the blade.

Followers of the Parents burned their dead. It had always been so. It was a small thing, that the ones Vatri gave to the flames were not yet dead. Enough time would make them so. A small thing, to cut the wick of their candle short. To let them burn, and sputter, and fade.

All things die, Vatri had told him, with flames bright on her flame-scarred skin. *There's no stopping death.*

Scal touched the blade to a pile of kindling. Far to the south, he had walked through a sea of grass with the fire-blade drawn, and the flames had brushed against the grass without burning. His hands, one holding ice and the other fire, had touched others without freezing, without burning. He was not only death. There was more in him than that.

But he had been named Nightbreaker. There was not space for anything else in this world. Not while the sun was gone.

Fire, he thought. His name and his will, and the sword-fire ate eagerly at the kindling. Jumped to the wood, and flames danced along its edges. Swallowed the dead things they were given, and reached for more.

For as long as he could, the preacher stayed silent. But he

was human, and pain could rob all bravery. Scal turned his back, so that he would not have to watch. So that he would not see the way the fire danced in Vatri's eyes.

Edro's boots crunched loud upon the ground. Heedless of deadfall, heedless of lingering snow. The man's voice was louder still, and Scal did not know why Edro had been brought. No—that was not true. He knew. He had seen the way Vatri looked at him, when they bent over a map and Edro thumped his fist against the folding table so hard its legs threatened to give while he proclaimed bold strategies, described the fierce battles he would lead. Scal had seen the way Edro's eyes shone back at her.

Little lordling, the others called Edro, but only when he did not stand before them. Fourth son of a nobleman, and little enough use to his family. "I have come to help restore the sun to its rightful place," he had said when the scouts brought him in. One hand on his hip, the other pressed to his forehead, and the Parents' fire emblem was carved into his breastplate. Scal had thought him foolish, had seen Deslan and some of the others making faces behind the little lordling's back.

Vatri had smiled wider, though, and said help like his would be needed. *Invaluable.* Scal had not forgotten that word. It rang in his mind, when he saw Edro's tilted smiles, when he saw the man brushing out his long hair where all the women could be sure to admire it. He thought of it each time Vatri called Edro to her side.

Little lordling, they called him to his back. But when Edro stood before them, they all smiled and bowed. He was a lord, and he was handsome, and he had a temper that flared like the Mother's own fire.

"We must flush them out," Edro said, punching his mailed fist into his palm. "Wherever the rats nest, we must burn them from their homes, and follow them where they flee. They'll lead us to their masters, never doubt it. And once we've found their lair . . ." Another mailed punch.

Deslan, walking silent at Scal's side, raised her bow. She held no arrow, but she drew the string back and aimed her lead hand at the back of Edro's head. Twisted her face into a grimace, tongue thrust between her teeth. Scal turned his startled laugh to a cough, and when Vatri looked over her shoulder, he was smooth-faced once more and both of Deslan's arms hung at her sides.

Their camp appeared sudden from the trees, well hidden by nature and by design. The tents were low as bushes or as thin as tree trunks, and painted with whites and browns. There were no visible fires to give them away—only thin threads of smoke, leaking from the pointed tips of some tents. Those moving within the camp were quiet, moving on skilled feet, speaking in low voices. Scal knew the scouts had marked their passage, would have alerted them if anything was wrong, would have stopped them if they were not familiar faces. Might have stopped them anyway to talk, if Edro was not already filling the night with his words. He was not the only reason, but certainly a large one, why there were always so many volunteers to take scout duty. That was, at least, what Scal told himself.

Deslan slipped away, her work for the night done. Went to

find the others from her village, most likely—she was not so much older than them, and she was not a mother, but she acted as though she were theirs. They let her, with gentle teases and fond head shakes. There was a deeper bond among all of them than Scal could understand.

"We should move camp at moon-set," Edro announced, squinting up through the overlapping tree branches. "We've stayed here long enough. That's the third group we've caught from here. If anyone realizes how many preachers have gone missing on this stretch of road, they'll start using a different road—or worse, come looking for what's been disappearing their friends."

Vatri nodded, and then she looked to Scal. There was still that, at least. *You're not alone,* she had told him, far away in the waving-grass Plains. *We're together in this.* Scal looked only to her, and not to Edro, when he said, "We should move." Edro was right. They had been still too long.

Vatri nodded again, and smiled, and walked away. Edro smiled, too, and followed her.

Scal turned instead to face the camp. Almost five dozen tents, scattered among the snow and the trees, and they held all those who, in all the villages Scal and Vatri and their first followers had passed through, had heard Vatri's heartful prayers. Had seen Scal with the ice-and-fire-sword held tight in his hands, and cheered, "Nightbreaker! Nightbreaker!" All those who had dug through cellars and barns for anything sharp or heavy to use as a weapon, had left behind their homes and their families to do what little they could in helping to end the Long Night. They all bowed to Vatri, pressing their fists to their brows, called her *merrena*, the highest title of honor given to any priestess. For Scal, they murmured when he passed, and he had not ever tried to hear the words they said.

"We'll need as many as we can get," Vatri had told him as they stared down at the map one of the villagers had given her, as though giving it into her hands was the greatest honor. It had been before Edro, when Vatri and Scal alone would look at the map, when Vatri alone would mutter plans and options and finally decisions. "Not knowing what the Fallen are up to, we'll need to be prepared for anything when they do make their strike, and the two of us alone can't possibly cover everything. And until we know what they're doing," and she had smiled at him, with no humor in her eyes, "we'll continue making it harder for them to have a plan." She never said the word "kill," never talked of murder. Spoke only of balance, and how to return it to the world.

Soft unspoken truths made the doing easier. Scal was the will of the Parents, Vatri had made him so, and he would do what they asked of him. He was only what he had been made. What he had let himself become. *Nightbreaker.*

Others had come—those who followed them from the villages, and those, too, who heard whispered tales and went stumbling through the wilderness until Scal's scouts found them, brought them to kneel before himself and Vatri. And they always stared, the new ones, stared at Vatri like a walking goddess, her deep-carved scars like a badge of the Parents' attention. Stared at Scal like a man stepped from legend, like the hero of a tale they had been told since childhood. Stared at him like they already knew he would save them all.

Scal liked it better when they murmured. Liked it better still when he could walk among the trees, his hands hanging empty at his sides, and not think of worshiping eyes or preachers' screams or the word "Nightbreaker" thrumming through his bones.

Scal went to his tent, to avoid the eyes, to avoid the murmurs. It was tall and small, only enough room to lie curled on his side. He could not count how many had offered him a bigger tent. Each time he refused, it put a glow in their eyes he did not intend. Once, when he had not closed his ears fast enough to the murmurs, he had heard, ". . . thinks he's not any better than us," and it had been said in a wondering tone.

There was a brass bowl at the center of his tent, and a small fire burning in it. It was not an everflame, for it was doused each time they moved camp, but it was close enough to one. Close enough to be comfort. Scal knelt before it, one hand wrapping around the two pendants, the fire and the ice.

The fire is always talking, Vatri had said, and she always told him to see its words. Told him, lately, with pride, to see how Edro stared deeply into the flames and proclaimed how he had seen their victory, had seen the sun rising once more and the Twins forever banished.

Scal stared at the flames, but he did not see anything. Only flames reaching fingerlike to brush the stars, grasping, and closing on nothing.

CHAPTER NINETEEN

The cellar was starting to reek bad as a place Rora'd found in the Canals once, a place where a few different streams met and swirled and didn't have anywhere to go. Wouldn't've mattered most of the time, there were plenty of places like it all through the Canals, only in this specific place, one of the streams happened to be the one that, farther back, Whitedog Pack used for dumping corpses of the other packs. The place'd been close to clogged up with bodies when Rora'd found it, bloated and rotting and reeking, and she'd just stood staring in horror till vomit had burst out of her, and then she'd gone running far away and not ever gone anywhere near the place again.

The cellar wasn't quite so bad, but the smells of refuse were getting stronger every day. Rora knew a good portion of that was from her, but there wasn't much she could do about it. The part that wasn't her was from too many bodies stuffed into a place that was made to store *things* instead of people, and adding all the pups into the reeking mix didn't do a thing to help.

The pups were doing their best to be quiet, and the biggers were doing their best to hush the pups when they got too loud, but the problem was none of 'em were scared anymore. They'd been sent down to the cellar for safety close to a dozen times by now, and every time that nothing bad happened during the fighting up above, they got less scared and more stupid. They'd started a new game the last time, and kept it going this time: seeing how big a thing they could throw at Rora before she got angry and snapped at them. They were up to splinters from a broken old barrel, and they had damned good aim—her face was peppered with little cuts and pokes, but she'd promised herself she wouldn't let them get to her this time. She didn't want to let them win, even for a thing that didn't matter. With everything that'd been taken from her, losing anything more was like . . . well, was like getting a shower of stones and splinters chucked at you.

They were little terrors, all the pups, and Rora would've swore she hadn't been anywhere near so foolish and awful when she'd been that young. But there wasn't much for them to do, and even Rora—grown as she was, even if she didn't have the height to show it—was getting plenty bored. Still, she wasn't ever bored or stupid enough to annoy the witches, which put the pups pretty high on the ladder of stupidity.

The witches couldn't do much, sealed up behind their not-wall, and they were mostly well behaved and careful when the pups were around . . . but Rora'd seen them when they weren't so well behaved, when they *couldn't* be careful. She'd seen fire race along the ground, cracks walk up the walls and make showers of stone-dust, seen one witch just scream and scream until he threw up blood, and seen others fight each other like they were cornered animals, tearing and biting and wide-eyed with desperate fear.

But the pups hadn't seen any of that, didn't know how much they were risking just by making funny faces at the witches through the solid air, and they sure as shit didn't listen to Rora when she told 'em to stop it.

A piece of wood about the size of her palm thunked against Rora's shoulder, and she ground her teeth together, ignoring the pups' giggles.

The ceiling opened up on firelight and stars, and the pups fled for fresh air like they'd been kicked. Used to be, Rora'd tried to follow them, just a stupid instinct to stick with pack, but the shame of clanking chains and smirks had taught her quick enough to stay put.

Her belly was knotted up with nerves—the last time they'd brought down a new witch, her brother'd looked half dead with tired, and then after the not-wall had fallen down and Anddyr had attacked him, Aro'd gone to looking most of the rest of the way dead. Rora hadn't had the time or the brain to do anything besides shout his name after him as the fists helped him up the ladder, and if he'd heard, he hadn't said anything back.

They hadn't said a word to each other since they'd got to this damned place.

Rora'd told herself she wouldn't be the one to break. It was Aro's fault things were like this—she'd made him choose, and he'd chose himself over her, when all she'd done her whole life was choose him. Anddyr and Joros'd broken him, and every piece of Rora'd been screaming to kill them both, and Aro'd asked her not to because he thought they could help him more than Rora could. Rora planned on letting him live with that dumb choice. Let him see how much help they were, a crazy witch and a man who cared only about himself.

And then she'd seen how sick Aro looked, how he'd cried

under Anddyr's wild fists, and her anger had cracked, just a little bit.

She'd decided that the next time he came down, she'd say something. She still didn't know what, it'd only been a few days since she'd decided and she hadn't been able to come up with anything good. She'd figure it out. The twisting in her belly would chuck out some useful words.

Rora sat up straighter against the wall, put her hands in her lap, where it was harder to see the chains around them. She stared up at the open cellar door, and she watched the small group come down the ladder. That was a good thing about it being near as dark aboveground as it was in a witch-lit cellar: it didn't take her eyes anything to pick out faces, and her hands clenched a little in her lap.

There was a new person, another witch by the looks of his crazy-wide eyes, with two fists pushing him forward. One of 'em was Skit, who knew how the cellar worked, brought food and cleaned up when things got really bad, knew enough to keep things from getting too bad most of the time. He was a good one, talked to Rora sometimes, though never if there was anyone important around to see. She could recognize the other fist's face, but didn't know his name, and following after the fists, in Aro's usual place, was Tare.

It wasn't that strange—Tare came down to the cellar pretty often, acting like it was to keep an eye on everyone and everything. Rora knew the real reason was that the Dogshead wouldn't let Tare kill Rora, so the best Tare could do was remind herself that Rora's life was pretty shit right now. Rora could understand that well enough. It was the same reason she sometimes glared over at Anddyr behind the not-wall when she was sure he wasn't looking. You had to keep your hate burning bright, and the best way to do that was to see the one you hated being miserable.

So Tare came around pretty often, that wasn't unusual, but what *was* unusual was that Aro wasn't there at all. He always came down to push new witches through his not-wall.

Tare glared over at Rora as she passed by, same as she always did, but didn't say anything. And Rora, all ready to blurt out some words at her brother, was left just staring with the nervous twist in her belly gone sour.

Tare and the fists pushed the new witch through the cellar, past Rora's little corner to the far end, the big space that probably could've held three wagons if you could figure out how to get 'em through the cellar door. Now it was holding seven witches, all spread apart and glary like territorial cats. The fists added the new witch into the mix, pushing him through the not-wall, making the air shimmer and ripple for just a few seconds. Seemed like they didn't need Aro for it, and the not-wall didn't fall apart like it'd done the last time. The witch stood on the other side, looking like he'd bolt if he could just figure out which direction to run in.

And Anddyr, who always sat pressed into the corner, he reached out to gently touch the new witch's leg. It made him jump, but then his eyes fixed on Anddyr like he was drowning and Anddyr was something floating by. He sat down next to Anddyr, and the not-wall did enough to muffle the sounds of their voices that Rora couldn't pick out words, but after a while Anddyr turned his eyes away from the new one, looked back out to the same place he was always looking: Rora.

She looked away before he could see she'd been looking in the first place. She had promises to keep, after all. Even if they were just dumb little promises to herself. In the cellar, there weren't many things worth keeping, but a promise might as well be one of 'em.

Tare was smirking over at her, that mocking little smile, like she thought it was the funniest thing in the world that the witch Rora hated so much loved her like an idiot.

Skit and the other fist started going around the cellar collecting filth buckets, working with the witches to get the special buckets Aro'd magicked up, the ones that could pass through the barrier. She hated those buckets; when the witches threw their fits, they weren't shy about throwing the filth buckets around, and a lot of them ended up on her side of the not-wall.

Tare, nothing better to do, moved toward Rora's end of the cellar, leaning back against the ladder and hooking her arms through the rungs. "You're almost starting to look like a girl," she said lightly, almost cheerfully. Rora still hadn't figured out which was worse: when Tare spent all her time spitting and swearing and taunting, or when Tare ignored her, acted like Rora wasn't even someone worth pretending was there.

Rora shook her head, felt her hair brush against one ear, and against the smooth skin where she would've had a second ear if Tare hadn't cut it off. It was the longest her hair'd ever been, since she was a kid and desperate to make her and Aro look different, and he'd cried when she'd tried to chop his hair off. "Get me a dagger, and I can look proper and boyish again."

Tare snorted. "Get you a dagger, and you'd just put it in my back. That's all you're good at."

That amount of distrust hurt too much for Rora to have any light comeback. "Or maybe Sharra will turn her back long enough for you to put one in mine."

"Maybe she will."

Skit and the other fist—hells, Rora should know his name by now—came back down the ladder, buckets clean and ready to be passed back through the not-wall. That meant they'd all be leaving soon, and it meant her brother really wasn't gonna show up. Softly, not really expecting any answer but a gob of spit, Rora asked Tare, "Is Aro okay?"

Tare frowned down at her, face twisted but not in any way Rora recognized. "He's . . ." Down at her side, Tare's hand turned over, palm out with the little finger tucked up, and wobbled a bit. It was one of the hand signs knives used to talk to each other, but Rora wasn't sure Tare even meant to do it. It seemed like it was instinctual. "He's just tired," she finally said, but that was a lot less of an answer than the hand sign'd been. Tare's mouth said *fine*, but her hand said *wrong*.

Rora swallowed a lump that fell hard into the tangled mess of her belly. "Can you . . ." What, was she gonna send Aro a message through Tare? Fat chance of that happening, and fatter chance of it even meaning anything that way. Anything she asked Tare to do, Tare'd probably take two jumps in the other direction just for spite. Rora sighed, pulled up her knees, and wrapped her chain-clanking arms around them. "Thanks," she muttered, meaning it but not sure why she bothered.

Tare looked down at her like she wasn't sure why Rora bothered either. It wasn't a glare, though, and Tare left without saying anything else, Skit and the other fist following after. Skit did look back at her like maybe he was sorry, but he didn't say anything either. Once they'd closed the cellar door behind them, she was just left with witchlight and Anddyr's eyes staring like he could see inside her, all the way down to the twisting and the rocks in her belly.

CHAPTER TWENTY

Harin was the first one to mention it to Joros, and so, later that night, Joros moved five silver gids from one of his pockets to another, and a single small copper back to the first pocket—the latter for his bet that, among those of the pack brave enough to talk to him, it would be Harin who broached the subject; and for the former, one silver coin for each moon-pass they'd let the nonsense carry on without saying anything.

As the only man in the entire place with more than a single coin to bite, Joros was reduced to betting against himself.

"We're getting worried, is all," Harin muttered, scuffing her tattered boot just outside Joros's door. She hadn't crossed the threshold—nerves, he imagined, or perhaps some misplaced sense of propriety.

"It sounds like you should be," Joros said heavily, smoothing over the layers of sarcasm and mirth with a topsoil of manufactured sorrow. He added, "I only wish you'd come to me sooner." He'd given himself fifty-to-one odds they came to him on the second day. "He seemed so troubled lately, I thought to give him some space to heal on his own." Really, he'd wanted to see if the boy was able to function on his own without Joros's correction. Clearly, the boy was not.

Harin kicked her boot lightly against the doorframe, leaving a faint smear of mud against the wood that she didn't seem to notice. "So you'll talk to 'im?"

"Yes," Joros said, sighing as he stood from his desk. "I'll talk to him."

Whitedog Pack had done what they could with a space not meant to live even half their number—there weren't more than a dozen rooms that could conceivably be called bedrooms, and most of those were crammed full of people; they'd turned the dining hall into communal sleeping quarters; they'd even turned the stables into the saddest excuse for a bedroom he'd ever seen. No, that wasn't quite right—he'd seen, briefly, where they'd all come from. The shit-reeking Canals, where they'd carved alcoves into mud walls and lined the spaces with flea-gnawed blankets. Hells, anywhere above water level had to seem an improvement to them.

Aro had been shunted into one of the dogpile rooms with six other people. The boy could have gotten a room to himself if he had any sense; between the Dogshead's favor and his *witchcraft*, Aro had both respect and fear on his side. His roommates had given him the room's only bed, and given him a wide berth between the bed and their mats. An overly loud sneeze from Aro likely would have sent them scattering.

But there Aro sat in a crowded room, little space to himself as he perched at the edge of his bed and steadily, methodically, drove the tip of a dagger down again and again into his palm. Blood pooled in his hand and dripped between his fingers, falling in slow spatters to the floor.

Joros stood in the doorway for a moment, watching with one eyebrow raised. Aro didn't take any notice of him, or of the others in the room casting nervous glances at him. Joros had seen him over the last few days, stumbling from one place to another and dragging his nails down his arms, red furrows that had grown deeper until they'd sprouted blood. He'd slapped himself, gentle wake-up slaps at first that had become ringing, neck-snapping things as the days went by.

The dagger, though—that was new.

Joros stepped into the room and walked a straight line toward the younger man, forcing the others in the room to scoot or twist out of his way. He stood before Aro, a careful distance away from the small-but-growing puddle of blood, and said, "Aro. Walk with me."

The boy's eyes snapped up to fix on Joros's face, as mad a look as Joros had ever seen in any mage's eyes. The pack was always so *careful* with their words around Aro, suggesting rather than commanding, cajoling instead of ordering. Joros had no such compulsions; his time was valuable, and he wasn't about to waste it pleading with a madman when he could far more easily just tell the madman what to do. There was something deeply gratifying about the way Aro lurched to his feet; it was the same feeling he got when he watched the pack slaughter preachers: his influence made manifest.

When Joros turned and walked from the room, Aro followed tight at his heels. He let Aro keep the knife and the boy left a trail of blood drops in their wake. He led the boy out of the house and then, as they walked through the crumbling gates to the road beyond, he called Aro up to his side. "They tell me you haven't been sleeping," he said.

Aro nodded jerkily, but said nothing. Joros made a soft noise at the back of his throat and kept walking. There was a place some of the pack had made, the feet and fingers who had been messengers and pickpockets and now found themselves with nothing to do. They'd decided to take up farming, or perhaps gardening, or possibly just dirt-turning for all the skill they seemed to have at it. There was a little cove among the surrounding fields, visible only from the estate walls, where the feet had stomped down grass in a circle, where the fingers had dragged logs from the other side of the road, where they could sit together and stare at the furrows they'd scratched in the ground and wait to see if anything would grow.

Joros had thought it beyond foolish at first—how did they expect to grow anything in a sunless world?—but the rest of the world was still growing and sprouting, spring beginning to bloom. Perhaps they could have grown a garden, if they'd known how.

Joros pushed his way through the head-high wheat stalks that had gone wild in his family's absence. To the foolish boy Joros had been, the fields had always felt a sprawling castle, endless halls and wild spires and ceilings that curved above his head.

Once he found the tramped-down cove—quiet and empty with the fingers and feet having apparently found something somehow more thrilling than staring at dirt—Joros sat down on the cleanest-looking log and waited for Aro to jerkily seat himself nearby. Too close; Anddyr had had the same habit, when he was lost in his madness, of not remembering that personal boundaries existed. Joros readjusted himself farther away from the boy and the trickling pool of blood he was still drawing from his palm. Staring together at the hacked-at ground, Joros asked, "Aro, why haven't you been sleeping?"

Aro turned wild eyes to him. "I can't." It came out some-where between a hiss and a wail, a vocal contortion that made Joros's own throat hurt. "If I—I'll—"

"Out with it."

The words practically exploded from Aro. "They'll escape if I'm not careful, escape *again*. If I don't hold the barrier, it'll fall, and I have to watch it. I can't let Sharra down." He stabbed his palm particularly hard, gave the dagger a twist, eyes bug-ging at the apparent pain though he made no sound and did not stop. "I have to keep her safe, I have to keep the pack safe, and if I don't, they'll—they'll—"

"They'll what?"

"They'll send me down there," Aro whispered, "and they won't ever let me come back up."

Genuinely curious, Joros asked, "Did they tell you that?" It seemed like something Tare, heartless bitch that she was, might say—precisely the same kind of motivating threat Joros might have used.

"I can see it in their eyes. If I'm not useful . . . if I'm *bad* . . . they'll get rid of me. They won't need me anymore. Same way they got rid of Rora." Aro made a choking, broken sob around his sister's name. The dagger fell soundlessly into the blood-watered soil as Aro curled around himself, doubling in two with his arms tight around his middle, leaving behind a dark smear of blood on his tunic that was hardly clean to begin with. A high, keening sound drifted up from where his head hung between his knees.

Joros looked up at the stars, blinding-bright without the moon to fight. Impatiently, methodically, he counted them. He did *not* draw the lines between the stars, did not make shapes in the night sky as he'd done when he was boy to pass the lonely hours. He counted the stars, quicker than a heart's beating, and he waited.

Aro raised his head, splotchy with unshed tears, to stare pitifully at Joros. "I hate it here," the boy whispered.

And opportunity flared its wings to land gracefully on Joros's shoulder.

Joros rested his hand lightly on Aro's back, in his best approximation of a fatherly way. "So do I. Aro," he asked gently, "do you want to leave this place?"

Aro's eyes went wide and then knit in confusion, and he made an inarticulate little noise.

"There's so much to be done beyond the walls of the estate, so many that need help. I want to go and give that help, but I can't do it alone. After Anddyr's betrayal—"

This time the noise was a plaintive sound of denial with no real conviction behind it.

"After Anddyr's betrayal," Joros repeated firmly, "I've been left as alone as you are. Foolish of me, not to see it earlier. We can help each other, Aro. I need a mage. And I can take you far away from here."

Aro rocked slowly, reached up to run one hand through his hair and grip it tight at the roots. That keening sound came from him again, his eyes wide and wild and lost when he turned his face up to Joros. "They . . . they need me . . ."

"Do they really?" Joros asked, low and implacable as only the cold truth can be. "Have they ever?" As Aro whimpered, Joros patted his back in that supposed-fatherly way again. "They've done you a disservice, Aro, treated you as little more than a tool to reach their means. They don't understand what you're capable of. *I* know you can be so much more." The boy looked up at him with red eyes and running nose. "If I go, Aro, will you come with me?"

He could have commanded it, used the madness and the drug that sluiced through Aro—but a change of heart wasn't the sort of thing the susceptibility to suggestion was meant for. He could order the boy to come with him, and Aro would, but as soon as the edge of sanity touched him he'd go racing back to where he belonged. No, it was far better to use the boy's weakness to convince him that Joros's way was the right one, and let Aro think he'd made the choice on his own.

Voice tremoring on the edge of breaking, Aro said, "If I go . . . I'll need to make sure they'll stay safe." There was an earnestness in his face, a need to explain and to be understood. "They're my family. I can't leave them to die."

"The mages?" Joros asked, and Aro nodded grimly. "You're a clever boy—you'll figure something out. I know you're capable of greatness, Aro."

Those offhand words were the ones to make him break, strangely enough, and so Joros stared up at the stars again as Aro curled himself into a small and shaking shape as he wept.

When the boy finally got his emotions under control, he seemed to be holding also a portion of his sanity; he lurched to his feet, and there was determination in his eyes. "I can do it," he said.

"We'll need to leave as soon as we can," Joros said. "So much time has already been wasted."

Aro's straight-backed resolve crumbled a little, shoulders hunching forward. "I . . . I'll need to tell her. Sharra. I . . ." He looked at Joros piteously, and Joros waited. This was something he'd needed to train out of Anddyr, too—the expectation that Joros would guess his thoughts or intentions. He waited for Aro to work up the courage and the words to ask in a whimpery whisper, "Will you . . . come with me? To tell her? I don't . . ."

"Of course," Joros said, rising to his feet and aiming himself toward the estate. He'd been speaking the absolute truth when he'd said there had been enough wasted time; he didn't intend to let another moment go by. Aro trailed in his wake, reminding Joros once again how often he'd compared the boy to a kicked puppy.

"Go collect your things," Joros told Aro as they passed through the gate, and he noted how the boy's back snapped to attention, his eyes going sharp. "Pack whatever you think you'll need, whatever you have, and then come to my room. We'll find Sharra from there." He hung back as Aro scurried off to do as he'd been told, for Joros had spied a familiar face lurking just inside the gate. Harin didn't need more than a finger-flicking summons to hurry to Joros's side.

"Well?" she asked. "How is he?"

Joros sighed heavily. "Truthfully? He's in a bad way. I've seen a similar sort of thing happen with mages before, when they're under too much stress, too much pressure . . . and it only gets worse if they're forced to carry on." It wasn't even a lie. Mages who'd been addicted to skura were broken enough that they were only ever a few precarious steps away from shattering. He lowered his voice to a conspiratorial whisper, and Harin leaned in eagerly. "I worry the Dogshead has become too focused on the short term. She can't have missed Aro's condition, and the fact that she's done nothing to lighten the pressure on him . . ."

Harin gnawed her lip, and Joros saw the unspoken agreement in her eyes.

"I'm worried about him," Joros said with another heaving sigh. He put too much heave into it, and felt one of his ribs twinge in protest. "I don't think this . . . *any* of this . . . is very good for him."

"But the Dogshead won't stop him," Harin said, "not with things going so well as they are. And Aro's got so much loyalty in 'im, he won't ever think to stop on his own."

"Just so," Joros agreed, and he started for the house with Harin tripping over her feet to follow after.

After a silent handful of steps, she prompted, "So? What're you gonna do?"

"I'm going to take Aro away from here, and give him the chance to heal."

Another few steps of silence. "And you're gonna fight the Twins, too, aren't you? With Aro's help?"

"If he's well enough," Joros allowed.

Harin's steps stopped following; Joros could feel her watching him, and he smiled. Word would spread throughout the estate by the time he finished crowing to Sharra. Aro was well loved, and added some much-needed legitimacy to Joros's cause. Joros would be sorely disappointed if there weren't at least a handful of pack members waiting beyond the gate to join him and Aro when they left.

There was something so deeply satisfying about pieces falling into place just so.

Joros had little enough he needed or wanted to take with him: the battered but serviceable gear he'd taken with him out of Raturo so long ago, his shortsword, plainclothes that didn't have a thread of black on them, all the jars and seekstones he'd collected.

Almost all, at least.

Joros stared down into the near-empty desk drawer. He'd packed away almost two dozen of the seekstones, all carefully cataloged in his mind and organized in his pockets and pouches, each one a starting point, each one like a smear of blood on the map in his mind. They would prove invaluable.

But there was the last one. The seekstone that had been linked to a boy—a boy who was surely dead now, and in the boy's place: a god. Anddyr had broken into convulsions the one time he'd touched that seekstone, and Joros had been careful never to handle it with bare skin since.

It was a direct link to a god—a direct link to his enemy. It was, potentially, the greatest weapon he had at his disposal.

Hovering above the near-empty drawer, his hand tremored slightly, and that made Joros growl. He wasn't scared of a rock. He wasn't scared of anything.

He wrapped the seekstone in layers of torn cloth and tight knots, and stuffed it deep into one of his robe's pockets, far away from all the others. It was important to keep powerful weapons safe, and secure.

CHAPTER TWENTY-ONE

Rora pressed the heels of her hands against her eyes, cold iron brushing against her cheek from the chain. The pressing made her see stars, but it didn't do a thing to block out the witches' chanting, though if she pressed *hard* enough. the pain could almost make her forget, just for a second or two, where she was.

"We are safe," the witches said all together, some quicker and some slower, some whispering it and others screaming it. "We are secure. We are strong." It was like one of the deeper hells had opened up its mouth and the awful chanting was the thing that came out. They were all saying the same words, but different enough that the sounds hardly even sounded alike. Like nails on stone, or like nails through a skull. "We have each other. We are safe . . ."

When they'd started the chanting, Rora'd put up with it for a while. It had to be a good few hours of nothing but the chanting, before it'd started to drive her mad as a witch herself. She'd screamed at 'em, then, told them they weren't safe or strong and that having each other wasn't worth a steaming pile of horse shit. It'd made her feel better, just for a little while—but the kind of crazy they'd gone after that had been a lot worse'n the chanting. She'd curled her arms over her head and rode it out, ignoring how she could feel Anddyr's reproachful eyes on her like a punch as he started the chant up again, worked one by one to get the witches to join him at it until it calmed them all down and the fires all went out.

"We are secure. We are strong."

It *worked*, she wasn't saying the chanting didn't work—but by all the fiery and bleeding and dripping hells it was damned annoying, and Rora didn't know how much more of it she could stand before she tried to break her own wrist to get out of the manacle, and then she didn't know what she'd do first: if it'd be better to slam her shoulder up into the cellar door until it or she cracked, or if maybe clawing down the not-wall would let her put her hands around Anddyr's throat and choke the chanting right out of him.

"We have each other . . ."

The cellar door creaked open, and Rora wasn't even ashamed at the sob that burst out of her. She was close to babbling thanks to every god she could think of, because even if other people didn't stop the witches from chanting, at least it'd give *her* something else to do—but then she saw who it was coming down the ladder, and her mouth just hung open, empty.

Tare was first, and then Joros, who Rora hadn't seen since they'd got to the estate, and a few fists, and the last one down was Aro. Joros was the only one among 'em who looked anything like happy, with Tare looking about ready to tear someone in half, but Rora didn't spend much more time thinking about either of them once she saw her brother.

He looked like he'd come out of a deeper hell than the one that the witches' chanting came from—his skin was gray, there were deep black smudges under his eyes, his arms were thin and crisscrossed with the red lines of dragging nails, and there was a bandage round his left hand that was half soaked through with blood. He walked bent over like there was something sitting between his shoulders, pushing his face down toward the ground.

And she remembered how she'd decided to talk to him, next time she saw him, and how she still hadn't come up with anything to say—but even if she'd thought up any words, they probably would've fallen right out her mind at the sight of him, half dead as he looked. Just like the last time, she couldn't think of anything to say but his name. If he heard her, he didn't show it.

Tare glared over at her, same as always, and even Joros gave her a look that was somewhere between smirk and sneer. But Aro just kept his dead eyes dead ahead as they all went to stand before the not-wall.

Anddyr stopped his chanting and rolled up to his knees, and if it weren't for his filthy clothes and ratty hair, he would've looked like any normal sane person. "What's happening?" he asked, but no one gave him an answer.

Aro raised his hands, the bandaged one leaking a slow trail of blood down his arm, and his fingers started weaving witch-signs. He closed his eyes, lips moving in soft mutters Rora couldn't catch. Anddyr watched him like a starving man would watch a feast, keen and suspicious, and he muttered along like he was trying to follow the shape of whatever Aro was making. All the chanting had stopped, all the witches staring, and the only sound in the place was the muttering.

One of the witches shuddered and moaned, an all-body

shiver that Rora could *watch* walk up his spine. Anddyr's eyes went wide and he said, just loud enough, "How . . ."

Aro slumped forward, leaning his whole body against the not-wall. All the witches close to him scampered backward, looking close to hissing like cats. Aro's hands, still now, pressed against the not-wall, too, and the one left a smear of blood on the solid air.

"Is it done?" Tare's voice cut through the silence like a gut punch.

Aro leaned back from the not-wall, back straightening, eyes looking ahead but not looking *at* anything. "It's done."

Tare stepped up to the not-wall and glared down at Anddyr. He was the only one who hadn't scrambled back. "Witch," she snapped, "try to get through."

She hadn't even finished talking before Anddyr pressed his hands against the not-wall, his lips moving. Rora saw the not-wall ripple out from where his hands pressed against it. Then, all at once, like the street chanters Rora'd sometimes seen in Mercetta, the witches all groaned. Some of 'em grabbed at their heads or their bellies, some curled up whimpering, some just flinched, and Rora remembered how Aro had always flinched, every time he was in the cellar and one of the witches threw their body or their magic at the not-wall. Flinched, like it'd been *him* they were hitting. Anddyr's mouth had dropped open to be wide as his eyes. "How?" he said again.

She couldn't see Aro's sad little smile, but she could hear it in his voice, picture it clear as if he was pointing it at her. "Guess I learned something, huh?"

Anddyr's smile, which she could see, looked closer to a snarl. "You've learned cockiness."

"Wasn't something he needed to learn," Tare snorted.

"You may think you're clever," Anddyr said, his fingers curling against the not-wall, "and maybe you are, maybe you're the cleverest one in the room." Joros and Tare both snorted at that, but neither Anddyr nor Aro seemed to notice—they were fixed on each other. "Maybe you've found a way to *benefit* from your informal training, from learning outside the strictures of the Academy. Maybe you have a more primal understanding of your powers than any mage with real training. But you are a *fool* if you think cleverness and novel solutions are enough. You are brash and thoughtless and naive, and mark me before God, before any gods you'd like—you will lose control if you do not learn it better, and your powers will consume you. And *he* will drive you to the edge of your control, and give you a hand down to boot."

He didn't need to say who *he* was, and Joros's nostrils flared to say he didn't need to be told either. "It's done," Joros snapped at Tare. "The barrier will hold, powered by your captive *witches* themselves. Aro's held up his end of the bargain. We're done here."

"Oh, we're done all right." Tare's voice dripped poison, a dagger that'd kill you with no more than a nick. "You're free to leave. I won't be stopping you."

"Leave?" Rora didn't realize the word'd come out of her until they all turned to look at her. All of them except Aro, whose shoulders curled forward like he was trying to make himself small, like he was the little boy who'd thought he could hide from all his problems if he made himself small enough.

Tare didn't answer her, and Joros just gave her that sneer-smirk again, and all the fists stared at the floor like they wanted to be anywhere else.

And then Aro said the first words he'd said to her since they got to the estate, since they rejoined their pack, since Rora'd got thrown in the cellar, and he said, "I can't stand to be here anymore, Rora. I can't."

"So he's running away, again," Tare piped up, glaring at Aro's shoulder same way she always glared at Rora. "Just like old times, hey?"

Joros stepped to Aro's side and put a heavy hand on his shoulder. Aro flinched under it. "He's not running. He has a greater purpose in this world than to swat at flies for your Dogshead. He needs to find his place within—"

Aro twisted out from under his hand, and almost faster'n blinking he was standing in front of Rora, his hands twisting and his eyes huge. He looked the same way he'd always looked: her own face but softer, without any of the worry or the hurt carved into it, the version of Rora she could've been if *she'd* had someone taking care of her, watching her back, making sure she stayed safe and healthy and happy. Their father'd said Aro was the older one by a minute or so, but Aro was the same thing he'd always been. Her baby brother. Scared and lonely and stupid.

"I have to," he whispered. He stood close enough she could hear him, but far enough that if she stretched her chains, she wouldn't be able to reach him. Just far enough away that it felt like he'd measured the distance. "I'm dying here, Rora, I am, and maybe I still will be out there, but I have to *try*, I have to be able to be more."

Rora'd spent so much time thinking what she'd say when she got to speak to Aro, when she'd got him standing right where he was now. She hadn't found the right words, not in all her thinking, but she'd thought of what'd happen when she did find them. How Aro's eyes would go soft in that way that meant he realized what she'd done for him, and he'd demand the key to her manacles from Tare, and then he'd pull her up and into a hug, and even though Rora'd never been much for hugging, she'd lean into it, because he was her brother, he was her other half. Because of something the boy-twin inside Mount Raturo had said to her: *Without me, she'd tip. Without me, she'd mean nothing.* He'd been talking about his own sister, but he might as well've been talking about Rora. She needed Aro, and so she'd forgive him, and he'd forgive her, and they'd bear their scars together, matching in everything.

Rora'd spent so long thinking of the words that could make it all happen, the perfect words that'd turn like a key in a lock. With Aro standing in front of her, looking half melted and desperate for understanding, what she said was, "Then go." And she turned to the side, her back to the others, her shoulder to Aro, and she wrapped her arms around her knees and pressed her face against the wall, and tried to make herself small enough she could disappear.

Wasn't much sound after that. Voices, Joros promising that Anddyr could fix all the witches, make them useful and less broken and worth the scraps of food they got; Anddyr being made to promise that he'd do it, that he'd make the witches well enough to keep the pack safe. Feet going across the floor and up the ladder, wood creaking under hands and feet and weight. Rora listened to all of it, because she couldn't hear anything else inside herself to drown out the slow and steady thump of her heart.

Footsteps stopped, in the same place Aro'd stood. Close enough to hear, but not close enough to reach. "I never understood why you stuck by him," Tare said. She sounded the same way she had when she'd been training Rora, so long ago, curious why she'd chose one window over another, disappointed she'd chose the wrong pick for a lock. "Why you kept sticking your neck out farther and farther when all you ever got for it was scars. Never understood what Sharra saw in him neither—I knew her son, and your brother was nothing like him, but she acted like he was Derro come back to life. I always felt like I was the only one who wasn't blind. Like I was the only one who could see that all he ever was was a selfish little shit."

Rora said nothing; just curled up into a tighter ball, pressing her face harder against the wall, against her arms, against the cold and sturdy chain that held her fast.

Eventually, Tare left, too. The cellar door crashed down behind her, raining dirt and leaving silence behind it. Leaving only the sound of her heartbeat, throbbing in her ears.

"We are safe," Anddyr said softly; of course he'd get the witches started back up again. Couldn't let her have even a minute of peace. "We are secure. We are strong."

Rora wiped her eyes against her sleeve. She knew the words were for the witches, and she knew they'd make her murdery the longer the chanting went on . . . but for just a little while, she thought maybe the words could be for her, too, that they could make her feel calm and cozy as a witch.

"We have each other."

CHAPTER TWENTY-TWO

When they came to the village, there was no one.

Scal raised his hand high into the air, and the others who were spread out behind him, obedient, stopped. In the surrounding trees, Deslan and the other archers would see, too. Would be readying their arrows and moving leaf-quiet to better range, to better sight.

Vatri touched Scal's arm, but even she was silent.

Always, when they neared a village, they were met—by cheering crowds, or by suspicious ones that took up cheering when they saw Vatri's robes, Scal's blade. By nervous councilmen, or by solitary, armored sentinels. There was always someone to meet them, to sob with joy over their coming or to demand to know their business.

But as Scal stood at the head of his band, on the empty forest trail that curved into the town, there was no one. The village, twoscore small and sturdy homes, was silent, was still.

Vatri's fingers curled tight around Scal's arm. Squeezed. Released. And she stepped back.

Scal drew his sword, fire-bright, and it lit the village around him. Made timber-sided houses stand bright and stark, the shadow of the village's well stretching through the center of the road until it joined the darkness once more.

"We bring peace," Edro called out. "We bring the Parents' hope, and the Parents' flame. We bring an end to the Long Night. If you are there, if you have ears and hearts to hear, we only wish to speak with you."

Silence was his answer, for a very long time. Long enough that the group gathered behind Scal grew restless, nervous, twitchy. Clenching fingers. Glances over shoulders.

And, finally, a door opened. A squinting man stepped out into the light. Face slack in the way of a man who had had meat on his bones that had faded quickly, and a jacket that hung off his frame. He stared at them, two steps from his doorway, with his hands deep into his pockets. Said, "We'll thank you to be on your way."

It was not what Scal had expected. Nor Vatri—she stepped forward, the hard lines of her face drawn tight, a frown deeply in place. "I know these are trying times, and strangers are a frightening thing, but—"

The man cut her words with a sharp chop of his hand. "Where was your kind when the sun fell? There's a priest, used to spend his weeks between all the villages in the area, came here every three or four. We haven't seen him since the Night begun, and Horem down Graston way said he saw the priest fleeing south with his tail tucked between his legs."

"These are trying times," Vatri said again. "It can be hard to keep the faith in the face of—"

"And Betha, she was burned up almost as bad as you, everyone always said she had the Parents' favor. She died three days after the sun did. Just wasted away."

Vatri shifted her weight to one foot. To the other. Her hands drew shapes at her sides, as though plotting a course, as though trying to cast a witch's spell. "I can speak only for myself and my companions, but I can assure you—"

"Old Nelis watched our everflame all his life," the man interrupted again, and Scal could feel the frustration begin to boil off of Vatri, "took the duty from his grandda when he passed, and Nelis tended it well. He was staring at it, he'd just fed it fresh herbs along with his prayers. He was staring *right at it* when it died. Smothered itself with no reason at all."

Heatedly, Vatri said, "Listen—"

"No, *you* listen. We've been good and faithful folk all our lives. Kept our everflame burning, kept our prayers, kept to the old traditions as good folk should. We kept our faith bright even after the sun fell, because we thought the Parents would make things right again, that they'd protect us same way they always have. But they haven't. They've forgotten about us, or didn't care in the first place. Either way, we're left on our own, and if that's the way it's to be, then that's the way it's to be. And so I say again: we'll thank you to be on your way."

If Vatri had listened to half his words, it did not show. Her words came from her in a rush, as though she hoped to get out as many as possible before she was interrupted once more. "Everything is harder these days, and faith most of all. I know that well. I thought the Parents would stop the Twins before they rose, thought they would save us all." She faltered slightly. Did not seem to have expected to be allowed to go on for so long, and longer still. But the man stared silent at her, his head cocked and squinting still. "I've had to look deep within myself for an answer to why they would let this happen, and I know now that it's because we were given *choice* and agency and the will to be whatever we wished. The same thing that

Sororra thinks makes us weak is what the Parents so cherish. They're giving us the chance to choose the world we wish to live in, and we must all make that choice for ourselves. To live or to die is not a choice that can be made for us. We must fight for our world, and for our lives. The Parents cannot fight this fight for us, or it is no choice at all."

The man stared at her, and chewed a corner of his lip. Seemed to consider her words, to give them weight against the fear and the anger in his heart. He said, "When I was a boy, my da taught me to swim by tossing me into the river. I learned it well enough. He taught my brother the same way, and my brother didn't learn so well. He drowned. Da couldn't understand it. It was the same way his da had taught him, and his da before him, and all the way back to the beginning. My brother should've swum beside me, but they burned him instead. My next brother, Da tossed him into the river as well, and he learned to swim fine enough, and Da spent no more time thinking on his drowned boy. When I was young, it seemed the cruelest thing. Still does. I taught my boy to swim a kinder way."

Vatri stared at him. Wordless, unsure.

"When I was a boy," the man went on, "I thought my da was a god. But it's harder to love a god once you've started thinking of them as cruel. My boy thinks I'm a god, too, but he'll not think of me as a cruel one."

Edro called out, "Do you think it a kindness that the Twins pulled down the sun?"

"It's a fact, nothing more. They stole the sun. The Parents burned them and knocked them from the sky. These are just things that happened."

"Just a *thing*," Vatri spluttered, "that *happened*?" She stepped forward, two steps in front of Scal, and her fists shook at her sides. "You speak of condemning the world—of condemning *your boy*—as though it were a spot of bad weather."

"Hardly condemned, are we?" The man raised one hand from his pocket, waved it to the houses, the forest, the star-dotted sky. "It's been months and we're all still alive. Or most of us, anyway. If the Twins wanted us all to die, they've done a poor job of it. And the Fallen have done more for us so far than your kind have."

Edro took a long stride to Vatri's side. "You've had preachers come through?"

"We have. And they were a kinder, more sensible lot than you."

"When were they here? Where did they go?"

The man eyed Edro. Put his hand back into his pocket. "I'll not be telling you that, I don't think. Now I'll ask you a third time, and it'll be the last. Be on your way."

Edro put his hand to his sword's hilt. Scal saw it, and the man saw it, and the man's eyes narrowed. His hand moved, faintly, in his pocket.

Scal grabbed Edro's arm to pull him roughly back. "We will go," Scal said. To the man, to Edro, to them all. The rest of their group turned back willingly enough. Vatri went with anger and confusion warring across her face. Scal did not release Edro's arm, dragged the man with him. Walked backward, watching the man who watched them go.

The village was silent, and still.

They went a long way before they made camp. Made their own twisting path through the trees, and even Vatri was quiet, even

Edro. Scal drew wide circles around the group, checking the scouts, checking their trail, standing still in the starlight to listen for sounds of following.

They made camp, and they made a meal of hard bread and dry meat, and around a fire sheltered by the tight ring of their bodies, Edro was the first to speak. "They'll still be nearby. We should hunt them down."

"The preachers?" Deslan asked. Her voice as hard and as dry as the food. "Or the villagers?"

"The preachers, of course. If they're so fresh in that fool's mind, they can't have passed through so long ago. And since they haven't been to any of the villages we've been to, there are only a few places they could have gone. We should be able to find them easy enough, and keep them from poisoning any other villages. They'll—"

"Pardon, masters," a voice interrupted. One of the scouts, Scal saw when he turned. "Seems we have a follower." She held a boy by the arm, a boy who looked sheepish and scared and determined.

The boy puffed out his chest and stepped forward, farther into the firelight. "The preachers were going on to Beston," he said, the words wavering. The breath it took to say the words snuffed his confidence. "Can I . . . can I stay with you?"

Room was made around the fire, and the boy sat beside Deslan, who gently, calmly stroked his hair as he ate. She had a maternal streak, though she laughed whenever someone pointed it out, and said she could not stand children.

Edro, too, proved good with the boy, and they slowly worked the story from him.

Seven preachers had come to the village, and found the

usual mistrust at first. But they found fear, too, and the Fallen had always known how to speak to fear. The village had listened. Listened to assertions of the Twins' mercy, that one need only believe to be saved when their judgment came. Listened to the gentle assurance that, though the Twins had taken the sun, they would not allow the world to die. It was not what they wanted. Only those who did not pass their judgment need die. Listened to the tale of how King Cordano had been pulled down from his throne, not by the Fallen but by the citizens of Mercetta, a seething mob. ("That can't be true," Vatri whispered, but there was no certainty in her voice.) Listened, to their vision of the world made dark, of the world made fair. Listened and, for many, began to believe. Belief made in fear was no less strong.

But not all came to believe. After five days of preaching, still some held their faith to the Parents, held their hope that the sun would return, that all would be made as it had been.

And so the preachers had left. And life had gone on in the village. And, slowly, the village had begun to die.

It began with crops and wildlife—apples withering, grains spoiling, rabbits dead by no hand, piles of birds fallen from the sky. And then it was the people. No rhyme to it, no reason. An old woman who had gone to sleep and not woken, whose faith in the Parents had never wavered. A young man who had been among the first to embrace the preachers, whose heart had burst in his chest as he stood talking in the village square. A child who had begun coughing blood and coughed himself to a grave.

And the only thing they could think was that it was punishment for not listening to the truth, when they had been given the chance. Only some had refused the way of the Long Night, but all would suffer for their refusal. A single rotting apple to spoil the bushel. The world made fair.

"They pray," the boy said, soft, staring into the fire. "Near every hour, they gather and they pray to the Twins, and they pray for the preachers to come back and save them. My mum and my da, they go and pray, too, but it's only because they're scared for me. But I'm not scared." His eyes lifted. Found Scal among the dancing shadows. "I had a dream about you, before you came. I saw your sword made out of fire, and how you lit up the night like the sun come back. And then you *did* come."

Around the fire and from the shadows the murmur came: "Nightbreaker." A dozen mouths, a dozen voices. Scal, silent, looked from the boy to the fire. Could not hold the weight of his gaze.

Vatri leaned forward, and the flames danced reflected in her eyes. She asked the boy, "Will you lead us to Beston?"

They could not see Beston through the trees, but the boy swore the village was there. Half a mile farther down the road, no more, and the village would spread around the road, sprawling and stretching and fading until the road carried on lonely through the trees once more. Beston would be no different from all the villages scattered through this forest.

Scal stood staring down the road, and he did not feel as though what he would find at the end of it would be a normal village.

He said nothing. Edro had announced his plan, and Vatri's eyes had burned, and he knew that neither would be swayed. There was little point in arguing. Not when all he had to argue was a growling pit in his stomach, and a bee-sting prickle at the base of his neck.

So he waited as Edro murmured orders. Vatri and a handful of others staying with the boy. Deslan and the archers to scatter through the trees. Edro would lead a group of their fighters through the trees, to approach the town from the side, unseen. Scal would lead the rest down the road, a direct approach, a naked attack, a march of death. And Scal said nothing, though unease chewed him like a dog.

With all the planning done, there was nothing else to do. Nothing left but to begin.

Scal walked down the lonely road, his followers at his back with their weapons held in steady hands. They were not nervous, not anymore. Scal had given them the real weapons of dead preachers, and he had taught them as best he could to use them. Vatri had shown them the meaning of justice. They did not need to fear what they knew how to fight.

Scal held his sword in his left hand, coated in shards of ice. No fire to give them away. Only the cold and hollow ice, and the pit of his stomach opening wider with each step. *Wrong*, his footsteps whispered. *Wrong. Wrong.* He walked on.

The village, when they came to it, was silent and still.

Twoscore houses, old and sturdy-built. Clustered at the edges of the road, ringing the village square, and growing sparser back from the road, like fading shadows. A rough stage was built in the village square, at the center of the houses, painted an uneven brown. Twoscore *empty* houses. And twice as many, or more, people laid out neatly before the stage.

Even rows of them, lying like game pieces in a tray. Arms and shoulders and hips and legs pressed to the ones beside them, hands folded neatly on chests. They lay in curving rows, arches that grew broader, like the rise of the moon over a hill. Like the shades of color in a sunrise.

Scal's footsteps echoed loud as he drew slowly closer. He did not want to, the wrongness pounding in his stomach and his ears, but he had to. Drew even with the farthest row, where he could see they all stared unblinking up into the sky, all their mouths hanging slightly open. And beneath, a second smile, longer and wider and sharper: the mark of a knife, drawn deeply across each throat.

He looked over the spread of bodies in their neat arches, to the stage. Painted an uneven brown, the center of it deeply colored while the sides looked to be raw wood.

Scal closed his eyes. *Wrong. Wrong.* He did not know if any of the others had followed him into the village, but he said, "Bring Vatri." In the silence, someone would hear, someone would go running, eager to be away from this place. He added, "Do not bring the boy."

The others came slowly from the trees. Edro and his group. Deslan and the archers. Those Scal had led. They stared, and the village was silent, and still.

Scal, alone, walked slowly through the bodies. His sword sheathed over his shoulder once more, his steps careful around stretching legs and tilted heads and circles of dry and brown blood that had stained the village square. He walked among the men and the women and the children, all with their staring eyes and their two smiles. Among them, at the center of the first arch, directly before the stage, he found a dead preacher. Black-robed, and eyeless, with two thumbprints of blood pressed beneath his empty eyes.

Scal pressed his hand to the stage. The wood had been cut recently, and quickly, the edges rough and uneven. At the center of the stage, where the wood was stained darkest, his hand came away sticky. In the light of the stars, the souls of all the watching dead, his fingers looked black.

He heard Vatri's choked prayers long before he could turn to face her. "Why have they done this?" she said, her faint words loud in the night. It was not a question any of them had an answer for. Not a question she expected to be answered. "Why did this happen?"

"We should burn their bodies," Scal said. It seemed the right thing to do. Seemed like the thing they would have wanted, in a world that had not gone wrong. Good and faithful folk.

No one else spoke, and so it was done. They moved in pairs, carrying the bodies at ankles and at shoulders, making a careful and gentle pile upon the bloody stage. Still, it was like stacking cordwood. Ugly, and unkind. But there was nothing else better for them that could be done. Not now.

There's always hope, Vatri had said, in a time when her face had not been the mask it was so often now. When fires had not burned so brightly in her eyes. *There has to be.*

When all the bodies had been moved and lay in new neat rows atop the stage and atop each other, Scal drew his sword. The right hand this time, so the flames lit the night. Making timber-sided houses stand bright and stark, their shadows stretching far and far down the lonely road until they became darkness once more. Scal touched his sword to one of the stage's supports, and he said, "Fire." His name and his word and his will. The stage burned, and the blood that coated it, and the bodies that lined it.

They all watched, silent as the night came brighter for the growing flames, as the village grew emptier. Its people gone now, truly gone.

"Why did this happen?" Vatri asked again.

Staring at the flames, Scal could see how it had happened. He had spent time with preachers; they were men and women like any others, who held their beliefs as tightly as any others. He had traveled, for a time, with a group of preachers, and had almost gone with them into their mountain. He knew the things they offered. Acceptance. Openness. Surety of purpose. All offered easily and without question, an offer made that expected nothing in return. Their certainty was powerful, and could be powerfully appealing.

He could see how it had happened, and in the dancing flames the bodies seemed to move. The single black-robed preacher, his body at the base of the pile, seemed to rise from among the others. Limbs bending, pressing, standing amid the flames and the death, and he stared out at Scal. And the fire-cast shadows seemed to fill the town square around him. The shades of the villagers who had lain stretched out upon the ground rose, too, their eyes lit with fervor, mouths open with prayer. Around the black-robe standing upon the stage, other bodies took on the shapes of more black-robes, six more of them rising through the corpses, through the flames. Mouths open wide in prayer, in entreaty, in certainty. Two of them held the first, his palms and face turned up to the sky. Embers sparked in the sky like prayers. And the fire, like a slash of the knife, flared across his throat. A second smile opened beneath the first.

And the shades surrounding Scal began to form a line, a cheering line, a praying line, a line of hope and promise, and they were taken to the stage one by one. Their arms held but not restrained, eyes staring up into the dark and sunless sky. The constant crackle of prayer. The knife. The rush of red across the rough-cut timbers. Another body laid out before the stage. Another person led forward. The line never faltering. The fervor in their eyes never dimming. Again. And again. And again.

Scal shook his head. Blinked into the flames, and all the bodies were lying down. None standing, none praying, and there were no shades beside him. Only his people, his followers. At his side Vatri stared deeply into the flames, as though trying to pull meaning from them. She was always looking, and it seemed she never saw what she hoped to see. Scal, who had never seen a vision in the flames, did not expect that he would find any more meaning in this place.

"They are still near enough," Scal said, shattering the silence, the stillness. Heads swiveled to face him, wide eyes and fear. "This was not done so long ago. The preachers will see what we have made of their work." Smoke from the fire rose high into the sky, the charnel-house air blotting out the stars. "They will run." He looked over them all, and the fear was not gone from their eyes, or the anger, or the grief. He looked to Vatri, and he left his question unspoken.

Shape me, he had asked her, and she had, and she still was. She had made him, and named him, and he would do as she asked.

He saw the jerk of her throat as she swallowed hard. The firelight carved the scars on her face deeper, making her features into a mask from a sculptor's nightmare, so that she hardly looked real. But her eyes. They were as scared, and as angry, and as grieving, as all the others. So human that it almost hurt to look. "We will find them," she said. Her voice never wavered when she spoke, whether surrounded by joy or surrounded by death. "We will show them the Parents' justice."

No one cheered, and no one argued. Only gave their silent acceptance.

"We can't leave them."

It was Edro who said it—Edro who was always seeking a fight, always seeking glory. But he stared at the pyre, and there was something in the line of him that Scal did not recognize.

There was reason to stay. Such a large fire, left unwatched at the heart of a forest, could be a deadly thing. It had been too long since they had slept. Their stores of food were low, and could be replenished in the village. There was reason enough. But, truly, the only reason that mattered was that Edro was right: they could not leave the dead yet. Could not leave them alone in their fate.

And so they sat before the pyre, and the village was silent, and the village was still.

CHAPTER TWENTY-THREE

Most of the pack had never been outside the city before Joros had rescued them, and that had only been a short trip beyond the walls before they'd found another set of walls to cower behind. It meant that those who had chosen to follow Aro, and by extension Joros, were even worse than simple country bumpkins. The pack panicked at every sound on the road, and their first instinct on seeing another human was rudeness because that was how one treated Not Pack.

It nearly got them lynched at the first town they came to, where Harin laughed outright at the admittedly silly custom of burying two eggs each moon-pass that the townsfolk had come up with to bring the sun back, and where Trip walked around gleefully nicking from every pocket and pouch he could reach. Joros had to herd his new flock away before the angry mob turned murderous, and when they made camp early, he spent a good amount of time shouting at them. "We could have slept in beds," he told them, kicking the leaf piles they'd be using as pillows, the rotting logs they'd pulled up to sit on around the fire, "at a warm inn, with ale and wine and fine company. Instead we're *here*." His shouting, though, only made them shout in turn.

Aro finally dragged himself far enough into sanity to explain in simple terms that even the pack could understand: townsfolk were like pups—stupid and wrong most of the time—but they should be treated like pack. People on the road should be treated like newcomers to the pack—good enough to have been allowed into the pack, but dangerous because they didn't yet have ties or connections or a reason not to start stabbing anyone; accepted, but worthy of mistrust. Joros grumbled an amendment that if they met anyone on the road, the rest of them should just keep their mouths shut and let him do the talking.

As luck would have it—or whoever that bitch Luck's cruel and petty brother was—the next moon-pass offered them a chance to test the pack's obedience.

Harin, who as far as Joros was concerned had well earned her position of eye, was the first to spot another group of travelers approaching down the road. She nearly sent the others into a panicked race for the woods until Aro, sane enough, reminded them in a furious whisper how to act. So the pack walked stiff-legged as cats ready to fight—and Joros almost did the same when they drew close enough that he could see that all the other travelers wore black.

Shit, he thought, and plastered a smile on his face.

There were four on the approach—few enough that Joros's group outnumbered them nearly two to one, which was a reassuring thing, but nothing about the Fallen would ever truly reassure Joros.

"Good night to you, Brothers and Sisters," one of the preachers called out when they were within reasonable sight—sight for normal people, anyway, since the preacher had removed her eyes.

"Hello," Joros said neutrally, keeping a sharp eye on them on the approach. The three preachers made no untoward moves, and neither did their guard, a solitary blade for the darkness, and no mage in sight. Joros stayed to the right edge of the road, his group lined silently behind him, and the preachers stayed to the left, and they passed without issue.

Joros looked over his shoulder at the four preachers' backs, and he softly asked Harin and Aro and his four others, "How many of you have weapons?"

Joros was used to the comforting structure of a plan. A single goal to achieve, with clearly chiseled steps leading up to it.

The last few months of his life, though, had taught him how to adapt. Still, he'd gotten better at "turning with a punch," as one of his older brothers used to say. He could look at the stepping-stones of a plan crumbling ahead of his feet, shrug, and find a hidden back staircase. He'd find whole webs of hidden staircases, if he needed to.

He had to have a plan. So long as he held on to his goal, he wouldn't have to face the fact that he had nothing.

The steps beneath Joros's feet now were the uneven skeleton of a staircase stretching up to the shining goal of destroying the Twins. Months ago, all that uncertainty would have driven him into a rage. Not now, though. Dealing with the pack had taught him how to hold his anger by a leash—ready to be released only when productive. He had at least begun the trek toward his goal, and for now, that was enough. He would keep climbing the steps so long as they held his weight, confident they would solidify into certainties, confident they were being built from the top down.

The only step that held his weight was that fewer Fallen could only make future steps stronger. He held one of the seekstones in his palm, and trusted that his chosen path would eventually, somehow, prove to be the right one.

This seekstone's partner belonged to the one he'd dubbed "the walker," who'd been weaving throughout the northern part of the country since Joros had obtained the seekstone. The walker had gone curiously still in the last handful of weeks, though. Not entirely *still*, for when he used the seekstone's sight, Joros saw feet and faces and a dull village, but the walker was no longer walking. The walker seemed to have settled, for some reason, in a village buried in the forest that bordered the Highlands.

And Joros aimed to find out what had made the walker stop walking. He'd find out with the point of his sword, and make sure the walker could never walk again.

The others thought it a fine enough plan—they were at least doing something different from bumbling around the estate, and they kept commenting that the air seemed to be doing Aro good. The boy still looked like shit, but Joros let them have their little lies.

Joros made a show of taking Aro aside whenever they made camp, leaving the others to make a fire and food, to lay out bedrolls and blankets, to set watch shifts. The brilliant thing was that none of them complained about it, they were so concerned for Aro's health and so certain that Joros was helping it. If the boy was in a sane state when Joros took him aside, they would walk and talk of inconsequential things, what Joros called a prescription of normalcy to offset all the abnormal Aro had been forced to deal with over the last few months. If he was in his madness, then Joros would sit and sharpen his sword and tell the boy of cleansing fires and sharp deaths and a path stretching to the sun.

The forest swallowed them and made foraging harder but hunting easier. Trip got sick from eating undercooked rabbit, and halted their progress for two moon-passes while the others nursed him back to health like grandmothers. Aro was no help—he'd learned to knit bones and keep a heart beating, but he couldn't figure out how to purge a disease from a belly. He wept and apologized, and the others coddled him as much as his sister ever had.

When they went back to fussing over Trip, Joros took Aro into the trees. He told the boy to hold his palms up, and indicated the healing tissue marring Aro's left palm, where the boy had driven a dagger repeatedly into his palm. "Why did you do that?" Joros asked.

Aro frowned like he was seeking the trap in the question. "To . . . to keep myself sharp. To stay focused."

"Indeed. And I'm unsurprised you proved an insufficient teacher for yourself. The lesson didn't stick." Joros ordered Aro to create a ball of soft-glowing light, floating in the space between them. When that was done, Joros pulled out his sword, and holding it in one hand and the back of Aro's hand with the other, he drove the tip into the center of the scar tissue. Aro's scream was delayed, and though he tried to pull his hand away, Joros held him tight. The ball of light winked out a moment after the scream began. He watched the boy's eyes for a flicker of that deadly spark, but he wasn't worried—Aro had spent his whole life suppressing the fire that boiled within him, letting it loose in only the most desperate situations. Joros had no intention of killing him, and so he strongly suspected the boy would return the favor.

Aro was already learning the lessons it had taken Joros years to grind into Anddyr.

Joros pulled his sword back and commanded, "Heal." The disconcerting slackness flowed through Aro, his scream stopping and his eyes going blank as he sought to comply. Still holding to the back of his hand, Joros watched the blood flow stop, the flesh knit, the skin seal over cleaner and smoother than when they'd started. Just as Joros had thought—the boy hadn't bothered to heal himself at all.

The lack of instincts was good in some cases, and frustrating in others. Joros ordered him to make the light again, and drove down his sword again, and was unsurprised when the light flicked out again. "You must learn to stay focused," Joros said as the boy healed himself once more, and the next time the light stayed for longer.

By the end of an hour, Aro could stare at Joros and, breathing hard through his teeth, hold the light steady no matter how deeply Joros drove the point of his sword.

Anddyr, when they'd left, had shouted something raving about Joros driving Aro to lose his control. But Anddyr had coddled the boy just as much as any of the others. The boy didn't need a kind and gentle teacher—he just needed to *learn*.

The road wound through the forest, a circuitous path, but so long as it kept going in the general direction of the walker, Joros was far more inclined to stay on it than to stray from it. It led them through the occasional village, where they could replenish their meager store of food and gather what little information there was to be had. The Fallen roamed the country, spreading the word of the Long Night, trying to seduce as many as they could to their side before the promised and swift justice of the Twins swept across the land. Everyone was waiting for someone else to stop them. It was no different from anywhere else in Fiatera.

Finally the seekstone's persistent tug brought them to the village where the walker had stopped walking. Joros prepared his people in advance: he had Harin scout out the best vantage points and posted one of his people in each of them, bringing only Aro into the village with him.

Joros walked down the road as it ran through the village, trusting to his feet as he gripped the seekstone, its tug leading him, the walker's sight blurring before his eyes. He stopped when he saw his own hip through the walker's eyes, and he blinked down to find a girl frowning up at him. Her black hair was done up in two plaits that wound around her head like a crown, Highlands blood written in her sharp features, and she wore a pale blue frock with yellow ribbons knotted down her right arm.

Joros opened his palm and held the seekstone out toward her, squinting through the double vision it gave him, the girl's image of Joros layered over his of the girl. He asked, "Do you have something that looks like this?"

Her face shifting into a variety of incredulous circles, the girl pulled out the matching seekstone. She'd wrapped a thin piece of leather around and around it so that it could hang around her neck. Likely she thought it made her look more adult.

"Where did you find it?" Joros asked her. One of his back teeth made a faint groan as he ground his jaw.

Her voice was high, even younger than he expected. "The Nightbreaker shrine."

Meaningless babble. Joros put his seekstone back into his pocket so that his sight was his alone. "Show me."

The girl led him out of the town, the rest of his pack falling in from the trees. The girl startled at each new one, but despite that she walked with a straight-backed fearlessness as she led them off the road and into the trees that shut out the sky. She grinned when Aro made a floating light—this close to the Highlands, she would be no stranger to magic. Joros almost smiled, too, for Aro had done it unprompted.

Though the forest was thick, and the undergrowth grabbed at his clothes, Joros began to notice that the girl was not choosing her path randomly—the ground beneath their feet was packed solid, a trail made by deliberate walking. The girl led them in silence, but Joros, behind her, could see that she clutched her seekstone with both hands, and that her lips moved in what he guessed was a silent prayer.

The trail ended at a wide clearing that Joros imagined had been a holy place even before this—the tree that stood at the center of the clearing was massive, its trunk wider around than Joros could have reached if his arms were twice as long, and he thought its spreading canopy might have blotted out the sky as thoroughly as the thick forest. The canopy was gone now, letting the stars stare down upon what was left of the tree— little more than the blackened trunk, a few skeletal branches reaching toward the sky. Posies of flowers were laid upon the scattered ashes that ringed the trunk, along with the occasional glint of coins or trinkets.

The girl walked across the clearing to kneel before the

burned tree, and her high voice carried back clearly. "This is where the Nightbreaker saved us."

Joros made her tell him all she knew. The Nightbreaker was a mighty warrior wreathed in flame, whose sword glowed with the power of the Parents. The Nightbreaker traveled through the Long Night like a star upon the earth, and he and his woman brought hope everywhere they went—hope, and justice. Preachers had been harrying the girl's village, and the Nightbreaker had killed them, here, with his righteous fire. "We celebrated him more than we did when Gerin come back from the Academy," the girl said, "and when the Nightbreaker and his woman left town to take their justice to more places, my auntie was one of the ones to go with them. All of us who were left, we come and found this place, where they killed the preachers and saved us all. People come from all around, even as far as Bentriver, to pray here and give thanks to the Parents for sending the Nightbreaker to us." She tugged at the seek-stone around her neck, running her fingers over the corded leather and the smooth pieces of stone that poked between. Joros felt a flare of something between revulsion and animosity, to think that she might have inadvertently seen through his own eyes. "I was here praying one day when I seen something in the ashes. I picked it up and I . . ." Her eyes filled and overflowed with tears. "I know I shouldn't'a taken it, but it didn't seem like tribute, it didn't seem like something anyone would've left here, and I didn't think anyone would miss it . . ."

Joros loosened his grinding teeth. "You should know the Parents are always watching." He managed not to snap the words, and he held out his hand, palm up, toward her. "They don't reward thieves."

Sniffling harder, she pulled the leather cord from around her neck, and shakily released her white-knuckled grip so that the seekstone fell into Joros's palm. He held the seekstone by its cord, and stretched his arm out now toward Aro; the boy stared and then, hand shaking as badly as the girl's had been, took the seekstone and put it around his own neck. With Rora safely contained back at the estate, Joros couldn't afford to lose this half of his twins. However he was to take down the Twins, he would need his own twins to play their part. *Like calls to like.*

Joros stood, his pack rising around him. Aro was the only one who looked shaken by the crying girl; the rest knew better. They would have hardened themselves to the world years ago, or had it forced upon them. All of them would have seen so much worse than a single sad girl. And if there was a pack rule Joros had learned, it was that one had to care for their pack, to the exclusion of everything else.

The ground was solid beneath his feet. It shifted, like steps stretching up toward the sun, firm enough to hold his weight.

He spared the girl a final look, and asked, "Where will we find the Nightbreaker?"

CHAPTER TWENTY-FOUR

*A*nddyr *watches, and is watched in turn.*

"Who are you?" Fratarro asks, and there is no animosity in his voice—only curiosity.

"How are you here?" Sororra asks, and hers is full of venom and fear.

Anddyr opens his mouth to speak, but no sound comes out. He is as ephemeral as a cloud, silent and shapeless; looking down at himself, he has no hands, no legs, no body—he is distilled down to his essence. The skytower surrounds him, ringing and wringing, insubstantial and solid. He wants to ask if they are dreaming, too—if gods sleep, and if this is where they come when they sleep. He wants to ask if this makes him a god, too.

"You should not be here," Sororra says, and her words surround him like a blizzard. He has no body to shiver, but the cold goes deeper than skin, deeper than bone, deeper than soul. "You do not belong here. You should not be able to find us."

"For so long," Fratarro murmurs, "we wanted only to be found."

"This is not the same." There is fire in Sororra's eyes, and there is ice, and there is no mercy. "Leave," she says, and the skytower opens beneath Anddyr, and he is falling.

And a voice calls after him, a screaming whisper that both is and is not Fratarro's voice: "Find me. You promised . . ."

Anddyr startled awake to the sound of thundering feet, a slamming door, and a creaking ladder. Blinking back sleep, he raised his head to stare through the barrier at the children streaming down the ladder to fill their place in the cellar, all full of quiet excitement and expectation.

Anddyr scrubbed his face with his hands. The Fallen must have been moving in greater numbers from the south, for so many of them to happen to pass by the estate, and that didn't exactly paint a pleasant picture of the pack's future on the estate. They'd done well enough so far, but one day they'd lure in a group that would overpower them, or a mage whose reflexes were quicker than Aro's, or—

Or they would face a group of the Fallen without a mage of their own.

Anddyr gaped at the settling children, shocked by the stupidity of their guardians. Without Aro to give them the advantage, without Joros to push them—Anddyr had thought the pack would settle into the quiet, peaceful lives they seemed to have always wanted. He'd thought they would hunker down and simply try to survive the Long Night, as they'd managed to survive every other messy thing in their lives.

But perhaps he'd been too idealistic. He'd heard Aro and Rora talk about their pack. They were like dogs indeed: faithful, and ruthless, and never ones to back down once they'd gotten the smell of blood.

He wanted to shout at them that they should know better, but the children *didn't* know better, and the adults who should were all beyond the cellar door, being unspeakably foolish.

And more importantly—to Anddyr at least, in this new

bubble of a life—Peressey was beginning to moan. She was one of the newest of his flock of mages, and she was having a particularly hard time adjusting to both her new surroundings and her skura withdrawal. Because he couldn't do anything about the pack, and because it would make his own life exponentially more unpleasant if he didn't, he went to deal with Peressey.

She had pressed herself into a corner made by the cellar wall and the magical barrier, her face jammed against the corner so tightly it had flattened the tip of her nose as she pawed at the ground before the barrier, as though trying to dig her way free. She was digging with her magic, too, though—a frantic, groping search for any weakness in the barrier. Every new mage always searched for a weakness and, when that failed, would try to batter it down. It never worked, though. The shield always held.

Still blinking sleep from his eyes, Anddyr sat down next to her—not touching, because touch could be a dangerous thing in the throes of madness, but near enough that she could see and hear him. "It's all right," Anddyr said. He tried to be pleasant-sounding, but he was no miracle worker. The best he could manage, sometimes, was a tone that at least wasn't actively hostile, that didn't betray his bone-deep exhaustion. "Peressey, we are safe. We are secure." The children beyond the barrier were staring and snickering, making mocking mewling noises. Anddyr didn't give them the satisfaction of glaring. "We are strong. We have each other."

Above, there were footsteps, and screams.

Peressey wailed, slapping at the barrier and wincing with

each slap. Anddyr winced, too—it was like a toothache twinge, sharp and brief, but the memory lingered. They all felt each blow, now that the barrier was linked to them, siphoning their power away to fuel itself. Anddyr remembered the ruthless glee he'd felt at seeing Aro twitch and wince whenever one of the mages had attacked the barrier; he could sympathize with something, without feeling bad for it.

Foolish, clever boy, he thought at his absent student. Aro had always defied definition—useless and brave, charming and desperate, cunning and thoughtless, cocksure and fearful. Anddyr still wasn't sure how he'd managed to survive without any training; most fledgling mages, left to their own devices, were very literally consumed by their uncontrolled power. Aro had somehow taught himself enough control to keep himself from burning, but he had no finesse. Though, for as clunky as Aro's siphoning barrier was, there was no arguing that it was perhaps the greatest magical innovation Anddyr had seen—he hadn't even known it was *possible* to draw on another's powers, to use someone else's magic to power his own spells. Such a thing would never have occurred to him, bound and trained by the strictures of the masters of the Academy. He would never have thought . . .

A long wail came from above, core-deep. Below, it was echoed by Peressey.

"We are secure," Anddyr muttered absently to her. For all his innovation, Aro still lacked control—he had kept his power from burning him alive *so far.* Anddyr had his doubts that the boy could maintain that level of control forever, especially since his control when using his power was so slippery. "We are strong." It didn't matter, though, not anymore—Aro was gone. He was Joros's problem now, for good and for ill . . . for both of them. "We have each other."

The cellar door opened, and they dragged down a wailing mage.

She was in worse condition than most of the captured mages: her long hair was a tangled mess, covering all of her face except her wailing mouth and its split lip; and beneath her stained robe, she looked absolutely skeletal. Anddyr felt his stomach lurch with disgust and pity at the sight of her, but he tried to bury both emotions—in moments, she would be counted among his growing flock. She would need him.

The pack was triumphant, singing their own praises, an orgy of self-congratulation. Some boasted that they'd never needed "that traitor Aro anyway," and Anddyr observed with a keen curiosity the way Tare's jaw tightened whenever one of her people said such a thing, the way her eyes flickered over to Rora after. That was something new. Rora, no less despondent than she'd been since her brother's leaving, didn't react to the words, and didn't seem to notice Tare's looks. Regardless, they all left Rora herself in peace, whether for pity or boredom or forgetfulness. She was allowed to stare at her wall, the only movement her thumb rubbing at the place where the manacle pressed against the inside of her wrist.

Skit and Badden came forward with the wailing mage and, with little ceremony, pushed her through the barrier. It was no different than it had been when the barrier had been Aro's— the same spell, the same quirks, just no longer powered by him. The new mage went sprawling, still wailing, and Skit and Badden turned away—no longer their problem.

Anddyr sighed and caught Travin's gaze. His second was shaking, not in a good place of his own, but his bad was significantly better than anyone else's, and even at his worst he knew his duty. Travin made his way to Peressey's side, to soothe her now-rising panic, so that Anddyr could tend to the new mage and try to calm her before she threw all the others into fits.

The new mage had rolled to her knees before the barrier and clawed at the solid air, wailing, "Why? Why? Why?" at the retreating backs of the pack as they made their way out of the cellar.

"It's all right," Anddyr said. A flat statement, probably not as comforting as it should have been, but by God he was tired. "My name is Anddyr. I'm here to help you."

"Why?" she wailed at the barrier. "Why?"

Because I'm even more unlucky than you are, he thought, but didn't dare say. "It can be a hard adjustment to make. I'm sure you're scared."

"Why?" She smacked her face against the barrier, and though her wild hair likely cushioned some of the blow, Anddyr winced in sympathy as much as in actual pain. "Why? W—" Her wailing stopped suddenly, her palms and forehead pressed against the barrier, and through her tangled hair Anddyr saw her split lips curve into a smile. "Oh," she said, and she began to laugh. "Oh, that's clever."

Anddyr scooted away from her without really meaning to. Her laughter sent a chill snaking through him: laughing was not uncommon among his flock of mages, roiling head-smacking laughter and desperate giggles and laughs that were half tears—but this was none of that. Her laughter sounded . . . genuine. *Sane.* It did not sound like the laughter of a person who had been wailing inconsolably and clawing at air a moment before.

The mage reached up to push her tangled hair back from her face, and the creeping snake in Anddyr's gut reared back and sank venom into his core. She had no eyes.

As she gazed with her empty sockets through the barrier, the mage's smile widened, and she said, "Hello, Rora. I thought I might find you here. What have you learned about shadows?"

CHAPTER TWENTY-FIVE

The shadows know your name were the words ringing in Rora's head as she jerked up to sitting, throat so thick it felt like she'd swallowed her tongue. Sometimes, when she didn't sleep well or when she slept too deep, she had bad dreams about being trapped in a cell under a mountain, because a cellar wasn't all that different from a cell. And when she dreamed of the cell, sometimes she dreamed of a woman on the other side of the bars, a woman with no eyes who whispered, "I am the shadows, and I know your name," as black smoke crawled from her blood-dripping hands to slide choking down Rora's throat.

Yes, she remembered that voice. And even though she was usually bad with names, she remembered the name, too: Neira. *My name, freely given.* She'd only talked to the woman once, but when someone tried to kill you, those kinds of memories stuck.

"What have you learned about shadows?" Neira asked as Rora twisted to face her, and she was almost spookier'n she'd been under the mountain. She was lit up from behind by witchfire, her face made of deep shadows. Except when she grinned, and the witchfire shone off blood on her teeth and lips.

Rora stared at Neira, and Neira stared back—didn't have eyes, but Rora could *feel* her staring—and Rora counted her heartbeats up to five before she opened her mouth and bellowed, "Tare!"

Neira's smile slipped a little, and her hands curled where they rested flat against the not-wall. She pressed her tongue forward, against the split in her lip, and blood welled up from it.

And all of the witches started to scream.

All at once, sudden as a punch, the witches all sounded like they were being killed. They acted like it, too—Anddyr doubled over holding his stomach, another one writhed around on the ground, another grabbed at his head like it might burst. "Shit," Rora said. "Shit, shit—*Tare!*" She didn't know if she'd be able to hear it over all the screaming, but it didn't sound like there were any footsteps up above, didn't sound like anyone coming to find out what all the screaming was about, didn't sound like anyone caring—

"I'm glad I found you," Neira said calmly, not seeming bothered by the screaming, or by the blood flowing freely over her lip and down her chin. "It hasn't been easy . . . you've learned how to hide—or, perhaps, someone's learned how to hide you." Neira kept one hand pressed against the not-wall, but she moved the other one, stretched it out unlooking toward Anddyr, who was nearest to her. She curled her fingers into a fist and Anddyr doubled over violently, his head slamming against the floor and his whole body going limp. Neira's empty eye sockets were still fixed on Rora. "There's so much we need to talk about."

Rora yanked at her chains, even though she'd done it a thousand times and the metal was sunk deep into the wall. She moved back, away from Neira and the not-wall and toward the cellar door as far as the chains would allow, but it wasn't far enough. The manacle bit deep into the base of her hand, catching under skin, grinding against her thumb, but her hand still wouldn't fit through. "Tare," she shouted again, her voice cracking like a boy's.

She saw Anddyr lift his head up, bleeding from a scrape on his cheek, and stare at Neira. "No," he croaked, reaching for her with a shaking hand. He managed to twist his fingers into his witch-shapes. But nothing happened at all, and he looked as horrified by it as Rora felt.

Another of the witches, his eyes full of fury and madness, made shapes of his own in Neira's direction, and his fingers lit up with witchfire. Neira pressed both hands back to the not-wall, and the witchfire fizzled out before it hit her. That witch fell over on his face, and then didn't move at all. None of the other witches were moving anymore either, their screaming stopped, so the only sound was Rora's heartbeat in her ears—

Neira smiled wider, and the not-wall flickered, and then it wasn't there anymore. Neira stood up, her robe trailing around her feet, her hands hanging at her sides. That smile was still on her face, blood still dripping from her lip, as she took a step toward Rora.

Rora felt like a kid again, trapped and scared and hopeless, only this time she didn't have a dagger to shove into her captor's heart. This time she didn't have anything. This time she didn't even have her brother.

Tears poked at her eyes, stupid, weak tears, but she couldn't do anything, and she was gonna die here, alone, because the family she'd come back for didn't even care about her enough to check on why she was screaming, because the brother she'd always done everything for had left her. Neira walked toward her, blurred by tears, and Rora thought how she'd seen a cat chew its own leg off once because it couldn't get unstuck. Thought about how, if she had a dagger right now, she might not've used it to throw at Neira but might've used it to chop her own hand off instead, or maybe the manacle would do that for her, cutting and twisting around the base of her hand, stretched back behind her as she strained toward the ladder and the cellar door. She gave another bone-straining yank and, amazingly, *felt* something—her hand, slick with her own blood, slid just a little farther through the manacle.

A sob burst out of Rora. She twisted her hand more, pulled at it more, the manacle scraping up skin and she was sure she'd feel a bone pop out any second—

Rora lurched forward as the manacle passed the thickest part of her hand, and she was free.

Neira was almost to her, but Rora scrabbled to the ladder, shimmying up it like a squirrel, and held on to the rungs with only her toes so that she could pound against the cellar door with both fists, screaming sounds that didn't even sound like words anymore.

"Rora," a voice said, disapproving as a parent, and a hand grabbed the back of her shirt to pull her down from the ladder.

Like a cat again, Rora met Neira with nails and teeth, the only weapons she had. Neira met her with the boiling black smoke, her magic that wasn't anything like the witch-magic Rora knew. The smoke was like a weight around her legs, pressing and dragging, making her knees want to buckle, but Rora fought it. She got a punch to Neira's rib cage, left three long scratches along one of her arms, and then Neira caught her wrist—the one she'd dragged out of the manacle. Even the grabbing hurt, but Neira's fingers were like ice. Cold spread down Rora's arm, and her head spun in that way it did if you stood up too sudden, and her knees finally buckled under the smoke.

"Last time," Neira said, still holding on to Rora's wrist, "you left before we had the chance to speak more. I don't blame you—Raturo isn't the most welcoming place." The smoke crawled up Rora's sides, snaking around her chest and pinning her other arm to her side, the smoke answering to the dance of Neira's free hand. "But there's so much you don't know—so much you *need* to know. You won't be any use otherwise."

Rora remembered the last time it'd been like this, when Neira'd trapped her with her eyes while her smoke had snuck down Rora's throat, sour and choking. She tipped her head back, straining as much as she could away from the weird, wrong magic, but she couldn't get away from her own body. Her voice like a gasp, Rora asked, "What are you?" If this was how she was to die, at least she deserved to know what killed her.

Neira smiled, and gave the same answer she'd given the first time Rora'd asked that question. "I am the shadows." She'd said they'd meet again, but Rora hadn't given her a bit of thought, had tried her damnedest to forget everything that'd happened inside the mountain—the same way she'd tried to forget the first man she'd killed, who'd whispered, *The shadows know you,* and *they will follow you to the ends of the earth.* Tried to forget it in the same way she'd tried to forget she was a twin, because if you pretended long enough that something wasn't real, it'd stop seeming real. And so she'd tried hard to forget Neira, deep inside the ice-cold mountain, telling her to *remember how far a shadow can stretch.* If you didn't remember something, it couldn't find its way into your dreams and wake you up in a cold sweat with a scream so big it couldn't find its way out.

Neira made a noise, and her fingers loosened just a little around Rora's wrist. Not by much, but it was enough for a little of the cold to seep away, enough for a little of the deadweight to fade out of Rora's limbs, enough for the smoke to loosen its hold, too. And Rora'd always lived her life by taking little chances when they were given.

Rora twisted her hand in Neira's grip, same way she'd twisted inside the manacle, only this time she grabbed on to Neira's wrist in turn. She dug in her nails, and felt her fingers go slippery with blood. Neira made another noise, but before her fingers tightened back up, before she could pull back whatever spell'd slipped for just a second, Rora swung up her other arm fast and hard. And when her forearm slammed into Neira's, she heard a wet *pop*. Neira's fingers fell away from her wrist like worms. Neira screamed, and the smoke boiled away, and Rora surged to her feet.

She saw, in the second she had to see anything else, Anddyr tangled up around Neira's feet. The distraction Rora'd needed to get free. Good enough—he was a witch with a lot of uses. Rora threw herself forward with a little jump so that she could get her arm up high enough, so that when she hit Neira she could hook her arm around the taller woman's neck. Her weight pushed Neira backward, pushed her stumbling against Anddyr, and she started to fall. Rora wrapped her arm tighter around Neira's neck, got her other arm up so she could hold on to her own wrist, pull her arm tight as tight could be, choking Neira as they crashed to the ground together.

Rora's elbow hit the ground first and took all their weight combined, or at least that was what it felt like—a sharp pain that made her whole arm go numb, but Rora didn't let go. She held on to her numb arm, using it like a garrote around Neira's neck. Neira clawed one-handed at Rora's shoulder and made fish-gasping noises in her ear, but Rora could feel the fight going out of her. Still, she had sharp nails, and they clawed through Rora's shirt, through her skin, drawing blood and sending the cold racing through her.

There was movement down by her legs—Anddyr, where she'd used him as a tripping block, screaming his magic-words and sobbing when they didn't work, screaming them louder and louder, and Neira wheezed a laugh in Rora's ear. "So," she rasped, "weak."

Then there were hands on Rora, grabbing her still-numb shoulder, pulling her away until she couldn't keep her grip round Neira's neck anymore. "No," she shouted, "please," but she was hauled up, thrown over a shoulder, driving hard into her gut, and when she twisted her head Neira was growing smaller—still sprawled, Anddyr wrapped around her legs, the black smoke beginning to rise—

Rora's head cleared the cellar door, and bodies blurred past her down the ladder, fists and knives all full of anger, ready to kill. And a painfully familiar voice directly above Rora shouted to them, "Kill them all." And Tare, carrying her, kept carrying her farther away.

"No," Rora croaked, but her voice was nothing under all the shouting. She pounded her good hand against Tare's back, but the older woman acted like she didn't even notice. "No!" Rora twisted her hips, kicked her legs, and like a fish she slid out of Tare's arm. She knew how to fall, Tare herself had taught Rora how to fall, so she didn't land on her head but the court-yard hit her hard in the back. She flailed around, even more like a fish, and scrambled back for the cellar door, dragging in enough air to bellow down into the cellar, *"No!"*

And they listened to her. For some gods-be-damned reason, they listened to her.

Or maybe it was only that Tare was right behind her, and took a harder look this time. At all the witches sprawled un-moving, except for Neira, who was sitting now, her not-broke arm raised and fingers drawing shapes in the air; and Anddyr, who was sobbing as he tried to fight her down with his hands, Anddyr who'd probably never had to fight with his hands in all his life. "It's her," Rora croaked, and wheezed a delirious laugh at herself when she tried to point with her numb arm. Maybe it was broken, broke as bad as she'd broke Neira's.

Maybe Tare believed her. Or maybe Tare just wanted some quiet and some stillness to get this giant mess all sorted out. Either way, she pushed past Rora and waded back into the cellar. Her hands moved, too, like the witches' but different, making words too fast for Rora's blurry eyes and fuzzy mind to follow. But the knives in the cellar saw, and they closed in with her.

Some grabbed Anddyr, twisting his arms and his hands even though he wasn't doing any magic, *couldn't*. Neira'd done something to all the witches, somehow. They pressed his face hard into the ground and sat on him while the others went for Neira.

Neira grinned at them, big white teeth under her empty eyes, and she raised both her arms up. The broken one flopped in that way that made Rora want to puke. Neira didn't fight when they grabbed her arms, didn't scream when they twisted the broken one, didn't call up any of her black smoke, didn't stop smiling for even a second. Tare glanced over her shoulder, eyes flicking to the cellar door, where Rora was close to pitching in with how far over she was leaning. Then Tare lifted up her dagger, and brought the hilt smashing down against Neira's skull, and finally her smile faded. The knives who'd held her let her fall to the floor.

Relief hit Rora harder'n Neira had, chasing all the blood-pounding terror out of her, so sudden that she almost *did* fall right through the cellar door as her whole body sagged. She was crying, but she wasn't sure if she had been for a while, or if that was new.

Rora rolled away from the door, sprawling onto her back. Her arm was still numb, and her shoulders and chest and face ached from all the places Neira'd hit her, but she could almost ignore all that. There were stars above her. It felt like a whole lifetime since she'd seen stars.

Rora turned her head at the sound coming up the ladder: Tare's head poked up and stopped, even with Rora's. Then she took another few rungs to put herself that little bit higher. She reached out to grab a twisting handful of Rora's hair. "What in all the bloody fecking hells happened here?"

Rora laughed, and cried, and told her.

CHAPTER TWENTY-SIX

Scal's people were always patrolling. Circling, cycling, looking for danger. Looking for prey.

They were looking especially for the preachers who had killed Beston, for Vatri had sworn they would find the preachers and give justice to all the dead villagers. But there was no sign of the preachers, no guess at the direction they had gone, no word in any of the other towns of passing preachers.

Within three moon-passes, it was clear that they would not find the preachers. They would not bring justice to the villagers.

It made Edro furious. He screamed at the scouts, and screamed loudest at Deslan, who had become something like the leader of the scouts. No one had asked her to, and she had not taken or been given any title. It was only that when she spoke, others listened. Deslan bore Edro's anger with tight-lipped silence.

Scal could not bear it. He stepped between Edro and Deslan, facing the little lordling. They were almost of a height, but Scal was taller. He said, "Enough."

Edro pushed him. Hands flat against Scal's chest, and his anger bursting forth from his arms. Not hard enough to hurt, but hard enough that Scal stumbled back a step.

It was silent in the camp. Silent as a village of the dead.

Vatri had told him once, *Anger is a foolish, prideful thing. A man who is quick to anger should be trusted with caution.*

Scal took a step forward, retaking the ground he had lost. It put his face close to Edro's, close enough he could smell the man's fury, see the creases anger had drawn in his skin. Scal said, "Enough."

He thought, for a moment, that Edro might hit him. He tried to decide which would be better—to hit the man back, to hit him until his face was nothing but red lumps, until Vatri would not want to look at his face; or to walk away, and show that he was better than Edro's petty rage. He knew which he should do, but he also knew which he wished to do.

But Edro did not hit him. He spit in Scal's face, and turned on his heel, and stormed into his tent.

Scal wiped the spittle from his face. His eyes found Vatri's across the camp. She frowned at him, and she looked away, and she followed Edro into his tent.

Deslan frowned at Scal as well, but there was more anger in hers. She looked like she had been making the same calculations he had been, if Edro had hit Scal. He thought it likely that she had come to the same decision.

"Come," he said to her. "We will scout again."

Three parties went out into the woods, different directions, different ground. None of them were likely to find anything, for they had already covered the same paths, again and again. Scal and Deslan and the three others of their party walked in silence. Even angry, Deslan's steps made no sound, and her longbow stayed tight around her shoulder, disturbing no more trees than she did. In time, her anger faded, drawn into the night sky like smoke.

She stopped, and so smoothly Scal did not see it until it was done, set her bow and drew an arrow back to her ear.

The others froze as well, and then Scal heard the footsteps approaching, and a soft voice running constantly as a stream. The others drew their weapons, soundless.

What emerged through the trees before them were ghosts.

One of them yelped, which covered half of Deslan's polite, "Your names and business?" They did not answer, for the one who led them simply stared openmouthed at Scal.

It was not often that ghosts followed Scal from one life to another. The last time it had happened had been Iveran, and then he had killed Iveran.

Joros closed his mouth with a click that was loud in the forest quiet. "I see you survived," he said to Scal. "How fortunate for us all."

Deslan's eyes darted to the side. "You know them?"

"I do," Scal said.

"Friends, or fodder?"

"I do not know yet."

"Scal?" The other ghost, Aro, stumbled forward and fell to his knees a dozen paces from Scal. He was pale, pallid, and far too thin. His hands were spotted with dry blood. "Is that really you? Is this real?"

Scal did not step forward to meet him. There was something *wrong* about him, something very wrong that made Scal's stomach churn. He hardly looked the same person Scal remembered—a ghost, indeed.

Aro began to cry. "Please," he said softly, "please tell me if it's you. Tell me if this is real or not." One of the others of their party moved forward, her empty hands raised pointedly toward Deslan, and knelt down beside Aro. One hand to his shoulder, the other rubbing his back, murmuring soft comforts that did nothing to calm him. "Please. You have to tell."

"It is me," Scal said softly, and Aro's replying sob made his stomach turn again. The boy curled against his comforter's shoulder, wetting her shirt with his tears.

Scal looked to Joros, who gave him a tight smile that was not truly a smile. "The boy has gotten rather sick, since the last time you saw him. Can you lower your weapons? We're no threat to you. We're only looking for someone."

Deslan did not lower her bow, though Scal could see the faint tremors in her arm from holding the arrow drawn for so long. She would hold it, though, until Scal told her not to. And he did not tell her not to yet.

Joros made a noise in his throat. "Perhaps you can help us, then. We'll leave and never see you again. Just tell me if you know how to find someone called the Nightbreaker."

The tip of Deslan's arrow dipped, and the uncertain look she gave Scal lasted far longer than a flicker. The others of his scouting party shifted, too. Their habit was to welcome any who sought the Nightbreaker. Anyone who passed through the woods and spoke the name in seeking was at least granted an audience. Was welcomed in, if they were found worthy. Until now, the name had been like a key.

"Why?" Scal asked. Deslan righted her arrow. She would follow him, in anything. Her unshaking faith made him nearly as sick as seeing Aro in his state.

"I believe the Nightbreaker would make a powerful ally." Joros smiled again. "We could all use more friends in these trying times."

"Where are the others?" Scal asked. "Rora. Anddyr."

"They're safe. This is Aro's venture—he wished to show the world what he's capable of." Joros rested a hand on Aro's shoulder. It was a mockery of support, of fatherlike pride, but Aro brightened beneath it. "I'm only here as a guide. But Rora and Anddyr are resting safely among friends." Joros shifted his jaw with a crackling noise, and eyed Scal sidelong. "Your merra. She left us some time ago. I can't tell you where she's gone. Doubtless terrorizing some other poor souls."

"She is not mine."

"I have to find him," Aro blurted suddenly. His back went board-straight, his chin tilting up so high he almost was looking up. "The Nightbreaker. He can help. He can save us all, that's what she said. He can help us, and he can help me. I have to find him."

Scal made motion to Deslan, and she dropped her arrow. Released it from the string and returned it to her quiver. She did not sling the bow back over her shoulder—she was not quite that trusting of these people who were strangers to her. Scal said to Aro only, "Come with me. I will take you."

Aro's eyes grew wide in his face. "You know him?" he whispered.

"Come," Scal said again. He had spoken only to Aro, but he was not surprised when Joros and the others in his group came as well. He did it for Aro alone. Aro, who thought the Nightbreaker could fix whatever was wrong with him.

Scal led them, with Aro and Joros at his back, and their people at their backs. Scal's scouts ranged in a loose circle around them, an escort. Scal had learned, in the span of his lives, the fine difference between an escort and a guard, and the difference lay mostly in the tightness of the surrounding circle. Escorts led, and would protect if needed, but escorts did not plan to be needed. Guards were protection. Guards meant danger—from without or within. Scal had taught the scouts how to walk, when guiding potential new followers.

He wanted to tell them to walk a tighter circle, now. But there was no way to do it without drawing suspicion.

Aro walked close to Scal's shoulder, truly a ghost from a lost life. The last time he had traveled with Aro, the boy had been full of energy and eagerness, often at Scal's side chattering. Scal had enjoyed his company. He chattered now, too, though his words were wild and uneven, as though his thoughts were leaves tossed in a wind. "I've heard the Nightbreaker is a mighty hero. As tall as two men, and he takes care of everyone he meets, and he's never afraid. Scal, how did you find him? How . . . how did I find you? They say the Nightbreaker's sword can cut through stone, and he can see the truth inside your heart. Will he help me even if he can see the truth? I just want to show Rora . . . Have you seen his sword, Scal?"

Scal walked silent. Deslan, close to him in the loose-ringed escort, was silent, too, but Scal could feel her eyes hard on him. Confusion floating off her in waves. But Scal said nothing, and so his people said nothing.

The camp, when they returned, was restless. All were unhappy about not finding the preachers, and a confrontation between two of their leaders had not helped to settle their minds. Those they passed greeted Scal's return with terse nods, or with smiles of relief, and looked with interest at the newcomers. Scal spoke to one of them, in a low voice that the others would not hear, and the young woman went off in search of Vatri.

"These are his people?" Aro asked, staring around in wonder. The camp was nothing to wonder at, but Aro looked at the tents as though they were castles, the people as if they were lords.

For all the wonder Aro showed, Joros showed disdain. "I'd expected something more . . . fitting."

Deslan snorted. "We can hardly live in manors, doing what we do. If we're easy to find, we're easy to kill."

Scal gave her a slow-blinking look, and she turned her face away, cheeks going red. Though Joros tried to pull more answers from her, the first who had told him anything, Deslan said nothing more.

"*Well.*" Vatri's voice cut through the quiet of the forest. Cut through the tension in the camp, and shattered it into a thousand sharp and brittle pieces that pierced and scraped. When Scal turned with the others to face her, she stood with arms crossed and a grin creasing her face, but there was a hardness in her eyes. There was a fire, in her eyes. "What an unexpected surprise." Edro, at her side, frowned. Hand resting on the hilt of his sword as he eyed the newcomers, as he tasted the sharp strain in the camp.

Joros sputtered. It was, perhaps, the first time Scal had seen him caught truly off guard. He spun to face Scal, fists at his sides. "What is this?" he demanded. "I came to see the Nightbreaker, not some—some dried-out traitorous shrew—"

Edro stepped forward, and the smooth sound of his sword drawing cut off the rest of Joros's words. "I think that's enough," he said, even so.

"It's all right, Edro," Vatri said, stepping once more to his side. Still smiling. "Joros is an old, *old* friend. An insult from him is a sign of the utmost respect."

"Hello," Aro said, meek, nervous. He raised his hand in a wave that stopped halfway, and fell. Vatri ignored him.

She went on, "You came to find the Nightbreaker, then? Of course you did. You can't keep away when there's a whiff of someone whose power you can twist, can you? Scal." She turned her dagger-point smile to him. "If you promised to show them the Nightbreaker, then show them." She knew. Knew he had wanted to hide it from them, and knew why. Her smile stayed in place.

And so Scal drew his sword, and its fire lit the night, and he did not look at any of their faces. He could not.

CHAPTER TWENTY-SEVEN

Anddyr's hands shook around the knots. He'd never tied up a mage before, but he'd had his own fingers bound often enough that he knew how to do it properly, to keep Neira from tracing any sigils in the air, to keep her away from her power.

He only prayed—and prayed vehemently, under his breath—that her wrong magic, her *blood* magic, worked the same way as normal magic.

He could feel the others staring—all the pack members who had charged down, ready to kill whatever stood before them and still looked ready to kill; Rora, who was free and hurt and had swayed on her feet so badly that Tare had had to catch her and steady her. If Anddyr hadn't spent the last months watching the two of them interact, he might not have seen the fury that flickered instinctually across Tare's face fade more quickly than usual, or the way she made sure Rora truly was steady. And he'd seen that Rora had seen both, too.

He could also feel the ones who weren't staring—or were staring in a different way. All his mages, fragile as newborns, nursed so carefully . . . and gone as suddenly as a candle's flame. Because of *her*, because of what she'd done—draining their power by twisting Aro's spell. The wall had been fed by a trickle of their power, a trickle that flared stronger when challenged so that the wall would hold. By continually channeling her unnatural power at it, Neira had forced the wall to pull more and more power from its sources, to pull until there was nothing left to pull.

The second thing a mage was taught by the masters of the Academy—after learning to control the wild power—was that a mage was nothing without their power. It was a foolish mage indeed who chose to or let themselves be drained of their power; one should always plan for the *next thing*, when a spell might be necessary and a mage, unable to perform said spell, would put their own life and the reputation of the Academy at risk. But there was something *beyond* drained, something not seen very often, where a mage poured out all the power they had and then gave *more*, gave the last that they had to give. And a mage who had given everything was dead.

Neira, using the wall, had pulled all their power, and then pulled a little more.

Now they all stared at Anddyr, the living and the dead, as he finished tying Neira's hands, tied them tighter, perhaps, than he needed to, tied more knots than were strictly necessary. He was unwilling to take any chances—it was only by sheer force of will, and no small bit of luck, that Anddyr was still alive.

I'm learning how to fight, he thought with grim pride, hoping that one day soon he'd be able to say the words to Etarro himself. Etarro had been the one to free him, and the one to teach Anddyr that freedom had to be fought for. Anddyr had been fighting every day since, against the poison in his blood, the madness in his mind. He had gotten so good at fighting.

Anddyr tied the last knot he could and sat back on his

heels, twisting his own fingers around each other to hide the way they still shook. There was a welling need in him to cast a spell, to cast *any* spell—but the shock of realizing that Neira had drained his power still resonated in him, and that empty feeling kept him from drawing any sigils.

He knew her, from his time in the mountain. She'd always been on the periphery of the leaders of the Fallen—an assistant to Dirrakara for a time, one of Joros's secretive shadowseekers, rumored to be the lover of a variety of the Ventallo at any given time, rumored to dabble in things that wiser people avoided dabbling in. Some had called her a true fanatic, and a small subsect of the shadowseekers had formed around her, secrets wrapped within the larger secrets. Others claimed she was mad, and that was why she'd spent so much of her time around the mages she'd helped enslave. Everyone had agreed that she was too smart for her own good, and not to be trusted, and an invaluable ally.

She'd been kind to Anddyr—mostly. Even the times when she had been unkind, she'd at least been polite about it—like adding a grinning "please" as she leaned away from whispering in his ear the command to seal a recalcitrant mage, still living, in a tomb of stone.

"She's trouble" had been the general consensus, and Anddyr had avoided her kind of trouble whenever he could.

Now, though, he knew the truth: she was *dangerous*.

"What now?" It was one of the fists, dependable Skit, who asked it. Anddyr didn't have to turn to know he would be looking to Tare for an answer, and his hands shook harder. She had no reason to believe Neira was what Rora claimed, no reason to believe that a single mage had overpowered all the others and broken free. Given how distrustful Tare was of *witches* in general, and of Rora in particular, she was just as likely to suspect Rora of colluding with Anddyr on searching for some loophole in the shield that her own brother had made. There was no reason for Tare not to leave them both trapped in the cellar with Neira and the corpses of his poor flock, to wait for her to wake up and have a chance at defending herself, but by that point it would be too late—

"Take them up," Tare said, voice hard as it broke through Anddyr's rising panic. He twisted toward her, knowing an expression of unabashed shock stretched across his face, but she'd already turned away to make her own way up the ladder. He found Rora's eyes instead, and she actually held his gaze for a few moments before hers slid away, and she moved to follow Tare up the ladder.

Anddyr's hands still shook, but it wasn't even noticeable when he wrapped them around the ladder's rungs. He climbed up, leaving behind Neira, leaving behind the mages he'd failed to save, and climbed into the clean air beyond the cellar.

He had almost forgotten what it was like. He stood with his eyes closed, feeling the wind against his cheeks, tugging at his oil-heavy locks of hair; feeling dirt under his feet that *moved* when he curled his toes, rather than dirt so hard-packed it might as well have been stone. He reveled in the smells of nighttime and growing things and anything that wasn't just stale sweat and urine; the smell of flowers nearby so heady he could *taste* them on his tongue. He almost laughed; he almost sobbed.

"Put him in the stables," Tare said. She stood some distance away, her arms crossed and her stance wide, as though she were waiting for a fight. But the only one near her was Rora, sitting cross-legged on the ground and holding her wounded hand, blood from her wrist making a sleeve down her arm. Anddyr's fingers itched with the urge to heal her, to stop any pain she might be feeling, but he couldn't do any of that, even if she'd let him.

Skit took a step toward Rora, hesitated, took another step, and hesitated again. "What about her?" he finally asked Tare.

"I don't care," Tare said, and one of the fists pushed Anddyr into the stable before he could see Rora's reaction to that.

When the fists closed the stable doors, though, leaving Anddyr enclosed in darkness that at least smelled better than the cellar, Rora wasn't there with him.

This time, the skytower comes to him. This time, the boy inside it is alone. And this time, the boy does not wear the eyes of a god.

He is only a boy, a boy Anddyr knows. He sits calm as summer, calm as sunlight, and Anddyr knows the things he holds as well: in one hand, a stuffed horse, lumpy and ragged and dirty; in the other hand, a small earthenware jar that Anddyr can smell, no matter that he is incorporeal, that he is dreaming. He can smell it, and it makes his insides try to tear themselves apart.

"Do you want to be free?" Etarro asks. He has asked Anddyr this question before, but the last time, Anddyr hadn't been in a place to understand what freedom meant.

He still doesn't, not really. "I don't know." It is the same answer he gave the first time.

"Free is something you have to fight for." Etarro extends his hand, the one holding the jar. His eyes are not the eyes of a god, but far older, and they see far more than they should.

Anddyr swallows hard. He can smell the skura, hear it calling to him, feel his stomach clawing toward the jar. He is not in this place, this place does not exist, but he can hear the roar and wail of his stomach. "I . . ." *The clouds from which the skytower is built are firm beneath his feet; if he has weight, the clouds will support it. But there are clouds at his back, too. He can't step away, and so the best he can do is press himself against the wall of the skytower. He says,* "No. I . . . I don't want that."

Etarro pulls his hand back, the jar and the horse at a level once more. He stares at Anddyr.

Anddyr swallows again, and whispers, "I'm sorry. I should have chosen you. You . . . you don't deserve this."

The boy's other hand moves forward, and his fingers are curled around the stuffed horse's lumpy neck. Her name is Sooty. It's a good name for a horse. "You have to come back for her," *Etarro says.*

All the boy's words are echoes from the past: words Etarro said to Anddyr inside Mount Raturo, the last times they talked. This isn't real, Anddyr realizes, none of it; it's only a dream, his sad and desperate subconscious spewing forth guilty memories. "You're not real," *he says out loud, because saying a thing makes it true. At the least, naming a thing as false denies it its power.*

"You have to come back for her," *the boy says again.* "Find me."

"They all said you're probably dead."

Etarro rolls to his knees, stretches the horse out closer to Anddyr. "Find me."

"I . . . I don't think you're dead, but maybe it would be better if you are. Dead has to be better than trapped."

"Find me." *Etarro stands, and walks forward, the horse brandished before him like a talisman.*

Anddyr remembers how, before, he sank through the wall of the skytower as though it wasn't there, or as though he wasn't there. This time, though, no matter how hard he presses himself backward, no matter how desperately he thinks, I want to leave, I don't want to be here, the wall stays solid, and he stays solid.

"Find me."

"I don't know how!" Anddyr wails as Etarro stands directly before him. "I don't know how to find you. I don't know how to help you."

The stuffed horse presses against Anddyr's hand, and his fingers close around it reflexively, around the horse and the boy's hand. But Etarro slips away, back to the center of the room, leaving Anddyr holding the stuffed horse.

"Find me," Etarro says, and the skytower opens beneath Anddyr's feet and returns him to the world.

Anddyr woke with damp cheeks, and when he lifted his hand to wipe away the tears, he found his hand was full.

He sat up, staring, silent and utterly dumbfounded. And Sooty, his old stuffed horse, stared back. Squeezing his fingers, he could find all the familiar lumps, could feel her dirty patches coarse beneath his finger pads. Either his madness had taken a sharp downward turn or she was, impossibly, real.

Anddyr slowly lay back down, stretching out on the pile of moldy hay he'd claimed for his own. He held Sooty cradled against his chest, the place she was used to sleeping. It wasn't her voice, but still, she seemed to whisper, Find me.

And Anddyr held her tight, and promised, I will.

Something poked into Anddyr's leg—it felt like a stick, or a broomstick, and when he cracked an eye open he saw it was the latter, wielded by a pack member he didn't recognize. She was smaller than fists usually were, and she didn't have the same coiled-spring strength as Rora and the other knives did. Digging through his memories, Anddyr managed to pull up a fragment of Aro babbling about the hierarchy of a pack, everyone with their assigned role, all working to be the most efficient their pack could be. *Eyes are for watching, nimble fingers can take anything they want, feet make distractions or run messages—*

Yes. This woman looked like a foot.

To emphasize it, she poked him again with the broomstick and said, "The Dogshead wants to see you. Don't make any trouble and you won't get no trouble."

"That's not accurate," Anddyr muttered, staying tightly curled around the lumpy fabric ball at his center.

"Feck you say?"

"Nothing." Anddyr tucked the stuffed horse—the impossible stuffed horse that was—into his ratty robe. It wasn't quite falling apart, and the waist was still tight enough that Sooty could sit down near his hip without needing to worry about falling out. Once she was secure, he uncurled and sat up, brushing hay away from his arm and side. The foot, holding the broomstick like she expected she'd need it for bashing soon, poked him again.

Anddyr stood up, moving slowly so he wouldn't startle her. He didn't want her need to bash something flaring up too suddenly. She brandished the broomstick at him and jerked it in the direction of the main stable door; he happily complied, walking to the open door with his fingers spread nonthreateningly at his sides. They itched with the need to weave a spell, because a night of sleep should have at least restored a modicum of his power and not testing it was almost like a physical pain, like a nagging toothache. He didn't think his foot escort would appreciate a magelight to guide their way, though.

The foot was replaced by two fists outside the door, neither of whom he recognized. They deftly tied Anddyr's hands behind his back, finger-winding loops and firm knots that did nothing to ease the itching, but at least made the urge to cast a spell a nonstarter.

Tucking the broomstick under her arm, the foot streaked off ahead, and Anddyr resisted the impulse to compare her to a flying star—madness lurked at the edges of such a comparison. Instead, he counted his steps as the fists led him after her trail.

The first time he'd been to the estate, Anddyr had hardly set foot in the house. Joros had declared the place belonged to the pack, and that they should keep it and themselves in good order, since they might both prove useful or even necessary. And then the cappo had whisked Rora, Aro, Vatri, and Anddyr away, along with their new complement of fists and knives. That first time, at least, sunlight had streamed through windows, lighting up the dusty halls, illuminating the corners of the large bedroom Sharra Dogshead had claimed as her own and from which she had negotiated terms with Joros. Now those same hallways were bathed in shadow, and the Dogshead's room was lit only by a flickering lamp whose light didn't reach the corners.

The Dogshead sat behind the heavy desk that dominated the room, looking more like a stern banker than a criminal leader.

The foot stood inside the door, broomstick planted at her side, and Tare leaned against the wall a few paces away. That one had a way of looking deceptively casual—her arms were crossed over her chest, and one foot was tucked behind her calf, but Anddyr had no doubt that, if he were to make any remotely threatening sort of move, she could put a knife through his throat before he had a chance to draw breath.

And on the other side of the room, in one of the lightless corners, sat Rora.

Anddyr swallowed. She'd clearly bathed, her ear-length hair clean if tousled, and the clothes she wore, though too big for her frame and certainly not new, were at least clean as well. Her hand was bandaged where she'd dragged her wrist free of the manacle, and the visible wounds along her arms and face and neck had been tended to. His eyes darting to Tare, Anddyr wondered if she'd been the one to nurse Rora's wounds, and a pathetic jealousy growled in his stomach.

The fists pulled him forward to stand before the Dogshead at her desk, and stayed at his side. He didn't like having Tare at his back, or Rora out of his sight, but there was nothing for it. The Dogshead cracked the knuckles of one hand, slowly, methodically, as she stared at Anddyr, and no, she wasn't like a banker, she was like a teacher, like one of the disapproving masters of the Academy, and he felt like a guilty-twitching student before her—

"What," she finally said, scattering his thoughts, "am I supposed to do with you now?"

Anddyr opened his mouth before realizing he didn't know how to answer, and realized when he closed it that he probably wasn't supposed to.

"Everyone tells me the woman now trapped in my cellar is dangerous, not to be trusted, and as crazy as you are. They say she's the one who killed all the witches . . . except you. So

I can't put you back in the cellar, not until I get her sorted out. But I'd be a fool to let you roam around my house, among my people, when I *know* you're dangerous and not to be trusted and crazy."

The Dogshead began to crack the knuckles of her other hand. Anddyr, his own fingers aching in their knots, still tried to flex them anyway. He looked back at her in silence, no answer to give even if she'd wanted one. Finally she reached her last joint, and then laid her palms flat on top of the desk, fingers splayed.

"Rora tells me I should trust you," the Dogshead said, and the words were nearly enough to knock him down. His eyes scanned over to Rora, but the Dogshead pulled him back with a sharp snap of her fingers before he got more than a glimpse of Rora's face, canted away. "She says you, at least, have a bit of sense behind your stupid eyes, and that you kept all the witches from killing each other or any of my people. That you kept 'em as organized and calm as you could." She looked over Anddyr's shoulder, to where he knew Rora was, but when he tried to look, too, her eyes snapped back to him with a fierceness in them that made Anddyr swallow hard. "She tells me neither of you is the traitor Joros branded you. Normally I wouldn't care to listen to a traitor squawking about not being a traitor." Another slide of the eyes, but this time Anddyr didn't twitch, staying focused on the Dogshead. "But I've had my own doubts about your master. There've been enough things he's said that haven't lined up with the things I hear from people I trust more. So when I have to make a choice between two people I don't trust, it comes down to the actions."

Anddyr shook with the need to turn, with the need to

weave his hands. And every shred of him ached to run, because there was an impossible horse at his hip, and the words *Find me* pulsed through his blood. "What is it you want from me?" he said, voice carefully inflectionless, the same tone he'd always used with Joros.

The Dogshead stared at him, level as his voice. "Right now I've got two witches in my home, and they're both a problem. That's one too many witch problems." The Dogshead stood slowly. Anddyr remembered she had a bad leg, but it didn't show in the measured way she rose to her feet. She wasn't taller than Anddyr, very few people were, but he still felt *loomed* over as she stared him down. "We can take care of the problem right now, if you want to be difficult—I couldn't give two shits if you die. Or you can prove that you're worth keeping around, and you go take care of the other witch—then I can stand having you be my problem. You do that, and I won't even put you back in the cellar when it's done. I'll let you roam free."

The words were like a double punch: the word "free" shuddered through him, delirium-hot, intoxicating—and then the price of freedom struck home. They would have him *kill*? Of course they would, they were cold-blooded, coldhearted, they thought nothing of taking a life, but—There was a third punch, or perhaps a parting kick: Rora had been a part of this decision. *She* would know how much the ultimatum would shake him, which meant that she hadn't cared, or that she had given it to them.

His hands shook where they were bound behind his back, but the skillful knots kept anyone from seeing it. He remembered a mountain, the bowels of the tallest point in all the world, and a boy who had told him, *Free is something you have to fight for.* Etarro's remembered words felt like a whisper from his half-remembered dream, the boy—the dead boy, surely he could not survive sharing space with a god—coming back to haunt him. *Are you ready to fight, Anddyr?*

He had gotten so good at fighting . . .

"Yes," he said, as loudly as he could manage without the word turning to a sob or a scream. "I'll do it. But I'll need more time."

And that was that. The fists untied his fingers—a show of good faith—and he stood there working feeling back into his fingers as the Dogshead spoke more words at him. He didn't hear any of them. When the fists led him out of the room, he was acutely aware of another who followed them out.

Surprise felt a distant thing, but he did not expect, when Rora said, "I'll take 'im," for the fists to leave. But they did, and Anddyr and Rora walked side by side through the dark and dusty halls.

"You're leaving, aren't you?" she asked softly, not even loud enough to disturb the swirling dust.

"Yes." There didn't seem to be any point in lying. Not to her. Not with no one else around to hear.

She stopped, and Anddyr stopped with her. When she turned, he turned. And, for the first time in what felt like an age, she met his eyes, and held his gaze. "We're not square, you and me," she said. "You helped me out down in the cellar, and maybe I'd be dead if it wasn't for you, but that doesn't make up for all the rest of the shit you've pulled. I still think my life'd be better if I didn't know you." She took a deep breath, closed her eyes as though she were counting, and still held his gaze when she opened them again. "But thanks. Thank you, for . . . for maybe saving my life down there."

Anddyr gripped the sides of his robe in each hand, clenching and unclenching his fingers. It helped relieve some of the itchiness, the need to cast a spell, the need to assure himself he wasn't broken, wasn't more broken than he already was. "Is that why you told them to trust me?"

She shrugged one of her shoulders. "Part of it, yeah. You don't have to leave, y'know. You can—you'd be useful."

"Useful," Anddyr repeated. It felt like a foreign word in his mouth, the shape of the vowels all wrong, nothing familiar in it from which he could parse meaning.

"Yeah. I think they've all got a taste for how useful a witch can be. Without—" She stopped, her brother's name hanging unspoken in the air. Her eyes went away for a while.

Anddyr gently cleared his throat, and her gaze sharpened back on him. She'd spent so much time avoiding even acknowledging him in the cellar that all the intentional attention was making him flustered, making his tongue feel heavy in his mouth. Carefully shaping the words, carefully holding her eyes, Anddyr asked, "Do you want me to stay?" Not if he would be welcome. Not if he would be useful. Not even if he would be free. This was the only question whose answer would matter.

Rora looked away and her mouth twisted, as though she were chewing something unsavory. "Like I said. You'd be useful."

Could one grieve for something that never had been, and never would be? Was that allowed? Anddyr straightened his fingers, smoothed them along the sides of his robe, gently calming the wrinkles. "You've never needed me," he said softly, and turned away. She didn't refute it, or try to stop him, or say anything at all.

None of the pack stopped him as he walked across the courtyard. It was dark, and few of them would recognize him as a danger. There was a muffled sound that filled the night air, an almost singsong, repetitive noise, and he followed it. It led him to where he'd been intending to go anyway.

Anddyr went to one knee beside the cellar door, spreading the fingers of one hand wide against the cobblestoned ground as he flexed the fingers of his other hand experimentally. Now that it was time, he was almost too nervous to check. Too nervous of failure, too nervous of knowing.

The repetitive sound came up through the cellar door: a voice calling, "Rora. Rora . . ."

His fingers wove sigils in the air, and his magic welled up from the core of his being, and flowed through his limbs and blood in a tide of relief. He wasn't broken.

With senses beyond his own, Anddyr explored the cellar. It was a great cavernous empty space, but for one small and pulsing light, pacing. *Neira.* Anddyr changed the movements of his fingers and he built a solid wall around her, a wall made of air and light.

The repetitive call stopped for a moment, and turned into a soft laugh. "Good-bye," Neira called up through the cellar door. "Good luck."

He didn't look back at the house as he left. Let them all think he was a coward. Let them all rot.

CHAPTER TWENTY-EIGHT

R ora waited for them to come for her, wondering if they'd send some nameless fists she didn't even recognize, or if Tare'd come for her herself. All she knew for sure was they'd send someone. They had to. She'd told them to trust Anddyr, and then he'd run away and left them with no kind of protection, and left Rora holding the blame for it.

In the Canals, all you had to live on were your words and your hands and your smarts. Rora's hands'd only ever been good at cutting, and all her daggers were gone, and she'd never been smart enough to do any better'n just getting by. Even when all the pack thought she was a twice-over traitor, at least she knew she wasn't, at least she still had the truth and the hope that someday they'd trust her again.

They had, and it'd lasted maybe five whole hours.

"Better'n nothing," she lied to herself as she sat in the little nook an old shed made against the crumbly wall. It felt weird, being under the stars and all the air, and having walls at her back and shoulder made it all feel a little less big. She wasn't hiding. She never hid from her problems. Hiding wasn't the same as just waiting for them to come find you first.

In the end, it was Tare. It had to be, didn't it?

The older woman's shadow hit Rora first, the rising moon

behind her turning Tare all to black. She just stood there, and Rora couldn't look up from her knees. "You knew he was leaving," Tare said, no question in the words.

"Yeah." No point in lying, and nothing she could say to defend herself.

"And you didn't stop him."

"No."

"And you didn't tell me."

Rora pressed her back a little harder against the wall, feeling a loose stone dig into her shoulder. "No." That'd be the end of it—with all the bad things Tare thought she'd done, admitting to another bad thing was like putting a knife to her own throat. Ever since Rora'd gone back to the pack, back in the Canals, Tare'd been waiting to kill her. One more betrayal was all the Dogshead'd need to let her do it.

Tare's shadow moved, and the shed wall creaked as she sat down against it. She was at an angle to Rora, so that when Rora looked up in surprise, she could see Tare's face clear in the moonlight just by looking straight ahead. With Tare staring up at the moon, Rora could stare at her and lie to herself that she wouldn't notice.

"That crazy bitch down in the cellar," Tare said, "she keeps calling your name."

"I've heard it," Rora said. It was part of why she'd chose her corner. It was far enough away from the cellar door she could pretend the sound was just the wind. Rora swallowed, and because another minute passed without Tare looking to kill her, she said the thing she hadn't been able to say in all the time so far: "Thanks. For . . . for pulling me out of there."

The moonlight made a mask out of Tare's face. "I can't keep saving you."

Rora reached up to rub at her missing ear, the one Tare'd cut off. If they'd been in the cellar she probably would've said something about it, but they weren't in the cellar anymore. "I learned how to save myself." It came out sharper than she'd meant it to.

Tare looked down from the moon, turned her head to meet Rora's eyes. Neither of them blinked, but it wasn't the dog-staring, ready-to-kill kind of unblinking. It was like seeing something familiar that you'd half forgot. Tare said, "You've got a lap full of problems, Sparrow," and she said it like when Rora'd been younger, when Tare'd been training her how to use her words and her hands and her smarts, before Tare'd thought of her as a traitor or a coward or a twin or anything except a scrappy pup called Sparrow. She said it like a challenge. She said it like a test. "What're you gonna do to fix them?"

Rora rubbed her palms against her thighs and looked away. She had to—if she kept staring at Tare any longer, she might say something stupid, like "Why aren't you killing me? Why do you care?"

For a long time, Rora didn't think much of anything at all. She just stared up at the moon, and she could lie to herself that she didn't notice Tare staring at her.

Rora finally cleared her throat, and said, "The biggest problem is that crazy bitch down in the cellar."

"And what're you gonna do about her?" The challenge, again.

Rora smoothed her hands down her legs again, just wasting

time, just waiting. The thing she was gonna say was something she couldn't take back, once she'd said it. It was something she hadn't expected to have a choice in, and choosing to do something stupid and dangerous was a whole lot worse than someone forcing you into it. But you could only waste so much time, once you'd already made a choice, once you knew there was nothing else to do. Rora put her hands to the wall at her back, and pushed herself up to her feet. "I'm gonna go see what she wants with me."

Tare nodded again, and she stood up, too. She was close to a head taller than Rora, but Rora'd never felt short next to her. She still didn't, somehow. "Then I'll go with you."

That took Rora so much by surprise that she blurted out the first stupid thing to pop into her head. "You don't trust me?"

"That's not it." She knew Tare well enough to recognize she was telling the truth—and anyway, why would she bother lying? You didn't put in the effort to lie to someone who didn't matter to you. "You always learned fast, but I might still need to save you again."

Rora felt her mouth hanging open and closed it quick. "I . . . I appreciate it."

Tare shrugged, and down at her sides, her hands were moving. "It'll be nice to remember when things were better. Back before you were up here causing trouble." Her hands were moving, the same movements over and over, so casual you wouldn't notice it if you didn't know the movements were trying to tell you something. The language of hand signs was a simple one: an open palm with the thumb tucked in. *Me*. A sharp jab down with two fingers. *Bad*.

Rora ran a hand through her too-long hair and held on to

the back of her head, because the spinning made her feel like it was about to float away. That was the closest she was ever likely to get to an apology from Tare, but for someone who'd been expecting to get drawn and quartered, anything like an apology was . . . unexpected. Rora laughed, surprising them both. "Yeah," she said breathlessly, dropping her hand back down to her side, "it'll be nice to see the place again. Been having trouble sleeping in a soft bed." With a circling finger, Rora's hand said, *No*. Two middle fingers tucked up said, *Good*.

The hand signs were simple things, meant to point out a mark or warn of danger or signal when the time was right. They weren't good for complicated things, like telling someone how you were going to hit a mark, or why they should stay away from a certain alley, or making a plan on the fly. Just simple signs for simple words. But simple words were easier, sometimes. Simple words could say just as much as the complicated ones.

Rora and Tare walked side by side to the cellar door.

As they got closer, Rora began to hear the calling again. It was irregular now, not the constant droning noise it'd been before; like someone drifting off and waking up with a start and calling out the first thing in their head, only this didn't sound tired at all. And it wasn't some random dream-word—it was her name. Over and over.

Rora took a bracing breath. She wasn't scared. She'd expected to be dead or dying by now, and instead she was standing with the expected killer steady at her side, and maybe that wasn't as reassuring as it'd seemed at first. But she'd cheated death. She shouldn't be alive, but she was. So she didn't have anything to be scared of.

"Wait," Tare said, even though Rora hadn't even leaned down to grab the door handle yet. She was still working up to that. But she turned to face Tare, who was fishing around under the hem of her shirt. Tare finally pulled her hands out and held them palm up toward Rora, and across each palm was the hilt of a dagger.

Rora recognized both daggers right away, of course—they were close as family. Her own daggers, the one with the big blue stone she'd broken, and the plain but sturdy one Tare herself had given her.

"She might still be dangerous," Tare said, holding both hands out, perfectly even. Tare looked at her steadily, silent, unblinking.

Knowing it was a test, knowing there was only one way to pass it, Rora reached for the plain dagger first. The one Tare had given her years ago. Rora'd borrowed a belt to hold up the too-big but clean pants she'd got from one of the fists, and she redid the belt now to give the first dagger a secure home on her left hip. Her left hand was the stronger one, since her right arm'd been broken as a kid, so Tare's dagger was the one she'd reach for first and fastest if it came to it. Rora held Tare's eyes as she took the jewel-hilted dagger next. It was a shitty sort of test if you both knew there was only one right answer, the sort of test that only told you if the other person was dumb enough to choose the wrong answer apurpose. But if a stupid test would help Tare trust her again, Rora'd do it. And she did feel better with her knives back at her hips, where they were supposed to be.

She faced the cellar door again, and she wasn't scared, and that actually felt closer to true this time.

Another breath, and Rora reached down to grab the door

and fling it open. The door clattered against the cobblestones, a sound that'd woke her up countless times when she was down in the cellar, a sound she didn't miss at all. The ladder stretched down into the darkness. They hadn't left Neira a light, and Rora hadn't thought to bring a lamp.

Didn't matter, though—a witchlight flickered to life down in the shadows, outside the square of cellar floor she could see, over by Rora's old corner where they'd left Neira. "Hello, Rora," Neira's voice said. She always sounded like she was a second away from a laugh, but the sort of laugh that made people back away from you. "Have you finally come to talk?"

Rora didn't answer her, but took the ladder down. As soon as her head ducked below the doorframe, a crazy panic rose in her that this'd been Tare's plan all along, that she'd slam the cellar door closed and leave the two of 'em trapped down there forever, both her problems taken care of in one swoop—

The ladder grumbled as Tare's weight was added to it, and Rora kept climbing down.

Rora turned as soon as her feet touched the ground— she didn't like having Neira at her back. Anddyr had tied the shadow-woman up in the same place Rora'd sat for the last few months—only that space was empty now, untied ropes hanging from the ring in the wall. And Neira wasn't there.

Rora froze, even though her blood was screaming at her to run, run, *run*—

"Hello," Neira said, and Rora's neck popped she turned so fast. The shadow-woman was crouched there among the dead witches, her empty eye sockets fixed on Rora, and a smile stretching her face.

Run, run, run—

Rora would've bolted back up the ladder if she hadn't noticed the way the air shimmered between her and Neira—the same kind of not-wall that'd sealed off the witches, only now it sealed off most of the cellar. She'd seen the witches try to get through the not-wall, seen how they couldn't no matter what they did. It didn't get rid of her heart's pounding, but it did let Rora keep her feet on the ground.

"A parting gift from your friend, I believe," Neira said, still smiling.

She can't hear my thoughts, Rora told herself, because that had to be true, didn't it? She'd just seen Rora's face and made a good guess that she was thinking about the not-wall.

"Who untied you?" Tare asked. She was right at Rora's shoulder, and even though it was stupid, it made Rora feel braver. Maybe that was mostly the threat in Tare's voice—she'd punish anyone who went against her orders, no matter who it was. Rora knew that firsthand. There weren't any empty threats with Tare.

Neira waggled her fingers. "I did. Your pet mage knows his knots, I'll grant him that, but, well . . ." She shrugged like they should know why the same knots that could make any other witch powerless hadn't worked on her.

Rora could feel Tare's anger rising at her back, but angry wouldn't get anything done. She took a step forward, closer to Neira, closer to the not-wall between them, even though her legs felt like stones, and she said, "You've been calling for me. You . . . you said there's stuff I need to know. Well?"

"Will you sit?" Neira asked. "I'd prefer to talk like civilized people." Maybe she didn't realize she was surrounded by the witches she'd killed.

"We'll stand," Tare said, back stiff as the words.

Neira sighed, and she moved in a way Rora couldn't quite follow, and there was a sound like a struck bell as something hit the not-wall. A dagger clattered to the floor on Neira's side of the barrier as the bell-echoes faded fast. The shadow-woman grinned wide and raised up her hand, showing the bloody slash she'd left across her palm, a new cut among old scars. That black smoke began to boil up from the floor beneath her.

Rora swore and stumbled backward, bumping into Tare, who hadn't moved yet, didn't know the danger, didn't know to run, run, run *to the ends of the earth*—

The smoke hit the not-wall, and it didn't pass through. It pooled on Neira's side of the barrier, around the corpses, around Neira's knees, full of restless reaching waves, but it stayed put. When Neira closed her bleeding hand into a fist, the black smoke faded away.

Rora stopped trying to run out of her own skin and stood still, even though her legs shook with wanting to flee. Close behind her, Tare'd grabbed Rora's shoulder when she'd tried to run and her hand was still there. It made Rora feel a little steadier, even though Tare let go and stepped a little away.

"See?" Neira said. That mad smile was still on her face. "I'm powerless here. Safely contained, and at your mercy. There's no reason we can't talk like reasonable people."

"Or it's all a witch's trick," Tare grumbled, not quietly.

Neira's smile slipped a little, her head tilting as her empty eyes turned toward Tare. "I don't believe I know your name."

"No," Tare said. "You don't."

"Very well." Neira spread her hands in front of her, not seeming to care that the one was still dripping blood over her dress, over the floor. She was still fixed on Tare when she asked, "Is there anything I can do to make you believe I'm not a threat?"

"No."

"I thought not. Then Rora," and she turned her head like Tare didn't matter anymore, like Rora was suddenly all the world, and the weight of those dead eyes made Rora shudder, "I have two favors to ask of you. They do not require you to trust me—they only require you to trust that your friend's barrier will hold. It will, unless he chooses to drop it or is drained of his power."

"Is that how you broke the last one?" Rora asked. Her voice tried to run up higher the same way she'd wanted to, but Rora swallowed it down. No matter what'd happened, she did trust that Anddyr wouldn't do anything halfway. If he'd put this bubble around Neira, she trusted it'd hold, and that meant she didn't have to be afraid. Easily said, harder done.

"Yes," Neira said without hesitating.

"So I also have to trust you not to do that again."

"It takes time to do. Enough time that you could be safely away before the barrier fell. And I promise not to."

Rora and Tare snorted at the same time.

Neira smiled like she thought it was funny, too. "There are two favors I would ask of you," she said again. "The first is a fire. A simple wood fire, built down here, on your side of the barrier. I do not need to touch it or interact with it in any way. It need only exist until the end of the second favor, which is that you listen to all the things I wish to tell you."

"And what is it you want to tell me?" Rora asked. "What d'you need me to hear so bad?"

"Oh, I'll tell you everything. Where the sun went, and how *you* can save it. Why the mages have been enslaved, and how they can be freed, and how they can be used. How to save your brother. Who I am, and how I can help you."

"Is that all?" Tare muttered.

Rora signed for her to be quiet, and kept her attention on Neira. There were already so many questions burning inside her—why in all the hells would one of the Fallen want to bring the sun *back*?—but she didn't ask any of them. All she did ask was, "And after all that? After I make you a fire, and listen to everything you'd tell me. Then what?"

"Then I leave," Neira said easily. "If you hear all the answers I'll give you and you still want me to leave, then I will, and you'll never see me again. I swear it, by my hands and my heart and my blood."

Rora weighed Neira's words, and she weighed the distrust she could feel radiating off Tare, and she weighed the steady pounding of her own heart. She wasn't scared. And this time it actually was true.

"I'll be back," Rora said. Promised it. "I'll need to get some wood for the fire." When she turned back for the ladder, she saw the unhappy line of Tare's mouth, the anger in her eyes as she stared at Neira. But Tare didn't say anything against Rora's words, and Tare followed her up the ladder, and Tare stayed at her side and showed her where the fists piled up firewood.

CHAPTER TWENTY-NINE

J oros had never liked leaders who were too cowardly to actually lead. Leaders who hid behind the guise of fairness, where each delicate opinion mattered and transparency was law and a leader could hide behind any decision by claiming it had been the will of the people.

Vatri was one of those leaders.

She made Joros *petition* her, publicly, before all the fools who thought she and Scal were anything special. Well—there was no denying that Scal's sword was unusual, and if even a quarter of the tales he'd heard about the Nightbreaker were actually true of Scal, then there *was* something there. But the Northman was attached to Vatri's teat and wouldn't so much as blink without her leave, so if Joros hoped to take advantage of the Northman-shaped gift that had fallen into his lap, he needed to convince Vatri.

A conniving bitch who hated him at least as much as he hated her.

He'd thought briefly that Aro, who could occasionally demonstrate miraculous social acuity, might be a help in that— until the merra's spitting and screeching reminded him that Aro's unexpected revelation as a budding mage was what had made Vatri leave their merry little band in the first place. No help from that quarter.

No, it was left to Joros alone—as usual—to save them all.

And so he stood with Aro and Harin and the others at his back, facing Vatri with Scal to one side and some lord's son named Edro to her other, and all the other followers of the Nightbreaker ranged around them, intrigued.

Joros began with a sweeping bow. "O kind and blessed merra," he began in a nasally, bootlicking voice, and he saw Vatri gnash her teeth. If she thought to make a mockery of him, the least he could do was return the favor. "I stand before you, humbled, seeking—"

"You will speak plainly," she interrupted, "or you will leave."

"As you wish." Joros bowed again, simply out of spite, though this bow wasn't as extravagant as the first. "We've been traveling in search of help—help in defeating the Fallen, and rebinding the Twins, and returning the sun to its proper place. From all we've heard, the aims of the Nightbreaker and his people are the same. There is a logical alliance to be made."

Vatri snorted. "Ignoring, for the moment, the fact that nothing in our shared history would make me want to ally with you again—what could you possibly have to contribute to an alliance? What could you provide that equals the power of the Nightbreaker?"

Joros raised a closed fist, and extended one finger. "I have knowledge of the inner workings of the Fallen. I know how they think, and I can anticipate how they will act and react." He raised a second finger. "I have seven—excuse me, *eight*, now—mages loyal to me. The Fallen have many more, but to try to go against them without mages of your own would be sheerest madness." A third finger, and Joros allowed himself to smile. "And I know a means of finding the Twins."

It had been quiet as he spoke, but after those words even the sounds of fidgeting and breathing died. They all waited, and Joros was not ashamed of preening under their undivided attention.

"Explain," Vatri said tersely.

"The sharing of sensitive information is typically reserved for allies . . ."

Vatri growled—*actually* growled, like a dog, and it was almost enough to make Joros laugh. "If you aren't willing to share even the most basic—"

"Wait." The man named Edro put a hand on her arm, and she fell silent. "I know there's . . . a history here. But I would like to hear what he has to say."

At least one of the three had something like a brain between his ears.

Vatri scowled so fiercely he thought it might strip bark from the surrounding trees, but at length she nodded and ground out, "Continue. Please."

"Perhaps," Joros said delicately, "a conversation of this nature would be better had in private." He flickered his eyes pointedly to the crowd that surrounded them. "I'm sure you trust all your people, but I don't have that luxury."

"He's not wrong," Edro murmured, though it was loud enough that Joros—and, likely, no few others—heard it. Joros liked the man more and more.

Vatri, though, didn't particularly seem to like him in that moment. Even so, she could see that he was right. She raised her voice and called out, "Everyone, back to your business. I believe dinner should have been started already, but I don't smell anything cooking. And doubtless there are some few of you who can spend your time searching in the trees for our *friends* in black."

They scattered obediently, save for a handful of what Joros guessed to be self-proclaimed bodyguards. Their number included the handsome woman with the longbow as tall as she was, who kept eyeing Joros. True, it was usually with distrust or uncertainty, but she *was* looking.

Vatri led them toward the largest tent their meager camp had to offer, which still looked hardly big enough to hold a handful of people. Vatri and Edro and Scal went in, leaving their bodyguards outside, and so Joros left most of his group as well—he brought with him Aro, and included Harin so that they wouldn't be outnumbered.

The tent was as small inside as he'd feared, and they had to sit knee to knee in a jagged circle, a ring of frowns—and Aro, who was slowly coming up from his bout of madness and smiling in pleasant confusion at the world.

"So," Vatri said. She and Joros had wound up seated next to each other, by some clever machination of . . . it must have been Edro, because Scal wouldn't care. It meant Joros didn't have to look at Vatri—instead he was across from Edro, the clever man. And Vatri got to stare at Harin, for whom she had no reason yet to harbor any ill will—though Joros expected that wouldn't take long. The merra could find fault with a rock, and wouldn't shy from pointing it out. Though she spoke to Joros, she did it without looking at him, and that suited him just fine. "We have privacy now. Our people *are* trustworthy, but . . . it is true that there is no harm in keeping delicate information to the fewest ears. So please, speak openly."

Over the years, Joros had needed to develop a number of techniques to express his derision inwardly while keeping any sign of it from showing outwardly. His favorite was a sort of mental snort. "Aro and I are one piece of a greater mission," he told Edro. "The mission, of course, being the defeat of the Twins. To that end, we have been seeking information on the Fallen—their whereabouts, their plans, their doings—while simultaneously collecting their mages and helping them recover from what the Fallen have done to them. In every case, the mages have proved so grateful that they've offered their help willingly."

From the corner of his eye, he saw Harin frowning. Rora had often had the same internal struggle written on her face, as she tried to parse if she'd understood his words right, and if the blatant lie was something she should call out. Rora, at least, had generally been smart enough to wait to question him until they were out of earshot. He had no such assurances with Harin.

He went on: "We've developed something of a stronghold, a safe place from which we can operate, but there are still too few of us. In order to combat the Fallen—in order to represent a true danger to the Twins—we must be stronger. And so Aro and I have come in search of allies, and when we heard of the Nightbreaker . . ." Joros shrugged. "It seemed the perfect solution. Almost as if the Parents themselves had crafted it."

"You do not *get* to speak of them," Vatri spat. Joros felt an immense gratification to see horror flicker across Edro's face at her venom. Let her people see what a snake she was.

"Forgive me," Joros said with no contrition. "But you must admit it's an elegant solution. Two groups seeking the same thing—"

"There are likely dozens, hundreds such groups across Fiatera. All strong-hearted people of good conscience would seek to destroy the Twins and return the sun."

"That may be true. But I would argue that few, if any, of these other groups have the actual *power* to accomplish those tasks. Mine does. It seems yours does as well. But neither of our groups can succeed alone. There is power in numbers, power in alliances."

From his own icy silence, Scal rumbled, "There is danger in being alone." He frowned as he said the words, face creasing as deeply as Vatri's fire-scars. He had the look of a man reciting something from a source he could no longer remember.

"Just so," Joros agreed.

Edro leaned forward, elbows on his knees. "I can see the sense in an alliance." Before Vatri could get out too much spluttering, he raised a hand. "It's not a decision any of us can make on our own, and I certainly don't mean to, but the idea has merit. I would hear more." He pierced Vatri with a stern gaze. "In a fight for the future of our world itself, there is no place for old grudges. You can hate him beneath the light of the sun, and not until then."

Oh, but that was nicely handled. Joros turned his head to look at Vatri, intensely curious how she'd react. And her reaction surprised him even more—though there was a tightness in her jaw, she stared down at her folded hands and, at length, gave a single nod of agreement.

Edro nodded in return, and fixed Joros with his attention

once more. "Now then. You say you have a means of finding the Twins. I understand you not wishing to disclose it yet. I won't press you for information on it. So instead: let us assume we are able to find the Twins. What then?"

Another skill Joros had developed was remaining calm in the face of rising panic. His plan was still little more than a few scattered steps in a long stairwell, pieces that might eventually connect, or might spiral off in different directions. There *was* no plan.

But there were facts, and there was always a safety in stating facts. "Since they rose, the Twins have only been growing in power. They may be too strong even now for us to truly fight. So they must be made weak before we have a hope of defeating them." His mind was racing ahead, laying down boards, stringing up ropes, rapidly constructing the skeleton of a staircase even as he stumbled up the shaky steps. "You have the power of the Parents—*doubly* so, with a sword made of their fire and one of their godmarked. If there's anything that can weaken them, it's the Parents' power."

Edro nodded along, his eyes gleaming. "And when they're weak?"

"I should think," Joros said slowly as the last step crystallized above him, shining, "that the power of eight mages and the power of the Parents combined should be enough to bind the Twins once more. Bind them in their mortal bodies, and let them waste away into husks. And if we destroy their *true* bodies, the ones buried beneath the earth, then they will have no hope of anything else."

Grinning, Edro pounded a fist against his knee. "There's a plan a man can sink his teeth into!"

Vatri, as usual, did her best to kill any joy before it had the chance to grow. "They were bound once, and freed. If they're bound again, who's to say they can't be freed again? After all, it was the power of the Parents that bound them in the first place, and that proved not enough."

Of course there are holes in the plan, viper. Joros spread his hands wide. "I have never claimed my way is the only way." He hadn't—but he'd often claimed his was the *best* way, because the plans of fools were not to be trusted. "You merely asked what I and my group had planned, and I told you. You've spent all these months searching for information on where the Twins are—if you've also developed some idea of what you'll do when you find them, please, I would love to hear it." He would mock it to oblivion, and then steal its best parts to bastardize into his own newly formed plan.

He watched Vatri and Edro and Scal exchange glances, and knew they had nothing.

"What is it," Vatri asked, "*exactly,* that you would want from us in this . . . alliance?" She said the word like it was a maggot in her mouth.

"You told me once that when you call on the Parents, they answer. I would have you scream yourself raw calling for them, until they answer with all the power they have. I would have our Northman friend here wielding the Parents' power to strike fear and death at the Fallen, and at the Twins themselves. I would use your people as a spear cast at the Twins, cleaving a hole through the Fallen so that we may reach the Twins, and destroy them."

Vatri nodded. "And what would we get in turn?"

"The location of the Twins. Mages, to supplement the

power of the Parents. My own fighting force to supplement yours. My years of knowledge of how the Fallen operate, and which of their weaknesses we can best exploit. And you get the only plan, so far, that has a hope of defeating them."

Vatri stared beyond Joros, at Aro. "The last plan of yours I knew," she said, "involved using your chosen twins as hosts."

Joros felt his lip curl. "If you wish to point out the clear failure—"

"No. Even the best plans can crumble. I understand that. But I want to know: you spoke of mortal vessels, and fighting the Twins on equal footing. I had a suspicion, then." She was still staring at Aro, and the boy met her piercing gaze with a wrinkled brow. "If things had gone your way. If Rora and Aro had played host to the Twins. Was it your plan to kill them?"

Joros shifted his jaw until it popped. She'd turned her attention to him, now, and her eyes said she knew full well what the answer was. She merely wanted to see if he'd admit it, and if he didn't, she'd have her argument against him and the shaky alliance he offered: How could they trust a man who could not tell an inconsequential truth about something done and gone? He could practically hear her shrill voice making the argument. And much as it pained Joros to admit it, he very badly needed her and her people—he had no willing fighting force, and mages that would only heed him because of the poison that had once run through their veins.

So he held Vatri's gaze, and he said, "I had always hoped it wouldn't come to that. But if it had, if the choice had been between the world and their lives . . . then yes. I would have done it."

She nodded, and had the grace not to look surprised at being given the truth.

Edro seemed to sense that Vatri had the answers she'd wanted. He clapped his hands together and said, "You've given us plenty to talk about. Will you now give us the time to discuss your offer?"

"Of course," Joros said. It wasn't really a request—to refuse them the chance to discuss him and his words would be as good as demanding they refuse his alliance—but Edro had clearly had some experience in etiquette or minor politics.

"Deslan will see that you're made comfortable. We'll speak again when we have an answer."

Joros stood, Harin a heartbeat behind him, and together they pulled the still-frowning Aro to his feet. Joros was pushing the boy toward the tent's exit when a voice rumbled, "What is wrong with him?"

Joros twisted around to face the Northman. "He's sick," he said easily.

"He's a *mage*," Vatri corrected, scowling. "He wasn't in such poor shape the last time I saw him. He's clearly been given the same drug as the other mages we've seen." Her eyes, fixed on Joros, were full of all the judgment he'd expect from a priestess. At Joros's side, Harin went stiff.

"It is true?" Scal asked.

Joros popped his jaw again and chose his words carefully. "An unfortunate mistake. I've been working with him, to help his recovery."

Scal said nothing more, and Joros ushered his people out of the tent. He wanted to think the suspicion in Harin's eyes was only imagined, but of all the pack with him, she had enough of a brain that she might begin to see the cracks in the story he'd told. He'd have to make sure to talk with Harin, smooth over the lies.

The group of Vatri's people that they'd left outside had formed a loose ring around the tent, a respectful distance away but close enough to respond if called for. Joros's people were peppered among them, and all talking animatedly. It was the first time they'd looked anything like happy since leaving the estate. They'd found other peasants who were passionate about their cause—likely down on their luck, simple folk who carried weapons they knew how to use to great effect. The pack were practically at home.

"Deslan?" Joros called, and it was the handsome woman with the longbow who turned at the name. She strolled over to him, bow slung around her shoulder. She looked less mistrustful than she had before, which was a mark in the right column. "They'll likely be talking awhile in there. Edro said you'd be able to see to our comfort as we wait."

She snorted. "'Course he did. I'm no steward . . ." She shook herself, and forced a smile at Joros. Even forced, it was a pleasant smile. "Right. I can find you food and a fire, at least. You lot," she said to the rest of her people, "stay here. The rest of you, come on with me."

As she led them through the camp, Joros tossed idle questions at her about the methods of the Nightbreaker's people, trying to separate the truth from all the legends he'd heard along the way. She answered everything willingly enough, and when she accidentally called Edro "little lordling," she blushed very charmingly. Joros replied with some offhand, scathing remark that made her laugh, and when she caught him eyeing her significantly, she only smiled.

She commandeered a campfire for them, informing its two occupants they'd now be sharing space, and they shuffled around willingly enough. Food would be brought around soon, Deslan promised, and by then the three likely would have come to some agreement. "I'll come back and fetch you when they're ready to talk again," she said.

Joros reached out and gripped her upper arm, and both her eyebrows shot up. "Why don't you stay," he said with his most charming smile. "Surely you need to eat as well, and I'm sure any meal would be made more palatable by your presence."

She laughed, and her eyes gleamed, and she opened her mouth to agree—

"Joros?" a wispy voice said, tugging at his sleeve. "Can . . . can we talk?"

Joros ground his teeth in frustration while not letting his smile slip or his attention waver from Deslan. Still, the moment had shattered. She smiled again, ruefully this time, and said, "We've both got business. The food's good enough—plenty palatable on its own. I'll be back when they're ready to talk with you." She gently shook off his hand, and disappeared back into the camp.

Joros rounded on Aro and nearly thumped the boy. "What do you want?"

"I . . ." He had the grace to cower. "Can we talk? Alone? There's . . ." His hands flailed, as if he could pluck the right words out of the sky.

With a growl and a terse nod, Joros turned to the two who'd originally claimed the campfire. "Will we get shot if we go into the trees?"

"Sentries are mostly looking out," one said, "so's long as you don't go too far, there's nothing to fear."

Joros could have thanked the man, but he was frustrated and ungrateful and looking forward now to beating his mage in private. He stomped into the trees, Aro trailing in his wake. Every tree looked much like the others, and so he chose one at random to stop beside, once there was a screen of trees between them and the fire. "What?" he demanded.

Shoulders hunched, Aro stared at his feet, but Joros could hear his words clearly enough: "You said you would've killed us."

Joros stood by that decision even more in this moment—hells, he almost wished it *had* come to that. "To spare the world this mess, yes, I would have killed you, your sister, and scores more. What of it?"

"You keep us around. Me and Rora. You're always so careful about it. You . . . you still think there's a chance you'll have to use us like that, don't you?"

Maybe his sister wasn't the only one who'd gotten a touch of cleverness, but as Joros wasn't feeling particularly charitable, any cleverness Aro had was rather like a candleflame that burned incandescently for one breath before dying. "The future could bring any manner of things. I try to be prepared for most of them."

"There's something else you said, a while ago. I remember it." Aro looked up, and there was still madness hovering in the boy's eyes, but there was clarity, too. "You said, 'Destroy one, and you destroy them both.' You said that, didn't you?"

Joros frowned, pushing his frustration down a touch. This was not at all the direction he had expected this conversation to go. "I did say that."

"Then . . . if it comes to it . . . I've got a favor to ask you . . ."

And he asked, and Joros—partly because of his frustration and partly because he simply *could*—agreed. When they returned to the camp, Joros saw horror and grief and green sickness written across the boy's face, but he didn't say, *No, wait, I take it back, don't.* He kept his lips together, even when some of the camp folk delivered around bowls of half-palatable food. Aro simply stared into the fire.

When the meal was done, Joros turned his back to the fire, staring through the camp the way they'd come. He didn't fidget, but he was very close to standing up and pacing when he finally heard someone approaching through the darkness. He plastered a smile on his face as he stood up, but it wasn't Deslan who stepped into the ring of their campfire's light. It was the Northman, and Joros was even gladder that he'd stood.

"You've decided?" he asked Scal. His stomach gave a twist—likely the food not sitting well; he wasn't nervous, he didn't *get* nervous. There was only one possible answer they could give. They were fools if they didn't, and he had no interest in working with fools.

"Yes," Scal said, and he took long agonizing moments to look from Joros to the eager faces of all his people, and to Aro, who hadn't moved, who still nursed his bowl of gruel and stared into the fire. Finally he turned back to Joros. "We will help you," he said, and his eyes slipped back to Aro halfway through the sentence.

Joros grinned, and shouted that there must be alcohol

somewhere in this camp, and altogether they managed to turn up a few bottles of cheap wine and a barrel of mead that didn't taste like pure poison. They made do. The camp celebrated the new alliance long into the night, and somewhere in the darkness Joros found Deslan for a celebration of a more private sort. His plan—any plan—would likely see her and all the others dead before it was done, but she wasn't dead yet. And there were things worth celebrating.

CHAPTER THIRTY

When she got to the bottom of the ladder and turned around, Rora saw that Neira was playing with the corpses, and that was just too much.

Rora hadn't *liked* the witches, had hated every minute she was stuck with them, but bleeding hells—they'd been *people*, people she'd got to know. She could recognize the look in Peressey's eye that meant she was about to start spewing fire, knew that when Soris started crying the best thing to calm him was singing, had heard Travin describe all the different kinds of plants in the Highlands so many times she'd probably be able to name them all on sight. They were people, and she'd known them, and Neira was busy cutting all their eyes out.

It pushed Rora right away from scared and into boiling mad.

"Get away from them," she snarled, and Neira's eyeless face twisted toward her. Tare, coming down the ladder still, bumped into Rora, nudged her stumbling forward, but that was fine. Rora stamped the rest of the way to the not-wall. She dropped all the firewood and slammed her hands against the barrier, feeling the sting from her palms to her elbows. *"Get away from them."*

Neira raised her hands, bloody and sticky, one still holding the dagger, and she easily stepped away from the witch she'd been picking at. Travin, the second cellar-witch, who'd been down there almost as long as Rora'd been. There was curiosity written on Neira's face, even without eyes.

"Go sit over there," Rora ordered, jerking her chin toward the space she'd been chained up for so long, the space they'd left Neira tied up in but she'd managed to get out of. Rora realized too late that Neira wouldn't see the chin jerk—but the shadow-woman did go over to the spot. Lucky guess, Rora supposed. The cellar was small.

Neira sat against the wall, folded her bloody hands in her lap, and waited.

It was hard to hold on to the boiling anger, in the face of that. Rora sent a sorry look toward Travin, toward the other witches whose eyes Neira'd gotten to, but it wasn't like they were doing any complaining or any forgiving. Rora picked up the firewood she'd dropped and, with Tare's help, went about building the fire Neira'd asked for.

There wasn't too much of the cellar not taken up by the bubble, so they had to build the fire close to the barrier, and close enough to the open cellar door that the smoke could find its way out without filling the cellar too much. Rora and Tare sat on the other side of the fire, and with the way the flames moved and the way the smoke played with Neira's witchlight, it almost seemed like the not-wall wasn't there, like they were just three normal people sitting around a fire in the night.

But Neira, at least, was a far way away from normal, and she proved it when the first thing she said was, "The sun is still there, you know."

Rora kept her mouth shut, but Tare barked out a laugh. "I told you this was stupid," she said, and she had—she'd kept saying it as Rora filled her arms with firewood, kept saying it as she told some of her knives where they'd be if things went wrong, kept saying it even as they climbed back down the ladder. Rora made the hand sign for *silence* at her again, and was amazed—again—when Tare didn't rip her throat out for it.

"It is," Neira said firmly, with the same calm confidence that Rora'd once seen in a madman explaining to a rock how rain fell up.

Rora folded her hands in her lap and stared at Neira over the tips of the flames. She'd promised she'd listen, and she would.

"If the sun was truly *gone*," Neira went on, "think what the world would be like. Plants would die, and the animals who eat the plants would die. It would be cold—there would be a thousand winters, all at once. The world would collapse, and crumble, and wither away to nothing. That might even be what the Twins truly want—a fresh start, an unencumbered place upon which they can build their better world . . ." Neira lurched up to her feet, so sudden it made both Rora and Tare shift back, hands to daggers—but Neira stalked off, away from the fire, prowling along the not-wall. "You've been outside now. It's *spring*. The snow has melted, crops are growing, and all the wildlife are doing their damnedest to see to the continuation of their species. The world goes on . . . just in darkness."

Rora frowned, because she'd never thought about it, but it did make sense that the sun being gone should've made things colder. It got colder at night, so the Long Night should've been cold. But she'd been wandering the estate with her new freedom, and she'd seen trees going green beyond the walls, she'd seen wildflowers someone had stuck all through the house for decoration, she'd seen baby birds clumsily learning how to fly. The world was getting warmer, not colder.

Neira was pacing now—pacing at the barrier's edge, pacing through the witches' bodies. Her hands were moving inside the sleeves of her robe, but Rora couldn't make out what she was doing. "If you throw a blanket over an apple," Neira said, "you can't see the apple anymore, but it still makes a noticeable lump. That's all they've done. The sun is hidden, not gone. They *lied*." She practically hissed the last bit, and that black smoke suddenly appeared and swelled out from around her feet, full of angry waves like reaching hands.

Tare glanced over at Rora, but Rora didn't take her eyes from the shadow-woman. She knew better than that. She didn't look away, and she didn't take her hand off her dagger. The plain but sturdy one, the one Tare'd given her.

Neira kept pacing, her steps short and sharp, but the smoke settled around her. It didn't go away—just died down and trailed after her. "Grumbling" was the word Rora thought of, without really knowing why. Neira almost seemed like she'd forgotten she wasn't alone.

Rora chewed the inside of her cheek, and finally cleared her throat. Neira's head spun toward her like an owl. Rora said, all careful, "You think there's some way I can help pull that blanket off the sun."

Little flutters shivered through the smoke at Neira's feet, and the woman grinned. "Oh yes," she said.

Rora was starting to feel like this couldn't end quick enough—the sooner Neira got through saying all the things she wanted to say, the sooner Rora could tell her to leave. The sooner Rora could find out if the shadow-woman had been telling the truth, or if she'd have to learn how to kill a witch.

Thinking back on it, Rora realized Neira'd never actually promised to leave peacefully—just that Rora'd never see her again. Sitting there in the cellar, in front of a crazy woman who could make smoke out of blood, Rora realized just how many ways there were to take that.

"Why?" Tare asked, before Rora could think through what to say. Rora was actually surprised she'd been quiet for so long—Tare was more used to giving information than listening to it. "Why would you want to bring the sun back? You're . . . you're one of them."

"You don't know what I am." Neira said it in such a flat, pleasant way, and that was what sent prickles crawling up Rora's neck.

Tare wasn't put off by it. "Then what are you?"

The black smoke writhed, stretching out from Neira to pool against the not-wall, and her grin suddenly looked much more like a skull's smile. "I am vengeance, and I am salvation. I am a power that can shake the world. I am the shadows."

Rora swallowed, and her hand still hadn't left her dagger, and she thought about pulling it even though she didn't know what she'd do with it.

Tare, though, just snorted. "Try that again, but without all the bullshit."

The smoke settled back again, no longer rising waves— but a bunch of it stayed pressed against the not-wall, and it'd shifted to loom directly in front of Tare. Like it was *staring* at her, even though Rora knew that was crazy. Neira's smile turned into just a normal smile. "I do like you," she said. "Your bluntness is . . . refreshing."

"Just say what it is you mean to say."

Neira made a soft, almost amused noise, and the smoke crept back from the not-wall, shrank and faded until it was just a shadow around her feet. Rora made a quick sign with her hand that she hoped Tare saw: *Thanks.*

"I am one of the Fallen." Neira spread her arms so the black robe billowed around her. "One of the truly faithful, one who saw the chance for the Twins to rise and did everything in my power to see it happen. But I have been lied to." She started pacing again.

Now that Rora had her heartbeat a little better under control, she could talk without feeling like it might turn into a scream. She asked, "Who lied?"

"Who hasn't?" Neira almost snapped it, but when Tare made a low growl, Neira *laughed.* "Yes, yes. *Speak plainly.* I am here now because the Twins themselves lied." The smoke was starting to lash again, creeping out to flow over the bodies of the witches. "They promised to tear down the sun." A wave of angry smoke filled her side of the cellar and crashed silently against the barrier. "More, they promised equality in the darkness. That no one should suffer because they were *not good enough.*"

Rora swallowed, trying not to look at the smoke, because doing that reminded her of when she'd last seen Neira, inside Mount Raturo, and she'd felt that black smoke crawling over her skin. She tried to just look at Neira's face, which—even without the eyes—showed the hurt under the anger. "So they lied," Rora said, as evenly as she could.

"As I said, the sun is still here." Neira's bitterness made the smoke swirl wildly.

"And everyone's not even."

"No. They're not."

Neira wasn't the normal kind of witch that Rora'd gotten used to, but it was getting clearer that she was just as badly broken as all the witches Rora'd seen. It was a different sort of broken—the kind that made you want to see everyone else broken, too, because then you wouldn't be the broken one. You wouldn't be not good enough.

"All right," Rora said. "Tell me how you want to stop them."

Neira'd been pacing, but she stopped—didn't turn, just stared off at nothing, at the empty cellar wall. "You've always been clever," she said quietly, still without turning or moving. The smoke still surrounded her but it was motionless as she was. "Resilient, too. Stronger than you think. Things might have been so different if they'd taken you instead . . ."

Neira moved so quickly it made Rora jump, the shadow-woman spinning around at the same time as she dropped into a crouch. The smoke, still unmoving, hid what she was do-ing, but Rora could *hear* it, and she knew the sound of a blade in flesh. It made her stomach churn, made her mouth go dry, made her skin go cold—but she didn't say anything. Dead was dead. The more she listened to Neira, the more interested she was in not pissing the woman off.

"There is a power," Neira said, her voice coming from just above the top of the smoke, "in sacrifice. There is power in blood. There is power in a life. There was a time, before the Fall, when preachers would go around the country making ritual sacrifices for the glory of their gods, and the Twins were filled with so much power. Until the preachers discovered that a *willing* sacrifice gave the Twins yet more power . . . and then they began sacrificing themselves.

"You were there," Neira went on, "when the Twins were freed. I know you fled, but perhaps you stayed long enough to see all those who fell to power their rise. Did you see scores and scores of the Fallen die, all at once?"

Rora didn't like thinking about that day for a lot of reasons. "Yeah. I saw it."

Neira stood, with the smoke swelling around her, and there was blood coating her hands. Rora was glad the smoke hid whichever witch she'd been working on. "There is a power in sacrifice. And on the night the Twins rose, all the Fallen gathered to free them, and all the Fallen were willing to do whatever it took to restore their bound gods."

Into her waiting pause, Rora said, "They were all willing to sacrifice their own lives for the Twins. To give them power."

"But it seems," Neira said with that smoke-swirling bitterness again, "that it was not enough. They needed mortal flesh to be free, but mortal flesh makes them weak. They don't have the power to tear down the sun, or to pass their judgment upon the world, or make all equal under their rule."

"They lied," Rora said softly.

And Neira agreed, "They lied." The smoke shrank back, like a tide slowly letting go of the shore, and Rora didn't take her eyes off Neira's face—didn't want to know what this tide would leave behind. "And now they must be destroyed."

"How?" It was Tare who asked the question that Neira'd been . . . not *avoiding*, but she kept circling away from it and rounding back and kiting away, like she was herding prey toward a trap.

"There is power in blood," Neira said. "My blood flows through all the mages who have been addicted to skura, and when my blood commands them, they will listen. Every one of them."

Rora thought of her brother, going crazy after Anddyr'd dumped the black paste down his throat, his shaking and how terrible he'd looked the last few times she'd seen him, how he'd hissed, *I'm dying here, Rora* . . . She cleared her throat and pushed her mind somewhere else. "How do witches help?"

Neira smiled that skull-smile again. "There is power in a life." She motioned both hands to the floor of the cellar, where the smoke had cleared, but Rora didn't look down. "Their lives, to fuel my power. Other lives, to fuel the Twins', but they're not doing what they should be—if they were enforcing their judgment as *they'd said*, they would have a constant stream of power, but all they're taking is a trickle. They are allowing themselves to be weak. That is what will let us destroy them. When I command it, every mage I control will give their life to me—and then I will have enough power to face the Twins."

"You . . ." Rora groped for the words to describe one of the particular things knotting her gut. "You talk about yourself and the Twins like you . . . like you work the same. Like you have the same . . . *powers* they do."

Neira laughed again, ripples flowing through the smoke. "I'm not the first one in history to wield the power Sororra once taught freely, but I am the first one in a very long time. I know how the Twins work. I know what they *could be*. That they are not taking the power rightfully theirs is the same kind of weakness Sororra has always despised in humanity, the same—"

"You said you'd face the Twins," Tare interrupted, sounding almost impatient. It was the same tone Rora recognized from all her years of training, and it got very close to putting a smile on her face—of course Tare wasn't scared. Didn't keep Rora from feeling the chills creep-crawling down her arm with every word from Neira, but she was glad she wasn't facing this alone. "What, just you against them, hoping you kill enough witches that you're stronger?"

"If only it were so easy. I will face them, and I will *push* them. If they are driven from their human hosts, they will try to return to their true bodies. I can send them fleeing, and then they can be caught, and *redirected*." Neira paused, and the empty holes of her eyes turned to Rora.

"Redirected," Rora repeated, wishing she didn't understand the word, didn't understand everything Neira was saying, "into me, yeah? Me and Aro."

"Precisely."

Rora didn't ask what'd come once she was playing host to one of the Twins. She knew. The answer was all in Neira's smile and her gone, dead eyes. Hearing it would turn it into something she couldn't pretend she didn't know. "So how are we supposed to trust you? How in all the hells do you expect me to think you're not just lying about everything? How'm I supposed to know you're not just trying to destroy everyone who might get in the way of the Twins?"

"I'm no liar," Neira said, her voice dangerous and low. She brightened up some when she said, "I've known you most of your life." Tare startled, but Rora didn't dare look away. "I've never hurt you, have I?"

Rora rolled her shoulder and felt the skin there stretch where Neira's nails had left deep gouges. "You did. After you—after the witches."

The way Neira laughed made it sound like Rora'd just told her favorite joke. "You were trying to kill me," she pointed out, all cheerful about it. Her voice changed to something almost like annoyed when she added, "You didn't even give me the chance to explain myself. You just assumed the worst of me. What would you have had me do?"

Killing a half-dozen people in the space of a breath was a damn good reason for not trusting someone, as far as Rora was concerned—but then again, Rora herself *had* jumped to killing Neira pretty quickly. Maybe that made them something like even. Rora couldn't quite bring herself to say that out loud, but she made a grumbling noise to show she understood.

"So excepting that dark moment in both our lives." Neira's smile was a little crooked, when it was an honest smile.

Rora thought about how much shadows had haunted her nightmares, but it was true enough. In all those years, Neira'd never done her any real harm. "No. You've never hurt me."

"I'm always fair and kind to those who serve my purposes."

"What about the people who don't?"

Neira smiled, softly this time. "Obstacles can always be overcome."

Tiredness washed over Rora all of a sudden. So much had happened in the last few hours, in the last few days, in the last few months. It had to've been close to a year since she'd run away from the Canals and the pack, and she just hadn't *stopped* since then. This—the crazy shadow-woman and defeating the Twins and witches that could be controlled with just a word from the right mouth—it all felt like one more step than Rora could manage. She put her face into her hands and pressed her fingers against her eyelids until all the world glowed white.

Neira didn't say anything for a while, and fabric rustled like she was sitting down, though Rora didn't look up to see. At least there weren't any dagger-in-flesh sounds this time. Neira's voice was soft when she finally said, "I only have one other thing to say to you, Rora. Those who follow the Parents believe that staring into the heart of a fire will show you the truth. So look into the fire, and tell me what you see."

It was stupid. It was so stupid. Rora dropped her hands from her face and looked over at Tare, but Tare was staring at the fire between them and Neira and frowning. The light hadn't touched the shadowy smoke around Neira.

Rora looked up to the shadow-woman, who was staring at her, or maybe at the fire. It was hard to tell, with the no eyes. Her smile was gone, and she just looked deadly serious. "Please," Neira said.

Rora sighed, and put her elbows on her knees, and leaned in to look at the fire.

It was just a fire. Just red and yellow and orange, and heat on her face, and smoke that made her throat feel thick.

"I see you," Tare said softly, and Rora could hear the frown in her voice. When she turned her head, Tare was staring at her instead of the flames. Tare acted like she'd got caught looking at something she shouldn't and turned back to the fire, frowning harder, her whole forehead wrinkling up.

"Rora?" Neira asked.

"I don't see anything." She looked back at the flames, but they were still just flames. She didn't see her own face in the dancing shapes they made.

"You have to open your heart, and clear your mind. You—"

"You can't believe this," Rora interrupted. She'd heard plenty of Neira's talking, and she'd had enough. She was ready to find out if the woman would leave like she'd promised, and how much blood she thought she'd be taking with her. "You don't believe in the Parents. Why would you believe some dumb superstition from gods you don't even care about?"

Neira's head tilted a little to the side. "I've seen so much, Rora. As much as you have, if not more. And I know the gods can choose strange ways to communicate with the world." She shrugged, opened her hands, and smiled with just one side of her mouth. It was the most honest smile Rora'd seen from her so far. "I have seen things when staring at a fire, and I know others who have as well, and I think it would be madness not to listen when the gods speak. *Any* gods."

Rora glanced over at Tare again, but the older woman was still staring at the fire. Rora couldn't tell if she'd even heard anything Neira'd said. But Neira was still staring at her, waiting, so Rora tipped up her chin and stared at the place where Neira'd had eyes once, and she asked, "What do *you* see?"

Neira looked away from her, down to the fire, and after a quiet minute she said softly, "I see an army. A small force, but powerful. And I see them cleaving through Raturo."

Rora rubbed her mouth and looked down at the flames, too. It was just a fire, just a stupid fire. "What'm I supposed to see?"

"I can't tell you what to see, Rora. I can only tell you how to look."

It felt a lot like getting drunk, only before you actually got drunk—when there was a group of you, all drinking your drinks, and everyone else started laughing and singing because they were feeling the drink, only you hadn't really started feeling it yet. But everyone else was getting good and drunk, so maybe you started acting like you were drunker'n you actually were, until you couldn't tell anymore if it was really the drink making you stupid or if it was just you.

Rora stared at the flames, squinted so that the edges blurred even more, and maybe—just maybe, just for a second—it looked like a cow floating through the fire. If she closed one eye, the way the flames moved looked like water in the Canals, running sluggish through old channels.

And then she saw a boy. Even though the flames still danced and flickered, they kept his shape. There were chains around his wrists, holding his arms spread wide open at one end and the other ends attached above, somewhere she couldn't see. He hung like that, just from his wrists, and blood streamed down his arms and sides and legs to float away into embers. His eyes burned like coals, but Rora knew that was blood, too, that his eyes were gone, same way she knew his lips were sewn together. But he stared at her out of the flames, and she knew his face, even as broken as it was: Etarro, the boy who'd saved her inside Mount Raturo. The boy who'd been sacrificed to a god.

He stared at her, and he tried to call out to her, but he couldn't with his lips sealed shut. He fought, tugging at the chains around his wrists, his skinny chest heaving, but he couldn't break free. Ash boiled out of his eyes, and his whole body went slack, and his head sagged forward, chin resting against his chest.

"What do you see?" Neira asked softly, and then the flames were just stupid flames again.

Rora must've leaned too close, the smoke'd made her eyes water and she rubbed at them hard. The smoke was thick in her throat, too, made her sound like she was half choking when she said, "Anddyr kept saying Etarro was still alive . . ." She couldn't look at the fire, and she didn't want to look at Neira, so Rora just stared at her hands. Her fingers were twisted around each other so tight they couldn't move, not even a bit, not even a tremble. "Is . . . d'you think he was right?"

"I don't know." Neira sounded sad about it, but Rora couldn't tell if she was sad over thinking about Etarro, or sad over not having the answer to everything. "In all of history, nothing like this has ever happened before."

Rora's fingers were aching, with how hard they were twisting around each other. A hand touched her wrist, and she looked over, surprised to see Tare sitting there—for a little while, the world'd melted down to just Rora and Neira and the fire between them. Tare pressed at the back of her hand until Rora opened her fingers, let her hands come apart. Her joints ached. Tare's hand didn't leave—her fingers curled around Rora's, holding without squeezing, gentle.

Rora closed her eyes. If she squeezed them shut tight enough, the world burst into white again, but she still saw Etarro's battered face screaming. And if she squeezed her eyes too tight, his face turned into Aro's, and she thought she'd be sick.

She blurted out the words that were stuck in her throat, because it was them or puke. "I'll help you."

Tare's fingers shifted, the two middle ones tucking up against Rora's palm—the hand sign for *good*.

Neira bowed her head. She was either a good actress, or more honest than most people Rora'd met. She didn't care anymore which was true. The nod of appreciation felt good. "Thank you," Neira said.

The cellar was filling with smoke, maybe that was what was making Rora feel so crowded, so small, so cornered. Maybe she would've tried to run, if Tare's hand wasn't keeping her grounded. But she did want to leave the cellar, leave it behind forever, seal the fire up inside it and let it burn away everything that'd ever touched the room.

"So how d'we get you out?" she asked Neira, because that'd put Rora the next step closer to being able to leave. "If Anddyr put this wall-thing up . . ."

Neira looked up, and gave an apologetic smile. When she stood, her smoke surged forward and hit the barrier, racing along it, covering it—and then the air shimmered, and the smoke fell like water from a broken cup. It pooled on the floor, creeping slowly toward the fire, creeping slowly toward Rora—

And stopped. Shrank back, and faded, and the sorry smile was back on Neira's face.

"You could've done that anytime," Rora said around the heart-sized lump of fear in her throat.

"I thought you'd be more comfortable with it in place."

Rora swallowed. She'd committed to working with a not-witch who was only a different kind of crazy than all the witches—she'd have to get used to doing that without running and screaming every time Neira did something crazy. Still . . . Rora said, "Leave your dagger over there." Neira laughed and raised her arm, the dagger held far away from her body. The sound when she dropped it made Rora's teeth hurt. Neira's empty eyes looked back at Rora, waiting, patient.

Rora opened her hand, and Tare let her fingers go. All three stood up at about the same time, and Tare kicked the fire to half-burning pieces. Rora led the way up the ladder.

It was still night out, of course, still dark. But the night was full of clear air, and stars, and a sliver of moon that looked like the sky was giving a crooked smile. Rora closed her eyes, not hard enough to see white, but enough to swallow down the image of Etarro trapped and trying to scream for help. Not like she'd ever forget it, but she couldn't walk around living any kind of normal life with that stuck at the front of her eyes. There were some things you had to bury, or they'd bury you.

She opened her eyes. Tare stood to one side, Neira at the other. Even a day ago, that would've seemed like the wrongest thing in the world—either of 'em at her side, much less both. And maybe it didn't feel *right*, but it was the best she had. Her fingers, which still ached a little, curled up, the two middle fingers tucked in. It was good.

CHAPTER THIRTY-ONE

The trees whispered as Anddyr walked, and when he caught pieces of their voices, he didn't like what they had to say.

"*You won't do it.*"

"*Coward.*"

"*You'll never find them.*"

"*You don't have the heart for it.*"

"*Worthless.*"

"*Never was very brave.*"

"*You'll never find him.*"

Anddyr hunched his shoulders against their cruelties, and hugged the stuffed horse tighter against his chest. Sooty felt very much like a shield.

He stopped when he found a quiet place, a stone outcropping that formed a cave that was sheltered from the chatty trees. Anddyr nestled into the little cave, and set Sooty carefully beside him. His impossible Sooty. She watched fearfully as he settled his limbs, adjusted his back to keep the stone wall from digging into it, shifted and twitched and wasted time.

The trees were right. He was scared.

Anddyr took a deep breath. Waiting wouldn't make it any

easier. He closed his eyes, blocking out Sooty's concerned face, and he thought of *Find me* . . .

The skytower builds its structure around him, intangible and solid. Fratarro kneels there, and Anddyr can't tell whose eyes stare up at him—the boy's or the god's.

Fratarro raises both hands, and a bundle sits in his palms, wrapped in layers of cloth, knotted tight. Anddyr feels its call even from where he stands across the skytower room. It's like a pulse, like a living thing with wants and needs, like a heart torn free and proffered.

Anddyr knows, now, how this place works. It's impossible, but it is. He walks across the room though he doesn't have legs, kneels before Fratarro, and reaches with hands that don't exist. He wraps his palms over the boy-god's, and Fratarro smiles a sad, terrible smile, and says nothing.

In the cave, Anddyr opened his eyes and stared down at the thing in his hands. As impossible as Sooty, but it was there nonetheless. Even wrapped up, he knew it for what it was, felt its summons like a pulse. *Find me. Find me.*

The last time he had held the seekstone linked to Etarro-who-was-Fratarro, it had burned through his mind—burned like fire, and it might have killed him if Joros hadn't knocked it from his hand. There was no one here now to save him. If the fire from the god's mind burned through his own, he would simply die, alone and unmourned.

Sooty stared at him with a hint of reproach in her button eyes—she'd always been so calm and self-assured. He envied her that.

"If it kills me," he said to her, reasonably, "then what will happen to you?"

From outside his shelter, the trees hissed, *Coward, coward, coward . . .*

Anddyr put his face in his hands. "I'm not!" he said into his palms. But they were all judging him now, Sooty and the trees and the bundle waiting in his lap. Still aloud, but only to himself, Anddyr said, "This is what I meant to do . . . I wouldn't have taken it if I didn't mean to use it. I will use it." He straightened his back, and called to the trees, "I *will*! You'll see." Sooty still stared at him, though, and so he amended, "Just not yet. I'm not ready yet."

Before he left his shelter, he ripped one sleeve off his robe and draped it over his head to tie beneath his chin, making sure the sleeve wrapped snugly over his ears. It did block out some of the whispering when he started walking again—not all of it, but enough that what he could hear, he could pretend was the murmur of his heartbeat in his ears.

"I will," he muttered out loud. "When I'm ready."

And so he continued walking, not entirely sure what direction he was going. It didn't matter—he needed to go the direction he hadn't learned yet. Once he was ready, he could fix his feet.

After a time, Anddyr pawed the sleeve from around his head, staring down at it, perplexed. His madness—leftover strains of the skura that had run rampant through his system—manifested in such strange ways. He usually had a hard time remembering, once he was clearheaded, why in the world he'd done something while mad. It felt, lately, like it was getting worse—the madness more mild overall, but *deeper*. More insidious.

He stuffed the sleeve into a pocket and paused, his fingers brushing against a different lump of fabric. The seekstone. The fear of taking it out, of trying to use it . . . that he could remember. It had seemed such a good idea when he'd taken it . . .

The ground and the trees sloped away suddenly, a rough incline down into a pocket of a valley where a perfect, idyllic village sat, rooftops lit by moonlight. Anddyr rocked to a halt at the edge of the basin, frozen by indecision. It had been so long since he'd been around other people, *real* people. It had been years since he'd been a free man, out among other free men, all doing as they pleased with no concern of losing control and sending a bolt of flame streaking out to kill anyone nearby. It would be so nice to feel normal again . . . but he *wasn't* normal. The fact he'd thought it necessary to tie breeches around his head more than proved that.

Still. He hadn't brought any food, or any water. He would need both, sooner or later. A village of any size should have some of both to spare.

Yes. He, a weary traveler, would go into the village and barter for supplies, and make small talk with people who didn't know what he was, and when he was done he would leave. Nothing harmed, nothing broken.

Anddyr started down the incline.

It was steeper than he expected at points, knocking him down to his rear to avoid pitching onto his head, and forcing him to scuttle down like a crab. Halfway down the incline he noticed the switchback trail cutting down into the valley. He likely could have found its head easily from up on the ridge, but now it was far enough away from him that he'd need to spend just as much time walking sideways to reach it as he would slipping down to the valley floor. It might save him a broken neck, though, which—as a root grabbed his foot and sent him stumbling a few terrifying, headlong lengths down the incline—was rather appealing.

He kept going down. He was almost to the valley anyway.

Anddyr half expected there would be villagers waiting for him—waiting to laugh in the face of the man who'd come flailing down into their village—but there wasn't anyone. Maybe they were all sleeping—he had no idea what time it was—did time mean anything anymore? Regardless, he managed to walk firm-footed into the village proper with what little dignity he had.

He expected someone to stop him, with a greeting or a rebuke or a curious gaze, but no one did. No doors opened, no windows twitched, no feet sounded upon the ground.

"—mentioned another village," came a soft voice from what Anddyr guessed to be the center of the town. "To the east by a day or so. He said there were enough people willing to hear his words that it may be worth our visiting."

Anddyr's steps slowed, and he moved deeper into the shadows against the houses as he continued forward. He couldn't name *why*, but it all felt wrong . . .

He came to the edge of a house, which let him peer into the village's small square. And then Anddyr froze.

Four people stood at the center of the village, and though they might have otherwise been unremarkable-looking people, they *were* remarkable in that they stood as the rest of the village, a few dozen people, lay prone along the ground before them. Even in the moonlight, Anddyr knew the look of black robes. Even in the moonlight, Anddyr knew the look of blood.

"How many?" another of the four asked.

"No more than this. But you know any are a help."

"A good hunter doesn't take only the easy prey."

"A good hunter must eat, like anyone. And if the choice is between a lean rabbit and starvation, even the best hunter will choose the rabbit."

Anddyr slowly, carefully moved back away from the square. A group of preachers, and they had slaughtered a village, and they spoke of the next one. He might have tripped over his own heart, for as deeply as it had sunk.

The need to flee burned in him, and as soon as he was out of sight of the square, he nearly did take off at a desperate sprint. But he stopped himself—if he went back the way he had come, even if he took the switchback trail up the incline, surely they would see him. It was a wonder that his near fall down the hill hadn't gotten their attention, though judging by the fresh sheen of blood on cobblestones, they'd been rather occupied until very recently. From up on the ridge, he'd noticed that the village sat in a little bowl, and though the far incline had looked slighter, there was still no easy way to leave the place unseen. And Anddyr very, very badly wanted not to be seen.

"We are safe," Anddyr whispered to himself, squeezing his eyes shut, willing the words to be true. "We are secure." He took a deep breath, which he could convince himself didn't tremor at all. "We are strong." He opened his eyes, and let the breath out, and reached for the door handle of the closest house. It was unlocked. Anddyr gave thanks to his god as he slipped into the house, and shut the door behind him.

The next stretch of time passed in a blur. Though Anddyr had felt at his sanest when he'd entered the village, his time in the cellar had taught him that stress could trigger the madness in his blood. He huddled in a swirling hell, hoping that the screaming was only in his head and not coming out of his mouth.

Somewhere within the madness, a realization struck him, and so when he returned to himself—minutes or hours later, impossible to tell—he was cradling the bundle that held the seekstone, and the realization still burned sharply in his mind.

He checked, first, to make sure the group of Fallen were gone. The village held only the dead, including one black-robed preacher among the neatly arranged corpses. Anddyr couldn't look at any of them for too long. He returned to his commandeered house, arms still wrapped tightly around his bundle, and wondered idly which bodies this house had belonged to. It didn't matter; with a little searching, he found the sharpest knife they'd owned.

He laid the bundle out on their roughhewn table, carefully unwrapped the layers from around the seekstone heart until the blue stone was allowed to breathe once more, sitting like a blue star in an endless black sky.

It was simple, really. He needed to find Etarro-who-was-Fratarro, and for that he needed to use the seekstone. But when he'd touched it, it had burned his eyes and mind quicker than he could parse any useful information. That was the part he'd been balking at: the pain. But he'd realized that the mind-burning was nothing to fear—his mind was already a burned and blackened husk. Damage to his mind was something he could handle. That left only his eyes to worry about . . . and seeing the preachers, with their eyeless faces, had given him the key.

He'd seen the ritual hundreds of times inside Raturo. He knew precisely what to do. The knife wasn't a spine of ice taken from the Icefall within the mountain's depths, but it would do.

"Guide me," he whispered. The words didn't matter; only the intent. "You keep asking me to find you. Let me." He raised the knife and looked past its sharp, shimmering tip. He saw its descent as though the world had slowed around it—without really *seeing* it grow closer, larger, sharper.

If the petitioner was faithful enough, and opened their heart to the judgment of the Twins, the sacrifice of one's eyes would give a blessing from the gods. No one had ever talked about it openly, but everyone knew the blessing gave them a *different* kind of sight. To see without seeing, to see what no one else could . . . that was what he needed.

An impulsive, instinctive blink fluttered his eyelashes against the knife's tip. Its point loomed before him, filling his vision, blurring as he still looked past it. Lower still—

Pain blossomed under the knife's gentle kiss, and Anddyr could not help but see. There was a wet *pop*, and a flood of fluid down his cheek, and his other eye watched the knife leave— tried to watch it with both eyes, and the shifting of muscles beneath the damaged one sent sharp, stabbing tendrils of pain throughout his body.

There was pain, but Anddyr knew pain. The pain didn't scare him.

He watched his hand raise the knife again. He could not help but see, and he could not stop what he had started. He had to *find me* . . .

It hurt less, the second time. Perhaps it was only the blessing of not having to see, from the corner of his other eye, the knife as it went in. He only felt it, sharp edges leaving behind clean and perfect destruction. Only heard the knife as his fingers finally released it and it clattered to the floor.

The darkness he found himself in was touched with red, like Sororra's Eyes that had hung watching in the night sky before she had been freed, red bursts of pain and fear and anguish. Anddyr waited, whispering, "Please," and "I am safe. I am strong," and still there was only the red-tinged darkness.

The bottom fell out of Anddyr's stomach, and the world rushed around him, and he felt like vomiting.

Pain had driven away any slow-lingering madness, leaving him feeling more clearheaded than he had in a very long time—leaving him to realize just how much of an utter idiot he was. Why, *why* had he thought the Twins would give him anything? He'd never been one of their followers, he didn't want to help them beyond what it took to help trapped Etarro. Of course they wouldn't grant him their blessing, and he'd been a fool to think they would—

The darkness changed.

Oh, it was still black, but now there were shades of black coming slowly into focus—a lighter black filling the walls of the house that surrounded him, a darker black for the knife upon the table. But the world, all the world that he could see again, was built from shifting smoke.

The seekstone flickered with dull blue lights, like candleflames glimpsed and gone through a swirling mist. When Anddyr reached for it, tentatively, he stopped and screamed, terrified until he realized the shifting blue smoke was what made up his hand. His heartbeat thrummed as he stretched out his arm, turned it this way and that, raised the other one as well, and watched the blue smoke swirl through him.

And then, before he had time to think better of it, because that had worked out fine already, Anddyr reached out to grab the blue of the seekstone with the blue of his hand.

It was instant, and agonizing.

Fire sparked behind his missing eyes and, when he didn't let go of the seekstone, spread to fill his skull. It raged and flared, and the way it flickered in his mind promised, *Let go, or it will be worse.* Anddyr clenched his teeth around his spiraling screams, and clenched his hand around the seekstone. He knew pain; the pain didn't scare him.

The smoke in his eyes swirled furiously, growling faces emerging and retreating, gaping maws that rushed toward him and dissolved. And the house around him disappeared, replaced by gentle hills that nearly melded with the sky, the swirling line between the heavens and the earth even further blurred. In the distance, piercing the skyline, were the towers and walls of a city. Blue-smoke people dotted his sight, wreathed in black flame, their forms flickering and blazing like the fire in his mind. And ahead was a shining beacon, a form made of light itself, and she smiled as she beckoned to him. Her face was indistinct, too bright to make out features, but he knew her nonetheless: *Sororra.*

And though his mind still burned, though the fire of it threatened to burst through his skull and pour from his mouth and nose and ears, through the searing pain, he still felt a *tug.* A beckoning, like Sororra's outstretched hand. He could find them, a map scrawled behind his eyes, drawn in arrow-straight lines of fire, and the screaming in his mind sounded almost like, *Find me . . .*

Anddyr's fingers loosened, and the seekstone fell from his hand, and he fell to the ground beside it. There was darkness, and it was absolute.

CHAPTER THIRTY-TWO

This is the place."

Keiro lifted his head slowly, exhaustion running through his veins. But he fixed his eyes on the preacher who had spoken, one of the informal scouts Sororra had requested. The woman was tall, and eyeless, and one of the most obstinately pious people Keiro had ever met. Sororra loved her. No—Sororra *was thrilled* by her. With Sororra, the distinction was important.

Keiro looked around slowly. The place Derra had led him was flat and featureless, likely some farmer's field at one point or another. He'd preferred the gentle, sprawling hills they'd passed through a few days ago—they'd reminded him of the hills near the Plains, where he'd been happy, before everything had changed.

Derra had led him ahead of their group, claiming to have found a place that met Sororra's exacting specifications. Looking around slowly—feeling almost too tired even to turn his head—Keiro suspected that this was, indeed, the place.

Secluded, but near enough to a number of surrounding towns or villages—they'd passed through two within the hour, and Derra promised there were others within the same distance. Featureless, and untouched by humans, and enough space for growth. Most importantly, within a day's walk of Mercetta, the capital city of Fiatera.

"Go," he said to Derra. "Bring them all here."

"This *is* the place, isn't it?" she asked excitedly. "It seems perfect, just the kind of place they—"

"Derra," he interrupted. "Go."

Still she hesitated. "You're . . . you're not coming back to tell them yourself?"

Keiro turned to look at her, his one remaining eye to both her missing ones, but she knew, or felt, or saw his look. She quailed before it. With her missing eyes, she had seen what happened to those who opposed him. Derra left, picking her way back toward the road, until the darkness hid her from his sight.

There was a mask he wore, shaped by all the things he needed to be. He allowed himself to take it off only when he was alone, only when there was no one to see him without his armor. He could not let anyone think of him as weak. As Derra walked away, Keiro let his mask fall, and the exhaustion hit him the same way it always did. He could keep his back straight and his head high for as long as he needed to, but as soon as he allowed himself a reprieve, the weight of it all came near to crushing him.

Keiro sat down on the ground. The grass was short, but soft, and it tickled at his elbows. He wanted so badly to sleep, but that would be dangerous—though it would be some time before Derra returned with the others, there was no telling *how* long, and no guarantee he would wake in enough time. And if they found him sleeping . . .

Keiro shook his head, half in denial and half to wake himself up.

"You can sleep," a soft voice said behind him. Keiro did not need to turn—that was a voice he would know anywhere. Cazi, who was always there, even if he was not always seen. The Starborn slunk to Keiro's side and lay at his side, tail curling around Keiro in comfort or protection. *"I will watch."*

It was so very tempting . . . "You won't know when they're close any better than I will. I'm fine. I can manage. I'll have to." He could not let himself slip, not even for a moment.

A rustling made Keiro twist, and another *mravigi* slunk forward through the grass—belly low to the ground, as though trying to move through the knee-high grass the same way they'd moved through grass that was taller than a man. Another followed, and more, and more—

"We will watch," one of them said. The pattern of the star-bright scales was unique to each *mravigi*, would identify who had spoken, but they blurred before Keiro's eye, the stars on the ground and the stars in the sky. Twins' bones, he was tired . . . *"Sleep. We will wake you before they arrive."*

It was easy to argue with Cazi—he was young, still, and his steadily growing vocabulary left him ill-equipped for any real persuasion. More importantly, he was only one, and loyal as optimistic as he was, Cazi couldn't do everything. But *all* the Starborn—the hundreds of them that had lived beneath the ground and watched over the sleeping Twins, that had followed the Twins on their circuitous journey from the hills to Fiatera, that had remained unshakingly loyal—Keiro could trust them with his life. They were, perhaps, the only ones who knew the stakes as well as he.

And he wanted so badly to sleep.

When he leaned back, Cazi was there, as he always was.

The Starborn curled around Keiro, a solid pillow of flesh and scale, and the soft glow of his star-speckled scales lulled Keiro quickly to sleep. He got so little of it that he could sleep almost anywhere.

He dreamed of fire, and of Sororra's eyes.

Entirely too soon, Cazi woke him. *"Be here soon,"* he said, and Keiro sat up, back sore, head sore, heart sore. He checked the position of the stars—it had been little more than two hours since Derra had left. They hadn't gone so far ahead of the group, and that likely meant they'd stopped in one or more of the villages. That very possibility was why Keiro had chosen to wait.

Keiro stood, twisting his back to feel his spine pop, stretching his arms. He felt more tired on waking than he had when he'd fallen asleep, but that was nothing new. Whatever sleep he did get was fitful, exhausting, plagued by dreams— nightmares, he supposed. Could it be called a nightmare when the night never ended?

The other *mravigi* were nowhere in sight, away in the grass or the fields or the trees, away wherever it was they spent their time. Perhaps they *were* still nearby—Keiro had long suspected they could dim their scattered glowing scales at will, but he'd never seen them do it, and if it was a trick Cazi had learned, he kept it a secret as well.

A snout bumped against Keiro's hand, and he looked down into Cazi's red eyes. The ember-glow of them was always comforting. *"Strong now,"* Cazi said. Like a child, the *mravigi* was still learning to speak, but he didn't need a large vocabulary to make himself understood. Keiro rubbed the small flap of Cazi's ear in thanks, and turned to face the direction from which they would approach. He waited, back straight, single eye fearless. His mask was firmly back in place.

And they came. Gods among men, and their loyal retinue.

Sororra and Fratarro led their followers, as they always had. Though they wore the bodies of children, there could be no mistaking them: as they approached, Keiro could feel the waves of their power radiating off them, pounding like a second heartbeat. He wondered, sometimes, how anyone could be near them and not be driven mad. He wondered why anyone would want to stay.

But those wonderings did not come often. Keiro had grown expert at quashing those sorts of thoughts.

"A fine place you've found for us!" Sororra called out. She was practically overflowing with joy, almost childlike in her glee, but that was a dangerous comparison to make.

Keiro bowed as they approached. "I thought it might suit your needs."

In the crowd of followers, Derra shifted but said nothing. Everyone knew she had found the place, but it had been Keiro who sent her looking, and so Keiro would get the acclaim. Such was the way of the world.

There were some new faces in the crowd of followers. Not very many, not many at all, but some. They must have stopped in two of the villages, then.

"Does it meet all your requirements?" he asked. As Sororra gazed happily around the chosen spot, Keiro tried to catch and hold Fratarro's eyes. If the god wished to speak against this place, or have Keiro speak against it, as he had the last likely spot, their time was running quickly by. Finally Fratarro gave him a glance, and a small shake of his head in the negative. Keiro felt his shoulders relax in relief—this leg, finally done!—but the feeling was short-lived. The tension he'd been carrying between his shoulder blades spread to suffuse his entire body. Fratarro would not meet his eyes again to answer Keiro's silent, desperate question: *Are you really ready?*

"Yes," Fratarro said, which made his sister crow with joy, "this will do."

They all cleared space for their gods, backing away until the Twins were little more than darker shadows in the night. Keiro couldn't hear what Sororra murmured in her brother's ear, and he couldn't see clearly the line of Fratarro's back to know if the words helped or hurt. But at length Sororra left his side, and came to join her followers, all watching with expectant eyes. She bounced on the balls of her feet, fidgeting with her hands before her. A feral grin covered her face, but didn't quite touch her eyes.

He can do it, Keiro thought fiercely, and he knew the thought was not entirely his own.

Fratarro spread his arms, and the ground beneath Keiro's feet began to tremble.

For a long while, nothing happened save the trembling, the earth growling a low warning like a threatened dog. When things did begin to change, it was so imperceptibly at first that Keiro didn't notice until he closed his eye against the pounding in his skull. When he opened it again, he startled to see that the ground before Fratarro had bulged upward, swollen, *swelling*, as though something were trying to break free—

Sororra crowed again, her laughter ringing bright, and the

boil surged higher. A hill, burst forth from the earth below, pulled from nothingness, shaped by Fratarro's hands and his powers.

Keiro's heart swelled with pride as the hill grew taller, wider, a Mount Raturo in miniature and growing rapidly. He really *could* do it. Even with his useless hand, and the lacking powers it represented, Fratarro could still shape the earth to his will. He had made minor shapings well enough, but *this*, this showed his true power, the power he had wielded centuries ago when he had pulled a mountain from the earth, when he had made a paradise and a race to populate it, the power of creation itself. It proved to Keiro and Sororra and to Fratarro himself that he was not useless, that it hadn't all been for nothing. It proved that there was hope, yet.

The mound grew quickly to a hill, to a small mountain, and then its growth slowed, until it stopped entirely. It was a mountain, there was no denying that, but it was nothing close to the size of Mount Raturo, and wouldn't even challenge some of the Highlands mountains. Keiro's heart sank as he watched Fratarro lower his arms, shoulders curving forward, spent. In their whispered conversations, Sororra had declared their new home would be far bigger than Raturo, a lance to touch the moon itself, tall enough they could see beyond every edge of the world. Fratarro, with a tight smile, had always agreed. And they had both looked to Keiro: Sororra's gaze daring him to challenge her, and Fratarro's alternating between begging him not to and hoping that he would.

Sororra was no longer crowing, and the smile had fallen from her face.

Keiro turned quickly to face their followers and raised up

his arms. "Look!" he cried. "Look at the glorious new home Fratarro has made for us. We will fill its halls—" Gods, he prayed Fratarro had shaped halls into the place, it would be his head if he lied to them now. "And people shall flock to beg entrance, and the citizens of Mercetta will quake with fear to see us looming over them." The followers sent up a raucous cheer—they didn't know the mountain was meant to have been bigger; didn't have desperate hopes that were so easy to dash; didn't need to wear a mask so crushingly tight.

Sororra forced a smile at them all and then turned her back, striding quickly toward her brother.

"Wait a moment," Keiro told the followers when they'd stopped cheering. "We must make sure everything is in order." He moved more slowly as he went to join the Twins where they stood together in the shadow of the new-made mountain.

As he approached them, he could hear Sororra saying, "—did perfectly fine." She had her arm around her brother's hunched shoulders, the sides of their heads pressed together. Keiro felt an intruder, but why did they keep him if not for moments like this? "You pulled a mountain from the earth! You made us a new home."

"It's not what we wanted," Fratarro said. Keiro heard the incrimination in his voice; heard *you* where he said *we*. But as usual, any anger Fratarro felt was twisted to point only at himself. His good hand was wrapped around the bad one, squeezing and rubbing as though it had only gone numb and would work again if he could just get his blood flowing through it. "If it wasn't for—"

"You knew this was a possibility," Keiro interrupted. He'd learned to redirect Fratarro before he could spiral down too deeply. "You knew it was a possibility, too, that *nothing* would happen. This is a success, by all counts."

Both Twins looked at him, and neither had anything friendly or particularly charitable in their eyes. But Fratarro sighed, and shrugged off his sister's arm. "We'll practice more," he told Keiro. "It's as you said. 'Practice will make all the difference.'" He forced a smile at his sister, brittle and already half broken. "One day, I'll be strong enough."

Fratarro turned to the mountain, and gestured expansively back toward their followers. The Fallen cheered and raced forward, eagerly going to the hidden entrances Fratarro showed them, learning the trick to opening the doors, exclaiming over the brilliance and the beauty of the home Fratarro had built them. It would be good for Fratarro, to receive praise unbidden. Keiro hoped it would take some of the brittleness from his smile.

At his side, Sororra murmured, "Do you have your doubts still, Keiro?"

"No," Keiro said instantly. "Never." Sororra would take her reassurances in any form, and didn't mind the lie beneath the spoken words—she knew the lie was there, and he knew she knew, and that was the kind of power she valued most.

"Good," she said, smiling the same brittle smile. "Then let's go see what my brother has made."

Part Three

If a twin is born, it is surely curs'd, and should better be drowned than suffered to live.

—from Parro Etani's *Thoughts of the Fall*, written 4 Years After the Fall

It felt strange, to be going south once more. The last time Scal had gone south, it had changed him—he had gone seeking Vatri, to show him his place in the world, and she had done that and more. The last time he had gone south, he had not stopped regretting it.

The forests that ringed the Highlands were not the snowy wastes of his early lives, but they had felt enough like it. Secluded, solitary, where a man could walk a straight line for hours and never see another living creature. In the forests, he was a man. Only a man.

There is danger in being alone. Someone had said that to him, but he could not remember who.

But now he had left behind the forests and the Highlands. The distant mountains were disappearing over his shoulder, seen only when the moon was bright enough as it rose. He could not see the forests at all, even when he turned and stared, even when the moon was full.

There were flat roads, and there were fields, and there were people all around him, and it felt nothing like a home.

He was their leader, he was the Nightbreaker, and so he walked at the front. Vatri was beside him, and Edro was beside her, always. Joros had taken to Scal's other side, and pulled

Aro with him, always. The others scattered behind them, loose ranks, a rough march. Deslan was wise enough to guard their rear, to send her people ahead and aside, scouts for any signs of danger.

"A group this big," Joros said, "traveling through the Long Night? We won't find any trouble."

"Better to be prepared," Edro said agreeably. Scal was not surprised that the two had found common ground to walk. He was surprised that Vatri allowed it. She glared, but said nothing to halt their talking.

And all the while they moved south, along roads that could have held their number five times, and they saw no one.

The first town they found sealed its doors to them. Even when Vatri nudged Scal to draw his blade, and its flame lit up the center of their town, they did not open their doors. He might have thought them dead, save for the moving and whispering they could hear within the houses. They slept in the town center, hoping to put its residents at ease, but when they woke they were still alone.

They moved on, and Vatri was more upset than Scal had yet seen her.

"The Fallen have no doubt passed through here," Joros said grimly. "We saw it on our way north: small bands of them corrupting villages. We did what we could to put an end to it, but the longer the Long Night goes on, the more people start to question, and to doubt . . ."

"They're not only making them question," Edro said. His face was stone-hard. "They're *killing* the people they corrupt. Entire villages, dead. We've seen it."

Joros frowned, and said nothing.

Scal spent his time watching Aro.

Vatri had said he was a witch. Dangerous. That he had killed a dozen people with witchfire. Scal had not wanted to believe it, but he watched Aro. And his shaking and muttering and flickers of madness made Scal think of Anddyr, the mad witch. It was hard not to.

He dropped back to talk to Deslan, soft-voiced. The ones who had come with Joros and Aro, the ones they called "the pack," had fallen in with those who followed Scal. They fit as though they had chosen to follow, too, or as though they had lived among the others all their lives. Scal had asked Deslan and her people to ask them careful questions, and she told him with certainty, "He's a mage. They say he's sick, just like all the other mages they've seen." She paused, frowned. "I've seen sick mages, too. Not many, but . . . it's not something you forget. It sounds like our new friends have seen a fair number of sick mages. Many more than I've seen. Many more than I would have expected." She did not look at him as she kept talking, did not look to the front of their column, did not look at anything but the stars above. "The only sick mages I've seen, and the only ones I've heard of, have all been with the Fallen. Seems a little strange to me, our new friends knowing so many."

Scal could see the shape of the question in her words. *Is it safe?* He had seen Deslan sharing a tent with Joros. Had seen her mothering heart stretch out toward Aro. Had seen her companionably comparing daggers with the woman called Harin. *Are they safe to love?*

And Scal did not have an answer for the silent question. "It is strange," he said. With Deslan's eyes hard on his back, he returned to the head of the column, where Joros and Vatri were bickering.

It felt like the old times, his old life, only it was nothing like it at all.

When they stopped, Scal asked Aro if he would like to help find wood for a fire. In that old life, when Scal had traveled north, all the way North, with Aro and Joros and Vatri and Rora and the witch, Aro had been eager to be useful. Offering to help when it was not needed. Scal had refused at first, but the younger man had often pushed past his refusals to help anyway, and he had been useful enough. Had been a good companion, even when he was not useful. They were memories from an old life, the bonds of a man who no longer was, but Scal had not forgotten.

No. He *had* forgotten. He had not thought of Aro since his end in the snows, since he had left the group Joros had assembled. But seeing Aro again had opened a gate to the memories of that old Scal. And he saw weak, sick, pale Aro next to the Aro of his memories, who was bright and laughful and eager, and there was something wrong there that Scal would not let himself forget again. The reborn Scal had no ties to Aro, but for his old self, the man he had been once, he would try to help.

And so he asked Aro if he would like to help find wood for a fire. In truth they had more than enough wood, but it was never a poor idea to find more when they could. It was a task Aro had liked to help with, before. And it would give Scal the chance to see him alone.

Aro did not answer right away—or his answer was to look to Joros. Request glistening in his eyes. Joros did not even notice it, absorbed in his conversation with Deslan. She did notice, and when she nudged him, he faced Aro with an impatient look. "What?"

"I . . ." Aro's mind had slipped—he made small noises that were not words. "Go—"

"I would take him with me," Scal said. "To collect wood for a fire."

Joros snorted, and turned away. "Why should I care?"

Aro looked back to Scal, uncertainty in his face. Scal made a motion for him to follow, and after a pause of a few heartbeats, he did.

In the grasslands and farmlands they traveled through, there were few trees to be found. Little enough wood to be picked or cut. It did not matter—it was not the point. Scal walked beside Aro, both searching, though Scal was also waiting. Waiting for his friend of an old life to begin chattering, as he always had when they had done tasks, constant talking and questions and laughter.

But Aro remained silent, his eyes fixed to the ground, scanning for stray pieces of firewood.

Finally Scal could not stand the silence. "Aro," he said, and the younger man's head swung up to face him. "What is wrong?"

Aro frowned. Forehead wrinkling as though in deep thought. "Nothing's wrong."

"You have changed. *Been* changed."

One shoulder shrugged. "Things happen, and people change. *You've* changed, too, you know."

Scal shifted his weight to one foot. Back to the other. "I have not."

Aro laughed, and it was the last thing Scal had expected. It almost sounded like his old laugh, though the differences crawled spider-light down his back. "Then maybe I have, too. Maybe we've both changed so slowly that we can't see it from the inside."

Scal did not like this direction. "Where is your sister?" Joros had not spoken of her, beyond to say that she was safe, and waiting for them.

"She hasn't changed. Not at all." Aro stared at the ground once more, but he was not looking for sticks. "Joros is so hard to face without her . . . *everything* is so much harder alone. I didn't think it would be. I'd been alone before, I could make it on my own. But I was wrong . . ."

Starlight showed tears on his cheeks. Scal reached out, and put a hand to the younger man's shoulder. "What has happened?"

"You left, and Rora couldn't protect us alone. You left, and it all had to change."

Scal was not the same man who had left them—it had been a different life, and he *had* changed. But he still felt the weight of responsibility, of blame, as heavy on his shoulders as the sword strapped to his back. One could crumble from the weight. Or one could learn to bear it. Vatri had told him once, *We all carry things with us we don't want to.* He said to Aro, "I will not leave again."

Aro stared at him, and there was something in his eyes that was familiar and frightening. Not from Scal's last life, but further back—to his second life, when he had been a boy plucked from the killing snows. When he had lived inside high walls and slept to the sound of clanking chains, and to the snores of a red-robed priest whose face he could not remember. He had lived with the prisoners of Aardanel, and they had all had haunted eyes. Eyes that knew death, and were themselves half dead. Aro's eyes looked like their eyes. "I want to help," Scal said.

Aro looked away. "I think it might be too late."

And Scal believed him. He bowed his head. "I am sorry." He had never known how to talk to the dead.

CHAPTER THIRTY-FOUR

Joros had to trust Harin when she said they were getting close to the estate; in the darkness, he couldn't tell the difference between one field and the next, but he knew the pack, in their boredom, had done a great deal of exploring the surrounding lands while the Dogshead refused to let them do anything worthwhile. If Harin thought she recognized one particular rock, or the bend of the road spoke to her of home, he'd have to take her word for it.

He called the group to a halt, and for those who gave him resentful looks for daring to assume leadership, he glared right back. If they could accept a disfigured merra as a leader, they could accept him. "My people back home," he said, ignoring Harin's raised eyebrow at "my people" and how it went higher at "home," "can be . . . *overeager*. They value their safety above all else—they're truly a pack, and like wolves, they will protect what's theirs. If they see a force of our size approaching, I worry they will take action before they know what they're doing. A group should go ahead."

There were nods of agreement, and Edro smiled—he seemed to like the idea of a pack of overeager killers on his side. Joros couldn't blame him, though he'd eat his boots if Edro managed to mobilize the pack into anything useful.

For the last hour, since Harin had started to point out what she thought were familiar landmarks and what were in actuality nothing recognizable, Joros had been juggling whether it was better for him to lead the warning party, or to stay with the main group. If he went ahead, he'd be able to oversee things, lay the groundwork to cover up that terrible, maddening, *impossible* emptiness in his pocket where the seekstone had sat secure. He didn't know who to blame for its disappearance, but the only certainty was that no one could know. If anyone found out that it was gone, that he no longer knew for certain where the Twins were, before he had his replacement plan in place, this fragile alliance would fall to pieces. On the other hand, staying with the group gave him control over his new allies, and kept them from conspiring against him in his absence. In the end, that was what swayed him—he trusted Vatri little enough as it was, and he was loath to give her any time to begin unraveling all the work he'd done. He would have time later to talk to Anddyr, to shove as much skura down the damnable mage's throat as necessary to get the mage to somehow find the Twins. He'd done it before, when they were sleeping lumps below the earth. He could find them again. He *had* to.

Vatri proved his choice to stay right when she regarded him with suspicion and said, "Deslan can lead some of our people."

He nearly snorted at her transparency, and at the idea that if he did have some grand ambush in mind, Deslan's presence would deter him. "Excellent," he said. "Harin can lead the way." He'd already given Harin her instructions, and trusted her as much as he could to see them through.

He'd debated, too, sending Aro—a show of faith for those pack members who so coddled their precious wayward son—

but that would leave Joros without any real protection. Though Aro had little of Anddyr's strike-before-thinking impulsivity, having a mage at one's side should make any would-be troublemakers think before any striking was necessary. So he kept Aro, and sent Harin with two of the other pack to lead Deslan and her three charges. They ranged ahead, moving quickly, lost to the shadows in little time.

The rest of their group continued forward at the same steady pace, walking in relative silence. At length, dim lights emerged from the darkness ahead of them, and when it became clear that the lights were torches, all stopped in silent agreement. Scal and Edro both drew their swords, the Northman's devoid of its flames, and stood ready at the head of their group. Behind him, Joros could hear other weapons being drawn, bows being strung, all readying for any attack that might come. At his side, Aro stood gawping until Joros drove an elbow into the boy's ribs. Aro darted his eyes around and then raised his hands hip-high, as though ready to fend off some short attacker. He likely thought it made him look prepared for spellcasting, the poor fool.

The torches moved closer, and from the pools of light they cast Joros could pick out Deslan's face, and the two pack who'd gone with, and a new face in the form of Tare, the ear-cutter. Harin wasn't with the returning group, and that was good— she would hopefully be tending to some of Joros's last-minute business at the estate.

"It's a safe place," Deslan called ahead. "They'll take us in." Their approach was accompanied by the sounds of weapons being sheathed and sighs of relief. As they drew closer, Deslan raised an eyebrow toward Joros. "They seemed surprised to hear you'd come back."

"We were that," Tare growled. Joros wondered how exhausting it was, to be so perpetually joyless.

"I found the answers I was looking for more quickly than I expected, and Aro has shown great improvement in his health. But he missed his family, and there are things here I still need. There are plans still to be made."

"So you thought you'd bring more mouths for us to feed, when we can barely keep our own fed."

"That's a matter I'll discuss with Sharra."

Tare laughed. "Oh, will you?" Her eyes lit on something behind Joros, and a frown creased her face. "I know you."

Joros twisted to see her staring at Vatri, who sneered. "And I you. I see we're all keeping fine company these days." Joros had worked so hard to block all memory of Vatri that he'd forgotten she'd been there when they whisked the sad remnants of Whitedog Pack out of Mercetta and installed them in Joros's old estate. And she'd been there, too, to see the truth of how the pack members they'd taken to Raturo had died—that was a tricky spot he might need to dance around. He couldn't remember Tare and Vatri interacting, but he would have been genuinely surprised to learn they'd liked each other. Neither of them was the sort who made friends easily or well.

"When times are hard," Tare said, "even a bad friend is better'n none."

Vatri's silence conceded the point—she was, after all, keeping company with Joros to a greater extent than Tare was. Limited room for judgment had never stopped the merra from spitting vitriol in the past, but perhaps she'd learned to pick her battles.

"Well," Tare said, turning her scowl back to Joros. And

then, alarmingly, the scowl turned to a smirk. "We should go back. A lot's happened since you left. I'm sure you'll want to hear all about it."

"Happened?" Joros demanded.

Tare's smirk deepened. "I think those are matters you'll discuss with Sharra."

She offered nothing more, and he wouldn't demean himself by begging, so Joros fumed in silence as they resumed the journey toward the estate. Deslan dropped back to his side, pulling him into the circle of her torch's light. "You've got a curious collection of allies," she said, to which Joros grunted. He felt her subsequent frown. "All right, then," she said, and added with no trace of malice or anger that he could detect, "I hope your thoughts keep you company well enough." She moved to walk beside Scal, and didn't expect any conversation from *him*.

The estate was as sparsely lit as it had always been before Joros and Aro had left: enough light to not need to worry about bumping into comrades, but not enough to turn the place into a beacon. There were more torchbearers at the gate, watching them with cold faces and curious eyes as they passed through.

And standing at the center of the courtyard with crossed arms, in what appeared to be a carefully well-lit position, was Rora. Her smirk matched Tare's.

Joros felt his mouth hanging open slightly and quickly snapped it shut; with its closing, he could feel his anger rising, as though his mouth had been a vent that, now sealed, threatened to burst. He stepped forward, fists clenched, ready to start throwing threats—

And from the corner of his eye, he saw Harin at the edge of the shadows, making sharp silencing motions.

Joros halted, and uncurled his fingers. His glare stayed in place, and he gritted his teeth hard enough to make his eyes ache, but he gave them no ground. He supposed he should have been like Vatri, and anticipated an ambush.

"Welcome back," Rora said with tight, forced cheer. If she heard the choked noise her brother made behind Joros, she gave no indication.

Joros had been gone less than three months, and somehow in that time, mortal enemies had managed to patch up their wounds. Tare strolled past him to Rora's side and rested her arm companionably against the younger woman's shoulder, their matching smiles giving him the same spine-shivers that the bloody spooky twins inside Mount Raturo always had. This, though, had the flavor of barely contained rage—the kind of all-consuming, illuminating anger he hadn't felt in so long.

The old Joros had always been able to accomplish anything he wanted to.

He pushed past the smirking bitches, and ignored Harin when she scrabbled to his side with hurried whispers—Twins' bones, but he was surrounded by too many damnable women. He marched into the main house, the merra and the Northman and Edro and Aro on his heels, Deslan's voice dimly calling out for her people to rest while the leaders discussed things, but he didn't care. There was just one last damnable woman to face.

Sharra Dogshead had taken Joros's parents' old room and turned it into an office his father would have loved: sparse and no-nonsense, with his father's abominably heavy desk dragged into the room and set at the very center, facing the door. The room had a single chair, the same chair his father had done all his business out of, which Sharra had claimed for herself. It did feel a great deal like being marched into his father's study to recite whatever minor wrong he'd been caught doing, and he let that comparison fuel his anger.

Joros marched toward the desk, enjoying the muffled curse Tare made behind him, too far away to do anything if Joros had had murder on his mind. He wasn't there—yet. He simply planted his fists on the desk and leaned forward, looming over the Dogshead, letting her feel his radiating fury. "We had an understanding," he snarled.

Joros's frame completely blocked the room's one lantern from her, throwing the Dogshead entirely in his shadow. She looked up at him with an infuriating calm. "So nice to see you again, Joros."

Joros lifted one fist and slammed it down, making the desk shudder, sending a few papers skittering to the floor. A hand grabbed his shoulder and wrenched him back—Tare, finally having shoved her way through the cretins filling the doorway. Joros let her pull him out of his looming stance before he twisted out of her grip.

"Understandings can change," a different voice said, and an eyeless specter stepped out of the shadows that had collected at the back of the room, "when you understand more."

"*You?*" Joros sputtered. Eerie, irritating Neira, who had thought herself the gods' will made manifest and had haunted the halls of Mount Raturo worse than the young twins. Whispers had always followed her, surrounding her like the shadows she conjured, which were unlike any magecraft anyone had ever seen. Joros, preferring to keep his distance, had never joined in the whispering, but he had *heard* them well enough— he'd led the Shadowseekers, had been the effective spymaster for the Fallen, after all. He'd heard of the strange noises coming from Neira's chambers at all hours, and the cloud that seemed to overcome one's memories when trying to remember anything seen beyond the dark door of her room . . . Joros had always avoided her as much as he could, and the few times their paths had crossed had done nothing to change his opinion on her. Dirrakara had always praised the woman . . . but Dirrakara had been wrong about so much.

Joros swung back to the Dogshead, to Tare and to Rora still hovering in the doorway, and couldn't help a peal of mocking laughter. "If you've been listening to anything she's said," he told them, "you should know she's a compulsive liar. She'll say anything to get what she wants."

From her position behind the Dogshead, Neira went utterly still, and her empty eye sockets fixed unsettlingly on Joros. Dimly, he could make out her surrounding shadows, beginning to writhe furiously. "What did you call me?" she asked softly, and there was a tilt to the words that filled Joros's core with ice.

"Enough." The Dogshead stood, which was a mistake—her bad leg gave out, and she had to catch herself on the desk, glaring Tare away when she moved to help. Sharra righted herself, and treated everyone in the room to that glare before saying, "This is my home, and if any of you hope to stay in it, you'll behave civilly."

Joros barked another laugh—*her* home? Had she spent her childhood tiptoeing through its halls, or staring through the shrinking crack of every closing door, or studying at the huge painted map of Fiatera and imagining what else lay beyond the crumbling walls? Her home, indeed . . .

"Those of you I haven't met," she went on, to the fools still hovering in the doorway, "I assume you're the ones wanting to help him. Come in, then. You're welcome here just as long as he is."

They all filed in to stand in a rough ring before the Dogshead's desk: Vatri and Edro and Scal, Rora who went to stand near Tare who stood near the Dogshead, Aro who had been utterly ignored and likely thought his frequent glances to his sister were subtle.

"Well," Vatri said to Joros, in some feeble attempt to lighten the mood, "isn't this nice. We're all back together once more—your whole merry band of lackeys."

"All except one," Rora corrected—she'd never miss an opportunity to point out when the merra was wrong.

Joros snorted and said stiffly, "I trust Anddyr is still enjoying his new flock?"

Tare spread her hands, grinning. "Like I said . . . a lot's changed."

Joros sat among the wreckage of a vicious storm made of his own hands and fury. The destruction had brought him no joy—only left him feeling the same dull sadness he'd felt while trudging away from the Plains and his failure there.

Surrounded by all the smirking women—Rora and Tare and Sharra and Neira and Vatri, damn bleeding *hells*, there were too many of them—he had had no reasonable outlet for the blinding rage within him. He'd stormed from the room as Rora explained Anddyr's absence, lest he be further tempted to kill them all, and had found himself in the room he'd claimed. *His* room, but one of the eyes had taken it over in his absence, and the man wisely fled before Joros was forced to commit bodily harm. He'd proceeded to smash everything in the room he could—it was that or scream his throat bloody. If anyone had dared enter the room at that point, he likely would have smashed their face in, too. But they were all wise enough to leave him to his anger.

Joros sat now in the middle of the debris he'd made and couldn't even muster up enough energy to want to be angry. He'd managed to build some small life in this place—a new room in his bleak childhood home, some vestiges of happiness and comfort despite the world continuing to fall apart around him. But it *did* keep falling apart. He had no way of finding the Twins now. The staircase had crumbled beneath him, his plan shattered like the furniture he'd destroyed.

Anddyr had always been more trouble than he was worth, but that was more a reflection of how much trouble he caused than how useful he was—the mage had been a scatterbrained idiot, but he'd been damned useful, and Joros didn't like admitting that he'd come to rely on him. But Anddyr was gone now, and he'd taken with him Joros's last bargaining chip: if he didn't have the seekstone linked to a god, at least he had a mage with an uncanny connection to both the god and the boy whose body the god had stolen. But no—it was all gone, all ruined.

"I did try to stop him," a voice said from the doorway, and Joros looked up to see Rora leaning there. The smirk was gone, her face as hard and unforgiving as he was used to. She didn't seem surprised by the destruction he'd wrought.

"That must have been terribly hard for you," Joros said flatly.

"I could've had them kill you, y'know? I thought about it, and they would've done it if I asked. Put a dagger right through your eye soon as you stepped foot in the courtyard. I thought about it for a long time."

"Then why didn't you?"

He could hear Rora sucking her teeth. "You've taken damn near everything from me, and even when I think there's nothing left for you to take, you find something and snatch it away. I hate you, and I want you dead, and I wouldn't mind being the one to kill you myself." She kicked at a broken piece of chair, sent it skittering off into a corner. "I want my life back, and I want everything back that I've lost. Only way I see of getting a *chance* to get it all back is if the world goes back to how it's supposed to be. The more people trying, the better I figure the chances are. I just want this all to be done."

"So do I," Joros muttered.

"Then come on. Everyone's talking. Vatri says you've got a plan, and Neira's got one, too, and Tare thinks the Dogs-head might even send some of the pack for help, with some convincing."

Joros blinked at her slowly, wondering why she was being . . . not *nice*, exactly, but more compassionate than he would have ever given her credit for. "Your brother," he started to say, but stopped. There was no benefit to telling her. A kindness did not automatically deserve a kindness in turn. And he *had* promised Aro he wouldn't tell.

"What about him?" Rora asked stiffly.

Joros chewed on the inside of his cheek and finally said, "He's not any better. You may be smart enough to have realized he was simply a convenient excuse for me to leave, but . . ." A partial truth balanced on Joros's tongue. "If there was a way I could make him well again, I would."

Her expression was that of someone used to swallowing their feelings—a peculiar blankness that showed cracks only in the twitch near the left side of her mouth. "Let's go," she said, turning away. "I'm fecking sick of the darkness."

CHAPTER THIRTY-FIVE

Anddyr thought it was a hallucination at first—though he knew it was far to the south and west, suddenly Mount Raturo was *there*, piercing the swirling sky ahead of him. He flinched and yelped and scrambled for the closest cover he could find, falling into a prickle-bush and curling up at its heart until his own heart slowed enough that he could peek through the thorns without tasting panic.

And sure enough, there was Raturo, a jagged spire scraping the sky. Like everything in his new sight, it was built from shifting smoke, but there was no denying the reality of it. He hadn't had a single hallucination since he'd taken his eyes, no matter how deeply into madness he sank. That was one change for the positive, at least.

But it meant Raturo was real, somehow, and here.

Though his heartbeat had returned to normal, it began to race again as he realized what he needed to do. He knew they'd be there, in the impossible mountain, how could they not be—but he had to be sure. He couldn't afford any mistakes.

Anddyr took a deep breath, and crawled backward out of the tangle of branches; he needed more space than it allowed him. He knelt on the ground, deadfall and detritus pricking his knees, and opened his pack before him. He pulled out Sooty first, and tucked her under his arm. Then he reached in for the blue-swirling seekstone, its smoke so similar to that which made his own form. He laid the bundle out before him and, after another deep breath, reached out to grab the seekstone. With his new sight, it looked as though the seekstone became a part of him, melding with the blue smoke of his hand.

Fire tore through Anddyr, but there was no light to it. There was only, ever, the darkness.

The beacon call burned through him, pointing and guiding, and he flung his body forward, arm outstretched as his fingers sprang open. He could manage that much, at least, before the gibbering madness took him.

It was a quick spiral down to the depths, where Anddyr dwelled screaming and raving and weeping, clawing at the ground and at his blue-smoke flesh, begging Sooty to help or to make it stop. But it didn't, not for a very long time. It seemed to last longer, each time he used the seekstone, his punishment lengthening for daring to touch the mind of a god.

When finally it released him, and Anddyr went floating sluggishly to the surface of his sanity, it felt as though hours had passed. He had no way of knowing—the stars were not present in his smoke-made world, and he couldn't find the moon, so all he had was the rumbling in his stomach, which rarely stopped anyway.

Anddyr did find the seekstone, though—flung out from him to land in the direction it had shown him, and he could draw a straight mental line between it and the earth he'd turned up in his mad writhing. Unsurprisingly, that mental line pointed directly toward Raturo.

He'd known, but he'd needed to be sure.

Anddyr collected all his things, wrapping the seekstone back up without touching it, and tucking loyal Sooty back into her bag. He returned to the road, then, and with his heart moving significantly faster than his feet, began walking toward the impossible Mount Raturo.

Anddyr had had to learn how to walk again. He'd stumbled from the hut of his rebirth, falling repeatedly, tripping over his own feet and finding plenty of other things to trip over. He'd ended up crawling out of the village—the crawling was not any kinder to his hands and knees, but it had at least saved them the repeated impacts of falling. Still, he'd crawled headfirst into a tree, and used that as a good enough signal that it was time to curl into a ball and not move for a while.

More accurate to say that he'd had to learn to trust his eyes again.

In his new world built from shifting smoke, seen through eyes that were no longer there, distances were not the same as they had been. A tree that looked to be the proper distance away for decent conversation was, in fact, much farther away when he reached out a blue-smoke arm to touch it. A shifting black village that seemed so far up the road as to not be a concern for another few hours suddenly rushed forward to meet him, sending him lurching off the road in a panic.

It was a different kind of sight, but it was still sight, and that was more than a fool could have hoped for.

Having learned many of the ways in which his new sight could trick his mind, Anddyr was almost—but not quite—surprised that, the closer he drew to Mount Raturo, the smaller it grew. From a distance it had seemed huge and hulking, the same scale as the real thing; but closer, he could see that it wasn't the true Raturo, that it was smaller and more straight-sided. It was still a massive earthen spire but, for someone who had cowered in the shadow of Mount Raturo, this was not as impressive a thing.

But it *was* where the Twins were. Or where Fratarro was, at least, and whatever was left of the boy whose body he had stolen. Whatever was left for Anddyr to try to save.

He got surprisingly close to the small mountain before anyone stopped him, but when he *was* stopped . . .

It burned like white fire across his smoke-swirling sight, like a star shooting through the night sky but shooting *toward* him, a flash of radiance that lingered and loomed and knocked Anddyr onto his backside with the sheer surprise of it. He squinted reflexively, though it did nothing—there was no way to stop seeing anything, and no way to block the burning light.

When it was over him, nearly on top of him, the light dimmed slowly to become something almost more wondrous: points of the same white fire scattered over the deep black of the thing's shape, with the points connected by thin and shimmering threads of fire. It was like a living map of the constellations, and from it he could begin to make out the shape of the thing—long and reptilian, and at the core of its star-map form, two red eyes glowed.

Anddyr gaped, unsure what he was seeing, unsure that he could trust his eyes anymore. From all his days among the Fallen, he knew well the history of the Twins, of all that had led to their Fall—he knew that Fratarro had shaped a living race of his own, and he knew that jealous Patharro had killed every last one of the new race. Yet . . .

The thing tilted its head, and said in a musical voice, *"You should not be here."*

Anddyr swallowed hard, and croaked out, "What are you?"

The head tilted the other direction. *"That is not the right question."*

"I . . ." Anddyr's hands were shaking and, desperate, he clawed his travelsack from his shoulder and dug in it until he could close both hands around Sooty's comforting form. The blue seekstone glowed invitingly, but he ignored it. He didn't need it anymore. Holding Sooty tight, Anddyr managed to control his breathing and, at length, push himself up to standing, where he was much taller than the impossible creature, where he felt taller than the impossible mountain in the near distance. "Will you take me to them?"

"That is a better question. Come." The *mravigi* turned toward the mountain and began to walk, and Anddyr followed after its constellation tail.

Maybe soon, he would wake up in the cellar back at Joros's estate and realize it had all been a dream, everything since before Neira, that it had all been a madness-made fiction. He rather expected it. It at least allowed him to enjoy the magic of the dream while he lived it.

As they drew closer to the mountain, more star-streak *mravigi* emerged and faded in his sight, their light so strange and beyond anything his new sight had yet shown him. It was always swirling shades of darkness, with people colored in blue smoke—or perhaps it was blood that shone blue for him, for seekstones were built from the old blood magics and swirled with the same blue as all the other people he'd yet seen. There had been no stars, no light at all, until now. He supposed it was fair that in the vision granted by the Twins, Fratarro's own creations should look so beautiful.

There were some people, but not so many of them. Most, like the other *mravigi*, ignored or avoided him until finally a hulking someone approached. The person nodded to Anddyr's escort, who trilled and then slipped away without so much as a farewell, leaving Anddyr feeling dazed and clinging all the more tightly to Sooty.

This was the first person Anddyr had really met since taking his eyes, and it was more confusing even than he'd feared. His new sight gave him very little detail—he saw only the shape of a face and none of its contours, only darker pits for eyes or mouth but nothing to give expression, nothing even to tell him if it was a man or a woman. He couldn't tell if they were angry to see him or pleased, if they were scowling at Sooty or smiling in understanding. Anddyr simply waited, feeling wretched, and not very much enjoying this part of the dream at all.

Finally the person asked, with a deep-throated but female voice, "Where are your robes, son?"

"I'm not a preacher," Anddyr said with inexplicable relief. Perhaps it was simply talking to a person again. Perhaps it was that, though he could likely assume this woman wore black robes, he couldn't see them and so felt none of the sick terror he usually did upon seeing any preacher.

He could feel her rising uncertainty, almost like palpable waves. "Then what are you?"

"I'm a mage."

"Who took your eyes?"

"I did."

If anything, that just seemed to make her more uncertain. "You . . . ?" She paused, and he could see her weight shifting from foot to foot, saw her head turn as she glanced around—he assumed, after she spoke again, that she was looking for someone else to make a decision for her. "I suppose you'd better come with me. The *mravigi* wouldn't have brought you if you were a danger, and . . . they can figure you out inside."

Anddyr nodded agreeably, and followed the woman toward the mountain. There were still so very few people, and none that acknowledged him, and none that his guide seemed to think she could foist him off on. Anddyr stared at the mountain's peak, dark against the dark-swirling sky, and had to tilt his head back farther and farther as they approached to keep it in sight, until he was staring directly upward and tripped over his own feet.

Finally they reached the mountain, and the woman pressed her hand against its surface. Anddyr watched some of the blue of her palm seep into the mountain, spreading like a halo before it dissipated—all but confirming for him that blue, in his new sight, was indeed blood. Just like it had been in Raturo, blood opened unseen doors, and his guide led him into the mountain.

It would be dark inside, he knew, likely utterly lightless, or as sparsely lit as could be managed. But that was another advantage to his new sight—there was no difference between dark and light. Had there been a sun, he imagined it would not touch the shifting black smoke at all. So though it was likely black as pitch within the hallway he stepped into, Anddyr could still make out the lines of the walls, stretching and twisting ahead. They were still hard to see, only dim, subtle differences in shading between the walls and the floor and the ceiling, but he could see them.

His guide kept one hand pressed against the wall as she led him deeper into the mountain, and he knew, then, that she still had her eyes.

The halls she led him down, past only the occasional person—like Raturo, it was a massive space for comparatively few people—were lit by occasional torches. Anddyr knew this because fire, too, shone differently from the black smoke—he could see the actual flame, flickering against the blackness, and burning almost as painful-bright as the *mravigi* had. He couldn't look at the torches for very long.

The halls eventually opened onto a wider room that had some small comforts—a few chairs, a hooded lantern whose flame didn't burn Anddyr's eyes so terribly, what were likely hangings on the wall but looked to Anddyr simply like darker squares against the walls. There was a person seated in one of the chairs, bent over a lap desk, and one of the star-map *mravigi* lying at his side.

"Godson," Anddyr's guide said softly, and the figure in the chair lurched upright.

"What?" it snapped in a man's voice.

"I . . . I wasn't certain who to bring this to. This man is a mage . . ."

The seated man seemed to make a frown. Inspecting his face as best he could, Anddyr noticed the man had a single dark splotch on his blue face—only one eye, where Anddyr was used to seeing two or none. The *mravigi* lifted its head and stared at Anddyr as well, with its two red eyes among its star-dotted form. The weight of both of their regards made Anddyr feel small.

"Why have you come here, mage?" the man called Godson asked.

Truthfully, Anddyr answered, "I've come to see the Twins."

"To what end?"

"I've heard their call. I . . . expected my purpose to become clear when I found them."

"What's that?"

Anddyr gawped, uncertain how in the world to answer that question, and the man motioned impatiently toward Anddyr's chest, to where Anddyr's crossed arms clutched— His cheeks burned, and then he berated himself. After her loyalty, after all they had been through, how could he feel any shame at Sooty? Anddyr uncrossed his arms and tipped his chin up as he held Sooty out toward Godson. "This is Sooty," he said, and his voice was warm with pride.

Godson stood up, the lap desk and its contents clattering loudly to the ground, and walked quickly to stand before Anddyr. He plucked Sooty from Anddyr's hands before Anddyr could process that she needed protection, and he made a keening noise as Godson turned her around and around in his hands. The splotch of his one eye was narrow, and the line of his mouth described a deep frown. "Where did you get this?" he asked.

Anddyr had to resist the urge to snatch Sooty out of the man's hands, and instead smoothed his palms against his legs in a self-calming gesture. "She's mine. She's been mine for years."

The man didn't give Sooty back, and turned to the woman still standing behind Anddyr. "Go fetch me some guardians," he said, and she hurried away. To Anddyr, he said, "It will be easier for everyone if you just tell me the truth. Where did you get this?"

"A friend gave her to me, and then gave her back to me."

"Who is your friend?"

Anddyr focused his empty eyes on the other man's single eye. "His name is Etarro." And the man went still as death, and utterly silent.

Four others stomped into the room at that point: three muscular shapes with weapons strapped to their forms, and a fourth that was roughly Anddyr-shaped. They all stood attentively waiting, until finally the man called Godson made a sharp motion and moved past Anddyr out of the room, the *mravigi* rising gracefully and following at his heels. The four newcomers, the guardians, closed ranks around Anddyr and escorted him out after. It was unnecessary; Anddyr would have followed anyway. The man still had Sooty, and, too, Anddyr suspected where the man was taking him.

This new mountain was very like Raturo, though on a smaller scale: its core was hollow and ringed by a path that spiraled from tip to base, full of branching passages and rooms through the sides of the mountain. Anddyr was led up, around and around the inside of the mountain, and the tighter circles made his head spin and his stomach grumble. He wondered and almost—but didn't—asked aloud if they'd named this place yet, and if they'd named it something silly like Orutar, but he decided that name actually wasn't half bad and almost—but didn't—suggested it as a fine name for the place.

They stopped near to the top of the mountain, or at least near to the top of the portion of it that was hollowed out. Godson pressed his hand against the wall, and Anddyr saw the blue seeping again, and another unseen door sliding open. But the man didn't enter the room until a voice from within beckoned him. Anddyr was pushed in after him, and almost immediately blinded.

It was much like when the first *mravigi* had approached him, too much light to bear without burning. It was like a beacon—yes, it was *very* much like what he had seen the first time he held the seekstone, a person-shaped beacon of pure and wondrous light. It faded more slowly—no, his vision adjusted more slowly than it had to the *mravigi*. Perhaps it was that there were two distinct beacons, two pools of unbearable lightness for his new sight to adjust to.

Anddyr stood before the Twins in silence, and as their light became easier to look at, he realized he could see their faces—*truly* see them, details and contours and expression, mouths and eyes and the wrinkles of frowns. And he knew their faces—of course he knew them. He had watched them grow. They had been his friends. Etarro and Avorra, Raturo's twin children.

But it didn't *sound* like Etarro who asked, "What is it, Keiro?" It was Etarro's voice, but for all that, there was little recognizable in it. If Anddyr's sight hadn't told him he was looking at Etarro, he never would have guessed it.

Godson—Keiro?—said, "This man, a mage, came to us. And he carried this." He held out Sooty toward the Twins.

Etarro-who-wasn't frowned, and stood up slowly to face them. He reached for the horse with one hand, and Anddyr noticed something strange about the other—there was no light glowing in his left hand, only the blue smoke Anddyr was used to seeing, as though the godliness didn't extend to that hand. Anddyr could guess why, for Anddyr had helped to burn Fratarro's hand, the real one that would have attached to his real body. Cappo Joros had said that would seal away part of Fratarro's power forever, and it seemed as though he had been right.

With his light-made hand, Etarro took Sooty from Keiro and held her gently around the middle. He stared at her, frowning deeper, and his face . . . *flickered* . . . Anddyr could think of no other way to describe it. The definition of his face faded, and the white light seemed to crack and fracture to reveal blue beneath. "This was mine . . ." Etarro-who-wasn't murmured, and he looked away from Sooty to stare at Anddyr with his shifting eyes.

Anddyr hardly dared even to breathe.

"Brother?" Avorra called softly, only there was no denying it wasn't Avorra, it was Sororra through and through. She stood as well, and touched her hand to Etarro's shoulder.

The blue cracks faded. Etarro's face solidified once more, features smoothing and clarifying. He looked to Keiro and asked flatly, "Why did you bring me this?"

The man called Keiro seemed taken aback. "You had this . . . or had one like it, in the hills. I thought . . ."

"You're mistaken." Fratarro—for it was abundantly clear that this variant, at least, was not the Etarro Anddyr had known so well—opened his hand, and Sooty fell to the floor. It was not so terrible a height, for the god was only boy-tall, but Anddyr still let out an involuntary cry and lurched forward to pick her up where she sprawled. One of the big guardians grabbed him and dragged him back, but not before he'd got ahold of her leg. As Anddyr was hauled back to where he had been, he looked up to see that Fratarro's face was flickering once more. Almost as though there were a battle raging within him, a fight between a mortal and a god.

Keiro cleared his throat. "Very well. There's still the matter of the mage himself, then. I'm told he took his own eyes, and he claims to have been called here."

"He's a mage," Sororra said, shrugging. "Put him with the others. We'll find use for him."

"As you say," Keiro murmured, but still he hesitated. It was because, Anddyr realized, Fratarro was staring at him—or, more accurately, was staring at Sooty, cradled in Anddyr's arms.

Anddyr's hand shook, and it felt almost as difficult as taking his eyes had been, but he held Sooty out toward Fratarro. "You can keep her," he offered, softly, and hopefully.

The blue cracks grew and spread, widening, chipping away at the mask of light, and Anddyr thought with grim triumph, *I found you.*

But then the pure light blazed brightly, brighter than before, and Anddyr yanked Sooty back protectively against his chest. The only blue was in his hand when Fratarro said, "What would I want with that?"

The guardians escorted Anddyr quickly out of the room and back down the spiraling path, Keiro trailing them in silent thought. Anddyr, confident that the close-packed guardians would keep him from stepping over the path's ledge into open air, spent a great deal of his time looking over his shoulder at Keiro, wondering why they called the man Godson. Not for the first time, he missed his true vision—he would like to know what the son of a god looked like.

"Take him to the keepers," Keiro said at length, his steps slowing as theirs went on. "They'll find a place for him."

"Aye, sir," one of the guardians grunted, and Anddyr was propelled ever farther downward. When he looked back again, the dim blue outline of Keiro still stood on the path where they'd left him, his face turned upward, unmoving.

CHAPTER THIRTY-SIX

I n the end, it was far easier than it should've been. The merra said it was the will of the Parents, that Metherra and Patharro had brought them all together to bring light back to the world. Rora thought that sounded like horse shit, but still, it was a little spooky the way the edges of all their plans lined up so nice, like a plate that'd broken into a few big chunks and hardly needed any figuring to piece back together. Even the part that'd frustrated Joros the most, Anddyr making off with his way of finding the Twins, wasn't a real problem—Neira laughed and said she knew exactly where they were. All the different pieces got knit together like a quilt that looked mismatched until you unfolded it and saw it was actually a beautiful design.

Maybe the reason she didn't like it was *because* of how Vatri said the Parents had done it. Rora'd never liked the thought of gods mucking around in her life, poking her where they needed her to go. Gods had caused her enough trouble just by having people believe in 'em, and thinking babies should be punished for what the Twins had done centuries ago.

"Then we're agreed," Neira said cheerfully. They'd all settled in the dining room, which had a long table and enough chairs for everyone to sit—though Neira had spent the whole conversation circling the room, one hand trailing against the wall in a constant soft scraping that'd made everyone a little twitchy. "We will find the Twins. We will weaken them. We will force them from their stolen bodies." Since most of the others were doing their best not to look at Neira at all, Rora was probably the only one who saw the black smoke surge up around her in a quick cloud of glee. "We will kill them."

It all sounded so simple when she said it like that—laid it out like each thing was just one easy step, like each thing wasn't near to impossible. She said it like you wouldn't have to be mad to think they'd all get through it alive—or like she knew they wouldn't, and it didn't matter.

"We're agreed," Joros said tightly. He wasn't happy about his plan being twisted, wasn't happy about not being the only one in the room with any idea of what to do, but it seemed like he'd accepted it. He'd chose the side fighting against the Twins, even if he'd grump about it not being exactly his way— he'd went on for a long while about how he thought they were risking everything by not destroying the Twins' true bodies. Neira'd promised him that with their stitched-together plan, there would be nothing left of the Twins to return to those bodies. Seemed like Joros was willing to let that be for now— though Rora'd bet anything he was already planning exactly how he'd gloat if it turned out Neira was wrong.

"We're agreed," Vatri echoed. She'd had all the same sus- picions about Neira that she'd had about Joros in the begin- ning, and then some more when she learned Neira was an extra-dangerous kind of witch, but she seemed to like Neira's plans better'n she'd ever liked any of Joros's. And Neira had been working hard to keep any of her smoke from leaking out.

"Agreed," Scal rumbled next to her. It was the first thing

he'd said, maybe since stepping into the courtyard. It was actually kind of comforting, knowing some things didn't ever change.

"Yes," the Dogshead said tiredly. She'd listened to all the planning, and Rora still didn't know if she was agreeing to help, or agreeing the plan sounded good so that everyone else would get out of her house and leave her people in peace.

Everyone else at the table didn't really matter. Everyone else was a follower, or a helper, people who'd do what they were told to do. There was a comfort, too, in knowing your place in the world. It was easier having someone make all the decisions for you—that way, when bad things happened, it wasn't your fault. There wasn't anything you could've done to stop it, because someone else had made all the choices.

Joros stood up, the legs of his chair scraping against the floor. He leaned his fists on the table, even though there was no one to lean over, and looked around at everyone—or at least the ones who mattered. "There's no sense in wasting any more time, then. The sooner we begin, the sooner we can finish this."

Tare got up from her chair and, after waiting for Neira to pass hand-scrapingly by, went over to twitch the curtains of one of the windows. "About an hour since moon-rise. Only a sliver, so there won't be much light no matter when."

"My people need to rest," Vatri said. "We've traveled a long way to get here. I wouldn't force them into another hard travel so soon."

"They're hardy stock," Joros said.

The big swordsman who sat on Vatri's other side, him and Scal looking almost like a matched set, raised a hand toward Joros. "They're *people*. And they've earned a rest, and explanations." He looked over at Scal, who wasn't looking at anything. "They deserve to know where the Nightbreaker's path leads next, and decide for themselves if they wish to follow."

Rora could feel some of the others trying not to snort—Tare and Joros, mostly. They all kept it to themselves, let the arrogant swordsman have his fancy words and his fancy thoughts. Rora almost told him it'd be better if he just commanded his people. She'd heard from an ex-soldier who'd ended up in the Canals that that was how it was in the army. Officers shouting at you where you needed to go, and not once telling you why. You didn't need to know, simple as that—all you were meant for was *doing*, and you didn't tell a hammer why it was putting a house together, or a horse why it was carrying you. Same way back in the Canals, on contract nights when Rora'd gone up into the city to kill someone and collect her payment for it, they'd never told her why the person was supposed to die. Someone had said they needed to, and Rora was a knife who could do it. You didn't tell a weapon why it was going to slit someone's throat.

Neira stopped her pacing, and stopped her hand dragging against the wall, and the sudden silence it left in the room was almost *worse*. She crouched down, staring at her hand, turning it front to back like her eyes could actually see it, like there was anything to even see. Tare, who was nearest by, took a few careful steps back toward the table. Everyone else tried not to look at Neira. "Two moon-rises from now, then," Neira finally said, and it took Rora a second to realize the woman wasn't just talking to her hand. "Will that be enough time for your people?"

Vatri murmured that it would, and then everyone just

stared at each other, meeting over but no one really sure how to end it. Joros managed it by turning, knocking over his chair, and leaving without a word. Aro followed after him—but no, Rora wasn't thinking about Aro. She'd felt him staring sometimes, but she'd never looked.

The merra and her matched set of fighters left, and Rora would've liked to talk to Scal—or probably talk *at* him—because she'd pretty much written him off as dead, and there was probably a good story getting from near dead to where he was now. But it seemed like Vatri had both men leashed like dogs, meaning Scal was still about as good as dead for all the chance Rora'd have to see him.

Rora left, too, then, because there wasn't anything left for her to do, and because she didn't want to spend a minute more around Neira. There was a plan, and she'd play her part in it. The time up until that started was like waiting for a show to start—sitting in front of a shoddy stage, the whole reeking crowd gathered and bouncing and excited, but nothing *happening*. All there was was the waiting.

The sooner it started, the sooner it'd be over.

Outside, Rora climbed up the crumbly old wall and found a spot where the stone had crumbled just right, making a little cup on the outside of the wall while the inside of the wall was still intact. Rora was small enough she could sit down in the cup and, if she leaned right, not even the top of her head would be visible over the wall. No one inside would be able to see her, and if anyone went walking along the wall, they'd probably step right over her without knowing it. It was a good place. Rora sat there, lengths above the ground, legs dangling, and tried her damnedest not to think about anything. There were so many things that, if she started thinking through them, she'd *know* them, and if she knew certain things she'd never be able to go through with it all. Easier not to think, not to know—they'd told her what she needed to do, and she didn't want to know why. A tool or a weapon didn't want to know why.

Tare had always been good at finding her.

Rora heard the footsteps coming along the wall and shrank down farther into her cup, waiting for whoever-it-was to pass her over. No such luck, though—the feet stopped near her head, and Tare asked, "Have you talked to him?"

"No." Rora sighed.

"You know you have to. He's your brother."

Rora could remember back before they'd all come to this estate, after Rora'd gone back to the pack and Tare had cut off her ear for being a traitor—Aro had gone from Rora to Tare, urging them both to talk, to apologize for their wrongs, but they'd both had too much pride for that. It felt weird to have it flipped now—Tare going between her and Aro. It wasn't quite the same, though. When it came to it, Tare was the second-closest thing Rora had to family, but she wasn't blood. You could forgive almost-family a lot more and for a lot worse than you could actual family. Wounds went deeper when it came to blood. "I don't have anything to say to him. And you don't even like him anyway, you said so yourself. Why do you care?"

Tare sat down on the wall beside Rora's cup, bouncing her heels against the wall. "I did say that, and I won't take it back. But he's your brother. You betrayed the pack for him—twice over, maybe. Anyone who knows you two minutes knows you'd kill for him, and *I* know you have. Most folks in the Canals don't have family of any sort—that's why we make packs, because the only way to get family is to make it yourself. You can't just give up your family and pretend he's dead when he's still right here, living and breathing."

"Maybe we make packs because it's better to choose your own family than to stay with the one you got stuck with." Rora didn't want to talk about Aro anymore—it made her want to punch something, and it put that tight feeling behind her nose that meant tears if she didn't do something to stop them. She cleared her throat to loosen up the tight feeling, and then asked, "You think the Dogshead'll send people?"

Tare sighed—maybe at Rora switching the topic, but maybe at the answer she had. "No," she said, "I don't think she will."

Rora just nodded. There was something hovering nearby— another thing she could keep from really knowing, so long as she didn't think about it. Rora'd leave again; and Tare would stay. Just facts, without any thinking or feeling behind them.

"Just because she doesn't send anyone," Tare said, "doesn't mean some of our people won't go with." Rora twisted around and up to look at Tare. The moon didn't give off much light to see by, but it was enough to tell that Tare was looking back at her. "Joros is a bastard, but he's been right about a lot. It's not right for Sharra to hold people back if they want to help . . . She's terrified of losing anyone else, but it's not living if we're just surviving, and it sure as shit isn't living if the world falls apart around us and we die without doing what we can to help."

It'd been a long time since Rora'd felt such a strong surge of hope. "Does that mean you're coming? You'll lead all the pack that wants to come with?"

And Tare . . . Tare looked away, and the hope went out like

a light. Tare didn't need to say anything for an answer at that point, but she did anyway, saying softly, "She's *my* family. I can't leave her."

Rora nodded, because there wasn't anything else to do, and looked back out over the dark lands.

After a while, Tare reached out to squeeze her shoulder and say again, "You should talk to your brother." Rora didn't answer, and there wasn't any other reason for Tare to stick around, so she left.

Rora supposed it was fair, for all the times she'd left Tare behind, and if those had hurt Tare as much as the grinding in Rora's chest now, Rora could see why Tare'd been so angry at her for so long. At least Rora got an explanation. It wasn't nothing, but for now, it sure felt like it.

She was right about one thing, though—you didn't leave your real family behind. It just gave Rora all the more reason not to talk to Aro: he'd left her for no good reason, left her chained up in a cellar and gone off to do gods-knew-what, and all that after he'd asked her to stuff down everything she wanted just so he could have what he wanted. The leaving was just the last crack in the wall that sent the whole thing crumbling down.

Rora kicked her heels against the wall she sat on, and wondered what it'd take to make it crumble.

Everyone else spent the next two days getting ready, but Rora didn't have anything to get ready. All she owned were the clothes on her back and all the daggers Tare had given back to her. It was about as much as she'd ever owned—only thing that was unusual was having the time to prepare, so of course she didn't need it when she had it.

Rora waited for the time to pass, and made sure to avoid anywhere Aro was.

And finally the waiting was over. It was finally time to leave, and time to take the first step to being done with all of this, one way or another.

The Dogshead holed up in her room, couldn't stand to see more of her people leave her, some of the same people leaving her *again*, but Tare stood at the gate wishing luck to all the pack who'd chose to leave. She gripped Rora's forearm with one hand and squeezed her shoulder with the other, and she forced a smile when she said, "You've managed to come back every other time you left. You're damned hard to get rid of."

Rora tried to smile, too, but couldn't really manage it. She left, walking out into the wild world touched by the barely there light of the sliver moon. All the others around her—the pack, and Scal's folk, who still stayed separate because trust didn't come easy in the always-night—were as quiet as Rora, maybe wrapped up in their own thoughts about leaving, too.

Neira led them, since she was the only one who knew where they were going. That hadn't sat right with Joros—he still didn't trust that she'd spent so long as a *zealot* and now wanted to destroy the gods she'd loved. He thought Neira was still loyal to the Fallen, if not the Twins themselves, and that she'd lead them right into a trap and handily destroy the biggest resistance against the Twins. Neira'd stared at him in her empty way for a long while as more and more smoke boiled out of her, slow but deadly dangerous, and everyone else had started sliding away from where the two of them were facing off. "I'm not," she'd said, and Joros hadn't brought it up again. So that put Neira leading their group, and no one else had any complaints to make about it.

Pacing in the courtyard before they left, Neira'd said, "We'll have to move quickly, but we must do our best to remain unseen." The dark out there in the courtyard hid her trailing smoke well enough. Seemed like she was having a harder time keeping control of it now that she was so close to getting what she wanted. "I'll do what I can to help with that, but we cannot let word of us reach the Fallen. If you see any preachers, if you even *think* you see black robes . . . do not think, do not hesitate. The Twins cannot be warned of our coming."

Aro put up one of the witch-bubbles to keep everyone hidden, even though it made him sweat and shake the longer he held it, even though he started to look as bad as he'd looked before he and Joros had gone away. He held up the bubble, though, even when they stopped to sleep, and he held it while he slept, too. Maybe his time with Joros had actually helped him. Still, even with the bubble, most everyone kept quiet as they went, because careful was better than dead.

"Three days, at most," Neira had said, baring her teeth in a grin. "They're so very, very close. Three days until we can put a stop to the liars."

Three days was all. It felt like a year, and at the same time, it felt like blinking.

Rora made her way to Scal's side sometime on that first moon-pass traveling, and for a while they just walked quiet together.

But the silence stretched out until it had to break, so Rora said, "I'm sorry about your cloak. The bear one. I lost it somewhere along the way . . ."

Scal's shoulders rose up and fell back down. "It was not mine."

Awful weird thing to say, since it sure as shit had been his, but Rora let it drop. "So what happened with your, ah . . . your atoning? How'd you end up back with the merra?"

"Aardanel is gone," Scal said, talking about the prison camp in the North where he'd chose to stay. "Aardanel will always be a place of the dead."

Both times she'd seen Aardanel, the prison camp buried in the North, it had been burning or burned, and all the prisoners had talked about how the place was always getting attacked. Sounded like that had happened again, only with Scal around this time, but she was guessing even he wasn't enough to keep the place from getting attacked. By the look on his face it'd gone pretty bad—he was always hard to read, but it was in little things like a muscle in his jaw and the lines around his eyes. "Sorry," she said, looking down at her feet.

"I am sorry," he said, "for your brother."

"Yeah." Rora kicked at a stone, sent it skittering down the road. Everyone up ahead turned to glare at her, and she glared back until they went back to their own business. Why had she bothered coming to talk to Scal at all? She should've known better than to think she could get anything like a story out of him, and his silences and funny ways of talking just made her feel . . . stupid, somehow. Like she should be talking more to say something that'd interest him enough to talk, or she should talk less to not embarrass herself, or she should give her words half the thought he did before he ever opened his mouth. She knew Joros had always thought he was just a big dumb Northman, not good at anything but killing, and it seemed like Scal was happy enough to let people think that. But it wasn't true. And maybe she'd gone to find him because there was damn near no one else in all this group she could talk to, and talking *at* someone was at least better than silence. And maybe if she talked at him long enough, she'd find the thing that'd make him really talk back. "I just want to get this all over with," she said. "We know what we need to know, we know how to do it, we've got the people for it. But now we've got days and days of walking before we can do anything. I just . . ." She trailed off, opening her empty hand like the right words would fall into it.

"Want to be done," he finished for her after a moment.

"Yeah. It's the waiting that's hardest, y'know?" Rora rubbed her hand against the hilt of one of her daggers—the plain one, the one Tare had given her when she decided Rora was all trained up, was ready to take her place in the pack and be her own person. "You ever feel like all your life is just waiting? Waiting for things to start, waiting for things to end, waiting for things to *happen*?"

He took his time to answer, same way he always did. "All of life," he finally said, "is waiting to die."

"You're in a right cheerful mood, aren't you?"

He looked at her then, the kind of look she wasn't used to getting from him. He wasn't the sort for eye contact. But that look reminded her that his people called him the Nightbreaker, that he had the power of the Parents in his hands, that he'd been touched by the gods. It reminded her that Scal had always been different, but he usually wasn't ever wrong. "You sound like a person who is waiting to die."

And that touched awful close to all the things Rora wasn't thinking on, close enough that she pulled up a quick smirk and a snort, the same sort of instant, unthinking reaction you got from a cornered cat. The kind of reaction that was supposed to prove you weren't feeling threatened, even as you were looking desperately for any kind of escape. "Well, you're like someone who's already dead."

"Perhaps." He turned his heavy look away from her, thankfully. Rora wondered, again, why she'd even wanted to talk to him. Back when they'd traveled together, it'd always been like this. He always said things that sounded dumb but cut deep. He always said things she had trouble forgetting.

Rora faded back without saying anything. He didn't stop her from leaving, and didn't look at her again. They just parted ways, like they both wanted to pretend they'd never talked at all.

All those months ago, when Joros had talked the Dogshead into helping him and the Dogshead had convinced him to find the pack a new home, they'd left the big city of Mercetta behind and gone out into the countryside. The same roads they'd taken then were the ones they took now, winding their way slowly back toward the center of the country, back in the direction of the capital city.

Rora recognized these roads well enough, even in the dark. It almost felt like she was heading home. It almost made her want to go back in to Mercetta, to go back to the place she'd lived all her life.

You sound like a person who is waiting to die.

Rora clenched her fist hard enough to dig her nails into her flesh. She'd bit the nails down to almost nothing, but they could still cut if she squeezed hard enough.

Neira stopped all of a sudden, staring ahead down the road. The fingers of one hand drew shapes at her side that made Rora's head spin until she looked away. Neira said softly, "There are a lot of dead people there."

They'd all heard the stories: how it was chaos inside Mercetta, the city guard holed up inside their towers to keep safe from the mobs outside, people stealing and killing in the streets without fear, people eating corpses just to survive, and some horrible disease tearing through the city. Some said the king had been hauled off his throne and dragged outside and beheaded on the steps of his own palace; some said it was commoners that'd done it, while others said it was his own bodyguards, and still others said it'd been the Fallen, that they'd had people hidden inside the king's court for years. Rora heard that all the gates of the city had been sealed shut, but no one was sure if it was to keep people out, or to keep the cityfolk in.

"Probably a lot of living people still, too," Joros said. "We're better off avoiding it." Still, he didn't start moving them forward. He didn't seem too eager to face off with Neira again.

She sighed. "Yes," was all she said, but her hand stopped drawing shapes, and she led them off the road, angling away from the city.

There was a big abandoned barn off the road where they stopped to sleep—the same barn they'd spent a night in when the pack was leaving Mercetta. It was the place where Rora, still loopy with blood loss and shock from getting her ear cut off, had made up some dumb fireside story to try to explain to Tare why she'd left without having to actually talk to Tare. They made new fires on the ashes of those months-old fires, and Rora sat with her arms wrapped around her knees and didn't look at where Aro was sitting, and half wondered if another dumb, made-up story could fix anything.

Sometime in the night, Rora got up to piss, talking to the door-watch before she felt her way out into the darkness. She was about to head back in when someone behind her said, "Rora?" and she was glad she'd already finished pissing or she might've embarrassed herself.

With the starlight and her panic, it was enough to make out Aro standing there. She couldn't see much of his face, but she could see he was looking down at the ground. "Shit," she said, pressing her hand over her pounding heart, "you scared me." And then she remembered she wasn't talking to him.

"I'm sorry." He sounded like he was talking around a mouthful of rocks or cloth, the words thick and jumbled.

"'S fine." Rora made a sharp motion with her hand and stomped past him. She didn't like being scared, and she didn't like being tricked, and she didn't like her brother all that much anymore neither.

Aro grabbed her arm as she went by, which was real dumb of him, because she'd always been so much stronger. She twisted out of his grip easy as breathing—and then he grabbed both her arms, *hard,* and leaned down so their faces were close together. His eyes were as wide as worlds, and he was crying. "I'm sorry," he wailed. "I'm so sorry, Rora. It wasn't me, I didn't—none of it should have happened, and I should have stopped it."

It wasn't often Rora froze up, but she did now, staring at her brother's sniveling face just a few inches away from hers, wondering all her *whys* and *hows* as he babbled. He was so broken, maybe broke beyond fixing, and if she could just—

No. That wasn't how it worked anymore. He didn't get to ruin everything and then come to her with big eyes and tears and let that fix everything because he knew she'd always bend for him. She'd always done everything to keep Aro happy and safe, and he'd learned a long time ago how to use that against her.

Rora unfroze. Close as they were, she didn't have the space for a good punch, but she drove her knuckles into the spot below where all his ribs came together. It was a good place for hitting, drove all the air out of him and sent him stumbling back. There was that hot feeling in the back of her nose again, all unexpected—she could count up to the number of times she'd ever hit her brother, and it made her feel just as terrible now as it had all the other times. "It's too late for 'sorry,'" she said, mostly because if she was talking maybe that'd help her keep the tears inside. It didn't work as well as she'd hoped—her eyes were starting to burn. She spun away from him before he could see, before seeing him made her break, too.

"I'm going to fix it," he called after her as he got his breath back. "Rora, I'm going to make it right!"

Rora scraped at her eyes before she reached the barn, and the door-watch didn't say anything, just let her back in. She found her corner, already far away from anyone else, and wedged herself into it tight as she could, curling up so small she felt like maybe she'd just disappear.

They saw it the second moon-pass, but only because of how the moon disappeared.

Once they knew to look, it was easy enough to pick out: the faint moonlight outlining the tip of a mountain against the sky. Only they weren't near anywhere that should've had mountains, and there'd never been a mountain there before.

"They wanted a new Raturo," Neira said. "A new home to rival the old one. Proof that their power was not false."

It was hard to tell with the distance and the poor light, but it didn't look like the new place was near as impressive as Raturo. Unless they were still days away—and according to Neira, they weren't more'n half a day—this mountain was a lot smaller. Still spooky as all hells, and Rora hated it right away, but it didn't make her guts clench like they had when she'd seen Raturo.

Smoke whirled around Neira like angry hands. "You see how they lie," she hissed.

They kept on going toward it, back on the roads now that they'd got past Mercetta without anything terrible happening. The mountain got bigger, but only slowly, like one of them was sneaking up on the other one. Rora was still so damned sick of the walking and the waiting. It felt like having something sharp stuck in your clothes, that you couldn't find no matter how much you dug and patted, but the second you stopped looking for it it poked you again. They were so close, Rora could actually *see* the end, but there was still waiting to go.

Scal's people made for good scouts, ranging up ahead, to the sides, and behind, keeping sharp eyes and reporting back if there was any trouble. Rora'd thought about joining them for a while, because that was stuff she could do well enough, but in the end there didn't seem like a lot of point to it. No sense in making friends for the three days they'd be traveling. No sense in looking for a different purpose when it was almost time for her real job to start.

You sound like a person who is waiting to die.

One of the scouts came back to report there was a town up ahead, and the whole group stopped. They'd avoided all towns so far, avoided anywhere even a small group of people might gather. This close to where the Fallen lived now, a town could be real good news, or real bad news. "Didn't seem like a lot happening there," the scout said doubtfully.

Neira looked grim, and some of the black smoke had started to lash around her hands and feet, if you knew to look for it. The words she muttered sounded an awful lot like "Dead town."

Joros frowned between Neira and the scout. "Go back," he told the scout. "Take a few others with you. Get as close as you can."

"What'm I looking for?" the scout asked, started to look almost more spooked by Joros's words than by Neira's smoke.

"Just see what you see, and tell me what you find."

Scal was one of the ones to go with the scout, no matter how angry that made Vatri, and Rora felt herself actually smiling a little. It didn't last long, though, because once Scal and the scouts left, it was just a lot more waiting.

They were back before too long, and the looks on their faces said everything. "Just like Beston," one of them murmured, and pressed the back of his hand against his mouth. Rora had a hard time getting her head around an entire town being dead, but it looked like it wasn't the first time Scal's people had seen such a thing, nor Neira either.

Into the grim silence, Neira said, "We'll be safe there."

Vatri went right to angry, same way she always did. "You're mad," she snarled. "If the Twins have *murdered* an entire town, I won't disrespect its people by—"

"She's not wrong," Joros interrupted, and he just sounded so tired. This whole trip was the thing he'd been working toward since before Rora'd ever known him, and he hadn't managed to look anything close to pleased since he'd got back with Aro. Maybe he felt the same way Rora did, and that'd be the first time ever. *You sound like a person who is waiting to die . . .* He said, "That town is the safest place for us to be. The Fallen have already taken what they need from it; they have no reason to go there, or pay it any attention. We can use that to our advantage."

Neira just smiled.

And so they went to a town of the dead. Neira said that was how the Twins worked—they had power and fear on their side, and the Fallen knew how to use those weapons well enough to turn entire towns into willing sacrifices for the Twins. Willing sacrifices gave the Twins the most power, that was what Neira had told Rora, and people who were scared of the Long Night, who were going mad without the sun, would be desperate for the promise of something better. They'd be easy to persuade, and they'd be the perfect sacrifices.

They left the dead where they lay, in neat rows on the village green, just past the last line of houses. They didn't want to draw any attention, in case the Fallen passed by. Edro raged for a while about not being able to put them to rest, until Neira demanded, "How would you do it? How would you see them honored?"

"They were followers of the Parents before the blasted

Twins came along," Edro growled. "They deserve a proper funeral, a burning as—" And he stopped, and looked toward the outline of the mountain, much closer now.

"Exactly," Neira said shortly, and turned her back on him.

The leaders gathered in the longhouse that'd served the town for exactly that sort of meeting. Rora locked eyes with Harin, who was maybe the closest thing to a leader out of anyone of the pack who'd come with, but Harin shrugged and looked uncomfortable. She wasn't really any kind of leader, and she knew it. Rora stared at the longhouse, where Scal and Vatri and Edro had disappeared, where Joros and Aro were heading toward. The pack should have some kind of representation. No one stopped her from walking through the door, and Joros was the only one to frown at her.

They gathered around a table, everyone else sitting while Neira paced, everyone trying to ignore when her smoke crawled over their feet as she passed by. She muttered to herself, but it didn't seem like she had much to say to any of them.

A few long moments went by, full of shifting eyes. Joros was finally the one who stood up, with his face still grim and his eyes joyless. "History will remember us as the people who brought an end to the world's nightmare. This is the moment," he said, "when the end of the Long Night begins."

The waiting was finally, finally over.

CHAPTER THIRTY-SEVEN

Keiro had always thought that leadership was mostly paperwork, or coordinating from behind a curtain—a relatively distant thing. That was what he'd always seen with the Ventallo: they'd spent far more time wrapped in their own bureaucracy, and less among the people they led.

Not so with Keiro's rule under the Twins. They wished him out among the Fallen, talking and listening and watching. Fratarro said it was the mark of a good leader. Sororra said it was the surest way to find any hints of dissent, and quash them.

"We must be as one," Sororra told him, pacing with her hands clasped behind her back, looking for all the world like a tiny field general. "Now more than ever. The weakness of mankind cannot be allowed to flourish here."

Earlier, Fratarro might have corrected his sister—he often had, when she spoke of humanity's inferiorities. She railed against them more often now, and he defended them far less. It was a thing Keiro had noted, but very carefully did not have any feelings or thoughts about.

So Keiro spent his endless nights walking through the mountain—Sororra had declared it was called Atura, and though Keiro used the name, it seemed far too grand for the empty and rattling space. The mountain was steadily filling, as the preachers who had spent the last months wandering the country and readying it for the Twins' arrival now flocked to their new home. But Keiro had seen the lines of corpses laid out in the hills. So many of the Fallen had perished in the Twins' initial rise, there were not enough of them left to ever fill Atura.

Keiro walked the mountain in great looping circles, with Cazi ever faithfully at his heels. They walked through the interconnected halls that Fratarro had shaped, around and around the central spiral, and—when he thought he could steal a moment for himself—through the doors that opened out into the night. Sororra had caught him out there once, standing at the ledge and looking to the ground far below. She had asked with a voice that was so artfully neutral, "What are you doing, Keiro?"

"I like to see the world made to your vision," he told her. "I like to remind myself what we're fighting for." The answer had pacified her, or she had thought the lie allowable.

Another time, Keiro had stepped through a door and found Fratarro already there, his toes curled over the edge of the winding outer path. "Hullo," he murmured, and it was not the voice Keiro was used to—different, somehow. Like it had been when the eyeless mage had brought the stuffed horse.

"Brother," Keiro said, carefully, neutrally. "It is good to see you."

Fratarro said nothing, and Keiro moved to stand at his shoulder—not quite at his side, for nothing in the world could have brought Keiro so close to the mountain ledge. They stood in silence for a time, watching the stars.

"I keep waiting for the sun to rise," Fratarro said, and did not notice the stab of panic Keiro couldn't keep from shuddering through his body. "It's like something keeps pulling me out here. I know it's dawn now, or . . . it would be . . ." He reached up and pressed his hand against his temple. Keiro did not move, or swallow, or breathe—for it was Fratarro's left hand, the hand that didn't work, only now his fingers curled and pressed against his forehead, raking through his hair. Fratarro didn't seem to notice, or to think anything of it, and Keiro was almost entirely sure that the shaking beneath his feet was only imagined. Fratarro simply frowned, consternation writ plain on his starlit face. "I don't know why I keep coming here."

Keiro remained silent and still. He knew there had been stories of Raturo's boy-twin Etarro, who had been raised in and by the mountain, and who had had an unsettling penchant for watching the sun rise. The boy whose body and life Fratarro had taken for his own. Keiro wondered sometimes—and more often, of late—if that boy was truly gone.

Fratarro shook his head and dropped his arm back to his side. "We should go back in," he said, his voice sounding once more as it always had. "There's no point in being out here." He used his right hand to open the mountain door, and before they walked inside, Keiro stared hard at the left hand—and it hung useless, as it always did.

Keiro talked when he could find people willing to talk to him, listened when the dark halls could hide his form, watched everything his one eye could see. He dealt with small things, accolades and punishments, decisions on where to house new arrivals, concerns over the *mravigi*. He reported it all back to the Twins, who spent most of their time in their room at Atura's peak. They were rarely alone: they had chosen seven generals, whom Keiro had not known before, and who did not trust Keiro. In theory, Keiro was in charge of the generals, just as he was in charge of all the Fallen; but in practice, Keiro strongly doubted whether the hard-faced, eyeless generals would listen to any command he gave.

In truth, he wondered if any of the Fallen would really listen to him. Keiro felt less and less a leader, and more a spy.

The generals spent long hours in planning with the Twins, because Sororra could not bear to sit idly by and wait, and there was little else they could do yet. The Fallen had gone out in groups of two or three, and each group had taken a blade for the darkness, and most had taken a mage. They needed the blades and the mages back, for they were the best power and protection the Fallen had, but the scattered groups of preachers were slow to return. They had gone to every edge of the country, and were returning at their gods' call, but feet could only move so fast. Until they all returned, the generals could only plan.

But their plans grew each day, and Keiro stood at the edge of their momentous decisions, and swallowed all the things he might have said.

"Mercetta is weak."

"It was a cesspool to begin with. It should have been cleansed long ago."

"A forest will grow stronger after it has burned. Mercetta has always been the heart of the kingdom the Parents would see carry on. If we destroy it, something stronger will rise from its ashes, and we can shape it into the Twins' vision."

"Then we're all agreed. Once we're strong enough, we take Mercetta."

Sororra's teeth shone in a feral smile, and it never ceased to amaze Keiro the things that people could will themselves to forget. If the Parents had not cast her down, Sororra would have seen all of humanity burn. Keiro doubted centuries of imprisonment had changed her thoughts on the matter. She would see something better rise from the ashes of all humanity, and he wondered how long it would be before the others realized it, but he only wondered that when Sororra was otherwise occupied.

He hardly even dared think what a foolish plan it was, that even if the rumors were true and the capital city was destroying itself from within, even if only a quarter of the population remained—it was still far more people than the Fallen had, even once all the wayward preachers returned with their blades and their mages. It seemed a fool's hope. It seemed a mission almost designed to spectacularly fail.

Fratarro was silent through most of the planning. He sat in his chair and shaped—minor things, like a wooden duck or a small but detailed building made of stone, but they were made with his powers rather than his hands. The generals always crowed over the things Fratarro made, eager to draw the eye of the more enigmatic god, but Fratarro rarely acknowledged them. Sometimes he met Keiro's eye across the room, for Keiro, at least, knew what the generals did not: that Fratarro should have been able to shape such simple things in a blink, not in the span of hours. But he did practice. Fratarro had only ever wanted to make beautiful things.

"Keiro," Sororra called, pulling him from his usual reverie. "Have you been to Mercetta?"

"Only a handful of times. And only very briefly—there were always too many people for me."

She laughed. "You'll be able to visit it soon enough without that problem. But there is a thing I would like you to do . . . You've proven yourself capable so many times, and you should have a place in this strike."

Keiro bowed low. "As always, I will serve as you command me."

"We have many advantages over our enemy: a powerful fighting force, a cadre of loyal mages; we have faith; we have the confidence that we are in the right; and we are not afraid of the dark. But these are all things the followers of my parents *could* match. They have their own fighters and their own mages, their own misguided faith and their own sureties, and they could learn not to fear the darkness. But there is one thing we have that they do not, one thing that they can never match. We have the *mravigi*."

Keiro felt a chill engulf him, and in the same instant, sweat speckled his brow and spine. He said nothing, and hoped the sleeves of his robes hid the way his hands curled into fists. At his side, Cazi's scaled nose pressed briefly against Keiro's fist.

Watching him intently, Sororra went on, "Your kind has thought them dead for centuries, and those who follow my Parents likely do not even remember that they once existed. They give us an element of surprise that nothing else can—but more than that, they have skills that will prove invaluable."

Fratarro held a lump of stone in his good hand, staring at it as he meticulously shaped its form. It was still just a lump, the shape he was trying to draw out indistinct, and he was either concentrating too deeply to hear, or choosing not to react to his sister's words. Or, perhaps, he had known and truly had no reaction to give. Keiro didn't want to believe that, didn't want to believe Fratarro would put his own creations at risk after they had suffered so much for each other, after the Starborn had remained so loyal through the centuries of his slumber and imprisonment . . . But Fratarro did not seem to hear, or to care.

"Keiro, you will lead a squadron of the *mravigi*," Sororra went on, watching Keiro with the same intensity with which Fratarro stared at his shaped rock. "You will be the first into Mercetta. The *mravigi* have adapted for tunneling over the long years, and we will use this. They can tunnel into Mercetta and, under your supervision, begin gathering the information we need to form the main of our attack. You've always been so close to the *mravigi*, and with your connection to young Cazi"—and her smile flickered down to the Starborn, who pressed against Keiro's leg, warm and shivering—"I don't doubt the *mravigi* will listen to you.

"They should remain largely unseen, except for strategic moments when their presence can further sow panic—the people will think them monsters in the night. And you, Keiro, will coordinate careful attacks, for the *mravigi* are powerful and deadly. Under your supervision, you and the *mravigi* will weaken Mercetta and prepare it for our attack. Your Cazi will be useful in that regard—he is quick, and can relay your orders to the others across the city. You should—"

"No," Keiro interrupted. He was surprised to hear his voice wrapped around the word, quiet but surprisingly firm. He hadn't thought he would ever speak—would ever dare to. But he had, and the word hung heavy in the air, sucking all other sound into it. Sororra had frozen, likely with the shock of being opposed, and the generals all held their breaths. Fratarro looked up at Keiro, and blinked slowly. So he had been listening.

Slowly, Sororra said, "I don't believe I heard you." Her eyes were bright and furious as fires, and her tone made it clear she was giving him a chance to backtrack down the foolish path he had just begun—and that it was the only chance he would get.

I should take it, hissed the voice in his head that sounded almost—but not quite—like his own thoughts. He had thought it was his own voice for a very long time, and had allowed himself to pretend even after he knew better. Sometimes a delusion made life more bearable.

It would be easier to take this offered chance. To weave another clever lie—that he had been disagreeing with the particulars of Sororra's plan, not the plan itself—and let the world spin on as it was, rushing toward darkness and destruction. There was life that way, at least, for as long as it was allowed. There was not the finality of an eternity spent among the stars. There was *something,* and that was not nothing.

Keiro had been choosing the easier thing for a long time, chasing the frantic demands of self-preservation—and it had gotten him here, to this moment, where he said to the twisting voice in his head, *No more.* There were so many he had failed to protect, so many lost lives who might have been saved if he had only said, *No.*

Preserving himself meant nothing if he became someone not worth saving.

Dimly, he thought he could hear the sound of a mask falling, and shattering. "The *mravigi* are not fighters," he said aloud, meeting Sororra's eyes and not looking away. "I won't lead them to their deaths."

And Sororra's voice in his head said, *So there is a limit to how far you will sink. I was wondering.* Outwardly her face was writ with fury, but beneath it there was a gleam in her eye. He had compared her before to a jungle cat toying with its food, and he had never forgotten the resemblance.

"Detain him," she said to her generals, and they leaped into action, eager to break the tension that filled the room. They grabbed his arms, pressed him hard against the wall so that the stone scraped his cheek raw, so that all his good eye could see were the fissures and cracks and imperfections in the rock. "I will not abide insubordination, least of all among my most trusted advisers. I think you forget, Keiro, the promises you have made. You said it not moments ago: 'I will serve as you command me.' I expected more of you."

Keiro said nothing; there was nothing more he could or wanted to say to her. She could have ordered anything of him, commanded him to any depravity, and he would have done it without more than a faint readjustment of the skintight mask he had become. But the *mravigi* . . . how could he stand by and let more and worse happen to them? They had been made for flying but had been forced to hide beneath the earth, and Keiro knew the reason for it. It was a *good* reason, he understood it, but he would never forget Cazi's screams as his wings were removed.

"I had hopes for you, Keiro," Sororra went on. Keiro couldn't see her, could only see the stone before him, but her voice moved like she was pacing. "You showed such loyalty, such promise, such *faith*. We placed our trust in you. I would never have expected your betrayal.

"But you prove the truths my Parents did not wish to hear: humanity is weak, and fickle, and flawed. Faithlessness runs in your blood, and your first interest always lies with your own skin. You should not be trusted with power, for it will corrupt you beyond recognition."

Sororra, in her time, had always been fascinated by humanity—so like her and her brother and their Parents, yet so different. She had studied them, and learned about them, and—in learning the ways they differed from the gods—grown steadily repulsed by them. She had never understood why the Parents cared for humanity more than their own children. It was part of what had led to the Twins' downfall, and it was the part that the Fallen always chose to forget. They liked to think that if they were only faithful enough, they would be spared her ire, or that Fratarro's peaceable nature would balance out his sister's rancor. They liked to think the lessons of history would not apply to them.

Sororra had always understood humanity too well . . . and Fratarro, still, did not understand his sister well enough.

"Traitors will not be tolerated," Sororra said, her voice pacing nearer. "All must know this. Keiro—once loyal, once elevated, once named Godson—must be made into a lesson. Take him away from me," she said to the generals, "and gather all who reside within the mountain. There is something they all must see, and learn."

They pulled him away from the wall, and as they marched him from the room Keiro twisted back and forth—not in some misguided attempt to escape, but to scan the floor for starspeckled scales. There was no sign of Cazi in the room. He caught Fratarro's eye as he twisted, the god frowning at Keiro, and though he looked entirely himself, there was something of the trapped boy in his eyes.

Two of the seven generals marched him down the winding spiral as the rest scattered, and throughout the long walk down, Keiro could hear their distant voices calling for all to assemble at Atura's floor. A steadily growing crowd assembled behind Keiro and his escort, and more streamed down ahead of them. There was an occasional hiss or jeer, if someone realized Keiro was the cause of the commotion, but there was otherwise silence—no one, it seemed, was sure of what was happening or why, and under the rule of the Twins, caution served one well.

Keiro hadn't forgotten that. It was only that he had to live with himself, and caution did not always make for the right decisions.

The floor of Atura was not like the floor of Raturo—there was no arch showing the Fall of the Twins, no chamber for the leaders to gather in, no path deeper down into the mountain's icy heart. There was only the floor, and a small dais from which Keiro or the generals or even the Twins had sometimes addressed small groups of gathered Fallen. It was strange seeing so many filling the floor now, a large portion of the Fallen's might assembled in one place—and still, Keiro remembered that there had been a larger crowd for his failed blinding. Nearly a decade ago, when he had been a nameless, unknown preacher seeking to bind his loyalty more fully to the unfound Twins, there had been more Fallen who had chosen to bear witness—whether from their own faith or boredom, there had been more free bodies in Raturo willing to sacrifice an hour of their lives than there were all the people within Atura.

And none of the other generals could see—or, perhaps,

chose not to see—that any plan to attack Mercetta was doomed from inception.

The generals cleared a path through the silent throng, leading Keiro to the dais and framing him as they all waited in nervous anticipation. Keiro scanned the crowd and saw no sign of any *mravigi*, who usually milled about in the mountain. Most tended to avoid people, but some, like Cazi, had found humans they were fond of and often stayed near. There were none of those around now, though.

Keiro's greatest regret was that, if they killed him now— and he had no delusions about what his punishment was to be—it wouldn't save the Starborn. Perhaps he should have continued to play along for a little longer, done his best to assure their safety . . . but what was done was done. He had a lifetime of regrets, and one more weighed only a little heavier.

The crowd parted again, allowing the Twins to pass through. They were shorter than most gathered, child-tall, and their faces weren't visible until they were very near to the front of the crowd. Keiro watched them come with his back straight and his chin raised.

"Keiro," Sororra called out when she stood before the dais, her voice ringing around the more-than-half-empty chamber. "You once showed loyalty and an enduring faith. We judged you, and we saw you were a shining example of what humanity could be. But now you have shown the truth at your rotten core: disobedience, faithlessness, and sedition. Keiro, you are judged a second time, and you are found wanting."

Sororra stepped onto the dais in a single wide but graceful step, and made a sweeping motion to her generals; one of them kicked the back of Keiro's leg, another drove his fist into Keiro's kidney, and he fell heavily to his knees, held upright only by the generals still holding his arms. Sororra stood before him, taller now than Keiro, though not by very much.

"You know our goals," she called out. She still faced Keiro, speaking to the crowd at her back. "In darkness, all are made equal. In the Long Night, all can be judged for who they truly are. We see Keiro now for what he has become: a different man from the one we once trusted, a man who seeks now to place himself above you all, who seeks to question our rule. Keiro has shown that he is no better than the worst of your kind, and his presence here makes the world a worse place for us all." She turned to face the Fallen, and raised her arms into the air, and called out, "What becomes of traitors? What is the reward for apostates? What waits for those who are judged, and found wanting?"

In one voice, the gathered Fallen answered, "Death."

"Death," Sororra agreed, and she was met with an explosion of sound: cheering and jeering and murmuring, a few cries of surprise, even fewer cries of outrage.

Keiro closed his eye briefly. He had known, but he still did not think he was ready. Could one ever be, though? He had chosen this path, and he would walk it with as much poise as he could muster.

He heard Fratarro whisper, "Sister . . ." and when he opened his eye, Fratarro stood at the edge of the dais before his sister, and there was a hard uncertainty written across his face.

She made a sharp, silencing motion, and Fratarro said nothing more. There was sorrow and sympathy in his eyes when he looked at Keiro, but those were not coins he could spend. Perhaps Keiro had hoped that all his time with Fratarro—working patiently with him, the long and scattered talking in the hills, the shared fears—he'd hoped, foolishly, that that might mean something. But Keiro was only a man, and what was one mortal life to a god?

Selfishly, he wished for Cazi at his side. The Starborn had been his truest friend, even at the depths Keiro had sunk to.

The crowd began to part again, this time to allow three blades for the darkness to approach the dais with heavy footfalls and hands on hilts. Keiro swallowed, and didn't let himself close his eye. He wouldn't let them remember him as a coward.

He did look, though, when a high screaming began near the back of the crowd.

"They're coming," the voice wailed. "All of them, they're almost here. Etarro, they're coming for you, they'll—they'll—" The babbling dissolved into a mindless scream, and Keiro saw the commotion as the screamer flailed forward, as others tried to hold him back. Keiro recognized the man's face—the eyeless mage, the one with the stuffed horse. Anddyr. Keiro had always known the mages' names.

Fratarro had half turned to see, but he was too short to be able to make anything out. He reached for the dais, perhaps meaning to climb up for a better view, but he went rigid all over, as though struck by lightning and frozen in place. His eyes grew huge and unfocused, and his mouth fell open ever so slightly. After a long moment as the screaming continued, Fratarro blinked rapidly and turned his head, finding his sister, meeting her eyes. It was a child's voice, rather than a god's, that whispered, "They're going to kill us."

Sororra had always protected her brother. Championed

him, fought for him, killed for him. All the old stories from before the Fall were full of inconsistencies and chaos, but there was always a constant, no matter the tale, no matter who told it: in all their interminably long lives, Sororra would do anything for Fratarro.

Sororra's voice snapped like a whip. "Go. If there is danger, find it, and destroy it." The generals moved rapidly, and Keiro's arms fell heavily to his sides as the generals leaped from the dais and into the crowd, pushing their way through, gathering aid as they went and racing up the central spire, scattering down various hallways. Much of the crowd dispersed, seeking to help or to hide. Some select blades and mages stayed nearby, moving closer to the dais, ready to offer their protection if needed. The mage—Anddyr—still screamed fragments of words and sentences that hardly made any sense, but the crowd had managed to restrain him though he still fought, straining toward the dais.

And amid it all, Sororra knelt down at the edge of the dais, and pressed her hand to her brother's shoulder, and leaned down to put her face close to his. Keiro couldn't hear the words she said, but Fratarro shook his head—not in denial, but as though to clear it, and his eyes looked once more as they always had.

"Something is coming," he said in his own voice, with conviction, but with a touch of confusion as though he weren't sure from where the conviction came.

"We will fight it together," Sororra said, squeezing his shoulder.

There was another constant, one that burned less bright, that often flowed by unnoticed: Fratarro never truly understood what his sister was capable of.

CHAPTER THIRTY-EIGHT

They had all gathered in the longhouse—there were few enough of them that it was possible, though space was tight. Joros would have preferred to gather outside—at least outside it wouldn't have smelled rank and sour with so many unwashed bodies, and outside the sound of everyone chattering and whispering wouldn't have echoed among the ceiling beams. Then again, the outside was full of rotting corpses . . . but at least the dead knew how to be properly peaceful.

Inside, though, gave the veneer of safety, and that was something their motley little army desperately needed, if only for a few moments. They were scared, all of them. They'd *been* scared, for a very long time, and that was no way to go into battle.

Joros had never led a fighting force of any size—but these weren't fighters, by and large. They were just ordinary people, farmers and peasants and thieves, and Joros knew people. There was no fire in their eyes, no surge of passion in their hearts—they would fight well enough, but they would break. Saving the world was too nebulous a concept, too *big* to latch on to. They were scared, and they had nothing concrete to fight for.

If they left this way, they would ruin everything he had worked so hard for.

Joros looked out over the restless, shifting, nervous, stinking crowd. Most of them hardly even knew him. Some of them hated him. But they all stared back at him, waiting, attentive. "I'm sure you don't need to be reminded what we're fighting for," he said to them. "But indulge me. We all have families and friends and homes beyond these walls. Perhaps they are waiting for us to return triumphant. Perhaps they were taken from us, and this is why we fight—for what has been lost. Either way, there is more—much more—than what is in this room. There is so much more than simply us.

"So fight for yourself. Fight for each other. But fight for your children and parents and siblings, fight for your friends, fight for your homes. Fight for the people and the places you love. This battle is not for us. It's for all the people we left behind, and all the places we hope to return to. Fight for them. Fight to see them again in the light of the sun."

They cheered as loud as they dared to. They were still nervous, but at least there was fire in their eyes now, the cause given a face in each of their minds. They would still die, but they would die fighting to their last breath, and die feeling as though it had been worth it.

The words felt like they had come from some hollow, empty place inside him. They might all have homes and families to fight for, but Joros didn't. He never had, and even defeating the Twins wouldn't change that.

He hadn't expected, teetering so close to the end of the world, to be overcome with simple melancholy.

Neira, curiously absent her usual cloud of smoke, stepped forward and urged them all to their posts—best to keep them moving while the passion still burned through them. As the longhouse began to empty, she approached Joros, her head tilted and an odd smile on her face. "That was nicely done."

Joros snorted. "Most of them can count. It's easy for them to figure the odds if they take a moment to think about it. They need to be reminded why the odds don't matter."

"As I said, it was nicely done."

Joros couldn't find the trap in the words, but that didn't mean it wasn't there. Rather than stumble into it, he simply grunted and waited for her to leave. She would be leading all the fire-eyed fighters still streaming from the room, leading them along with Scal and Edro into the heart of the newly made mountain itself. She would be gone soon.

Joros stayed in the longhouse, along with the few others not going to directly assault the mountain. Aro, who stuck to Joros like a burr, and Rora who, catlike, was trying to pretend it was all some cosmic coincidence she happened to be in the same room. Vatri was also staying, but if she could channel the power of the Parents as she claimed, it would be worth putting up with some of her nonsense.

Just the four of them—they couldn't afford to trim the numbers of the main force any more than they had to.

Joros's scanning eyes found someone staring at him, and he briefly met Deslan's gaze across the room. She quirked her mouth and gave him a single nod, which he returned. Strange, that he found himself hoping she returned; stranger, he realized, that the feeling extended to the other familiar faces— Harin and Trip and the other pack who'd gone with him at the start, Edro giving bracing shoulder slaps to those who streamed out the door past him, even Scal, who always looked so tormented. They were only pawns, pieces on the game board of his grand machinations, tools to be used and discarded. None of them mattered.

Still. He hoped they returned.

The realization made him feel uncomfortable—Twins' bones, melancholy would turn him to a weakling—and so he summoned his three charges. "We should go outside as well. We have preparations of our own to make, and we don't want to be caught unprepared."

None of them said anything, but he couldn't blame them, not really. They followed him out, and that was the important thing.

They stood watching until everyone else had left, watched until the night swallowed their backs, and then they got to work.

There was a clear space just outside of the village and back from the road, where they could see the road in both directions and see the smudge of the new mountain against the sky. Neira had said it would be the best spot for them, and Joros had reluctantly admitted she was right. She'd planned everything out, obsessively, and cornered each of the commanders to go over each piece of her plan in exhaustive detail. Her spitting intensity would likely give Joros the crawling chills for all the rest of his life—whether that proved to be five hours or five decades.

As they began to walk, a hand gripped Joros's arm and Aro's voice hissed, "Remember," and then the boy peeled away. Joros stared after him, and felt a surge of anger. He had made a promise. Did the boy think he was so dishonest that his word meant nothing?

He tamped down the anger. It hardly mattered anymore, and wouldn't matter for much longer anyway. He had already spoken to Vatri, and her eyes had been hard and strange when she'd nodded agreement. Joros had made a promise.

At their designated spot, Joros set down the small pack of supplies he carried. He paused, then—Neira's obsessive planning hadn't covered who would do the actual physical labor, and so Joros was left waiting for one of the others to offer themselves. It didn't happen, though—Vatri began to arrange wood for a fire, and Aro stood slack-jawed and twitchy, and Rora had put her back to the entire affair. Muttering unhappily, Joros retrieved the eight heavy wooden stakes and a mallet to begin pounding them into the earth. After a moment, Aro joined him, surprisingly, retrieving the other mallet but not making eye contact with Joros. Each blow of the mallet seemed to say, *Remember. You. Promised.*

As the steady thumping filled the night, Rora sat down with her back to the rest of them, wrapping her legs inside her arms and staring at the mountain. Vatri, frustratingly, began to murmur prayers—but Joros quelled his anger at that. He needed her, and he needed her supposed link to the Parents to work. They were all dead otherwise. If that meant withstanding some of her prayers, then so be it.

The stakes were in place. Joros pulled the lengths of rope from the pack, and cleared his throat. That got no reaction, so he finally said, "It's ready."

Rora pushed herself up to her feet and spent an inordinate amount of time brushing dirt off her breeches for someone who was about to go lie back down on the ground. Aro dithered even longer, and Joros couldn't tell if it was his creeping madness or if the boy was ten steps from fleeing. To be safe, he commanded softly, "Aro, go lie down." The boy obeyed. Joros saw how that made muscles jump in Rora's clenched jaw, but she said nothing. As Joros began tying Aro's wrists and ankles to the stakes, she lay down in her space beside him. It was the closest Joros had seen the pair to each other in months.

As he finished tying them, Vatri was lighting her small fire. She'd carried tinder and branches and a few small logs, and when Aro had sheepishly offered to carry more, she'd said she wouldn't need much. A small fire would do. Its light gave their spot an eerie cast that Joros didn't care for at all.

Joros finished his knots on both twins and stepped back, hovering near their heads. There was nothing left for him to do yet—nothing for *any* of them to do yet. Now it was waiting, and that could be the hardest part.

"Rora," Aro whispered, but among the four of them and the silent night, he might have been shouting. "I'm scared."

For a long while, his only answer was silence. Joros, deeply uncomfortable, kept his back to both of them and wished he could seal off his ears. This was his command, his post, his subordinates, but he felt like an intruder.

Finally Rora said, "I know, Aro. Me, too."

Vatri's praying continued, and they all stared at the mountain, and waited.

CHAPTER THIRTY-NINE

Quick as breathing and quiet as hope, they moved to the mountain.

Scal led. It did not seem fair, to ask others to go where he would not lead. And though there were some hunger-pained faces of the pack, these people were Scal's. They had chosen to follow the Nightbreaker.

The blind preacher Neira walked at his side, though he did not need her direction. The mountain was a hard thing to miss, dark shadow against dark sky, calling. He would need her when they got closer, need her to get inside the mountain, but for now she was a distraction. Scal wished to be alone. He was preparing to die.

There was a thing he had said to Rora. *You sound like a person who is waiting to die.* Always they had understood each other. Always he had seen a piece of himself in her, and of her in him. They could fight, and they could survive, and they could bear a great deal. There was an understanding, among those whose lives were shaped by the blood of others. Things that were true of Rora could be true of Scal as well.

In the village of the dead, where they had rested before marching on the mountain, Scal had chosen a small house to sleep in. He had looked at all the trinkets, all the collected pieces of a life lost, and he had started a fire in the cold hearth. In the North that had birthed him and shaped him, a dead man should be burned, and his most treasured belongings beside him. Scal could not burn the man who had lived in the borrowed house, but he could burn the man's belongings.

Later, when he was alone in the empty room, in the sinking light of the well-fed fire, the door to the house had opened. Scal had been praying prayers without words, soundless hope and silent fear, and so he had not turned to see who entered. Yellow-clad legs had knelt at his side, and after a moment a hand had covered his own. Heavy with old scars, fire-seamed.

In the night before the end of it all, Vatri had sought out Scal, not Edro.

"There is so much danger here," Vatri had said, and in Scal's mind a different voice had whispered, *There is danger in being alone* . . .

"There is always danger," he had said.

"If we fail in this," and her fingers had tightened around his, desperate, "then we will all die."

"We will all die anyway."

She had whispered, "I'm not ready to die yet." It was easy to forget that she was so young, still, hardly older than Scal himself. She had never seemed young, not before.

"Then we will not, yet." Scal had turned his hand so that she could twine her fingers through his, gripping his hand as though he were the tether holding her to life. Together they had prayed, before the flickering fire that had eaten the remains of a dead man's life.

And Scal had seen the flames move. Scal had seen his own death, rolling toward him like a quiet storm.

Vatri had told him anyone could see their future in the flames, if only they believed.

He had always thought his death—his true death, the end of his last life—would be waiting for him among the snows of the North. That the snow and the ice would swallow him, and would not spit him out once more. Perhaps, when the Parents had given him their fire, they had changed the shape of his death.

Scal had prayed—not for himself, knowing what the fires had shown him. He had prayed for Vatri, and for those who followed the Nightbreaker. For those who had lived in the village and thought death a better chance than the Long Night. For those who still huddled in their homes, doors sealed to the darkness. He had never, in all his life, asked the Parents for anything. But there, kneeling beside Vatri, he had asked them, *Let me do this one thing.*

The fire had not answered. After a time, Vatri's fingers had slipped from his. She had said, "The gods ask so much of us, but they never ask more than what we can bear. They want us to succeed. We can't ever forget that." She had smiled at him, a tight and brittle thing, a crack in a mask. "I'll see you after it's over. Once more, in the light of the sun." The door had closed behind her.

In the night before the end of it all, she had sought out Scal, and then she had left him to his empty silence.

The mountain rushed closer. The end raced with it. All things ended, and Scal had faced his death often enough that he was not afraid. The ground would split, and mountains would fall, and the sun would rise once more. Scal would not see it—*I'll see you after it's over*—but that did not matter. There was only one thing he had left to do.

To the left, a quiet clash of weapons, quickly silenced. "They have scouts," Neira murmured, teeth flashing in a grin. "Yours are better."

It was colder, in the deep shadow of the mountain. Scal had not yet drawn his sword. The fire or the ice that lined its edge would respond to his will. His will was, *Not yet*.

Neira moved forward, pressed both hands to the side of the mountain. For a long while she was silent and unmoving, as though listening for something very quiet. Or looking for something, with her eyes that somehow saw.

A door into the mountain slid open, and Neira stepped aside. "They're ahead," she said softly. "They're not alone." She smiled, that way she had of smiling when she should not. "Good luck."

Scal stepped inside the mountain, and his army followed.

It was a hallway, and it was empty, but sound called Scal deeper. Voices. Footsteps. Screaming. The faintest light, but in the Long Night, any bit of light was not to be ignored. Scal drew his sword finally, holding it before him in both hands as he willed, *Not yet*. He did not need its light—it would give him away, and the way the distant screams bounced off the walls around him was as good as a map. He wondered if this was how Neira and all the other blind preachers saw with their missing eyes: by simply paying attention.

The light spread, and the screams echoed louder, and the hallway opened, and Scal saw them.

A wide room, and nearby a writhing cluster of people, one of them screaming endlessly. At the far end, a dais, and on it a girl—only she was not a girl. Scal knew it without knowing her, for the way looking at her made the blade want to burn in his hands. There was a boy below her who shared her face. There were swordsmen and witches and black-robed preachers scattered, but they did not matter. Scal fixed his eyes on the Twins, and willed, *Now*.

Let me do this one thing.

Fire licked along the blade, twisting around the spines of ice that lined its edge, and both the fire and the ice seemed to strain across the cavern, toward the Twins. Scal's army streamed into the room behind him, ready to fight for their homes and their families, ready to die for the sun. They wasted no time, and the one screaming man was soon not the only one. Scal began to walk across the cavern.

The witches in the room shuddered and stuttered as Neira's voice called out a single, meaningless word. Every witch as one turned to face Neira where she stood at the entrance to the cavern. They faced her with open mouths and fingers splayed wide, unmoving. They faced her as she began to laugh. They faced her as black smoke began to boil from her hands and mouth and missing eyes.

The Twins both watched Scal's approach with wide eyes. Sororra with fury, the deep-burning anger that flared within her, so like the fire that Patharro loved in the humans he had shaped. And Fratarro's eyes were wide with horror and, deeper, with relief.

CHAPTER FORTY

Keiro stood frozen in shock as the unexpected battle swelled around him. The Fallen and their mercenaries clashing with the thin-faced invaders, all unarmored and poorly armed. Keiro would call them common stock, his own brethren who had grown in hovels and fields and on dusty roads. But they were *fighting*, and they were not losing.

The mages, all the mages that the Fallen had worked so hard to collect and twist—they stood more frozen than Keiro, their backs rigid, all staring eerily openmouthed in the same direction. Keiro didn't recognize the woman they faced, but she was black-robed and eyeless, a preacher by any measure— save for the terrible, spine-scraping smile that stretched her face as she watched the mages all powerless before her. Even the screaming mage had stopped, pinned beneath a dwindling group of frantic Fallen torn between deciding the greater threat.

The woman who was not a preacher spread her arms, palms up to the peak of Atura, and her echoing laugh turned to a defiant shout. "You have no power over me." She hadn't spared so much as a glance for the Twins. If she spoke to anyone in the chamber, Keiro had no idea who it was.

He might have kept watching her, horrified and entranced, if it hadn't been for the swordsman approaching him.

No—not approaching Keiro. Approaching the Twins.

Sororra had pulled her brother up onto the comparative safety of the dais, where they at least had height, had a barrier from the surging battle. The mages who had stayed to protect them were frozen, useless; the blades for the darkness were occupied, already engaged in their own fights, unable to break free. They couldn't turn, not even to face the huge swordsman who walked slowly through the fray with an impossible sword held before him, shards of ice and tongues of fire weaving along the blade. No other fighters approached him. He simply walked toward the Twins through the fighting, his steps steady, his face resolute.

And Keiro realized he was the only one who had any hope of getting between the swordsman and the Twins.

Keiro stood frozen to the spot.

Sororra's face was twisted with concentration and with fury, doubtless reaching with the fingers of her mind to try to shape the swordsman's will, but his steps did not falter, and the stone of his face did not crack. Fratarro's hands twitched at his sides, both of them, spastic and frantic, but the battle raging within him looked as much a stalemate as the battle without. The swordsman approached unimpeded.

Still, Keiro did not move. If he could . . . what would he do? He had spent so long keeping his mind a careful blank, so long tamping down any dangerous thoughts. Now, when he was free to do as he wished, he had no idea *what* he wished.

He watched the swordsman approach, watched Sororra

push Fratarro behind her, making herself a shield. It would never occur to her to flee, not from one of her Parents' imperfect creations. "Stop," she snarled as the swordsman stood before her, but he didn't.

The sword went through her stomach with a twist, and she fell as it pulled free. The swordsman was quick: Fratarro had time for only a small, aborted cry before he fell beside her.

Keiro's legs stuttered forward on their own, hand reaching to do gods-only-knew-what, but it was already too late. It had been too late the moment he had stood rooted to the spot, the moment he had defied them, the moment he had killed for them, the moment he had found them. It had always been too late for Keiro.

"I am sorry," the swordsman said in a deep rumble. He still held the sword in both hands, but it looked a normal sword now, no fire and no ice along the blade.

The Twins' stolen bodies sprawled at the edge of the dais, empty and bleeding out, the Twins gone, leaving them only the young twins who had filled Keiro with such hope years ago. Avorra and Etarro. Avorra, who was too clever by far, and Etarro, who had a secret penchant for watching the sun rise.

Their eyes were empty, though. Even Etarro's, who had fought so valiantly to make his presence known, to hold on to a piece of what he had been. But his body was still, blood flowing more sluggish from the mortal wound, and Keiro felt his knees give way as something broke within him.

CHAPTER FORTY-ONE

The command screamed inside of Anddyr, unlike anything he'd ever felt before; a single word that froze him utterly, rendered him incapable. *Stop.* It wasn't audible, it was only in his mind, but it sounded as though it were both screamed in an echoing room and whispered intimately in his ear.

There was nothing, nothing at all, he could do to ignore that command.

His mindless, desperate flailing toward Etarro ceased, and the scream that had been shredding his throat silenced. He twisted his head in sick compulsion, unerringly finding the source of the command: she glowed with the same blue light of humanity, but black ink wound through her like snakes, and the edges of her form were jagged, incomplete.

Even as far away as Anddyr was, he could make out the smile on her face.

The preachers and blades pinning him down faded away to nothingness, the battle around him disappeared, his own body seemed to disintegrate. All that was left was the command, and the woman with her hand like a vise around his soul.

A second command came, just as simple and just as unrelenting: *Give.*

Anddyr felt all his power, everything he had, begin to flow

from his hands toward the woman, a trickle at first and then a terrifying rush. It had been the same in the cellar, when Neira had pushed at the barrier so that it pulled and pulled, drawing his power from him like a thread—

Thoughts raced desperately through his spinning head, frantic and keening, whirling and colliding and dying. His body was gone, his limbs were dead, and all he was capable of was *giving* her everything that was in him. Dread crawled sickeningly through Anddyr, made all the worse by the knowledge that there was nothing he could do.

Neira glowed with flickering and flashing lights now, blue and black and white and colors that had no names, colors that existed only in the smoke-swirling world of unsight. She was incandescent, coruscant, glowing brighter than gods—lit by a hundred lives, and more and more flowing into her, filling her, *overfilling*, so the light-spark colors swirled and swelled around her, a tempest, a resplendent and a terrible beauty. Anddyr ached to give her everything he had even as something in him wailed and railed against it, but Anddyr had always been weak.

Dimly—so, so dimly, like little more than a tickle—Anddyr became aware of something pressing into his stomach, right below his ribs, pressing just hard enough to make a hitch in his already labored breathing. And he knew what it was: a stuffed horse that he had been given and had given away and had found again, impossibly. Knowing Sooty was there with him, at least, gave him a shred of comfort—and then a flurry of mind-searing hope.

Anddyr had learned how to fight from the very best. Not with a sword—that was something he'd never learned how to use or wanted to—nor with the magic he'd been given by his god and his blood—with that, he'd only ever been good at destroying things.

No, Etarro had given him Sooty and Etarro had taught him to fight, and the young boy-twin had so much experience in fighting for his own freedom.

The compulsions of *Stop* and *Give* pulsed through Anddyr like the beating of a second heart, ceaseless and inescapable—and yet.

Anddyr ground his teeth, and his fingers turned to claws, and tears streamed from the eyes he had taken for a different kind of freedom, and slowly he began to scream, *No.* He had fought so hard for so long, and he had gotten so very good at fighting.

His body returned to him piece by piece, and the hands pinning him were gone, busy fighting, raging and racing. The woman glowed with more light than she could hold, more life than anything could hold, and still she demanded more. It flowed from inside the mountain and from without, the mages who had filled the room fading or faded, the light gone from their forms; and more spilled into the cavern, seeping through the walls of Atura, pulled somehow from mages beyond the mountain, *how—?*

A small cry stabbed into Anddyr's ears, and he twisted to see the dais, and the end of the scene playing out on its stage.

A small body, no longer glowing, sprawled clumsy. Another form, almost identical, still standing and still resplendent. A giant of a man before the much smaller one, and in his hands a sword that devoured the darkness from the world around it, a glow so bright that shadows could not hope to withstand it.

And the sword cut through the small form, the shadow-killing light burning through the beacon-glow, and the body tumbled beside the first. Its light was gone, and so was the sword's, and Anddyr felt a new scream tear from his throat.

His limbs would not move fast enough.

A new light hovered over the fallen forms, bright and furious, twisting into two matching shapes that pulsed with a seeking anger. The Twins, expelled from their stolen hosts, searching for new life, new freedom—

A lance of swirling and varicolored light shot through the cavern and pierced them both, and Anddyr saw their mouths open in fear and impotent rage as Neira, holding unspeakable power, bore them out and away.

Anddyr was part stumbling, part crawling, part dragging himself along the floor. The battle swirled around him, steps and swords missing him somehow, a cosmic choreography that brought him scrape-handed to the edge of the dais. He dragged himself up, his whole body shaking—he felt so weak, she had taken so much from him already—and he grabbed at the small bodies before him. They were identical in death, Etarro and Avorra indistinguishable.

Stop, something in him wailed. *Give*. It was not a command, but a plea.

Anddyr felt himself pouring from his fingers once more, all his power, everything he had left, a trickle at first and then a relieving rush. "Now fight," he said, before the shadow-swirling world dissolved around him, and there was only a silent nothing.

CHAPTER FORTY-TWO

R ora knew when it all started by the way everything went
so still. And she knew when it all went wrong because
Aro went too still, like all his blood had turned to ice.

Aro, where he was staked down next to her, strained
against the ropes, twisting his head and arching his back, his
eyes unblinking, and his face was skull-white. Twisting like he
was trying to face the mountain, like something was pulling at
him that he couldn't ignore.

Neira had promised, "When I claim the mages, I can leave
Aro untouched. We'll need him, after all. I'll ensure he isn't
affected by my command."

She'd lied. Of course she'd lied.

Rora was screaming, fighting against her ropes, tearing her
wrists and ankles to shreds, but the damned ropes held. Joros
was swearing, shaking Aro by the shoulders, shouting in his
face. He'd taken all of Rora and Aro's weapons, and now he
pulled out one of Rora's own daggers, the one with the shattered blue stone in the hilt, and he slammed the dagger's point
into the palm of Aro's hand.

Aro screamed, and Rora's voice matched it.

"Wake up, damn you!" Joros shouted, his nose nearly
touching Aro's, one hand shaking her brother's shoulder while

the other pressed his thumb harder and harder into the wound he'd made in Aro's hand. "We need you—"

Through it all, Vatri just kept praying as she knelt in front of her tiny fire.

Rora couldn't remember who it'd been who had asked Neira what would happen to the witches when she *claimed* them, but whoever it was had made sure to ask it when there weren't any witches around to hear. "I'll need an incredible amount of power to battle the Twins," she'd said, "even in their weakened state. I'll need all the power I can hold." That hadn't really been an answer, which was almost as good as an answer, in a way. Witches were their power, it was in their blood, and if Neira needed as much power as she could get, if she needed to take everything a witch had . . . A witch with nothing left was just dead.

And Rora watched her brother, and she couldn't see it happening but she knew it was, knew that Neira was pulling out all his power the same way she was with all the other witches. Knew that Neira'd kill him, and it wouldn't even be for anything except her own stupid revenge.

Neira would kill him, and he'd die thinking Rora still hated him, and that cut deeper than any blade ever could.

Rora could twist her hand, the ropes digging farther up her arm. They were close enough, staked right next to each other, close enough that she could stretch her fingers and wrap them around her brother's stiff-fingered hand. All she could say was his name, "Aro," his name that matched hers, their father's favorite joke, "boy" and "girl" in the Old Tongue.

Aro blinked.

The mountain exploded.

It was like a hundred suns rose at once, all in the same place, a burst of light that made Rora's eyes burn just for the little look she got before she squeezed her eyes shut. That didn't block out the screaming, like cats yowling, like people dying, like gods fighting—

Something hit Rora in the chest, and then everything was fire.

She hadn't ever asked what would happen if everything went right, if Joros and Neira and Vatri's plans all came together. She hadn't wanted to know. The rough outline was enough: *You're the bait. You're the trap. They'll go looking for new bodies, and*—that was enough. She didn't want to think about what would come after that, because thinking about it would make her run screaming until she found the end of the world.

She figured, if it happened, she'd learn about it when it happened. The best way to learn was by doing.

So Rora wasn't prepared for the moment when her body wasn't just her own anymore. She wasn't prepared for when she had to fight a god.

Fire burned inside Rora and made her scream, a scream that matched the one someone else was screaming with her mouth. She could feel claws under her skin, behind her eyes, like a swarm of rats crawling and clawing and trying to tear her to pieces, to get her out of the way, to *take* and take and take. Rora tried to hold on, tried to grab for anything, but how do you hold on to something with just your mind? All she had was her fingers around Aro's hand, all she had to hold on to was her brother, and he was slipping, too, she could see the fires burning along their flesh, the ropes burning and falling away. The fire faded from her skin but it still tore through everything inside, and Rora felt like she was smashing herself against the walls of a cage, looking for a door or a flood or any way to stop the pain.

And then Rora stood up, only it wasn't Rora choosing to do it. Aro stood next to her, and when she looked over at him, it didn't even look like Aro anymore. It was like someone else had put on his face and it didn't fit right, the angles were wrong, the *eyes* were wrong—

There was still the sound of praying, and Rora turned to look at it without wanting to. There was a priestess, and a fire, and a searing anger welled up in Rora, an anger that wasn't her own, an anger at her Parents and their world and all that they had made and all that they had taken.

She would kill them all. Take their lives to fuel her radiance, take their lives so she could rise once more in her true form, her Brother ever at her side.

She was Sororra, and she would see the world burn to ashes.

Her Brother's hand was around hers. They had been tricked and betrayed—of course they had, the cursed humans couldn't be trusted. Humans could only be trusted to care about themselves, and damn the world. It was the truth her Parents had never wanted to see, that even the most loyal of their humans were rotten at their very cores. They could never truly love a thing that was not themselves, they would turn their backs when they were needed most, they would break and they would break you—

Fratarro was the only constant, the only loyal creature in all the world. He was screaming in fury and in heartbreak, grieving for his former host and the new one even as he raged against all his hard-won power being torn from him. He had worked so hard, *tried* so hard, and the humans had taken everything from him.

She was Sororra, and with her Brother at her side, there was nothing they could not do. Together, they would see the world burn to ashes.

Somewhere deep, deep down, there was a wailing. Sororra's host, still clinging to the shell of her body. Strange. Was this what her Brother had felt, with his last host?

She heard the praying, words to her Parents that stabbed like knives into her ears, and her roving eyes found the priestess robed in their yellow. She knelt before a small fire, a puny thing, as though she thought it would be enough protection. It wouldn't be. It would only be the first flames to fuel the Twins' destruction.

There was a man who stood in stark terror near the priestess, his body quaking and his thoughts practically screaming to Sororra. Usually she had to actively listen if she wanted to know a human's thoughts, but this one might as well have been shouting them aloud. *This is wrong* and *How?* and *Please please please* and *I'm so sorry* and *I promised.*

He would be the first. His life would give her power, and it would silence the inane babble of his thoughts. His life would be the first to fuel the second rise of the Twins.

The praying stopped, the priestess falling silent, and Sororra turned back to face her in the same moment the priestess punched one hand into the fire, like jabbing a spear.

All the world went silent.

And from above, from beyond, from a place that only Sororra and Fratarro could hear, two sharp voices reprimanded in unison, "*No.*"

And the power of the Parents burst forth from the fire. A massive wave of flame that shot toward Sororra and her Brother, growing huge, burning, burning . . .

One breath.

The man's babbling thoughts: *I promised Aro, selfish Aro, coward and fool and so used to being protected. Did Vatri listen? Destroy one . . .*

Her Brother's fingers in hers, a faint tremble beginning. He was screaming, but it did not sound like his voice. It sounded like the scream that reverberated within Sororra, the scream of her host, and both voices melded into a single plea: *No. Please.*

The fire raced toward them, enormous, powerful, unstoppable.

Sororra reached for her power—she had to try. She had to protect her Brother. It was all and the only thing she had ever needed to do. But there was no power to pull from. All her reserves, painstakingly shored up, had been robbed from her with the death of her last host. She was weak. She was powerless.

A second breath.

The priestess's scarred face seamed into a smile, grim and triumphant.

The babble again: *He knew his sister would give everything for him, and I promised. Destroy one, and you destroy them both. I'm sorry. I promised.*

The wave of flame narrowed, sharpened, became an arrow, shooting straight and unerring—

Fratarro squeezed her hand. Her Brother. Her other half. The only loyal creature in all the world. So long as they had each other, there was nothing they could not do. She had always believed that.

A third. The final breath.

He asked me, he was scared and horrified and grieving and resolved and he asked for a promise: "If it comes to it, and you only need to kill one of us . . . please . . ."

Fratarro had begun to turn toward her, his eyes full of fear and of understanding and of acceptance. He still screamed with the voice that was not his own, but beneath it she heard him say, "Sister. I—"

The flames rushed forward in a blazing spear, and the fire pierced through her Brother's chest without touching Sororra.

The clamor of the world resumed.

The fire burned through her Brother, dissipating into him, dissolving him. Sororra grabbed him as his legs buckled, cursing, sobbing, shouting, the second voice within her echoing her words, but the Parents' fire glowed beneath his skin, and it ate the light from his eyes. He clutched at her arm with what little strength he had left, and Sororra screamed a scream that shook the world. She was weak, she was powerless; she had not been able to protect her Brother, all and the only thing she had ever needed to do. She had failed him, she had failed him . . .

His fingers fell from her arm. His light faded and was gone, truly gone, burned away by the power of their Parents, who had given him life and denied him the freedom to create.

Sororra fell, still screaming, still clutching the body that had housed her Brother, and it was both voices in her that screamed. She shuddered and wept and the world continued to shake around her, until her voice became only one very mortal voice sobbing.

Destroy one, and you destroy them both.

Rora knelt clutching her brother's body, and if she had had the power to do it, she would have seen the world burn to ashes.

Above the still and meaningless world, the sun began to make its slow reappearance.

CHAPTER FORTY-THREE

The battle within the mountain ended with Neira.

Scal had not spared much attention for her as he stalked across the cavern, ready to do the last thing he needed to do. He did not even think to look to her until after the Twins lay at his feet, and the sword had gone dark in his hands.

Light filled the mountain, blinding. It cleared and Neira was gone—simply gone. Everything had stopped. Everyone blinking or rubbing their eyes. Even when sight cleared there was no rush to raise weapons once more. There were Fallen and Scal's own fighters, many still standing close for combat, but instead they all stared.

Stared at Scal's feet.

He looked down, and there was a third body at his feet. One he had not put there. A blue-robed witch, unmoving as all the witches whose powers and lives Neira had pulled. The witch's hands rested on the Twins. And beneath his still hands, the Twins moved.

Scal held his sword before him. It was lifeless, or he was lifeless—no fire left, and no ice. He would face them alone, as he was. A final stand. One last thing, before his death took him.

Sororra rolled onto her stomach and vomited blood and bile, and then lay still. Fratarro sat slowly, his hand pressed to his eyes, and when he lowered his hand and saw the witch sprawled before him, tears welled in his eyes. He whispered, "Oh, Anddyr . . ."

Scal's sword lowered by a length. This was not what he had expected, not at all.

Another voice said wonderingly, unbelievingly, "They're gone." Huddled at the back of the dais, a man with one harried eye and years piled upon his face. He started forward, paused. Started again and knelt next to the boy—who seemed, truly, to be just a boy and not the body worn by a god.

Scal's sword dropped lower. The Twins were not here. He had done his part, he had done the one thing he needed to do. He had done the last thing.

And his death had not come for him.

"Look at me," the one-eyed man said to the boy, gentle but firm. He knew some medicine, perhaps, or knew at least what wounds to look for. "How do you feel?"

The boy croaked, "You need to tell them." His hand made a weak motion and, turning, Scal saw that the entire chamber stared. Both sides frozen in shock and wonder and horror, waiting to know, waiting to see.

Waiting to hear what had become of the world.

Scal heard the one-eyed man swallow, and he bowed his head. Whispered, "I can't . . ."

There were footsteps, growing fainter, and Scal looked to see Deslan's back. Down the tunnel they had come through, going to look at the world outside.

In the almost-dark of the cavern, it was hard to tell one side from another. Common clothes could look almost black. Black robes could be any color. They were only men and women who eyed each other warily, waiting to see if they needed to raise weapons once more, to draw lines once more. But for a few moments, they were united by uncertainty, and there was no telling one side from the other.

They stood among the dead and the dying and the changed, and they all waited.

The boy-twin dragged himself over to his sister, and when he moved, it jostled the witch who still sprawled over them. Scal got a glimpse of the witch's face. He had thought that he had misheard the thing the boy had said. Even missing eyes, though, Scal knew the face.

He did not know how or why the witch Anddyr had come to be among the Fallen and in the mountain. But Scal knew that he had killed the children to drive the Twins from their bodies. He could see that the mortal wounds he had given them were gone. And he knew that witches had powers beyond telling.

Running footsteps, loud in the waiting silence. Deslan burst into the cavern once more, eyes wild, grabbing at arms whether they wore common clothes or black robes. "The sun!" she cried, and then raced away again.

There was a wild chase—all who had heard, streaming through the tunnel, hurrying to see what had changed in the world.

Soon it was only the dead, and Scal, and the one-eyed man, and the children. There was so much here Scal did not understand. The children should be dead. *Scal* should be dead—he had seen his death in Vatri's fire. She had always told him the flames showed truth. He had been ready to die.

"You should leave," the one-eyed man said urgently to the boy. "They'll return soon, and they'll . . ."

"They won't do anything, Keiro," the boy said. "They're broken. They have no strength left."

The man glanced to Scal and away. "I'm not talking about the Fallen."

Scal wanted to say that his people would not kill children. He realized the lie before he said it. *He* had killed children—the same children. He did not doubt that most among his fighters had helped to drown twins at some point in their lives. They would all kill children, if it meant their safety.

Perhaps it would be for the best. These children had been the Twins. There was no telling what that had done to them, what they could still do. Perhaps they were still dangerous.

The girl lay weak and unmoving. The boy sat trembling at her side. They did not look a danger, and killing them once was as much as Scal could stomach. He had needed to, the last thing he needed to do. He could not do it again. He should be dead, and they should be dead. It was all wrong, and yet it seemed to have gone right. The sword fell from his hand, and clattered loudly to the stone at his feet.

"I will take them to safety," he said. The words came from his mouth as he thought them, wrong and yet right. The last thing he had needed to do had not been the last thing. There was something that could keep a man going, even after he should have rightly stopped.

The one-eyed man stared. He might have been close to laughing, but he did not seem like a man who laughed. "You."

"He will," the boy said, and the man turned his stare. The boy gave a weak smile that shook so badly it looked ready to fall from his face. "Have faith, Keiro."

The one-eyed man stared at Scal for a very long time, his

face hard. Scal knew his face. A man who had seen too much. Done too much. A man who had been ready to die, and did not know what to do with the breath in his lungs or the life in his hands. He finally nodded. "Then we should go—"

"You can't come with us," the boy interrupted softly. In the empty cavern, full of the dead, even a whisper was loud. "You know that. There's a different path for you."

Scal had never seen the end of the world—even the sun's leaving had not been the end. It had not taken everything, and smashed it to pieces too small to ever be put together again. But he watched the world end, for the one-eyed man. Pieces so small they turned to dust.

"I'm sorry," the man whispered, tears streaming silent from both eyes. "For . . . I'm sorry I wasn't . . ."

The boy reached out to hold the one-eyed man's hand. "You're a good man, Keiro. You always were, and you always will be. The gods ask so much of us, but they never ask more than what we can bear."

The same words Vatri had said to Scal.

Releasing the man's hand, the boy turned to Scal. "I think I can walk now. Will you carry my sister? I . . . she's not well enough to walk."

Scal nodded. A thing, finally, that he could do. He paused as he bent down toward the girl, paused over the sprawled witch whose half-turned face stared up sightlessly. Scal had known Anddyr so little. The witch had frightened him, for what he was and for his madness. Scal hoped he had found peace in death, finally. Words had never come easily to Scal, and they would not pass his lips now, but he thanked the witch. Perhaps the dead would hear a thought better than the words.

Scal lifted the girl, and she was motionless. Breathing, but asleep or unconscious or exhausted. He carried the slight weight of her gently as the boy rose shakily to his feet, took a few unsteady steps. Breathed, righted himself. Learning, perhaps, how to control his own body once more. He paused, too, over Anddyr's body. Turned him gently, reached into his robe to retrieve something that he passed into the one-eyed man's hands. A stuffed creature, lumpy and misshapen. The man clung to it as the boy turned away.

Scal walked at the boy's side, through those who had fought and fallen. Two small armies had fought, but even a small battle could leave behind so many dead. A hand grabbed weakly at Scal's ankle as he passed, but he did not pause, did not look to see the color of the clothes. With the boy he walked down the tunnel he had come through so recently, ready to kill one last time before he died.

All wrong, and yet.

Scal had to squint as he went farther down the tunnel, for light—true light—reached along the ground as he walked it. Blinding-bright, and he stepped blinking from the mountain and into sunlight.

Though it hurt, though he could hardly see through the watering of his eyes, he could not help but stare up at where the sun sat once more in the sky.

He stood, unbelieving. He had been ready to die. Had not thought that, if they did somehow win, he would ever see their triumph. Had thought he would go from the dark world to the dark of the afterlife, among the stars in the night sky.

"—see their power is gone," a voice was shouting, and it was familiar: Edro. "*They* are gone. The Twins are no more.

They have fallen, and they will not rise again. You have lost." Scal blinked his eyes, and could make out Edro standing atop a pile of rocks, tall enough that all who had gone streaming from the mountain could see him. In the light of the sun, it was very easy to tell black robes from common clothes. Easy to see who had won and who had lost, and not only by the despair on some faces. "If you still wish to fight," and Edro paused to draw his sword, holding it ready before him, "then we are ready to face you. But know that you're fighting for nothing. Winning a single battle means nothing after you have already lost the war."

Some of the black-clad mercenaries twitched for their swords, but did not draw. They had fought for the Fallen, might have even believed in the fighting, but they had only ever been hired blades. Looking for someone now to command them, they found no one. They did not draw. They would not fight.

The Fallen themselves had always been peaceful enough. They fought when they had to. Even against the makeshift weapons of Scal's fighters, their chances of winning were low. They were wise enough to see it.

There were no witches left.

Silence was Edro's answer, and he took it. He leveled his blade, swept it in a circle before him. "Kneel. Surrender to me, and I may let you keep your lives."

They did, all among the gathered crowd who wore black. It was not all the Fallen; there would still be many within the mountain, and they would need to be rooted out. Seeing the looks on the faces of his people, Scal knew they would take to that task eagerly. He wondered, if Edro turned his back, would the others still tear their new prisoners to pieces faster than blinking? The looks on their faces said they might.

Scal did not share that fire. His limbs ached, and he should not have been alive, and there was still one last thing he needed to do.

As Edro supervised the Fallen being taken prisoner, Scal put his back to the scene. He walked from the mountain of the dead, toward the town of the dead. He did not know what he would find there, but waiting would not make the learning any easier.

You sound like a person who is waiting to die.

Rora, Aro, Vatri, Joros. He needed to know what had become of them.

He was not the only one who left Edro to his work. There were steps behind him, and a glance showed him a number of the pack, who had come to fight with and for Rora and Aro, who did not care for the fallout of the victory they had helped bring. There were some of Scal's people, mostly the older ones who did not have the same hunger as the young ones. There was Deslan. He wondered if she followed for him, or for Joros.

She came to his side, and her eyes widened when she truly saw the boy at his side, the girl in his arms. She froze for a moment, Scal walking on without her, and then she rushed forward again, demanding a question she did not have the words to ask, a frantic and worried babble of sounds.

"It is done," Scal said, silencing her confusion and her concern. "They are not what they were made."

For a time she remained silent, and she remained at his side. She was studying the young twins. Intently, intensely. Scal waited, and finally she reached the same end he had. There had been enough killing. These children were not a danger. They had suffered enough. Deslan, for all that she did not have children of her own, had a mother's heart. She pulled a waterskin from her belt and offered it to the boy; when he had had his fill, she made Scal stop so that she could work water down the girl's throat as well. Gently she asked their names. Etarro and Avorra. Sensing the boy's wish for silence, she asked nothing more.

The dead-town approached, roofs shining in the light of the sun. All the villagers laid out, given to the darkness, given needlessly, and now lying under the sun. It was obscene. Heartbreaking.

At the outskirts of the dead-town, Rora knelt weeping over her brother's body.

Etarro rushed forward, still unsteady on his feet, but determined. Joros, standing nearby with his back to Rora, startled when he saw Etarro. Fumbled at his waist, had his shortsword half drawn before he noticed the others. Noticed that the boy did not charge with fury, did not charge to kill. Etarro dropped down next to Rora and flung his arms around her waist, and their heads pressed together, and new sobs tore out of Rora. The pack joined them, making a loose circle of grieving around their fallen member. Someone, he did not know who, had told him that their packs were closer than family.

Scal looked for a place to set Avorra down where it would not look like he was laying out another corpse. Deslan took her, kneeling down and cradling the girl half sitting, speaking softly to her of normal things though the girl still slept.

Only one of the pack had not joined the grieving circle, a woman he thought was called Harin, though there were tears clear in her eyes when she marched to stand before Joros. She was not angry at him—not yet. Scal knew, by the lines of her body, that she was looking for a reason not to be angry. "What happened?" she asked.

Joros, for once, seemed unwilling to meet her eyes. Unwilling to stand before a battle of words. "What happened was what was necessary." All the leaders—Joros and Vatri and Neira and Edro, and Scal and Rora and Aro at the edges—had decided it was best not to tell their people of the deaths they knew would come from the battle. Everyone knew some would die—a war could not be fought without deaths. But the leaders had known that certain lives must be given to win. They had known from the start of this path that Rora and Aro would need to die for the Twins to die.

Only Rora had not died. Like Scal, like the one-eyed man in the mountain, she stood with breath in her lungs and life in her hands when she should not. She lived, and there was an emptiness beside her where her brother did not.

"He asked me," Joros said, "made me promise. They didn't both need to die, and he wanted—"

Rora had always moved so fast, when she wished to. Scal blinked, and she had borne Joros to the ground, screaming and tearing and choking. Scal was not alone in trying to pull her off, but she was strong for her size, and she had nothing to lose. She did not stop fighting him and them until Etarro said softly, "Rora, stop. It won't change anything."

The words reached her, somehow, and she slumped as though they had robbed her of the last of her energy. She let herself be returned to her brother's side, and Joros was wise enough to say nothing more.

So much was wrong, for a day when everything had gone right.

And a last thing: Scal did not see Vatri. Among the four they had left behind in the dead-town, there was no sign of her. He knew, somehow, that he would not find her if he looked for her. He had asked her to shape him, and she had. Shaped him to her purposes, shaped him to something useful. Her purpose was complete, his usefulness done. There had never been anything more.

"There is nothing left here," he said aloud. The words were for the others scattered around in their small and their large griefs, and the words were for himself as well. Words that would move past his lips, words that he could bear to speak. There was a breaking here. A fracture in a slab of ice, spidering slowly but unstoppably outward. There was an ending waiting for him, somewhere. He had done all that he had needed to do, all that he could do.

He watched them stand slowly. Watched them gather the dead, and gather the living. There was nothing left for them here. The others left at the mountain would follow. Some few began the long walk back to the looming shadow, to share the rest of what had happened, to help with what still needed to be done there. The rest went in the other direction, away from the mountain, away from the death. Rora helping to carry the body of her brother. Etarro beside Deslan, who carried his sister. The pack. Joros, lingering, and following.

They would be the first to share the story with the world. *They will sing songs of us, and our names will be carved into the stone of history.* People would ask, happy and unbelieving, and they would tell the tale, because they must. *We will be remembered as the ones who brought back the sun.*

Scal did not want to be remembered. He turned his eyes in a different direction, as all the others faded away.

He had always thought his death would be waiting for him among the snows of the North. That the snow and the ice would swallow him, and would not spit him out once more. Perhaps it was not his death that waited for him there, but something waited. Something called to him, strong and powerful. He would find it, or he would find his death there after all.

CHAPTER FORTY-FOUR

Keiro sat where they had left him, alone at the heart of the mountain the Twins had built—their new home, their show of defiance, their reminder to the world that they were back and would not be forgotten.

All for nothing, in the end. All of it, everything Keiro had done—everything he had been forced into, and everything he had done by his own choice. He had let himself become something other than the man he had always wanted to be, let himself change until he could no longer recognize his own self, and it meant nothing.

The victors would return soon—the Twins' mountain was like a boil on their world, and they needed to cleanse it. They would round Keiro up with all the rest of the Fallen, and if he was very lucky, his punishment for being a traitor to the country and to the world would be service in a prison camp for the rest of his life. He couldn't stand the thought of just sitting there, waiting for them to find him, waiting for them to shape the course of the rest of his life . . . but he couldn't think of anything else to do. There were scores of exits from the mountain, but none of them would allow him to leave unseen. What, then, was the point? If he could have gone with the young twins, gone to ensure their safety . . .

There's a different path for you, Etarro had told him, but Keiro could not see the road, could not find his way out.

He sat holding the stuffed horse Etarro had taken from the dead mage, stroking his thumb along its yarn mane. He didn't know what it meant, didn't know what he was meant to do with it. But Etarro had wanted him to have it, and that was more than nothing.

Something pressed lightly against his elbow, and Keiro turned to see stars amid the darkness of the mountain.

Cazi stood there, with a dozen other *mravigi* arrayed behind him. *"Come,"* Cazi said, gently, expectantly. Since they had met, Cazi had been trailing behind Keiro, always following, always ready. It seemed only fair that Keiro follow when asked. He tucked the stuffed horse into his robe, where it sat securely above his hip.

There was a place at the edge of the dais, hidden in shadow, where the wall of the mountain had been dug away—dug away by sharp claws that had not been shaped for digging, but that had served well enough when survival was at stake. Keiro followed Cazi into the tunnel that was barely big enough to fit him, crawling on elbows and knees, scraping his shoulders and hips as he went. The other Starborn followed, smooth and lithe and blessedly patient with Keiro's scramblings.

"Where are we going?" he asked at one point, and the simple answer he was given was, *"Away."*

The tunnel ended at a cavern, and the cavern was full of *mravigi*—all of them, he would hazard, every last one who had followed them from the Plains, every one who had survived Patharro's scorching fire, every one who had searched so long to find their creator . . . only to lose him again. Keiro felt a thickness in his throat. Had they gathered to mourn Fratarro's passing yet again?

No. Cazi had told the truth when he'd said they were going away. As the last of Keiro's escort filed into the room, a pair of *mravigi* began pawing away at the far wall, scraping the stone and dirt that had been piled there to reveal the mouth of another tunnel, this one sloping upward—and this one filled with sunlight. And as Keiro sat staring, the Starborn began to file into the tunnel, one by one.

"You've been preparing for this from the start," Keiro said wonderingly, to no one in particular.

His answer, though, came from the giant white-scaled Starborn who stood supervising it all. *"We have been preparing for many things,"* said Straz, first of the *mravigi*, who had been shaped by Fratarro's own hands so long ago. *"We had been hoping for many different endings. This one will do."*

"Why? Why . . . me?"

"We have been so long gone from the world. What we have seen of it has not made us wish to return. You know the world; you have traveled far in it. We are hoping you know of a place that will not revile us."

Dumbstruck, Keiro watched the rest of the *mravigi* filter from the cavern, until it was only he and Straz and Cazi. The younger Starborn nudged him gently toward the exit, and Keiro went obediently, crawling up the tunnel, shielding his eye with one hand as he went against the brightness of the sun that felt so unfamiliar. When he emerged, they were far from Atura, the mountain a looming shadow in the distance. When he emerged, all the Starborn were looking to him, waiting, patient, expecting.

All of Keiro's life had been walking. He had found such peace in a journey without end, a road that could lead anywhere. His heart had never been so happy as when there was firm ground beneath his feet and the sky stretching endlessly into the distance.

He hadn't thought to have that chance again. With everything he had done, everything that had changed . . .

Keiro swallowed, and straightened his back, and began to walk toward the slow-setting sun, with all the Starborn arrayed at his back. He didn't know where he was going, where he would take them, but he knew this was the path he had been meant for.

CHAPTER FORTY-FIVE

As they walked, Joros held a hand over his chest, finding it hard to breathe even an hour later. And he knew that an hour had passed, because *it had worked*. Somehow, it had worked. The sun had returned, and the Twins were gone for good. It hadn't come without a terrible cost, but what were a few lives when held against the sum of the world? That was an arithmetic his father had taught him well, one of the precious few things he'd taught Joros. A single life was nothing. A handful of lives had no significant cost. The number of deaths before it began to matter, before it began to *mean*, was a high number indeed.

There had been a high cost for this. In the great ledger book of life, it had all been worth it ten times over. But Joros felt very much like he had been robbed at knifepoint, and what had been paid did not feel insignificant.

All those around him looked similarly plundered, and some more than others. Those of Scal's followers who hadn't wanted to return to the madness of the mountain looked dazed—they'd likely seen a large number of their fellows fall in the battle, perhaps people they'd become friends with over the long weeks of traveling. Because they hadn't gone back, they were easy to identify as the sort for whom grief was like a smothering shroud, rather than a spark to tinder.

And the pack . . . they all had the look of people who'd been beaten and left for dead. Joros had wondered if Aro would make any sort of farewells to those who had been so ardently interested in his well-being, and if he had, he'd done it subtly enough that they hadn't been prepared to find him a corpse.

Rora, of course, was worst of all, but that was only to be expected. They'd managed to convince her she didn't have to help carry her brother's body, so now she stumbled along ahead of it, where she wouldn't have to see the body, the boy Etarro walking at her side with his hand in hers.

His own sister was still unconscious, still in Deslan's arms. She must be getting tired—she was a strong woman, Joros knew that well, but Avorra was practically old enough to be called a woman rather than a girl, and she'd never been skeleton-thin like her brother. Joros adjusted his steps slightly to move to Deslan's side. "I can carry her for a time," he said, softly, because breaking the grieving silence that surrounded their group felt like irreverence.

Deslan glanced over at him and then away. "I'm fine," she said just as softly.

Joros felt his jaw tighten. He'd caught a glimpse of her face, back in the dead-town, where she'd sat cradling Avorra as all the others had pulled Rora off him. There had been so much in her face, and he'd looked away before his mind had a chance to process all of it, but there had been so many similarities with the looks on the faces of the pack. He'd been hoping he'd imagined it all on her face, at least.

He wondered if he should have stayed—gone with the hotheaded youngsters back to the mountain, to wreak havoc and revenge. So long ago, before all his plans had shattered to pieces, that had been his goal—position himself for greatest advantage once the Fallen had fallen to their lowest. It would make it so easy to step forward and place himself as their leader, a veritable army to do his bidding, to do anything he wanted, to accomplish all his goals—

But what would he do? He had no goals—the only thing, the last thing, he had planned for: accomplished and done. The Twins were gone, he had done that—but what next? He had no path and no purpose; nowhere to go, and no one to go to. He had nothing.

The melancholy had sunk deep into his bones.

Ahead, Rora stuttered and stopped. Those walking immediately behind her barely managed not to run into her. Joros saw what had brought her to a halt: the sunlight, shining off the rooftops of a town ahead.

They'd avoided all towns on the way to the mountain, on the way to battle. But returning . . . it was Deslan who gave reluctant voice to what no one else was willing to say: "We should rest for a while. We haven't slept or eaten in . . . gods know how long. And"—she shifted her arms significantly—"someone should look at the girl."

They all nodded or murmured agreement, but still, no one moved. A town meant people, and people meant talking and explanations and celebrating when they all felt half dead. Perhaps worse, there was the potential they would find another dead-town, and more death seemed unbearable. The safer thing would be to avoid this town and all others, to simply make it back to the estate, where they could nurse their wounds and bury their dead.

Etarro finally tugged gently on Rora's hand, and they started forward once more, toward the town.

They could hear the celebration even from far off, which at least meant the townsfolk were alive—mixed curse and blessing as that was. It swelled outward to draw them in, and then faltered. Joros wondered what it was that gave the townsfolk pause: whether it was the corpse, or all the grim looks, or the unavoidably matching faces of two sets of twins.

The Long Night was only an hour gone. It took longer than that for people to refind the trust that had been stolen from them in the darkness. It took longer than that to refind humanity.

Joros stepped forward from the cluster of their group. Robbed as he felt, he was wise enough to know he was in far better condition than most of his companions.

He swept his arm back in the direction they'd come, where, in the far distance but still disconcertingly visible in the sunlight, the mountain lay dormant. "The Twins are dead," he told the townsfolk. "The Fallen are broken. We were there when it happened; we are part of the force that defeated them. If you can give us an hour of rest, and if you have a bit of food and water to spare, we will tell you all we know."

That was a safe trade, and an easy choice to make. From the perspective of the townsfolk, at worst they were looking at feeding, housing, and being entertained by a ragtag group of vagrants who were in no condition to fight. There was little at stake for them.

As food and water were passed around, and the town's bone-cutter was trotted out to take a look at Avorra, Joros sat at the center of the crowd of townsfolk, weaving the tale for them, mixing the grandeur of killing gods with the reality of a battle hard fought. He could have held their attention for as long as he chose to—they all gaped like fish, and his hands held the lines that had hooked them. It gave his people the time they needed to rest, largely ignored by the townsfolk. It gave them the relief of not having to tell their own part in the story.

When Joros ran out of tale to tell, his people were happy to leave, and the townsfolk were happy enough to see them off—Joros wasn't entirely sure any of them had actually believed a word he'd said, but it didn't matter. They'd gotten food and rest, the bone-cutter had pronounced nothing severely or overtly wrong with Avorra—and, too, the townsfolk had given them a shroud for Aro, and a sling to make carrying him easier. Rora had watched them wrap her brother with a stricken look on her face, as though realizing his death all over again. It was a hard thing to see.

Most importantly, his people had all learned they could survive human interaction—which was good, because there was more of it to come.

They could avoid some towns, but the tale needed to be told. The people needed to hear, and know what had happened, and know who had saved them. And, when the sun set, they needed to believe that it would come back.

When Avorra woke, she simply blinked, and said nothing. If she was spoken to, she would turn to face the speaker, but she wouldn't answer. *Couldn't*, perhaps.

It distressed Etarro far more than Joros would have expected—there had always been so much tension between the twins, like oil and water mixed. He would never have described them as close. But when his sister wouldn't acknowledge him, would only blink at him owlishly, he choked on a sob and fled her side.

When they resumed their journey, gentle tugging could pull Avorra to her feet, and she would walk where she was directed. Where before Rora and Etarro, hand in hand, had silently led the group, they now added Avorra. Just as silent, walking with her hands strung between the two of them, walking wherever they guided her.

Like everything had been since they'd defeated the Twins, returning to the estate was as terrible as it was a relief.

It finally gave them a true and well-earned rest, but meant telling the tale over again—and for the first time, Joros had no part in it. That was with good reason, as he'd played the largest role in Aro's not returning to them alive. The rest of the pack, Sharra Dogshead particularly, could hardly stand to see Joros there even when he remained perfectly silent. He couldn't blame them for it, not really. Maybe one day they'd accept that it had been Aro's doing, Aro's choice, but the wounds were too fresh for that sort of acceptance. Let them have their hatred.

Rora was given the open-armed welcome she hadn't received from her pack for more than a year. Grief, it seemed, was enough to wash away any lingering grudges. No telling if that would last, but Joros saw relief on enough faces that he suspected it might. Somber Etarro and silent Avorra were given similar welcome—for all their harsh ways, Joros had noted a particular softness among the pack when it came to children. Sharra Dogshead, weeping openly, crouched before the twins—a slow and painful process with her bad leg. She spoke to them too softly for Joros to hear, her eyes drifting frequently to Rora, to Aro's shroud. At the end of it, she held both her hands out to the young twins. Etarro gripped one with tears standing in his too-old eyes, and then reached over to lift his sister's hand into Sharra's other.

Joros remained at the periphery of it all. For the first time, he hadn't been thinking past the next step, the most immediate goal. *Get them back to their home.* With that done, Joros wasn't quite sure what to do with himself. He had no more plans, no more goals, nowhere else to go.

Once she'd finished her weeping, the Dogshead stood on her crippled leg and called for everyone's attention. "You're all welcome to stay here," she said to those who were not her pack, "for as long as you need." Her eyes settled on Joros, and immediately communicated two things: that the invitation did not extend to him, but that she would not call him out specifically. She would only make him *feel* unwelcome, without the trouble of actually throwing him out the door. If he wanted to, he could choose to ignore the first part and impose on her hospitality. It was his home, after all.

But he looked at the others in their little knots of grief and camaraderie, and he knew that staying would never draw him into any of those circles. He was sick of being scorned and abhorred until he was needed to do the difficult things they couldn't stand to do; he was not some tool that could be kept locked away until he was useful.

His eyes found Deslan in the crowd, but she wouldn't look

at him. She'd been avoiding him, intentionally, ever since she returned from the mountain.

So he left, feet re-stirring the dust that had just begun to settle on the sun-touched road. He had no path and no purpose; nowhere to go, and no one to go to. For the first time in longer than he could remember, he was alone. That was fine; he didn't need anyone but himself. Other people had only ever gotten in his way.

He had won, he had succeeded—and all it had cost was everything he had, everything he was. It was simple arithmetic. It was the way of the world.

EPILOGUE

The ocean stretched before Keiro, waves lapping gently at soft sand. He wore heavy clothes, fur-lined, but they didn't completely fight off the chill in the air. Still, the cold was worth it—he didn't want to miss a moment.

Out in the water, sea monsters frolicked. At least, that was what the locals called them every time they caught a glimpse of the *mravigi* playing in the waves.

They had taken to the sea of their new home more happily than they ever had to the grass of the Plains. They could burrow into the soft sand, or bask on its sun-warmed surface. The forest nearby was full of tall trees that never lost their foliage, no matter how cold it got, no matter how deep the snow that covered the sandy beach. Their claws were good for climbing, too, and for perching. Keiro knew that the higher they climbed, the more they could feel the sea-born wind racing past their faces.

There were some in the trees even now, no doubt, but many of them had taken to the water, slim bodies winding like otters, diving down and then surfacing with great sprays of water. It would be too cold soon even for them, winter on the approach, and they were enjoying their fun while they could.

Keiro watched them, smiling, one hand shading his eye from the orange light of the setting sun. Its reflection stretched across the water, and turned the waves into the bright colors of a painting—yellow turning to pink as one of the Starborn breached, ripples of orange and purple to mark where one had disappeared.

The Starborn were in high spirits. Across from the slow-setting sun, a pale disk against the pink sky, the rising moon was full.

The sand shifted behind Keiro, but he didn't turn. He knew the sound of those feet. The familiar form lay down beside and behind Keiro, curved loosely around him, and Keiro leaned back companionably against Cazi's flank. The Starborn made a good cushion—he'd grown over the years, and was now nearly as big as any of the others.

"You should be out there," Keiro chided gently.

The forked tip of Cazi's tail flicked against Keiro's knee, less gently. *"I am fine here."*

They watched together until the sun had gone beyond the far edge of the sea, and pulled its painted blanket behind itself. There was always a small, quiet moment of fear in Keiro's chest when it left, even now.

The *mravigi* emerged from the water, singly and in groups, the salt sea traveling in rivulets among their star-dotted scales. They flowed by Keiro with murmurs or nods, all moving toward the forest at his back. Cazi rose to join them, wordless, but Keiro waited a few moments longer. The beach was quiet and peaceful, and the cold had sunk into him so that he could hardly feel it.

Keiro finally stood and stretched, shaking feeling back into his hands and feet, and turned to the forest. The moon, nearly at its zenith, showed him his path. His bare feet slid on the sand, and crunched over twigs—old habits were hard to break, though he had boots at home awaiting the first snowfall.

Within the forest was a clearing, and in the clearing, the *mravigi* gathered.

Their black scales were turned gray by the moon's light, but the white scales glowed to rival the moon. They stood eternally patient, faces turned skyward. Keiro did not cross the border of the tree line into the clearing—this was a part of him, but he was not a part of it.

When the moon hung directly above the clearing, broad and beautiful, its light shining down like a gentler sun—then the Starborn began to sing. At their center, voice raised proudly, loudest, was Straz, first of the *mravigi*, who had spent centuries below the earth guarding his bound gods. He sang of lost years and found hope and the ever-flowing tides, and his vast family sang with him.

The locals might hear; let them. Let them hear beauty. Let them hear the sound of joy.

At the height of the song, a small form shot up from the center of the Starborn. The gray-scaled body of a youngster, though her white scales glowed as brightly as any other's. Breathless, Keiro grabbed at his throat, at his pulse pounding a frantic hope. And as the song crescendoed, the young *mravigi*'s wings snapped out and caught the breeze from the sea. They bore her ever upward, and her happy scream threaded through the song below.

Keiro fell to his knees and could not help the laughing sob that burst out of him. If he could sing, he would have sung with them. Instead, he simply watched the young *mravigi* discover the joy of flight, of the wind racing past her face. He watched her discover the wonder she had been made for, and in that moment, nothing else in all the world mattered.

ABOUT THE AUTHOR

Living in the cold reaches of the upper Midwest with her beast of a dog, Rachel Dunne has developed a great fondness for indoor activities. Her first novel, *In the Shadow of the Gods*, was a semifinalist for the 2014 Amazon Breakthrough Novel Award and was followed up by *The Bones of the Earth*.